THE IRON SWORD

Books by Julie Kagawa
available from Inkyard Press

Each series listed in reading order. Novellas complement
the full-length novels but do not need to be read to enjoy the series.

The Iron Fey

The Iron King (special edition includes the "Winter's Passage"* novella)
The Iron Daughter (special edition includes the "Guide to the Iron Fey"*)
The Iron Queen (special edition includes the "Summer's Crossing"* novella)
The Iron Knight (special edition includes the "Iron's Prophecy"* novella)
The Iron Prince
The Iron Traitor
The Iron Warrior

The Iron Fey: Evenfall

Shadow's Legacy (ebook novella)
The Iron Raven
The Iron Sword

Shadow of the Fox

Shadow of the Fox
Soul of the Sword
Night of the Dragon

The Talon Saga

Talon
Rogue
Soldier
Legion
Inferno

Blood of Eden

Dawn of Eden (prequel novella+)
The Immortal Rules
The Eternity Cure
The Forever Song

*Also available as an ebook and in *The Iron Legends* anthology
+Available in the *'Til the World Ends* anthology by Julie Kagawa,
Ann Aguirre, and Karen Duvall

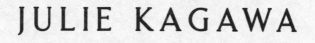

JULIE KAGAWA

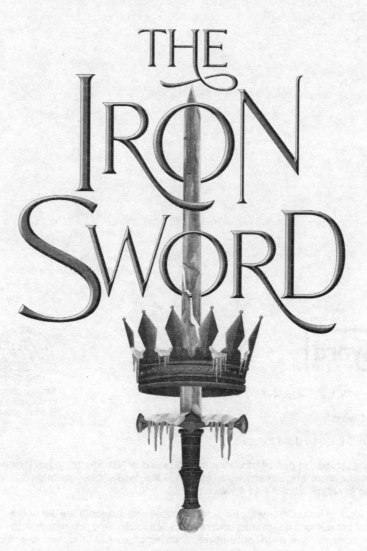

THE IRON SWORD

inkyard
PRESS

ISBN-13: 978-1-335-41864-7

The Iron Sword

Inkyard Press
22 Adelaide St. West, 41st Floor
Toronto, Ontario M5H 4E3, Canada
www.InkyardPress.com

To Nick, always.

PART
I

THE MISSING KING

I've lived a long life.

Not as long as some in Faery. Robin Goodfellow, for example, is older than me by several hundred years (though you wouldn't know it by the way he acts). King Oberon, Queen Titania, and Queen Mab are older still, ancient beings with the power to rival anything in the Nevernever. I'm not as old or as powerful as the kings and queens of Faery, but even by fey standards, I've lived a goodly while. I'm known in the Nevernever; my name is recognized and even feared, by some. I've been to the farthest reaches of Faery. I have seen things no one else has. Nightmares, dragons, the End of the World. I've passed impossible tests, triumphed in unwinnable challenges, and killed unbeatable monsters.

None of it prepared me for being a father.

Meghan stared at Glitch, her face pale in the sickly light of the wyldwood. At the Iron faery who had just turned both our worlds upside down with his announcement.

Touchstone is no more. Prince Keirran, King of the Forgotten, has vanished.

"Explain, Glitch," Meghan demanded. Her voice was calm, steely, though I caught the tremor beneath. "What do you mean, Keirran has vanished? What has happened to Touchstone?"

"Your Majesty." Glitch bowed his head, the lightning in his hair flickering a subdued purple. "Forgive me, I only know what the messenger told us. That Touchstone has disappeared, and Prince Keirran is gone. I wish I could tell you more."

Keirran. Fear twisted my insides. Not for me, but for the son who, despite all his assurances, couldn't seem to keep himself out of trouble. Even before he was born, he had a prophecy hanging over his head that proclaimed him either a savior or a destroyer, and the entire Nevernever watched to see which he would become. For years, Meghan and I raised him with that knowledge, trying not to let it influence us, but knowing that one day, we would have to face the consequences of Keirran's decision.

The prophecy finally came to a head when a powerful new foe rose up to threaten all of Faery. The Lady, the first queen of the Nevernever, furious that Faery had moved on without her, gathered the Forgotten to her side and waged war on all the courts. She promised them a new world, a world where humans would fear and worship the fey again, and where no faery would Fade away from being forgotten. She demanded the courts be dissolved, and that the rulers of Faery step down and acknowledge her as the true and only queen of the Nevernever. Naturally, the other rulers refused, and the war with the Forgotten began.

At that moment, Keirran made his choice, and it was Destroyer. He betrayed his court, turned his back on his family, and joined the Lady in her quest to conquer the Nevernever. And even though I had known it could happen, even though the prophecy had foretold it, it was still a devastating blow for both Meghan and myself. Keirran was stubborn, idealistic, and once he set his mind to something there was no changing it, but I hadn't thought him capable of betraying his entire court.

Meghan took a quiet breath. I could sense the struggle within; the desire to know what had happened to our son, balanced against the duties and obligations of the Iron Queen. Faery wasn't safe. We had just returned from the wyldwood, after battling a vicious new monster that nearly killed us all. I still ached, muscles battered and bruised, from the power of the creature's attacks. There had been five of us: myself, the Iron Queen, Robin Goodfellow, an Iron faery named Coaleater and a Forgotten called Nyx, and even then we barely managed to bring down the creature. Only to discover the threat to the Nevernever was far from over. In fact, it was only beginning.

Meghan knew this. A shadow had fallen over Faery, the echo of a new prophecy hovering over it like a storm. *The end has begun. Evenfall is coming. Faery and every living creature that exists under the sun are doomed.*

I stepped close to Meghan and put my hands on her shoulders, feeling them tremble beneath my palms. Leaning in, I murmured, "I can find him, Meghan. If you need to return to Mag Tuiredh, I'll take Puck and Grim, and we'll go look for Keirran. Grim can lead us to Touchstone, and from there we'll see what happened to the capital and where Keirran could have gone. You don't have to come with us this time."

"No." She reached up and squeezed one of my hands. "I need to know what happened to Touchstone, why it suddenly vanished. If another one of those monsters is responsible for its destruction, you'll need my help to take it down. Besides…" She paused, a shadow of pain crossing her face. "If something happened to Keirran, if one of those creatures got to him like they got to Puck, I want to know. I want to see it for myself. If both of us are there this time, maybe that will be enough to bring him back."

My insides felt cold. The Monster we had fought and killed was unlike anything I had ever seen before: a physical manifestation of hate, rage, fear, and despair. It poisoned the land around it, tainting everything with dark glamour and negative emotions, and worst of all, it was able to bring out the shadow side of any living creature it touched. I had seen this firsthand with Puck, where he had been transformed into a faery consumed by jealous anger and vicious spite. The Robin Goodfellow of old. The Robin Goodfellow who was still furious with me for stealing away Meghan, who held a grudge for all the times I tried to kill him.

Not that I blamed him.

Fortunately, Puck had been able to fight through that darkness and return to his normal, carefree, irreverent self. But I knew what Meghan was thinking, and I shared her fear. Keirran had already shown himself capable of turning on and betraying everything he loved. Would we venture into the Between to find our son had turned into a soulless enemy once more?

I leaned close to Meghan, feeling her grip on my hand tighten. "We'll find him," I said quietly. "We'll find him and whatever it takes, we'll bring him home."

She nodded once, then stepped away to gaze down at the still-kneeling Glitch. "You've done well," she told the Iron lieutenant. "Return to Mag Tuiredh. Keep our people safe. I am going to search for Prince Keirran. I will return as soon as I am able."

"Of course, Your Majesty," Glitch said, though I knew he wanted to protest. The First Lieutenant never liked it when both rulers of Mag Tuiredh left the Iron Kingdom for unknown amounts of time. But he had been with Meghan long enough that he simply bowed his head and replied, "Good luck and safe travels to you both. I will keep the city safe until you return."

Meghan turned, her gaze seeking the rest of the party behind us. Puck stood under a tree with his arms crossed, bright red hair making him stand out in the gloom. Beside him, a cloaked, hooded figure watched the proceedings silently, seeming to blend into the shadows. It took Meghan a moment to locate her. "Nyx," she said, "you are a Forgotten, and a member of Keirran's court. Right now, it appears Touchstone has disappeared, and the Forgotten King has vanished. Can you part the Veil and take us into the Between?"

The silver-haired fey with the twilight skin and golden eyes raised her head, a steely expression on her face. "Yes, Your Majesty," she answered. "If Keirran is in danger, I must find him right away. When do you wish to go?"

"Right now." Meghan turned her gaze to the others, to Puck and Coaleater, watching intently. "This is an uncertain time for all of us," she said. "Faery is under threat. Something is coming, and none of us know what it is or when it could arrive—only that it is close. The rulers and leaders of Faery must be made aware of this threat. Coaleater…" She glanced at the large Iron faery, who straightened as her gaze fell on him. "I know you want to help us find Keirran, but I need you to return to the Obsidian plains and warn Spikerail of what happened. He needs to be aware, and should the time come when we must call on the Iron herd, I want him to be prepared."

"Yes, Your Majesty." The big man bowed his head, and I saw the shadow of his real self behind him: a huge warhorse made of black iron and flickering flame. "The Iron herd will stand ready to aid you against all threats. You will have our support for as long as you need it."

Meghan nodded gratefully, then turned to the red-haired fey beside him. "Puck?"

"Come on, princess." Robin Goodfellow flashed his toothy smile. "You know where I stand. You don't even have to ask."

"I believe I will come as well."

A fluffy gray cat sauntered into view, waving an exceptionally bushy tail. His golden eyes regarded us all with bored appraisal. "If Touchstone has disappeared, I would like to see it for myself," Grimalkin said. "Someone with an ounce of intelligence should be there to make sense of things and point out the obvious. And to point you in the right direction should you become lost. Not that I doubt the Forgotten's abilities, but you will need a guide should you happen to lose your way."

The Iron Queen gave a decisive nod. "Then let us go," she said. "I fear time is slipping away, and the longer we wait, the more difficult it will become to find Keirran. Nyx..." She gestured toward the Forgotten. "Whenever you are ready, take us into the Between."

Nyx immediately stepped forward. Closing her eyes, she put out a hand, fingers spread wide, as if searching for something that could only be felt. "Keirran showed me how to enter the Between," she murmured, taking a few steps forward. "He said that only the Forgotten remember how to do it, and that the Lady gave him the gift when she was alive. You have to find a spot where the Veil is thin."

"Like a trod?" Puck asked, referring to the magical paths that led into the Nevernever from the mortal realm.

"Similar," Nyx murmured, still walking steadily forward with her hand up. We trailed the Forgotten as she continued to search. "The Veil is like a mist," she went on, "constantly moving and changing. Those weak spots you find might not be there when you return to them. But, if you search long enough, you should be able to find... There."

She stopped. Paused a moment. And then, as I had seen Keirran do only once or twice before, pushed her fingers into the fabric of reality and drew it back like a curtain. A narrow gash appeared where she parted the Veil, and beyond that tear was darkness. A few tendrils of mist curled out of the hole and writhed away into nothing.

Standing at the mouth of the gash into the void, Nyx shook her head. "The Between," she murmured. "It feels...different. Angrier than it was before. That's not good." She opened her eyes and looked back at us. I saw concern on her face, but it was overshadowed by a somber resolution. "Guard your emotions," she warned. "Calm your mind, and your feelings. The Between can manifest physical representations of strong emotions. So, if you are not careful, we might be facing your worst fears, or the darkest parts of your anger."

I took a furtive breath to quiet the tangle of emotions, searching for the cold, empty calm of the Winter prince. It didn't come as easily as it did in the past. Before Meghan and Keirran, when I only had myself to worry about, I feared very little. I wasn't afraid of venturing into the unknown. Whatever came at me, whatever monster, nightmare or horrific abomination I would face, the worst that could happen was that they would kill me. And I was exceedingly hard to kill. Fear for my own life had rarely been a concern.

Things were different now. I had a family. I had a wife, and a son; two people that meant more to me than anything, in any world. If they were in danger, my entire being was consumed with wanting to protect them, to utterly destroy whatever evil they faced so it could never threaten them again. I could feel that anger in me now, rising up to dominate my thoughts, and breathed deep to find my center. If Keirran was out there, we would find him, and I would cut down anything that stood in our way. Simple as that.

Puck gave a loud, noisy sigh and glanced at me. "Well, ice-boy," he said, "here we go again. Another adventure through the worst Faery has to offer. Oh, wait, you've never been through the actual Between before, have you?" He grinned, green eyes shining with mischief as he stepped toward the gateway. "You're in for all sorts of fun surprises."

2

THE HALF-THERE CITY

Puck wasn't entirely correct. I *had* been through the Between. A couple times, in fact. Both instances were with Meghan when we visited Touchstone, the capital of Keirran's new realm. Keirran could no longer come into the Nevernever, but that didn't prevent us from going into the Between to see him. Though more often than not, rather than take us into Touchstone, the Forgotten King preferred meeting us in the mortal realm. I suspected he didn't want us to worry about him. It wasn't that Keirran was ashamed of his kingdom or his subjects, but Touchstone, at least the few times I had seen it, was a city of perpetual night and shadow. It was bleak, gloomy, and had a somber, melancholy air that was evident in the many Gothic-inspired buildings that made up the city. Parapets, soaring archways, and leering gargoyles were common themes in Touchstone, and the Forgotten slid through the murky streets and along the rough stone walls like creatures from a child's nightmare.

I would admit, Touchstone was a rather dismal place, which was why I suspected Keirran asked to meet us in the mortal world most of the time. But though the city was dim and shadowy, with a melancholy air that could practically be felt, it was still a city. It still had streets and buildings and recognizable structures.

It was nothing like the flat, empty void I found myself in now.

"The Between," Meghan mused, her voice barely above a whisper. Around us, the featureless landscape of fog and mist stretched on until it vanished into the void. There was no source of light, no smells, no sounds except our own voices. "So this is what it really looks like."

"Cheery, ain't it?" Puck said, his voice ringing loudly in the total emptiness. "Oh, but don't let the morbid peacefulness fool you—the Between can spit out some pretty horrific beasties if you're not careful. Tell 'em, Furball."

Grimalkin gave Puck a look of cat disdain, then turned to us with a sniff. "Goodfellow is correct," he said, though he sounded annoyed admitting such a thing. "The Forgotten has already warned you of what could happen, but I suppose it is up to me to elaborate...again." He raised his head in the cat equivalent of a sigh. "The Between is alive," he began. "Not sentient—it has no particular feelings of malice or ill intent toward those who venture inside its borders—but it can bring things to life around you. The Between has the ability to manifest physical creations based on how you are feeling at the time. So, sentiments like anger, fear, grief, despair, and any strong emotions I would advise keeping at a minimum, as much as you are able, unless you want to run into a creature crafted from your own nightmares. Though I fear asking fey to control their emotions is like asking a dog not to drool." The cat twitched his tail in an almost resigned manner. "Do give it your best shot, at least."

I glanced at Meghan, and saw the veiled fear and anger in her eyes. Worry for Keirran, anger that something was attempting to take him from us yet again. Determination that we would find him no matter what. The Iron Queen, though she had grown wise in her rule over the Iron Kingdom, still struggled with burying and shutting off her emotions, particularly when it came to family. I had more practice, a lifetime of freezing out memories and emotions, and yet, I was finding it difficult to remain impassive. My son was missing. I needed to find him, but after that, I wanted nothing more than to track down whatever threatened him and destroy it completely.

I felt a chill at my back, and turned to see a section of mist curl away, revealing a bleak scene on the other side. Frozen bodies, both human and fey, were piled carelessly atop each other, eyes glazed and wide with terror. At the very peak of the grotesque mountain, a familiar sword had been shoved point-first into someone's back. Standing brightly against the gloom, the blade glimmered with an icy blue light. As I watched, unable to look away, the corpses' eyes opened, hard with accusation, all blankly staring at me.

I jerked up, but as I did, a curtain of mist fell over the bodies, hiding them from view. A moment later when the fog lifted, they were gone.

"Ash." Beside me, Meghan let out a soft breath, and I knew she had seen it, too. "Are you going to be all right?" she asked softly.

Get a hold of yourself, Ash, I told myself. *The Between can bring your darkest fears and emotions to life. No one wants to see that, least of all you.*

Anger stirred again, and I pushed it down. Focus on finding Keirran, then deal with the threat, whatever it was. Meeting Meghan's gaze, I gave a faint, reassuring smile. "I'm fine," I told her. "Don't worry about me—let's just find Keirran."

Nyx stepped forward, her eyes glowing yellow in the eerie nonlight. "Touchstone is in this direction," she said. "Follow me."

We did, trailing the assassin silently through the void. I wasn't certain how long we walked. The Between looked the same wherever you looked; a gray landscape of eternal fog and mist, coiling over nothing. Occasionally, the tendrils would curl back to reveal strange shapes in the fog; everything from trees and bushes to snowmen and bleached animal bones. But, while some of these were mildly disturbing, nothing came to life, nothing leaped out of the mist to attack us, and we continued through the Between without incident.

But, while the Between was silent and still, it *was* angry. I could feel it, just as Nyx had said. Or perhaps these were my own emotions, reacting to the looming threat of this place and the uncertainty with Keirran. Why was my family continuously in danger? It seemed we had just finished a war where I not only had to fight an army of fey and one powerful ex-queen of Faery, I also had to watch my own son betray everyone he knew. And now, another threat had risen up, attempting to rip everything I loved away from me. Would I constantly be fighting to save my family knowing that, one day, I might fail and lose everything?

Anger shifted quietly into rage, but at that moment, Nyx paused, frowning as she stared into the nothingness of the Between.

"This isn't right," she muttered. Turning in a slow circle, she peered intently into the void and shook her head. "No, I'm not mistaken. Something is definitely wrong."

I stared into the mist as Nyx had done, but could see nothing. "What do you mean?"

"This is the edge of the capital," Nyx explained, turning to me with a somber expression. "We would have passed the perimeter a few seconds ago." She pointed a slender finger at nothing.

"There's supposed to be a gate, and a road that leads through the city to the town square. We should be in Touchstone right now."

I felt a chill go through my insides. Meghan gazed at the spot Nyx indicated in distress and alarm. "Glitch reported that the Forgotten capital was gone," she said in a shaky voice. "I didn't realize he meant it had simply vanished from existence."

Nyx looked pale, but before she could reply, something flickered in the mist, right in the spot she was standing. The Forgotten leaped back, and I drew my weapon, as an archway of stone appeared, parting fog as it materialized in front of us. Two leering stone gargoyles perched at the very top of the pillars, baring oversize fangs as they stared down at us.

Puck sighed, lowering his daggers and glaring at the structure that had suddenly decided to join us. "Dammit, I'll never get used to that," he muttered. "So, whose manifestation is this, and why are you afraid of archways? Or is it the gargoyles that are the problem here? I mean, they *do* hit really hard..."

Nyx blinked. "This...is the gate to the city," she said in confusion. "Or part of it, anyway." She glanced to either side, as if looking for a wall that was supposed to be attached to the archway. "I do not understand what is happening."

"It is the gate," Grimalkin confirmed, observing the sneering gargoyles with bored contempt. "And I think I can answer that." He leaped onto a broken stone block and sat down, curling his tail around his feet. "In the Between," he began sagely, "when an anchor is destroyed, everything attached to it vanishes as well, correct? But what if the anchor was only damaged? What would happen to the world around it?"

"Probably what we're seeing now," Puck guessed, indicating the gate, which suddenly sputtered like a dying candle and winked out for a moment, dropping Grim to the ground. When it solidified again, one of the gargoyles that had been crouched at the top was missing. "A city that can't decide whether it wants to be here or not."

"But, if something has damaged the anchor…" Nyx jerked up, her face going pale. "The anchor is at Touchstone Manor," she whispered. "Keirran—"

A shriek rang out in the mist ahead.

Everyone drew their weapons, and Grimalkin immediately blinked out of sight like the gate. We hurried forward, passing beneath the broken, flickering gate and into the city.

Or what used to be the city.

Beyond the gates, Touchstone seemed to be on the verge of fading back into the nothingness of the Between. Looming stone buildings flickered in and out of existence, there one moment and gone the next. Structures were fraying apart at the edges, looking fuzzy as tendrils coiled slowly into the air. A fountain in the center of town appeared nearly transparent, the water spewing from the top turning to mist before it struck the basin.

But the city wasn't just fading. As we ventured deeper into Touchstone and drew closer to the mansion, I began to see the chilling signs of an attack. Structures had been destroyed, buildings had collapsed or been torn down by some massive force. Several trees lining the road had been snapped like kindling, and one was nothing but a burned, charred skeleton, branches crumbling to ashes in the wind. Everything was eerily silent, lifeless, like this was a photo someone had shot in the aftermath, not a living, breathing city.

"Where are the Forgotten?" Meghan wondered, blue eyes scanning the destruction. When I had last come to Touchstone, the Forgotten weren't exactly swarming the roads, but there were at least a few skulking about in the shadows. Now, the streets were empty and silent, seemingly abandoned. "Have they all left the city? Everyone can't be gone."

I didn't answer. At the moment, I didn't really care about the

Forgotten. My present concern was finding Keirran; when he was safe, I would worry about his subjects.

Touchstone Manor shimmered into view in the mist, an old mansion sitting atop a hill overlooking the city. Inside the manor it was very nice; well-lit and comfortable, if a little empty. Keirran's Forgotten staff were a reticent bunch who shied away from being seen, so visits to the manor usually only involved us and Keirran. But the outside of the manor resembled a classic Gothic mansion, with pointed arches, spiky turrets, and soaring windows. It stood silhouetted against the moon, imposing and ominous, looming over Touchstone like a gargoyle.

"The manor is still intact," Meghan observed as we made our way up the long, winding road to the mansion. She sounded cautiously hopeful. "Perhaps Keirran is still inside."

I wanted to share her optimism, though all signs pointed otherwise. The damage wreaked upon the streets and buildings. The empty city. The way Touchstone itself flickered and wavered as if it was struggling to hold on to existence. But I knew Keirran was strong, both in will and magic. I held out hope that we would find him, alive, in the smoking ruins of his city.

Because if we didn't, I wasn't sure what I would do, but something, somewhere, was going to pay.

We reached the top of the hill, and my hopes died a little as I saw the massive hole that had been torn out of the front gate. Stones had been crushed, trees uprooted, and the ground had been churned to mud by something enormous and powerful. The manor itself was dark, and that same dead stillness hung over everything. We slipped through the gate into the courtyard, staring up at the mansion, searching for a monstrous silhouette perched on the roof, but nothing could be seen in the mist and shadows. Whatever force of destruction had come through, it was gone now.

Nyx drew in a quiet breath, her attention suddenly shifting

to one corner of the manor, where a few stones lay behind a low fence. It looked like a simple pile of rubble to me, but Nyx shook her head solemnly. "The anchor has been damaged," she murmured, "but it doesn't look completely destroyed. Maybe Keirran was able to save it."

"But where *is* Keirran?" Meghan wondered as we walked toward the looming front doors. "If he's still here, we would have seen him by now."

"Also," Puck commented, "is the fog getting rather aggressive, or is it just me?"

The mist around us was growing thicker, creeping over the ground and sliding forward at a concerning rate. In seconds, it had surrounded us, turning the courtyard white, making it impossible to see more than a few paces ahead. And it felt...angry. The mist was a writhing cauldron of rage and hate, ghostly tendrils clawing at us as it billowed forward.

I drew my sword in a flash of blue light, seeing Meghan do the same. Beside me, Puck pulled his daggers, and Nyx raised her arms, twin blades of curved moonlight appearing in the hands of the Forgotten.

Shadowy figures began rising from the carpet of roiling fog, hands reaching out of the mist like grasping zombies. The whispers grew louder, turning into growls and snarls of rage, as hordes of shadowlike things emerged from the fog. They looked like Forgotten—black, featureless silhouettes with glowing golden eyes—but their frames were twisted, literally bent out of shape. Their bodies were contorted into grossly impossible positions, limbs stretched and wrenched out of place, yet somehow able to move. One creature crawled toward me with its spine bent backward, long arms twisted at the elbows like a grotesque spider. Another staggered toward me, jaws seeming to dislocate and distend like a snake's as it wailed. Whispers rose into the air, tangled and fragmented, snatches of words lost in the storm.

Nyx recoiled, her own golden eyes filling with horror as the misshapen creatures staggered close. "Are these Forgotten?" she whispered in disbelief. "What did this to them?" A Forgotten stumbled close, neck bent at an awkward angle, its head hanging down by its knees. Nyx backed away, her expression haunted as she gazed at the approaching shadows, before it hardened. "What happened here?" she called into the horde. "Where is King Keirran?"

"Imposter."

I couldn't tell which of the shadow creatures had spoken, but the rest of them exploded into sibilant whispers:

"He is not Forgotten."

"Not one of us."

"You are not one of us, either."

"Traitor."

The twisted shadow fey pressed closer, their voices growing louder, angrier. *"You stand with those who would destroy us,"* they hissed. *"Who shut us away in this void to Fade and be forgotten. But we will not Fade. We will not forgive. We will rise up and take back what was stolen."*

I narrowed my eyes. This was treading very close to outright war talk, and apparently Meghan thought the same, because the Iron Queen stepped forward, her power filling the void like the energy before a storm. "We are at peace now, Forgotten," she said, as a tide of blank yellow eyes turned on her. "The war has ended, and the courts no longer consider you a threat. There is no cause for another conflict between us."

"Queen of Iron." The motley assemblage of shadow creatures hissed, and the depth of anger, fear and loathing in their voices made me clench a hand on my sword hilt. *"Ruler of corruption. You would damn us to Fade, just like your kin."*

Anger stirred. A cold, dangerous anger that I hadn't felt in years. The fury of the Unseelie prince.

"No one wants you to Fade." Meghan took a step forward, earning an outbreak of wails and hissing from the gathered mob. "No one desires your destruction. The Lady is gone, and the Nevernever is at peace."

"We were here before you." It was getting harder to understand them now; the wailing and gnashing was rising in tenor, drowning out the Forgotten's words. *"We existed, and the Nevernever was ours. It will be ours again. Free from the corruptors, the poison spreaders, the plague that holds it now. By doing nothing, you allow us to Fade. You are Queen of Nothing, like the king who once ruled the Between."*

"Where is Keirran?" Meghan's voice was stern; she was done asking nicely, and I was right there with her. "Where is the King of the Forgotten? Tell me—now."

"Imposter!" the shadow creatures hissed in return. *"Not one of us! He is yours, a king of nothing. A ruler of nothing, who does nothing. We know the truth. We will pull down the oppressors! We will rise up to take it all back!"*

The rage flared, a cold rush through my veins, freezing any thoughts of kindness or mercy. These creatures, though they had once been fey, were monsters now. They knew where Keirran was and refused to tell us. Worse, they had actively threatened my family, the queen fighting at my side. They deserved death. And I would give it to them.

I took a breath, drawing in the hate-drenched glamour around me, and drove my sword into the darkness at my feet, releasing a surge of Winter magic as I did. With a pulse of cold, the shadow creatures closest to us turned to ice, becoming twisted statues posed in grotesque formations. I yanked up my sword, and the crystalline forms shattered with the sound of smashing icicles.

"Ow! Jeez, ice-boy!" Robin Goodfellow yelped and backed away, shielding his face from the explosion of frozen shrapnel. "Went right to the nasty magic, didn't you? What happened to trying the reasonable approach? I don't think Keirran will be happy with us turning his subjects into Popsicles."

I inhaled slowly, feeling the violence within, the cold anger coiling around my heart. "They might have been fey once, but they're lost now," I said, as the remaining shadows cringed back from the lethal display of glamour. "There is no reasoning with them."

I gestured and, with another pulse of magic ice spikes, punched through the foggy ground, impaling several shadow monsters and causing them to instantly erupt into coils of smoke. Wailing, they vanished into nothingness. Striding forward, I lashed out and cut a nightmare in two, then stabbed another through a mouth that had grown half as large as its body. Both howled and disappeared on the breeze, leaving only a few tendrils of shadow behind.

"Ash, stop." Meghan's voice cut through the icy rage, making me pause. "They're leaving," she said as I lowered my weapon. "They're running away. No need for more death."

I looked up and saw she was right. The horde was drawing back. Wailing and snarling, they lurched away into the fog and were lost from view. Though their fragmented whispers floated back to us, venomous and hateful.

"Imposters."

"Not one of us."

"We will rise, and the courts will fall."

"We will take back what is ours."

I sheathed my sword and breathed deep to calm my anger, feeling it settle coldly in the pit of my stomach. We were alone in the mist once more, though I knew the shadow things, the once Forgotten, were still out there, watching us. A stony resolve settled over me. If they attacked again, they would die on my blade. I would tolerate no one threatening my friends or family, not even the subjects of my own kin.

"Well, that was disturbing." Puck's voice shattered the somber silence. "Really gives new meaning to the phrase 'bent out of shape.'" He sighed, raking a hand through his spiky red hair. "Dammit. I was going to ask what got them all riled up and angry, but I'm afraid I already know the answer. And I'm not going to like it."

"The Monster was here," Nyx said. "Or something similar was. The glamour taint here feels the same as last time. Those Forgotten...weren't like that before." Her voice shook for the barest moment, but she took a breath and the tremor was gone. "How many of these things are there?" she murmured.

"I don't know," Puck said, his voice uncharacteristically solemn. "But I do know I don't want to have to fight it again. Do you think the big ugly is still here?"

"The king wouldn't leave the city defenseless unless he had to," Nyx said quietly. "If the Monster *is* still here, that means Keirran..."

She trailed off, and Meghan briefly closed her eyes. Shoving down the cold fear clawing at me, I stepped forward. "We won't know for certain unless we find the thing that did this," I said. "There has to be something left. Someone who can tell us what happened here. Nyx..." I glanced at the Forgotten. "You lived here. Is there anywhere we could go that would still be intact? Anyone who could still be around?"

"I believe I can help with that." It was Grimalkin's familiar voice. I had forgotten about the cat when the shadow creatures had appeared, since he always vanished if a fight was imminent. I glanced down as the cat materialized out of the fog, his wispy fur nearly a part of the mist itself. His eyes, floating in the gloom, were the only part of him that seemed real.

"I found someone," Grimalkin announced, padding lazily into view. "While the lot of you were futilely threatening the

27

local population, I discovered one who had not currently lost her mind. I believe you should all listen to what she has to say."

Only then did I notice a shadow behind Grimalkin, nearly invisible in the darkness. She edged forward: a willowy Forgotten with slender dragonfly wings, though just like the others, she was a featureless silhouette in the murkiness. Her golden eyes were wide with fear as she stared at us all.

"Iron Queen," she whispered. "You have come." She gazed at Meghan, and the wings on her back shook. "Please forgive me, Your Majesty. I tried to help the king. I tried…but everything happened so fast. I'm sorry."

"What happened here?" Meghan asked, and though her voice was calm, her expression was steely. "Where is the Forgotten King?"

"The king." The Forgotten trembled. "He isn't here," she whispered. "He's gone. He left the city with the survivors, after—after the attack.

"My name is Elaith," the Forgotten continued into the silence that followed. "I was King Keirran's personal assistant. The night it happened, I was here, performing my duties here at the manor. The king was in his office, with instructions not to be disturbed. Suddenly, the door banged open and he rushed out, looking alarmed and angry. He told me to gather up as many Forgotten as I could and take them to the edge of the city. It was then…" She paused once more and covered her face, seemingly overcome with shame or fear. Meghan waited patiently, though I had to stifle the urge to prod her along. "It was then," Elaith whispered again, "that I felt it coming. I can't explain it. It was just…"

"Yeah," Puck sighed. "*It*. We know what you're talking about, unfortunately."

Elaith trembled, and though her features were veiled in darkness, her eyes were huge with terror. "I didn't even see the creature plainly, whatever it was," she whispered. "I just…felt it coming. I felt its anger, its absolute rage and hate for all living things, and I was terrified. But Keirran told me again to gather our people, as many that would come, and meet him outside of Touchstone. He then rushed out, into the city, to confront the Monster. That was the last I saw of him."

I narrowed my eyes as the Forgotten stumbled to a halt, looking anguished and guilty. "What happened?"

"I—I don't know!" The Forgotten let out a wail and covered her eyes again. "Please forgive me, I was too frightened to leave the manor. I could sense what was happening outside, and I couldn't make myself leave."

"You disobeyed a direct order," Nyx stated in disbelief. "The king told you to gather the survivors, and you betrayed him."

"You don't understand." Elaith looked up, her eyes huge. "I could hear the screams, sense the fear and terror, and when I peeked outside, Touchstone was in chaos. Forgotten had become monsters, twisted versions of themselves, and they were attacking anyone unlike them. I couldn't go out into that. And then…" She shook violently. "I saw it. The Monster. It was huge, and all around it, Forgotten were turning into twisted versions of themselves. Didn't you see them?" she asked, gazing up at us. "They're still out there, roaming the city. Some of them even tried destroying the anchor. If I left the manor, they would attack me, too."

"What happened to Keirran?" Meghan asked, and her voice was not gentle anymore.

"He fled," Elaith admitted. "Away from Touchstone and into the Between. Near dawn, while the creature was still decimating the city, I felt a rift being torn in the Veil, bigger than any I've felt before. I think that was Keirran, opening the Veil and taking everyone he could gather out of Touchstone and away from the Monster." She sank to her knees, her arms around herself, dragonfly wings vibrating as she trembled. "I am sorry, my king. I wanted to serve you, but I was just too frightened. If I had heeded your orders, I would be with you now."

I met Meghan's gaze, saw worry mingling with cautious hope. Keirran had been here, and the last anyone saw, he had been alive. Being pursued by an unkillable monster was not ideal, but I knew my son. Before his exile, when he was doing something foolish and didn't want to be found, I had chased him all over the Nevernever, through the real world, the wyldwood, and the Between. I knew firsthand how difficult he was to catch.

I had to trust that he was alive now.

"So," Puck ventured at last. "How are we going to find Keirran? The Between is a big place. In fact, I think Keirran once mentioned that it was eternal."

"Correct," Grimalkin said, looking up from washing his tail. "There are fey that have become lost and have wandered the mist for centuries. Tracking someone through the Between when we have no idea of where they are or where they are going would be most unwise. However," he went on, "there *is* someone who knows the Between far better than any of you. Who has been here longer than any except the Forgotten. Who owes me a rather large favor at the moment."

Puck winced. "Oh, no. Are we thinking of the same person? She might be a tad annoyed with me right now." He thought about that statement for a moment, then shrugged. "But, then again, she's always annoyed with me."

"Leanansidhe," Meghan said. "Of course. She lives in the Between. And she has a whole network of informants and spies who keep an eye on pretty much everything."

"Yes," Grimalkin agreed. "If anyone has information or news regarding the Forgotten King and his whereabouts, Leanansidhe would be your best hope. And she would be happy to share her information. For a price, of course."

A price. Anger stirred again. Even though I had been in Faery a long time, even though I knew this was how things were done since the beginning of the Nevernever, the thought that I would have to pay a price for information about my missing son still galled. Worse that it was Leanansidhe. The Dark Muse, as she was called, wasn't as strong as Mab or Titania, but she was still a queen. A self-made queen, perhaps, but still quite powerful in her own territory. She ruled a court of exiles, outcasts, and half-breed fey, and hoarded information like Grimalkin hoarded favors.

The cat was right; Leanansidhe was the perfect person to ask about Keirran. But the price she would charge was going to be very high. I would pay, of course. I would pay any price for the sake of my family. I just hoped it wouldn't affect Meghan or anyone else.

Nyx looked solemn. "I have heard of this Leanansidhe," she said. "The Exile Queen? Keirran mentioned her once or twice. Unfortunately, I have not had the pleasure of meeting her, so I don't know where her court resides. I could find it, eventually, but the Between is very large and it will take some time. Unless you or someone else knows the way...?"

"Worry not," Grimalkin sighed, and rose with an air of exaggerated patience. "As usual, I will lead you to her. We need to find the trod to Leanansidhe's, and the fastest way to do that is through the real world."

Meghan looked at Elaith, who was still kneeling on the ground with her arms curled around herself. I could see the turmoil inside the Iron Queen, but she finally held a hand out to the Forgotten. "You are welcome to come with us, Elaith," she said, and I admired her for not sounding begrudging at all. "Leanansidhe is the Exile Queen—she is very used to taking in fey that have nowhere else to go. You could stay with her and return to the Between when we find Keirran."

But the Forgotten shook her head. "I know of this Leanan-sidhe. The Exile Queen is not fond of us Forgotten," she said. "I am afraid of what would happen should I stay under her roof. No, I will stay here, and wait for my king to return. As long as Touchstone does not disappear completely, I will be waiting for him when he comes back."

Meghan nodded. "If that is your decision," she said. "I won't force you. But we need to go. Let's hope the Exile Queen can point us to where Keirran disappeared. Grim…" she said, turning to the cat, who watched her with lazy eyes. "Take us to Leanansidhe."

Fat drops of water pounded my head and shoulders as we left the void of the Between and stepped into the real world. For just a moment, the sensation of the rain combined with the feel of the wind and the sounds of the real world was almost overwhelming after being in the Between for so long. The sky was dim and cloudy, and I saw the hazy glow of a streetlamp overhead, the gray shapes of buildings blurring into view as I gazed around.

"Of course, it's a city," Puck complained as Grimalkin darted past him to take shelter beneath an overhang. In the distance, a car horn blared, and Nyx jumped, muscles tensing in an instinctive fight-or-flight reaction. "It's never a sunny meadow or a delightful fruit orchard. There goes my hope of grabbing a snack before we head back into the void."

"Where are we?" Nyx wondered. She relaxed slowly, never letting down her guard as she gazed around. "What is this place?"

"Oh, right. You've never seen a city, have you?"

"Not like this." The Forgotten continued to stare, taking in the many new sights and sounds. "Are they always so...noisy?"

"Some more than others." Puck shrugged. "But, yeah. It's no peaceful forest grove, that's for certain. Why does Leanansidhe insist on plopping her trods down in overcrowded cities and not in the wilderness like any rational faery?"

"I would guess more exiles and half-fey gather in cities," Meghan replied. Almost casually, she gestured with a hand, and small scraps of metal and steel particles swirled around her like metallic insects, until they formed a glittering parasol over her head. Nyx's eyes widened, but Meghan didn't seem to notice. "Cities are where most of her informants come from—it makes sense that she would have more trods there."

"That's a neat trick, princess." Puck blinked, gazing at the umbrella the Iron Queen had seemed to conjure from thin air. Nyx was staring at it in active alarm. "Doesn't really work for a human disguise, though. I take it we're not going to be doing much blending in."

The faintest of smiles crossed Meghan's face. "I barely even thought about it," she confessed. "I've been in the Iron Kingdom a long time now—certain things just become habit. But, no, we're not going to be doing any blending in." Taking a few steps toward me, she held up the parasol and I wrapped my fingers around the handle, shielding us both from the rain. "We're not going to be here for long, just until we find the trod that will take us to Leanansidhe's. I plan on staying glamoured until we're back in the Between."

"Which we will do faster if we start moving," Grimalkin commented, observing us all from atop a dumpster, plumed tail waving impatiently. "Follow me, if you are finished discussing the seriousness of the situation. The trod should be close."

"Right." Puck grimaced, then unexpectedly reached down and grasped Nyx's hand. She blinked at him, startled, but didn't pull away. He gave her a crooked grin. "Into the heart of oblivious humanity. Don't panic, stay close, and try not to stab anyone. No matter how much you're tempted."

Following Grimalkin, we stepped from the alley onto the sidewalk, and were immediately surrounded by humans striding past us in both directions. They couldn't see us, of course. We were all glamoured and invisible to mortal eyes, so unless we ran into a human with the Sight, we were free to walk down the street as we were. Which was fortunate, because I was not in the mood to deal with humanity today; I wanted to get to Leanansidhe's and discover if she knew what was happening in the Between, and where Keirran could have gone. I wanted to find my son; running into a rude or hostile human right now would try my patience and could end very badly for the oblivious mortal.

"So many humans," Nyx muttered. She had pulled up her hood, hiding her hair and most of her face, and even glamoured and invisible, her entire posture was tense. "Keirran told me there were thousands of these cities all through the mortal realm, but I found it hard to believe." She peeked up, watching as a young person rushed past, a notebook held over his head. "Maybe I could just meet you at Leanansidhe's—I'm sure I could find my way there on my own."

Puck chuckled. "Oh, no, Miss Stoic Assassin," he said, and raised their joined hands. "This is a team effort, and you're part of the gang now. If we have to endure the throngs of humanity, you have to suffer with us."

She frowned at him. "Is that how this works?"

"Yup." Puck grinned cheekily back, ignoring the assassin's glare. I had seen the Forgotten's abilities, both on the battlefield and off. I doubted Puck could have kept Nyx with us if she truly wanted to leave, but she let out a small sigh and pulled her hood up even farther.

"I'd fear what would happen if I wasn't present, anyway," she muttered.

I saw a small half smile flit across Meghan's face, though her eyes remained shadowed, her expression worried and far away. It had been a long time since anyone had come along who could keep up with Robin Goodfellow. Nyx seemed like one of the rare few who could not only handle Puck and all his quirks, but could also give it back. It was obvious my best friend was falling for her, and I hoped it would not end badly for him. She was, after all, a primordial faery assassin who had been around before the courts even existed. That was going to be a challenge, even for Puck.

"What are you looking at, asshole?"

A shout suddenly drew my attention. Across the street, a trio of younger humans seemed to have gotten into an argument. Two young men stood a few feet apart, pointing angry fingers and making sharp gestures as they shouted expletives, while a young woman, perhaps a sister or girlfriend, looked on angrily. I didn't know what had caused the argument, but from what I could tell, one human had looked at the girl in a way the other didn't like, and he had taken offense.

Normal human behavior, especially between two younger males. What was not so normal was the creature clinging to the girl's shoulders.

It was unlike anything I'd seen before, which in itself was astounding. I wasn't as well traveled as Puck, but I had been to the farthest reaches of the Nevernever, to the End of the World and back. I'd lived a long time, and seen creatures of all shapes and sizes, from towering giants to the tiniest threats. But this creature, much like the Monster we'd fought before, was something completely new.

It was tiny, the size of a piskie or large dragonfly, and had a humanlike frame despite long, spindly limbs and hands tipped with curved nails. Its body was emaciated; bones pressed sharply against dark, oily skin, giving it a skeletal look. From this distance, its features were difficult to make out, but I could see a gaping mouth with jagged, protruding fangs and pointed ears jutting from a bulbous skull. Thin, wasplike wings buzzed and vibrated against its back, only adding to its insectlike appearance. When the tiny creature turned its head in my direction, I saw that it had no eyes, just bulging lumps of flesh where the sockets should have been.

But most disturbing, threads of shadow kept coiling from its body and writhing into the air, like the tentacles of the Monster. I could see them coiling around the arms and neck of the girl the creature was perched on, sinking below her skin. Both the girl and the others around us seemed oblivious to the creature that was obviously out of place in the mortal realm. The three humans were drawing some looks of alarm from those nearby, but it was more a reaction to the shouting match than from the tiny monster clinging to the girl's back.

Beside me, I felt Meghan shudder. "What is that?" she whispered. "It looks like a piskie, but I've never seen its kind before, have you?"

"No," I murmured. "I never have." I didn't want to say what I thought it could be, to voice my suspicions out loud. Apparently, I didn't have to.

"It feels like the Monster," Nyx remarked grimly, confirming my fears. "It's smaller, much weaker, but I can sense its hate. It projects the same negative glamour the big creature did."

"But why is it here in the mortal realm?" Meghan wondered. "They're not from the Nevernever, and I haven't seen one in the Between. Where are these things coming from?"

"I don't know," Puck muttered, and gave me an evil grin. "Maybe we should go ask it, ice-boy."

I gave a serious nod. I doubted the creature would tell us anything, but I wanted to see what it would do, what kind of new threat I was dealing with. Resting my hand on my sword hilt, I started across the street with Puck beside me.

As we approached, the argument between the humans seemed to be escalating. Both boys had puffed out their chests and were standing on their toes, glaring at each other and motioning aggressively. The girl stood a couple paces away, arms crossed, watching the showdown to an obvious fight.

I could feel the menace in the air, the violent glamour flickering around the humans, prodding my own anger to life. On the girl's shoulder, the piskie-esque creature crouched like an enormous winged spider, dark wisps curling from its body to writhe into nothingness on the breeze.

Suddenly, its head jerked up. The tiny eyeless face swiveled in our direction, and its waspish wings buzzed in alarm. Curling its lips back, the creature bared thin, needle-like teeth in a snarl that stretched all the way around its head, then darted into the air. Zipping over the roof of a building, it vanished from sight.

The second it left, the air of tension and anger around the trio of humans faded. The girl stood there a moment, blinking, then stepped forward and grabbed the boy's arm, trying to tug him away. Almost in relief, the males backed down. Though they continued to threaten and posture, it was just to save face now, and gradually, the gap between them widened as they moved away from each other. Finally, the humans turned and went in opposite directions, leaving Puck and I to gaze after them in rising concern at what we had just witnessed.

"Well, that was…highly disturbing," Puck remarked as we returned to Meghan and Nyx. "Did you guys see what I did, or am I just imagining things?"

"That creature," Nyx mused, staring in the direction the piskie thing had fled, "was both radiating anger and feeding off it. When it left, the humans both backed down."

"Just like the Monster we fought," I added darkly. "But now they're here, in the real world."

"But where did it come from?" Meghan wondered. "That creature wasn't anything from the Nevernever. Is this an entirely new breed of faery no one has noticed until now?"

Once again, Nyx frowned, looking both thoughtful and frustrated. "It *was* fey," she admitted. "I could feel it. And it was… familiar somehow. Like I've seen it before, though I can't remember from where." She thought a moment longer, than shook her head. "Or perhaps not. I can't seem to recall anything about it."

"I think," Grimalkin said from somewhere behind us, "that these are questions that we need to pose to Leanansidhe. Perhaps she knows about the comings and goings of these fey in the real world and can tell us more. Which is what we were planning to do in the first place before you all became predictably distracted. This way." The cat yawned, waving his tail as he glanced back at us. "If you are finished talking and would follow me, the trod to her mansion is not far."

4

"Hello, darlings," the Exile Queen greeted from atop her double grand staircase. Tall and pale, in a glittering evening gown and holding a cigarette flute between two gloved fingers, Leanansidhe the Dark Muse beamed down at us, strands of copper-bright hair floating around her face. "My goodness, today is a momentous day indeed. The Iron Queen, the son of Mab, Robin Goodfellow, the Lady's assassin, and Grimalkin all decide to pay me a visit at the same time?" She gave us a brittle, razor-sharp smile. "To what do I owe the pleasure?"

I stifled a flare of impatience. Dealing with the Exile Queen would be the same as dealing with every powerful faery in the Nevernever: with bargains and word games and each player trying to one-up the other. There was always a price. Always a deal to be worked out, no matter how simple or vital the information. I was growing tired of it. Furthermore, that Unseelie part of myself, the side I hadn't felt in a while, was growing tired as well. In the past, I'd made bargains with Leanansidhe and paid her price because I had to. Now, with Keirran's life on the line, I wasn't nearly as inclined to be patient.

"I think you have an idea, Leanansidhe," Meghan stated, walking forward. "The Between is your kingdom, much as the Iron Realm is mine. You know that something strange has happened."

"Something strange?" The Dark Muse feigned ignorance, twiddling her cigarette flute as she glided down the stairs. Her gown and hair billowed behind her as if in a breeze, though the air in the mansion was perfectly still. "Whatever could you mean, darling? This is Faery. Strange things happen every single day."

Impatience ticked ever so slightly to anger. Setting my jaw, I stepped forward. "We are not in the mood for games, Leanansidhe," I said, which caused Leanansidhe's slender eyebrows to arch. "Touchstone was recently attacked by a new kind of monster, and Keirran was forced to flee the Between with the survivors of the city. No one could tell us where he is or where he has gone. We were hoping that you might be able to shed some light on these events, both in Touchstone, and on this new creature we've been dealing with."

"Right to the point, as always. That's not a good way to tell a story, darling. You lose all your dramatic punch." The Exile Queen pursed her lips, then sighed. "Oh, very well," she grumbled, tossing back her hair, which drifted lazily behind her in a defiant rejection of gravity. "This way, if you would. If we are going to discuss such matters, I would rather do it out of earshot of every gossiping faery in this place, which is all of them. Follow me, and Puck, darling —" she gave the Great Prankster a smile that was sharper than a blade "—if anything mysteriously vanishes and ends up in a bizarre location, for any reason, I will be very cross. The redcaps nearly broke their skulls, and my bust of Mozart, trying to get it down from the roof."

Puck gave her his innocent "who, me?" look, but didn't comment this time, and we followed Leanansidhe down thick carpeted hallways, through elegantly decorated rooms, and past countless musical instruments hanging on the walls or propped up in corners. I knew from past visits and dealings with Leanansidhe that this impressive collection didn't just stem from her love of music. Some were unfortunate humans or fey who had displeased the fickle Exile Queen and ended up on her wall.

We entered a smaller, cozier room with a crackling stone fireplace and a variety of plush sofas and chairs surrounding it. Several paintings hung on the wall, and an easel sat in the corner with a human in front of it, the man humming loudly as he moved his brush back and forth. Though his movements were frantic, the painting itself was quite detailed and beautiful. Leanansidhe snapped her fingers as we swept through the door, and the human's head jerked up.

"Out, Charles," the Dark Muse commanded, and the man fled. His brush dropped to the floor and left green spatters against the red carpet. Leanansidhe wrinkled her nose at the stain, but then turned to us with a smile.

"Now, darlings, have a seat, why don't you?" She waved a slender arm at the sofas arrayed around the fireplace. She stode to the largest one, then sank down into it and crossed her legs. "Make yourselves comfortable, and I will tell you what I know about what is happening in the Between."

Meghan calmly took a seat across from the Exile Queen, sitting up straight but looking confident and unruffled. I did not sit but took my normal place behind her, while Puck slouched on the other end of the sofa, looking the opposite of regal. Nyx also chose not to sit, sliding into a darker corner of the room with her back to the wall. Grimalkin sauntered over to an empty chair, curled up with his tail over his nose, and appeared to go to sleep.

"So, our darling Keirran is in trouble again, is he?" Leanansidhe sniffed. "How terribly shocking. That didn't take long at all, did it? No offense, darlings, but that boy of yours is almost a bigger headache than Robin Goodfellow. At least Puck hasn't managed to *completely* destroy my house and collapse everything I've built over the past hundred or so years."

"Yet," Puck added with an evil smirk. Leanansidhe ignored him.

"Keirran was exiled from the Nevernever and is paying for his crimes," Meghan replied in a far calmer tone than I knew she was feeling. "That is not the issue today, Leanansidhe, and it is not the reason we've come. Do you know anything of what has been happening in the Between, and the new threat we're facing now?"

"I do." Abruptly serious, Leanansidhe took a long drag on her cigarette flute, then blew a puff of green smoke into the air. It coiled into the wispy image of a dragon before writhing away into nothingness. "Possibly more than you want to hear, darling. The Between is getting...well, *angrier* is the best way to put it. You already know it has the ability to sense your emotional state and churn out manifestations that are the representations of your feelings. But lately, it feels like there is such an excess of negative glamour, it's starting to affect the Between itself. I don't know what it is or where its coming from, but all this anger, rage, fear, and hate is seeping into the Between like poison. If it continues, it might start affecting the Nevernever as well."

"Do you think our big nasty is the one causing it?" Puck wondered after a moment of tense silence.

In the corner, Nyx shook her head, the movement barely visible in the shadows of her hood. "The Monster leaves a trail of corruption behind it," she said, "but it doesn't feel powerful enough to taint the entire Between. Whatever this is, it is bigger than that."

"I did feel a large, shall we say, *emptying* of the Between several days ago," Leanansidhe went on. "A mass exodus of sorts, many creatures going through the Veil at once. If you say Touchstone was attacked recently, that was probably the moment when they all fled the city."

"That matches what Elaith told us," I mused. "She said Keirran opened a gate in the Between for the Forgotten to escape the Monster. Do you know where they came out again?" I asked Leanansidhe.

"Sadly, no, darling." The Dark Muse fiddled with her cigarette flute. "But since Keirran has been exiled from the Nevernever, and since I did not feel them reenter the Between, I would guess that he took them into the mortal realm. Where, you ask?" She gave a helpless little shrug. "That is anyone's guess."

"It might be anyone's guess," Meghan replied, "but you could help us speed the process, Leanansidhe. Your network of spies is extensive, and I know you have informants in many cities throughout the mortal realm. If Keirran took his people and fled to the real world, someone would notice. Eventually, word would get back to you."

"Oh, you have my network all figured out, do you, Iron Queen?" Leanansidhe gave Meghan a cheery, slightly brittle smile. "I do hope you also remember all the damage your son has caused in the past, not only to the Nevernever, but to me, personally. I helped him, took in that Summer girl he was so enamored of, protected them both at great cost to myself, and how does he repay me?" She waved a hand at the elegant surroundings. "By tearing away the Veil and causing the Between to vanish. Which, in turn, destroyed my mansion in the process and caused me to lose all my servants, spies, *and* all my Charleses." Leanansidhe gave a dramatic sniff, wiping away an imaginary tear. "I'm still rather miffed about that."

Meghan gave no outward sign, but I could feel her tense beneath my palms, and gently squeezed her shoulders to let her know I was there. At the same time, anger toward Leanansidhe stirred. We both knew Faery did not forgive, and the fey often held grudges forever, but from the day Keirran had been exiled, we had both been reminded, constantly, of what he had done; the harm he had caused to everyone in the Nevernever. It was a heavy burden, particularly for Meghan; she was the Iron Queen and still had to abide by all of Faery's laws. No matter how difficult they were.

"So, this is going to cost you, darling," Leanansidhe went on, with a grave look at both Meghan and me. "While I have no qualms with the Iron Queen, that boy still has much to answer for. So, if you want me to help you, I'm afraid I'm going to need a favor."

Meghan paused. I knew she was mentally preparing herself for the most dangerous part of this meeting: the bargaining. "What kind of favor?" she asked after a moment.

"A large one," Leanansidhe said unapologetically, and I tamped down my growing anger. The Exile Queen knew we would do anything to find Keirran, and she was using that knowledge to her advantage. It was an expected tactic in the faery bargaining game, but it still made my blood boil. Keirran could be hurt, captured or in danger, but all Leanansidhe saw was an edge in making a deal.

"I'm going to need more information than that." Meghan remained poised and unruffled, though the muscles beneath my fingers were taut. "What is it you actually want, Leanansidhe?"

The Exile Queen settled back in her chair and smiled. "I want out of the Between, darling," she said. "I believe I've been banished long enough, and as you can see, the Between is becoming...rather unstable. It is dangerous for me to be here any longer, what with all the chaos and uncertainty happening now—monsters running amok through Touchstone and turning fey into nightmares. No, it is time for me to leave. I wish to return to the Nevernever and the Summer Court, and I can only do that if the one who banished me rescinds the order. So, I need you to talk to Titania and convince her to lift my exile. Do that for me, and I will help you find your son."

My blood chilled. Titania, Oberon's wife and Queen of the Summer Court, was the last faery any of us wanted to deal with. Not only was she fickle, petty, and arrogant, but she also hated us—all of us: me, Meghan, Puck, and Keirran—with a fiery passion. She was one of the most spiteful fey in the entire Nevernever, and enjoyed toying with both humans and fey just because she could. But she was also one of the most powerful faeries in the Summer Court, second only to Oberon himself, and crossing her was a very dangerous proposition.

Meghan went very still, though her tone remained even. "That is an extremely risky favor, Leanansidhe," she said. "One that will likely be impossible. You know this."

"Yes, darling." The Dark Muse gave her a smug look. "I do. I also know that you and the others in this room are all very clever. If you put your minds to it, I am certain you would figure something out." She leaned back, crossing her long legs. "But, that is my offer, my dove, in exchange for telling you what I know about Keirran. Take it, or leave it."

Enough of this.

I felt something in me break, like a film of ice over a raging sea. I was done being patient. This request, if not impossible, would be a waste of time and resources trying to appease yet another fickle faery queen. Bargaining was not the only way to achieve information, and Leanansidhe was not the strongest faery here, not anymore. It was time I reminded her that, not long ago, I had been an Unseelie prince, and the Nevernever had feared me.

"No."

46

I stepped away from the sofa, letting my winter glamour fill the room. The temperature dropped, the fire in the hearth sputtered and died, and a sheet of ice spread over the ceiling with sharp crinkling sounds. Puck straightened quickly, his breath coiling into the air around his head, and Nyx went perfectly still in the corner. Meghan and Leanansidhe remained in their seats, both of them feigning calm, though I could feel Meghan's surprise as I loomed over the Exile Queen, my gaze cold as I stared her down.

"I'm afraid it is you who misunderstands the situation, Leanansidhe," I said in a frigid tone. "This is not a request. Our son is missing, the Between is in chaos, and the entire Nevernever may be in danger. You will help us—now—or you will come to regret it."

Leanansidhe's eyebrows arched, and the barest flicker of surprise and fear crossed her face. But she drew herself up and gave me a challenging smile. "Well, well, someone has gotten a little big for their britches," she commented in an equally cold, dangerous voice. "May I remind you, Winter prince, that you are in *my* court, my realm, and there will be consequences for threatening a queen in their own territory."

"You are not a queen, Dark Muse." I didn't break eye contact, and the ice on the ceiling lengthened to foot-long spikes, glittering and deadly. "You may call yourself one, and command the fear of exiles and half-fey, but you sit in a room with a true queen of Faery, Robin Goodfellow, the son of Mab, and a Forgotten assassin who is older even than you." Deliberately, I rested my hand on my sword hilt, the threat perfectly clear. "Should we wish it, there will be nothing left of this realm. We will tear it down and scatter it to the Void, and you will become a fading memory that no one remembers. Until you, too, are forgotten, and the name of the Dark Muse vanishes from existence."

Leanansidhe drew in a slow breath. I could feel her gathering her power, drawing in the glamour around her, and felt my own winter magic swirl in response. If she wanted a fight, I would happily give her one.

Then Meghan stood up, energy and glamour flickering around her like a storm, causing the lights to flutter and dance. Leanansidhe paused, the barest note of apprehension crossing her face, as the power of the Iron Queen filled the room.

"This benefits no one, Leanansidhe," Meghan said again, her voice softer but no less firm. "Keirran's city has been destroyed, his people lost, and a monster threatens the Between and the lives of everyone in the Nevernever. You will help us, because if the Between disappears, it will take your kingdom with it. It is in your own best interest that Keirran is found, and found quickly. Please." She gestured, and the power level around her eased, though it didn't vanish entirely. "Help me find my son."

For a few heartbeats, Leanansidhe stared at Meghan, her expression unreadable. I curled my fingers around my sword hilt, as Nyx hovered in the corner and Puck casually shifted to a better position on the couch. Meghan's gaze remained locked with the Exile Queen, as the silence stretched out and the tension in the room soared.

Then Leanansidhe threw back her head and laughed. "Oh, bravo darling, bravo," the Dark Muse exclaimed, rising from her seat and clapping her hands. "A standing ovation for you, my dove—I was expecting the son of Mab to show his true colors again soon enough, but I was wondering when the mantle of power would start to affect you." Leanansidhe's lips twisted in a pleased smirk. "It's intoxicating, is it not? Having all that power at your fingertips? Congratulations, you've finally learned how to act like a queen. Titania would be so proud."

Meghan didn't respond, but her jaw tightened. "Where is Keirran?" she asked once more, her voice carefully controlled.

"Tell me, Leanansidhe. I know you at least have an idea of where he could have gone."

The Exile Queen pursed her lips. "I really don't know where your boy could have gone, darling," she stated airily. "But I know who might. And I'll tell you, my dove, but do remember…" She angled the point of her cigarette flute in Meghan's direction. "I will not forget this. If you're going to act like a queen, know there will be consequences when you throw your royal weight around in another queen's territory. I've taken on Mab and Titania before—don't think I'd be afraid to throw down with the Iron Queen as well.

"Keirran has gone into the mortal realm," Leanansidhe went on, leaving that unsubtle threat hanging in the air between us. "That is the only logical conclusion—he cannot stay in the Between, and he has been exiled from the Nevernever, so the mortal realm is the only place left for him to flee to. The question is…*where* in the mortal realm could he have gone? Especially with a large group of Forgotten in tow. The human world isn't safe for the Forgotten. They're in constant danger of Fading away from the lack of glamour and the effects of iron and banality. Keirran knows this. Cut off from the Between and the Nevernever, he'll be looking to find a safe spot for them, wherever he can. If he is trying to avoid detection himself, he will be in hiding. Finding him could prove difficult.

"However—" Leanansidhe raised two long fingers "—there are two people in the mortal realm whom he might try to contact. I believe you know them both, darling. They were instrumental in the last war, though one of them was the catalyst for the whole debacle with the Between temporarily vanishing."

"Ethan," I murmured. Meghan's half brother. Ethan was fully human, but he had been born with the Sight, able to see the hidden world of the fey even when they were invisible. Admittedly, he had hated both me and the Nevernever for a long time, blaming us for taking his sister away, but was finally able to come to terms with Meghan and make peace with the faery world he despised. In the last war with the Forgotten, Ethan had become a champion of Faery, and might have singlehandedly stopped Keirran from doing the unthinkable.

I didn't know what truly happened in those final moments between Keirran and Ethan Chase. I did know that Ethan had been Keirran's friend, and they'd helped each other several times in the past. Perhaps it was an age thing, but Keirran had always preferred to drag a reluctant, begrudging Ethan into his problems rather than come to us.

Leanansidhe nodded. "How is our darling Ethan, by the way?" she asked. "Still as grumpy and surly as ever? That boy could give a medusa a run for its money."

"Ethan is fine," Meghan said cautiously, wary of giving too much information to the Exile Queen. "He moved to a small town with Kenzie and opened his own martial-arts dojo."

"Ah, Mackenzie," Leanansidhe sighed. "Such a darling girl, so unlike her perpetually scowling better half. I *heard* they were married sometime last year. I would've gone to the wedding, but sadly, I wasn't invited." She sniffed, looking like an offended faery grandmother for half a second, then smiled at Meghan again. "Did you know that, when we first met, Mackenzie made a bargain with me?" the Dark Muse continued. "I bet Ethan never told you, did he? Mackenzie wasn't born with the Sight like your brother—she had to bargain for it. Ethan didn't want her to, of course, but we worked out a lovely little deal for her to gain the Sight."

Meghan stiffened. Mackenzie St. James had been sixteen when she was first dragged into the Nevernever with Ethan, and bargaining with a faery queen was a dangerous proposition for even the most experienced fey. Granting a mortal the Sight was a huge request, and the price for such bargains was always high.

"What did she promise you?" Meghan asked quietly.

"A month of her life," the Dark Muse responded. "Really, it was one of my more generous offers. Ethan nearly went through the roof, but Mackenzie had no qualms making that deal. Of course, this was before I learned that she had leukemia." Leanansidhe shook her head. "Funny thing with humans who don't think they're going to live much longer—they're much more likely to risk everything. The point is, because of that and the nature of our deal, I've taken to checking up on our darling Mackenzie from time to time. And recently, I've noticed something odd happening in the real world. Have you seen those obnoxious little piskie creatures, hanging on to humans in the mortal realm?"

Meghan stiffened, and I narrowed my eyes. So, Leanansidhe had seen them, too. Or at least, her network of spies and informants had.

"Actually, we did have the pleasure of running into one," Puck said. "You wouldn't happen to know what they are, would you, Lea?"

"Not a clue, darling." Leanansidhe made a disgusted gesture with her cigarette flute. "I suspect they're a new type of fey, and that is all I know. But, according to my informants in the real world, these creatures are not only spreading, they are everywhere now. At first, it was just a few, and no one really paid much attention to them. But then, they started to multiply. And you can find them throughout the mortal realm, now. From what I can see, they are attracted to negative emotion—anger, fear, rage, despair—and spread it among human and fey alike. Like hateful little moths, fluttering around human lamps, making everyone cranky and stupid. They really are getting to be quite the menace."

"How long has this been going on?" Meghan asked.

"Well, that's the interesting thing, darling. I did some research, asked around, paid off a few favors, and you know what I discovered? These creatures, these *nightmare piskies* as they're being referred to by the exiles, first appeared a few months after the war with the Lady and the Forgotten ended. Now, what this means...?" She shrugged. "That is anyone's guess. But these creatures started appearing not long after the Between disappeared the first time. When your darling son made the sacrifice to rip away the Veil."

Anger flickered, and Leanansidhe shot me a look, as if she could sense my thoughts. "Regardless," she went on, "my prediction is that something happened the night when the Veil disappeared. Perhaps these creatures are appearing from a part of the Between that we don't know about. Which begs the question—if these nightmare piskies are coming through, what else is out there? And how much of a threat are they?

"So, I would very much appreciate it if you would look into that, darling," Leanansidhe remarked. "Maybe get the other courts in on it as well. They don't concern themselves with anything that is happening in the real world, and I think that perhaps they should. At least for this problem."

"I will." Meghan nodded wearily. "After we find Keirran. I'll return to Faery and let the other rulers know about this new type of fey. Though I feel we should know a bit more about them, first."

"Well, if you are in the human world, I'm sure you'll see a few of them," Leanansidhe said. "I'll put out feelers in the mortal realm, see if I can dig up any information on our missing Forgotten King. But I do believe your best bet will be your brother and his wife. Those two know more about what is happening than I suspect the rest of us might think. Besides, in the past Keirran has gone to Ethan and Kenzie. There's no reason to think he wouldn't try to contact them again."

Meghan groaned. "I don't want to drag Ethan and Kenzie into

this," she sighed. "I promised I would try to keep faery politics out of his life. But it sounds like we're running out of options."

"Ethan understands what being the Iron Queen's brother means now," I told Meghan. "Family is the most important thing to him, even if he has to deal with the faery madness that comes with it. I think we should trust him at his word and see if he and Kenzie have heard from Keirran, or have any idea of where he could be."

"And I'm sure he'll be thrilled to see us," Puck added, grinning from the other side of the couch. "We make his life so much more exciting. Hopefully, he's gotten over that slight miscalculation with the doves at his wedding."

Meghan sighed again and rubbed a hand over her eyes. "I'm sorry, Ethan," she murmured. "I don't want to do this, but I think we're going to have to upend your life one more time."

She turned, but suddenly put her hand against the sofa back, as if to brace herself. Alarm flared, and I stepped forward, catching her elbow. Her muscles shook under my fingers.

"Meghan…"

"I'm all right," the Iron Queen said calmly. "Just tired, I think. The fight with the Monster took a lot out of all of us."

That was putting it mildly. We had almost died, battling one of the toughest creatures I had ever encountered. It wasn't superstrong, it wasn't the most powerful monster I'd ever faced; it just seemingly couldn't be killed. Eventually, we did discover the secret to bringing down the creature down, or rather, Puck did, but not before it had inflicted some serious damage of its own.

"If I may, darling." Leanansidhe twiddled her cigarette flute, a dubious expression crossing her face. "You don't look so good. Right now, it is a few hours until dawn in your brother's part of the world. The Chases are likely sound asleep. A few hours of waiting is not going to make much of a difference, and you look like you could use the rest. I will send a messenger to the

Chases' house first thing tomorrow—he knows the way to get around the antifey defenses your brother has in place."

"That's awfully nice of you, Lea." On the couch, Puck crossed his arms and gave the Exile Queen a wary look. "Why so helpful all of a sudden?"

"I'm always helpful, darling." Leanansidhe waved an indignant hand. "I won't have anyone who comes to my home accuse me of being inhospitable—it's bad for business. If it gets out that I was rude to any of my important guests, despite how they threatened me, that would impact my bottom line. Don't worry, Puck darling." The Exile Queen gave him an evil smile. "If I want revenge, I take my time. While within the walls of my home, you're perfectly safe, I assure you."

Puck grimaced. "Funnily enough, I don't feel reassured."

"Regardless." Leanansidhe waved off his comment and turned back to Meghan. "Meghan, dove… I can still call you Meghan, yes? The offer stands. Please use this time to rest and heal and do whatever planning you need for the next step. I'll have a minion show you the guest rooms."

Meghan hesitated. I could sense the struggle within. We hadn't had a chance to rest since we'd started the hunt for the Monster, and the last battle with the creature took a lot out of us. Everyone, even Puck and Nyx, was mentally and physically exhausted. I myself still ached from where the Monster slammed me several times into a stone floor. The bruises and broken ribs had almost healed, but they were still painful. A few hours' sleep sounded very tempting right now.

But Keirran was still out there. And there was a new type of fey on the rise. The Monster that had destroyed Touchstone and the tiny nightmare piskies flitting around the real world might look vastly different, but both creatures had one thing in common: they attracted and spread negative emotions wherever they went. Clearly, they were connected somehow, and I didn't want Keirran to have to face them alone.

As if she could sense what I was thinking, Meghan glanced at me, and her eyes shadowed in concern. "Maybe some rest is a good idea," she admitted, turning back to Leanansidhe. "Everyone is tired. I don't want too long of a delay, but we won't be able to help anyone if we're so exhausted we can't function."

"Exactly, darling." Leanansidhe clapped her hands, and a redcap slid into the room, seemingly from nowhere. The short, squat man with the jagged shark teeth and wool cap drenched in the blood of his victims gave us a surly look, then turned his attention to the Exile Queen. "Take our guests to the VIP quarters," she instructed him. "Make sure they have everything they need. And minion, if I hear anything of Razor Dan harassing my guests for favors again, all of you will be spending the next few months regrowing your teeth, after I yank them out of your head and sell them to the goblin market."

The redcap cringed. Turning to us, he gave a rather jerky bow and growled, "Follow me, if ya would," in a slightly less surly tone than was expected from a redcap. We followed the short faery down more elegant corridors until he stopped at a pair of arched doors and grunted for us to go inside. He then fled our presence without looking back, leaving us alone in the hall.

"Only two guest rooms?" Puck gave the doorways a dubious look, then raised his eyebrows at Nyx with a faint grin. "Huh. Guess that means we'll have to share one. Unless you object."

The Forgotten's voice was dry. "Well, I was not planning on sharing a room with the queen."

Surprisingly, Puck hesitated. Glancing at me, he looked as if he wanted to say something, and a flicker of worry crossed his face. But then his gaze shifted to Meghan, and something on the Iron Queen's face caused him to nod and turn away. "All right, then," he announced, following Nyx into the first guest room. "But if you snore, I can't be held responsible for what happens."

There was a disdainful sniff near our feet. "Clearly, you have never heard yourself, Goodfellow," Grimalkin remarked as the door to the guest room closed. The cat shook his head, then padded away with his tail in the air. "I will return when it is time to depart," he said without looking back. "Do not wait for me."

Rounding a corner, the cat disappeared.

I entered the second room with Meghan, then closed the door and locked it firmly behind us; probably a useless precaution in this mansion of rogues, exiles, and outcasts, but one I did out of habit. I wasn't planning to sleep regardless; any faery that tried sneaking into this room unannounced would find itself with a sword at its throat. If it was lucky.

I could feel Meghan's gaze on my back, and turned to find her watching me with worried blue eyes. "What happened out there, Ash?" she asked quietly. "You've never threatened Leanansidhe before, and we knew we were going to have to bargain with her for information. This isn't like you."

"What would've happened if we tried to reason with Titania?" I asked. "She is never going to lift Leanansidhe's exile, and she would have demanded something impossible from you, something that you would not be able to grant. We would have ended up in a worse situation than before."

Inside, that same anger stirred. The Unseelie within still raged, annoyed that I hadn't made good on my threat to destroy the Dark Muse and her entire kingdom. I had never fought a queen before; part of me wished I had remedied that today.

I shoved down that voice, and the bloodlust faded somewhat. "I know there were other options," I continued as Meghan frowned. "But I made the call, and I'm sorry if I overstepped. Although, sometimes, I think Leanansidhe sees us as mostly human. She wouldn't try these games with Oberon or Mab."

"I suppose you're right," Meghan said, and her lips tightened. "And she conveniently didn't mention that she didn't even have any real information, either. She was just going to send us to Ethan and Kenzie."

"I did notice that as well, yes."

"I hope they've seen Keirran," Meghan sighed. "I don't want to drag Ethan and Kenzie into another faery mess, but… I keep having these terrible thoughts. What if…?" Her breath hitched, and she closed her eyes. "What if this new monster turns him back into the Soulless One?" she whispered. "It was able to change those Forgotten, and it even turned Puck into the old, sadistic Robin Goodfellow. If the Monster brings out Keirran's shadow side…" She trembled violently, shaking her head. "Ash, what if we have to fight him? What if he goes and does something unforgivable again? I can't… I don't think I could go through that a second time."

My throat tightened. I knew what she was thinking of: that terrible night when Keirran betrayed us all by killing Ethan and destroying the Veil. The moment when the prophecy finally came to a head. In her quest for power, the Lady had discovered that the way to tear down the Veil, which would allow all mortals to see the fey, was to sacrifice a human who possessed blood ties to all three courts of Faery: Summer, Winter, and Iron. Ethan Chase, with his relation to Meghan, Keirran, and myself, was the only human who fit this criteria. At the time, he was also Keirran's closest friend, but that didn't stop Fate from playing out that night. Within a site of power, surrounded by Forgotten and urged on by the Lady herself, Keirran stabbed Meghan's brother in cold blood and left him to die.

Thankfully, destiny did not play out exactly as the Lady envisioned it. Somehow, Ethan was revived, saved by a mysterious magic that baffles me to this day. And though the Veil did fall for a few minutes, causing chaos and panic in the mortal realm, it reformed when Ethan Chase stubbornly refused to stay dead. But that betrayal, that moment when Keirran made the decision to kill his best friend, was the catalyst for the war that came after, and our son turning into the enemy.

Meghan shivered again. I pulled her close and held her tightly, feeling her ragged breathing as she struggled with her fears. Pressing my lips to the top of her head, I closed my eyes, wanting to take that burden she carried onto myself. She was a faery queen with tremendous power, but she was also a human mother whose whole world had been shattered by Keirran's betrayal. In the war with the Forgotten, she had been forced to hide her grief and heartbreak when dealing with the other courts, or even her own people, but in the quiet moments when we were alone, her walls would come down and she would sob in my arms.

"We'll find him," I told her. "Keirran is strong, and he's trying to make up for everything he's done in the past. We must have faith that he'll stay true to himself. And if he does turn on us again…we'll just have to change him back. There is a way to beat the Monster's influence—Puck has proven that already."

Her arms around me tightened. "You never gave up hope, even when Keirran seemed completely lost," she mused. "You always believed he could be saved." She paused. "You never let me give up hope, either."

"You and Keirran," I said quietly, "are the most important parts of my life. I would do anything to protect you."

And destroy anything that threatened them. Monster, demon, or Exile Queen. It didn't matter who they were or how powerful; if they put my family in harm's way, I would show no mercy whatsoever.

Drawing back, I nodded to the large, four-poster bed against the far wall. "Why don't you try to get some rest?" I suggested. "We've been running around nonstop since we left Mag

Tuiredh. Who knows when we'll get the chance to catch our breath again."

"What about you?" Her eyes regarded me in a worried fashion. "You took a couple of nasty blows from the Monster. I can't imagine they're fully healed yet."

"They're not," I said truthfully, and shrugged. "But I'll live. I can still fight, anyway."

Her hand slid down my chest, as if she could sense the bruises below my shirt. I shivered as those soft fingers caressed my skin. "Leanansidhe has healers," she said.

"And would probably charge us a favor to use them," I replied. Catching her hand, I trapped it under my own, squeezing gently. "I'm fine, Meghan. I don't want to put us in her debt, especially now. I don't want to jeopardize any chance of us finding Keirran."

She sighed, giving me a faintly exasperated look. "All right," she said. "No healers. On one condition—that you take your own advice and get some rest while you have the chance. We're safe enough here—Razor Dan isn't going to sneak into the room to steal our livers while we sleep."

"I wouldn't put it past him," I muttered. Razor Dan, the leader of the redcap motley that worked for Leanansidhe, was sneaky, violent, and surprisingly ambitious for a redcap. He was, rightfully so, terrified of the Exile Queen, but that didn't stop him from trying to take advantage if he thought he could get away with it.

Meghan shook her head, but took my hand and drew me across the room with her. "Humor me, then," she ordered, sinking gracefully onto the bed. "At least lie down and pretend to rest. I know you're not going to be able to sleep, but keep me company for a while? I'll get too wrapped up in my own thoughts otherwise."

I climbed atop the mattress with her and sat back against the headboard, facing the door. Meghan curled up against me and closed her eyes, and I listened to her breathing as she relaxed.

"I'm afraid, Ash," she murmured into the silence. Her voice was barely a whisper in the empty room. "This whole situation with Keirran, with the Forgotten, with this new monster…it feels different. Something is out there. What I discovered beneath the roots of the Mother Tree…" She shivered and pressed closer. "I can't even explain how massive it was. It was almost like encountering a sleeping god. It was ancient. Older than the courts. Possibly older than the Nevernever itself. And it's starting to wake up."

She shivered violently. Shifting on the bed, I put my arms around her and held her close, and she fisted a hand against my shirt. Her fear was suddenly palpable, which made my adrenaline spike and my senses sharpen. I wanted to protect her from all threats, to destroy that fear so thoroughly it could never return to shadow her, but there was nothing here to fight.

Instead, I stroked her hair and kept my breaths slow and even, trying to ease some of her worry, to take it onto myself. "We've faced threats to Faery before," I told her softly. "There have been wars where the entire Nevernever has been in danger. How many prophecies have we already been a part of? We've fought the Iron King, Machina, the Lady, the Forgotten, even Keirran himself. Faery is still here, and so are we."

"I know," Meghan whispered. "And I know this might be dramatic, but it feels like—like this could be the big one, Ash. Evenfall. Dusk settling over the world. The twilight of all living things."

Evenfall.

A cold resolve settled through me. "Whatever this threat is," I said, "whatever it plans for the Nevernever, we will fight it, like we've always done. You, me, Goodfellow, Grimalkin, and everyone we've allied with along the way. And if it really is the end of the Faery, we'll face it together."

Though I would not let that happen. No matter what I had to fight, I would protect my home, my family, and my queen with everything I had. I would destroy all that threatened them, and if that meant leaving mountains of bodies behind, so be it. I had been an Unseelie prince. I was the son of Mab, queen of the Winter Court. Despite having a soul, death was still a part of me.

Meghan didn't reply, and after a few minutes, her breaths grew slow and even as she drifted into sleep.

In the silence, the Unseelie side rose up again, turning my thoughts ominous and violent. Meghan slept on, but her breath coiled into the air before her, and frost spread slowly over the walls and ceiling, until we were surrounded in glittering ice.

"Father."

I turned, my steps muffled by the heavy layer of snow on the ground. Around me, the world was cloaked in white; flakes fell so heavily from the sky it was difficult to see more than a few feet ahead. I couldn't discern the owner of the voice, but I knew he was here.

"Where are you, Keirran?"

Silence throbbed in my ears. The snowfall eased, and my son materialized from the white, standing across from me. He wore a white cloak, his pale hair and steel sword blending into the surroundings. Icy blue eyes regarded me without expression over the snow.

Then he smiled, and it chilled my insides. I had seen that smile when he had stood with the Lady in the last war; that cold, vicious smile of a killer. I drew in a breath, and smelled coppery blood drenching the frosty air. The snow around us was suddenly streaked with crimson. I glanced down and saw Puck staring up at me, green eyes wide and unseeing, the entire front of his shirt red and glistening.

"It's too late." Keirran's voice held an edge of cruel laughter. I glared up at him, and he raised his arms, both of them soaked with crimson. Blood covered him, spattered across his face and streaked through his hair.

"You can't save me," Keirran said. He started forward, making no sound as he stepped over bodies and frozen corpses, his sword glimmering red at his side. "You've already failed once. You couldn't protect me from the Lady, and now I'm going to destroy everything we both love, because you made me what I am. An Unseelie monster, just like you."

The snow swirled around us, and in the shadows behind Keirran, something moved. A head, rising to an impossible height, the skull crowned with antlers, eyes glowing a blank, soulless white in the gloom. It watched impassively, and I saw thin, nearly invisible tendrils of shadow writhing around it. I glanced at Keirran again, and saw the wisps of darkness attached to him, trailing back to the Monster like a puppet on a string.

Rage flared. I drew my sword, and Keirran lunged at me, sweeping his blade down at my head. I knocked it aside, and the clang of two blades echoed into the night and reverberated over the trees.

"Keirran." I backed away, and my son followed me, teeth bared in an ugly grin. "Stop this," I told him, raising my sword to parry another blow. "This isn't what you want."

"Wrong." Keirran slashed viciously at my face; I jerked my head back to avoid the edge that would've split open my skull. "I have always been like this," he snarled at me. "Because you have the same darkness inside. You've always struggled with your Unseelie nature. What makes you think I don't have that same bloodlust within me? I am you!"

I dodged another stab, circling around him. For a moment,

his back was unguarded, but I didn't take advantage of the opening. Keirran spun, eyes glittering, the scowl on his face revealing he knew I wasn't fighting him fully. "You can't save me," he said again. "You can't save anyone. Evenfall is coming, and no matter how hard you fight, nothing you do will prevent it. In the end, you're going to lose us all."

He lunged at me, and the rage soared. Knocking aside the blade, I stepped close and drove my weapon through his center, the point exploding out his back. Keirran jerked, stiffening against me, as his skin turned blue and iced over. I yanked my blade free and the frozen statue of my son shattered, raining to the ground with almost delicate chiming sounds, as the Unseelie within howled with glee.

5

THE MESSENGER

I jerked awake, my heart slamming against my ribs. An unfamiliar room, Leanansidhe's guest quarters, greeted me as I opened my eyes. I hadn't meant to sleep, but I guess I must've dozed off after all. Annoyance with myself flickered. If Razor Dan and his crew had decided to sneak in here, I did not want to be caught sleeping and unaware by a sadistic redcap motley.

Beside me, Meghan stirred and sleepily opened her eyes. "Ash?" she murmured. "Are you all right?"

I nodded, shoving the nightmare with the soulless Keirran to a distant part of my mind. His words, and the look on his face, made my blood run cold, but I would not lose hope. "I'm fine," I said quietly.

Her hand slid up my chest, leaving tingles where it passed. "Your heart is pounding."

"Just a dream," I murmured. "I'm sorry I woke you."

"Nightmare?"

"It was nothing," I soothed, and kissed the top of her head. "There's still maybe an hour until dawn. Go back to sleep."

Meghan sniffed. "Don't be bossy," she chided, but her eyes closed again, and a few minutes later her breaths grew slow and even once more. I lay there, awake, my mind churning over the dream with Keirran and the Monster, and if it did come down to it, could I really kill him to save everyone else?

A pounding came at the door, several blows in rapid succession. As quickly as I could without jostling Meghan, I slid off the mattress and put a hand on my sword. Meghan jerked up, instantly awake, power and magic immediately crackling around her as we both stared at the door. But it didn't burst open with redcaps swarming into the room, and after a few moments of silence, the pounding came again. Meghan and I exchanged a look, and I walked across the room to open the rattling door.

A redcap stood there, sullen and scowling, in a blood-drenched hat and a pink bow tie under his chin. He was a bit larger than the one we'd previously met, with glittering yellow eyes and jagged fangs protruding from his lower jaw like he had a mouthful of broken glass. A bone fishhook was shoved through his lumpy nose, which was quivering with distaste.

"Sorry to bother you, Majesties," Razor Dan said with a growl and a curled lip, as if he begrudged every word. "But Leanansidhe requests your and the Iron Queen's immediate presence in the meeting hall. Said it's extremely important, and that you should come as soon as you can. Oh, yeah." He scratched the side of his lumpy nose. "Also, don't wait up for Goodfellow and the Forgotten—they're already with Leanansidhe."

"Tell Leanansidhe we'll be there soon," I replied, and Razor Dan turned away without acknowledging the answer. Anger stirred, and for just a moment, staring at his slouched, unprotected back, I contemplated hurling an ice dagger between his shoulder blades. Just to remind him that one did not just casually turn their back on certain faeries, especially the rulers of the Iron Court. But Meghan slid off the mattress and walked toward me, and the violent thoughts toward disrespectful redcaps faded.

"That was quick," Meghan said hopefully. "Leanansidhe has always come through in the past. Maybe she's found something on Keirran's whereabouts."

"Let's hope so," I said, holding out a hand to her. The images from the dream rose up to haunt me, and I shoved them down. I would not let that fate befall Keirran, or Meghan. "Maybe she'll have some good news."

"There you are," Puck announced as we approached the double doors to the meeting room. For a moment, I thought he was alone, until I looked closer and saw Nyx leaning against the wall next to a pillar and a vase. She was so absolutely still, it was difficult to see her at first. "Did you guys have a nice nap? I have to say, I'm a bit envious. Try sharing a room with an assassin faery who doesn't sleep at night."

Nyx arched a thin silver eyebrow, looking faintly amused. "Forgive me, Goodfellow. I was under the impression that the last thing you wanted to do was sleep."

Puck loudly cleared his throat. "Uh, anyway, Leanansidhe is waiting for us," he said, jerking his thumb at the meeting-room doors. "Any clue as to what was so important she had to…erm, drag us out of bed in the wee hours of the morning?"

"Why don't you come in and find out, darling?" said Leanansidhe as the doors swung open dramatically, revealing the tall figure of the Exile Queen in its frame. "Instead of lurking out here in the hallway like gossiping gnomes?"

"Have you found Keirran?" Meghan asked as we headed into the meeting room once more, Leanansidhe firmly shutting and locking the doors behind us. I took notice of Grimalkin sitting in the center of the long table, his tail curled tightly around his feet. The cat gave us an impatient look as we came in, as if we were hours late for a scheduled meeting, and not dragged out of our rooms in the middle of the night.

Leanansidhe shook her head. "I haven't, darling, but I think you'll be very interested in what I did find. While you were resting, my minions discovered someone wandering the Between outside the mansion. I believe he is a messenger of sorts…from our missing prince himself."

I straightened. "A messenger… Where?" I demanded. "If the message is from Keirran, why didn't it come directly to us?"

Leanansidhe gave me a tight smile, then turned to the redcap waiting in the room with her. "Go bring in our 'messenger,' if you would, minion."

The redcap scurried out a second door on the far side of the room. A few moments later, a shriek rang out, making me tense and Puck jump. Meghan waited calmly, her expression a cool, unruffled mask, as another high-pitched yowl cut through the stillness.

Three redcaps entered the room with a body between them, a featureless shadow wrapped in chains. A Forgotten, wrists bound by manacles, hissing and snarling at the redcaps that held its leash. I noted that both the shackles and the chains were made of silver, not iron or steel, which was both a relief and a surprise. Some of the more sadistic fey would bind their captives with iron, killing them slowly and prolonging their torture. I was glad the Exile Queen did not feel the need for such baseless torment. Then again, she had many more interesting ways to punish those who displeased her.

"This is the creature we discovered sneaking around outside the mansion," Leanansidhe told us as the redcaps dragged the captive forward. "As for why I did not allow it to deliver its message, well, see for yourselves, darlings." She waved an arm in the Forgotten's direction, and the redcaps dragged it forward.

The Forgotten struggled, digging in its heels and jerking futilely against the chains. It looked like all the Forgotten in Keirran's court; a silhouette with glowing yellow eyes in a featureless face. This one looked almost rail-thin, with long fingers that curled into themselves like butterfly tongues.

As soon as it saw Meghan, the Forgotten straightened. "Iron Queen," it hissed. Its fingers uncurled, the flash of a blade appearing in its palms. "Message from King Keirran!" it shrieked, and lunged.

The redcaps braced themselves, yanking the faery up short. It howled, struggling against the chains, obviously trying to get to Meghan. "The Forgotten King sends his regards," it snarled, then suddenly burst into high-pitched laughter and collapsed to the floor. "Message for the Iron Queen," it giggled, making stabbing motions with the knife it still held. "Message for the Iron Queen. King Keirran sends his regards, Your Majesty."

"Wow," Puck remarked into the stunned silence. "Someone is taking the 'don't kill the messenger' saying a little too far."

I felt cold, the echoes of the dream rising up to crowd my mind. Meghan was rigid, staring at the Forgotten with a mix of horror and pity. Leanansidhe gave a loud sniff and raised her hand, pulling her cigarette flute out of thin air.

"Take it away, minions," she told the redcaps, who yanked the Forgotten to its feet and pulled it out of the room. "I'll decide what to do with it later. There, darlings. Now do you see why I didn't really want it delivering its 'message'?" The Exile Queen inhaled and puffed out a cloud of lilac smoke. "I tried talking to it, but it just repeated that it had a message for the Iron Queen from the King of the Forgotten over and over again. Of course, given the fact that it brandished a knife every time it said the word *message*, I thought maybe I didn't want an unhinged Forgotten rampaging through my house, stabbing the minions while it was looking for you."

"What does this mean?" Meghan whispered.

"You tell me, dove." Leanansidhe shrugged. "This is your son, after all. Surely you would know if our darling Forgotten King was sending assassins after you."

"That wasn't an assassin," Nyx said immediately. She shook her head, her expression torn between disgust and pity. "Its emotions were too chaotic. It felt confused, almost fractured." She hesitated, glancing at Meghan as she chose her next words carefully. "Keirran once told me he would never have use of my 'particular talents,' but...if he were to send an assassin, especially after someone so powerful, he would make sure they were capable of getting the job done."

I felt a dangerous, murderous rage at the thought of an assassin being sent after Meghan, and took a furtive breath to push it down. Only the most foolish, desperate, or mad would try to assassinate a queen of Faery, and if they did find themselves facing the Iron Queen, they would quickly realize they were in over their head. But Meghan tended toward mercy, and doing only what was necessary to eliminate the threat. If the assassin ran in to me first, they would soon wish they had never been born.

"I don't believe this was an attempt on your life, Your Majesty," Nyx continued, as I tried to keep my anger from bleeding frost all over the carpet. The temperature in the room dropped a bit, but thankfully no one seemed to notice. "I think Keirran might've sent this Forgotten to find you but it was somehow twisted, by the Monster or something else. Much like the Forgotten we saw in Touchstone."

"I hope you're right," Meghan said. Her voice was calm, but I could sense her concern; the worry that ate at her. Because, along with the rage, it was plaguing me as well. What if Keirran had changed? What if we found our son, and he had turned into the enemy again? "At least we know Keirran is out there," Meghan continued, "and that he's trying to contact us. That's good news, anyway. Now we just have to find him."

"Maybe Ethan will have had better luck," Puck added. "He attracts the same kind of trouble—if anyone has seen our wayward princeling, it would be him."

"That's what I'm hoping," I muttered. Keirran's relationship with Meghan's brother was a complicated one; they had been part of the same prophecy, but more than that, Ethan had always been the one Keirran went to for help in the past. Why Keirran had chosen to drag a very reluctant human into his world I had never been able to figure out, but when Keirran started down the road that would turn the Nevernever upside down, Ethan had been with him nearly every step of the way. They had been everything from best friends to bitter enemies, much like a certain jester and Winter prince, and even though Keirran had literally stabbed Ethan in the back, their friendship had somehow survived.

Leanansidhe sighed. "Grim, darling, you know the way to the right trod, yes?" she asked the cat, who yawned and flicked an ear in response. "The one that takes you close to Ethan Chase's new house? Be a dear and show them the way, would you? I have to decide what I'm going to do with a slightly deranged would-be assassin."

The Exile Queen left the room in a fluttering of copper hair, trailing wisps of violet smoke behind her, and we were alone.

Grimalkin gave a leisurely stretch, leaving white claw marks in Leanansidhe's polished wood, and hopped off the table. "Follow me, then. The trod to the human world is in the basement. Do be wary of the boggart that lives under the stairs."

It was still dark when we climbed the rickety wooden ladder in Leanansidhe's basement and found ourselves at the bottom of an old dry well in the mortal realm. As I climbed out of the ancient stone structure, a cool breeze blew against my skin, smelling of leaves and pine needles. Trees surrounded us, and the sky through the branches was navy blue, with a few stubborn stars still clinging to existence.

"What is that smell?" Puck asked. "Oh, right, fresh air. I *knew* there were some places in the mortal realm not covered in concrete and garbage." He took a deep breath and let it out slowly, smiling as he gazed around the forest.

I hadn't been to Ethan and Kenzie's new house yet, but I knew they lived on a small plot of land a few miles away from everything. Ethan preferred the isolation, not because he was antisocial (though there was a bit of that, too), but because he had the Sight, he had to deal with the fey constantly. And it was easier to deal with a faery if you didn't have other humans close by to worry about. From what Meghan told me, growing up, Ethan had been harassed and tormented by troublesome faeries to the point that he shut himself away from everyone to keep them safe; it made sense that he would want a place where he could have some relative peace.

"This way," Grimalkin said, trotting past us with his tail held high. "The house we are looking for is not far."

We followed Grimalkin through the forest, the only sounds being the leaves crunching under our feet, until the trees opened up and we found ourselves gazing at a modest ranch-style house in the center of a clearing. The front lawn was neatly maintained and had a white picket fence around it. A battered truck sat next to a sleeker blue car in the driveway. It looked like a perfectly normal human dwelling, which surprised me. Given Ethan's wariness of the fey, I was half-expecting iron fences and trained rottweilers prowling the front lawn.

"Huh, that's weird," Puck remarked, echoing my surprise. "Is this really Ethan Chase's house? I was expecting laser fences and killer attack hippos. This place looks perfectly normal."

"I don't see a house," Nyx stated quietly.

We blinked at her. "Uh, what do you mean you don't see a house?" Puck asked, and pointed to the dwelling straight ahead in through the trees. "I mean, modern houses might look kinda strange to you. It's not a mud hut, but it is a house."

"I have seen the houses of today," Nyx said flatly. "I know what a modern building looks like. I do not see anything in the clearing. There is no house for me."

"I see a house," Meghan said. "Puck, Ash, and Grim can see it, too." She gazed at Nyx, looking thoughtful for a moment. "I do know that Ethan set up defenses against the fey—maybe this is part of his security system. He knows the four of us, but Nyx is an unknown entity. So she doesn't even see the house."

"There are more defenses set up around the house and front yard," Grimalkin told us, and gave a sniff. "Powerful, but easily navigable, if one knows how to deal with them. Follow me, and do try not to trip over anything."

We trailed the cat through the woods and toward the Chases' front yard, which looked completely innocuous in the coming dawn. However, as we neared the fence gates, Nyx drew in a sharp breath and stumbled to a halt, frowning at the building in front of us.

"Nyx?" Puck cocked his head, giving her a concerned look. "You okay?"

"I…don't know." The Forgotten took a step, and her frown deepened. "The closer I get, the harder it becomes to continue. It's hard to explain, but I feel like I shouldn't be here. I don't want to keep walking in this direction."

"More anti-fey charms," I murmured. "Sounds like a powerful one, too. I've heard of spells that actively repel and prevent fey from crossing a circle drawn on the ground. This seems very similar."

"Here." Puck held out a hand to Nyx. "Just hang on to me. Close your eyes if you have to. And don't worry—there hasn't been a charm, spell, or faery repellant crafted that can keep out Robin Goodfellow. I'm an expert at getting into places that don't want me to get into them."

Nyx gave a weird little smile. "I am, too," she said, and placed her fingers in his palm. "The only difference is, if your charms didn't work, you would be dead the next morning."

"Oh, that's a cheery thought," Puck said, and turned back toward the house. "Maybe we shouldn't mention the little fact that you were an assassin to Ethan quite yet."

"It does seem to make humans nervous," Nyx agreed.

We continued toward the house. Nyx didn't say anything more, and continued clutching Puck's hand tightly as we walked across the lawn and approached the front door. Her jaw was set as we climbed the brick stairs onto the porch. Meghan didn't hesitate; raising her arm, she knocked loudly against the wooden barrier.

A booming bark immediately sounded from inside, making Nyx flinch. A few seconds later, the door swung open, revealing a haggard, immediately familiar face on the other side. Ethan Chase, Meghan's half brother and chosen champion of the Nevernever, gazed at us with wary eyes through the doorframe. His brown hair was mussed, as if he'd just rolled out of bed, and there was a five-o'clock shadow across his jaw and chin. For a moment, he stared at us, the expression on his face teetering between alarm and resignation, before he shook his head.

"Well, this can't be good."

"Ethan." Meghan smiled at him, and a corner of his lip quirked up as he returned her greeting. "Sorry to barge in on you so early. We need to talk."

Ethan Chase sighed and scrubbed a hand through his hair. "Yeah, I figured," he sighed. "Come on in. Just let me disable a few spells and I'll be right with you."

We stepped through the doorway into a cozy living room that looked like an ordinary human abode. Worn leather sofas sat in a half circle around a coffee table, and a small kitchen stood off to one side, a coffee pot bubbling in the corner. No strange magic could be seen or felt, though I knew there was protection and anti-fey charms completely laced throughout the house. Whatever Ethan had done, it was subtle. His home looked like a completely traditional, faery-less dwelling in the mortal realm.

"Ethan? Who was at the door...? Oh." Soft footsteps echoed outside the room, and Mackenzie appeared in the hallway, blinking in surprise as she saw us. Small and slight, her jet-black hair pulled behind her, she did not seem at all concerned about four powerful faeries and a cait sith appearing in her living room very close to dawn. I felt a pulse of magic when she entered the room, and noticed the silver bracelet on her left wrist appeared to be endowed with some sort of spell. Probably a protection charm of sorts to shield her from hostile glamour. She was trailed by two large black dogs—enormous shaggy beasts that looked like they might have been crossed with a bear. Amazingly, the dogs did not explode in a cacophony of barking when they saw us. Their plumed tails waved back and forth as they shuffled forward, their eyes lazy and kind as they circled us with wet snuffs. Grimalkin flattened his ears and winked out of sight, and Nyx withdrew farther into her cloak.

"Oh, wow," Kenzie said, gazing at all of us. "Everyone is here. This is going to be big, isn't it? Stewart, Mouse, enough. Don't drool on the royalty."

"Hello, Kenzie," Meghan greeted, as the girl clapped her hands, and the two enormous dogs padded back to her. "I hope this isn't too much of an imposition."

"Nope, not at all." Mackenzie grinned cheerfully, her gaze sliding over each of us in turn. "I just hope we can help. I just assume that when the Iron Queen and company show up on my doorstep, something is about to happen. Oh, hello," she went on, catching sight of Nyx standing a little behind everyone else. "I didn't realize you had someone else with you. Sorry about the repel charms—they're for a particularly annoying band of goblins that like to hang around the area. I'll have Ethan disable them."

"Already done," Ethan called from somewhere out of the room.

"We appreciate it, Kenzie," Meghan said. "This is Nyx, by the way. She's part of Keirran's court."

Kenzie nodded. "Any friend of Keirran's is welcome here," she said immediately. "But I'm being rude, making you guys stand in the hall. Let's sit down, and you can tell us what's going on. I assume something is going on. Is this about InSite and those weird piskie creatures we saw inside?"

"InSite?" Meghan frowned. "What is that?"

I frowned as well. From what Leanansidhe had said, the nightmare piskies appeared to be spreading, so I wasn't surprised that Kenzie knew of them, but this InSite was new.

"It's a social-media platform," Kenzie explained, motioning us toward the couches in the living room. "Let's see, how do I explain this? I have an online channel that does stories on big tech companies and what they're coming out with next. Recently, a new social-media platform called InSite has gotten hugely popular. In just the space of a couple months, they've exploded online. Can I get anyone anything, by the way?" she asked, as we all took seats on the sofas arranged around a low table. Meghan sat down, and this time I sat beside her, feeling much more comfortable in the Chase house than in Leanansidhe's mansion. "I have tea, if anyone wants it," she went on, as Ethan returned from whatever he had been doing and nodded to us all. "Or water? I'm never sure if faeries like coffee."

"Coffee would be nice," Meghan sighed, showing how tired she was for just a moment. Puck wrinkled his nose.

"Never understood how you could drink that stuff, princess," he remarked as Ethan immediately headed off toward the kitchen. Giving me a sidelong glance, a faint smirk crossed Puck's face. "I guess you've always liked dark, bitter things."

Meghan silently rolled her eyes. Nyx blinked once, probably having no idea what any of us were talking about, but she didn't say anything.

Ethan returned, handed Meghan a mug, and dropped into the love seat across from the sofa. Kenzie perched beside him, the two dogs curling up at her feet like enormous bear rugs.

"So, anyway," Kenzie went on, "InSite. I was curious. I made an account on their platform, logged in—" her nose wrinkled "—and the amount of vitriol, hate, and toxicity just about took my breath away. It was absolutely suffocating."

Puck snorted. "I don't get computers," he said, "and I don't go online very often, but from what I've heard, that's nothing new."

"Maybe," Kenzie admitted. "But this felt different. It seemed like InSite was deliberately trying to make people angry, or sad, or terrified, with what they'd post. Their daily 'insights'?" She shook her head. "Nothing but fear, accusations, and hate-mongering. It was disgusting, but people seemed to swallow it whole.

"So, naturally, I asked for an interview," Kenzie said. "I wanted to know if this was just a product of the internet, or if InSite really did have an interest in generating outrage. And they agreed to meet with me, but here's where things get weird. I went to their office building, which is located in Washington D.C., by the way, and…" She hesitated. "It just…felt strange. I can't explain it, but it was like the building was there…and it wasn't at the same time. I know that makes no sense, but that's closest explanation I can come up with."

"Faery magic?" Meghan wondered.

"That's what I was thinking," Kenzie agreed. "It got even weirder inside. There was hardly anyone there, but there *were* these tiny creatures flitting around the entire building. They looked like…"

"Like Tinker Bell had a baby with a demon?" Puck interjected.

Kenzie nodded. "Close enough," she muttered. "They kept buzzing around my head, trying to land on me, and got very angry when I slapped them away. I got my interview—the guy I talked to was pretty typical and said all the typical things, answering questions without telling me anything. It would've been normal, except for the hostile little piskie thing glaring at me from his collar—that was kind of distracting. But by that time, I didn't want to be there anymore. The whole place just felt *wrong*. And I swear, I could feel something watching me the whole time." Kenzie shivered and shook her head. "I know fey and technology don't mix, but if that place doesn't have some kind of strange magic attached to it, I'd be shocked."

"We were thinking of sending Razor to the Iron Realm with a message," Ethan added, glancing at Meghan. "But we weren't entirely sure it warranted action from any of the courts. Then, more of those piskie things started showing up not long after Kenzie's visit. Regular humans can't see them, of course, so we figured they were some kind of fey. Maybe a new kind of Forgotten."

"They're not Forgotten," Nyx said.

"Currently, we're not sure what they are," Meghan added. "They do seem to be a threat, and we'll have to discuss what their presence means for the Nevernever at some point, but…"

She paused, put down the mug, and sat up straighter in her chair. "That's not the reason we came."

Ethan and Kenzie exchanged a glance. "If it's not about the piskie creatures, I'm almost afraid to ask," Ethan sighed. "Is there another war on the horizon, or is it something even worse?"

"Keirran is missing," I said.

"Again?"

Ethan groaned, then grunted when Kenzie elbowed him in the ribs. My heart sank a little at his reaction. While Ethan wasn't exactly surprised that Keirran had gone missing, he hadn't been aware that the King of the Forgotten had disappeared. Which meant he did not likely know where Keirran was right now.

Kenzie shot her husband an annoyed look, then turned to us again. "What happened?" she asked seriously.

"Touchstone was attacked," Meghan said, causing Kenzie to straighten. "A creature came through and began laying waste to the city, and Keirran was forced to flee with the survivors."

"One creature," Ethan began, "was able to take down a whole city, *and* the King of the Forgotten? How big was this thing?"

"Its size doesn't matter," I told him. "We fought one of these Monsters before—they grow stronger from negative emotions like fear, anger, and despair, but that's not the worst of it. They have the ability to twist regular fey into shadow versions of themselves. Think of it like a negative glamour overload. Affected fey become angry, violent—"

"Or just really sadistic," Puck said, interrupting. "Also, they might grow horns and shaggy pants. The point is, getting hit by one of these Monsters is bad news."

"Keirran had to flee Touchstone because the Forgotten were turning on him," Meghan explained. "He decided he had to save as many of his people as he could, so he opened the Between and took them into the mortal realm. From there, they vanished."

Ethan frowned, crossing his arms. "And you think we might know where he is," he mused.

"He's come to you before," I said. "And now that he can't return to the Nevernever, you and Kenzie might be the only ones he can go to for help."

Ethan shook his head. "Sorry, Ash," he said to me, and he sounded genuine. "We haven't seen him since the wedding. And, trust me, after everything we've been through with Keirran, I would tell you if we had."

I clenched a fist on my leg. Another dead end. Ethan and Kenzie had been our best hope of finding Keirran, but now we were back to square one.

"Leanansidhe thought that he might be trying to get to you," Meghan said, and I could hear the faintest tremble in her voice. "She felt a large group leave the Between and enter the mortal realm. Do you have any idea where Keirran might be, if he could be close or trying to contact you? Any information at all would be helpful."

"We haven't seen him," Kenzie admitted reluctantly. "But… I know someone who would. She knows everything that happens in or around the city, particularly if it has to do with Faery. If an exiled King of the Forgotten came through, she would know where he is, or at least how to find him."

Ethan groaned, and Kenzie gave him an apologetic look. "I know, I know," she went on. "We said we were going to avoid contacting her, if possible, but I think this case is an exception. She has resources. She knows how to get information. And we need to find Keirran. I don't think we have many other options."

"Who is this person you're talking about?" Meghan asked.

"Her name is Dreamer," Ethan said, still wincing a little. "She runs her own little business downtown, and much like Leanansidhe, she mostly deals in information. Her network isn't as extensive, but she does specialize in finding things that are hard to find."

"Dreamer is *here*?" Grimalkin materialized on a high shelf, eyeing the dogs with obvious distaste. "How interesting," he said. "I was almost certain she had perished ages ago. With her talents, she has been doing a very impressive job of staying out of sight."

"Who is this Dreamer?" Meghan asked. "Is she an exile? A half-fey?"

"Neither," Kenzie said. "Dreamer is…unique. From what we've been able to gather, she was actually human, once. I don't know how old she is, but I think pretty old. A long time ago, she either tried to screw over a faery, got the bad end of a bargain, or was just the victim of fey spitefulness. She was stuck with a pretty nasty curse and couldn't go back to her normal human life. You'll understand when you see her. *If* she'll agree to meet with us."

"Why wouldn't she?" Puck asked. "I mean, ice-boy and grumpy cat I would understand, but I'm me. Everyone loves me."

There was a very loud snort from Nyx's direction, which almost made me smile. Even the Lady's assassin, who had been around before the rise of the courts, who was older than all of us and didn't even know the name Robin Goodfellow before she met him, understood the ridiculousness of that statement.

Kenzie just rolled her eyes. "As lovable as you are, Puck, Dreamer is pretty wary of full fey and anyone from the courts," she explained. "She deals mostly with exiles, half-fey and humans who have the Sight, like me and Ethan."

"One of her policies is no court fey," Ethan disclosed. "She was even distrustful of me at first when she found out I was related to the Iron Queen." He rolled his eyes. "And by distrustful, I mean she tried to poison me to make sure I wouldn't give her location to anyone in the Nevernever. She's terrified of being discovered by any full fey, especially if they're from the courts."

Kenzie regarded me, Meghan, and Puck appraisingly, then frowned. "The three of you might have to go in disguise," she mused. "Having the rulers of the Iron Realm *and* Robin Goodfellow waltzing through her territory might cause her to freak out and go into hiding."

"Honestly, she probably already knows you're here." Ethan sighed. "Going to see her in her lair could be...interesting."

I nodded. "Whatever it takes," I said. "If she can give us something on Keirran, it will be worth the risk. When can you set up a meeting?"

Kenzie rose, the two dogs heaving themselves to their feet after her. "I'll have Razor send her a message," she said. "He can get there faster than any of us. With any luck, we'll have an answer from Dreamer sometime tonight."

6

CALLING ON DREAMER

Razor was Kenzie's pet gremlin. Originally, the spindly, bat-eared creature with a taste for electrical wires had been Keirran's, but after the war with the Forgotten and the Lady, Razor had decided to stay with Kenzie instead of returning to the Iron Realm. Like all gremlins in the world of Faery, Razor had a rather hyper personality, the attention span of a cricket, and caused havoc wherever he went. He also hated Grimalkin for some terrible offense only he could remember, which Grimalkin seemed unfazed by. But Kenzie had been able to work wonders with the Iron Realm's most chaotic fey, and after coaxing Razor down from the bookshelf, where he'd perched on the corner and shrieked that he was going to drown the "bad kitty" and feed him to the dogs, Kenzie was able to convince him to deliver a message to the mysterious Dreamer. He returned a few hours later, clutching a tattered note in his claws, which he immediately handed to Kenzie.

"Dreamer has agreed to a meeting," Kenzie informed us, dark

eyes scanning the paper. "Tonight, at midnight." She glanced at me, Meghan, and Puck over the paper's edge and pursed her lips. "That doesn't give us a lot of time to prepare."

"What are you talking about?" Puck said. Raising his arm, he snapped his fingers, and instantly vanished in a puff of smoke. When the cloud cleared, a regular-looking human stood there, wearing Puck's trademark grin. "There, poof," he said, raising both arms. "I'm clearly a human, certainly not Robin Good-fellow, the most famous faery in the Nevernever."

Ethan sighed, and Kenzie shook her head. "Not gonna work, Puck. Dreamer can see through glamour. Faery magic isn't the answer this time." She considered us, brow furrowed thoughtfully. "Wait here. I still have some cloaks and hoods from that one meeting with the gorgon. I think we're going to have to make do with those."

"Cloaks and hoods?" Puck repeated, and snorted. "What are we, in the Middle Ages? Are we going to a séance? Hoodies were invented for a reason, you know."

"Yes, because two-legs were never smart enough to grow fur." Sitting on the back of the love seat, Grimalkin gave a sniff. "I am glad to be a cat so that I never have to worry about such nonsense."

Kenzie returned with an armful of fabrics. "Here," she said, holding them out. "Try these on. I know it's not ideal, but Dreamer gets some pretty shady customers from time to time. You should fit in fairly nicely."

"I'm not going to ask why you have these," Meghan sighed, shaking out a dark green cloak before swirling it around her shoulders. She pulled up the cowl, effectively hiding her face and hair from view. "And I'm going to ignore that 'meeting with the gorgon' statement. I know you and Ethan can take care of yourselves just fine—I am not going to wonder about things I don't need to be wondering about."

I followed her example and drew on a long black cloak, pulling up the hood. It was a familiar sensation; in the Nevernever, there had been many times when showing my face as Prince Ash would've been less than ideal. Cloaks and cowls had always been an efficient way of hiding your identity when glamour didn't work. They were popular in shady places like the goblin market for a reason.

As I pulled up the hood, I immediately felt different. A cloaked, hidden stranger, watching the world from the shadows. If this Dreamer person knew anything about my son, they would tell me. I would not take no for an answer.

Ethan walked in wearing a solemn expression, as well as a heavy jacket that almost obscured the pair of short blades he was carrying. Unlike Kenzie, he did not appear to be wearing any sort of protection amulet, and I was reminded that Meghan's brother was immune to nearly every type of glamour. Except for Iron glamour, faery magic simply could not touch him. That made him extremely dangerous to most fey, as he ignored any type of spells, illusions or charm effects being cast on him. Of course, he was human and could still die from a sword point through his center, but for a mortal Ethan was a competent swordsman, having trained all his life to protect himself from the Hidden World and all its dangers. Even the most vicious of fey would have a difficult time cutting him down.

Kenzie observed us all with a critical eye, then gave a satisfied nod. "Okay," she announced, and plucked a backpack off the table, swinging it over her shoulders. I suspected it was full of anti-faery charms and bargaining items. "I think we're ready to go meet Dreamer."

"And how are we getting to this place, exactly?" Puck asked. "Call me pessimistic, but I don't think the six of us are going to fit in Ethan's truck. And I'd love to keep the iron interaction at a minimum, if possible. I'd hate to hurl my lunch all over an Uber driver's leather seats."

He glanced at Nyx as he said this, and I suddenly understood. Puck wasn't worried for himself; he had dealt with the fey's iron intolerance for a long time, and had adapted to the human world fairly well. But Nyx, being from ancient times, had not been in the mortal realm for long. She might still be sensitive to the amount of iron in the world.

"Don't worry, Goodfellow." Kenzie gave him a knowing smile that was just the tiniest bit smug. "I've been saving a favor for this kind of situation."

I caught Ethan's gaze as she said this, and he winced. It seemed Kenzie was still making deals and driving bargains that made Meghan's brother slightly uncomfortable, but he knew better than to try to stop her. Mackenzie would do what she thought was best, and his only duty was to support and protect her as best he could.

I knew the feeling.

Kenzie's "favor" turned out to be a pair of goblins who took us through an elaborate series of underground tunnels that, somehow, led to a drainage ditch close to downtown. From there, Kenzie led us through an old, seemingly abandoned warehouse, though I spotted bogies in the shadows and gargoyles on the rooftop, keeping watch. After several minutes of walking down a long, spiraling staircase, we finally entered a dim, narrow room with thick red carpet and black curtains hanging from the walls. Plush sofas and divans lined the room, all of them empty, though a marble counter sat against the back wall. A skeletal bogey with a pale face and shiny, bulging eyes watched us over the smooth surface.

"Madam Dreamer is expecting you, Mrs. Chase," the bogey

hissed, gesturing to a narrow black door behind her, nearly invisible against the wall. "Please, go in."

Kenzie nodded, and we stepped through the door into a room much like the first. Elegant sofas and chairs were placed throughout the room, and though there were no windows, lacy curtains rippled against the walls.

I couldn't be sure, because of the way they billowed out, but I thought I saw movement on the curtains as we came in. As if the cloth might be covered in hundreds, maybe thousands, of tiny black spiders, watching us as we stepped through the frame.

I decided not to voice that observation to Puck.

"Ah, you have arrived."

From behind a large wooden desk, a figure raised its head as we entered the room, then rose with liquid grace and stepped around the desk to glide toward us. She was tall and painfully thin, wearing a black dress that hugged her nearly emaciated ribs, then billowed out at the waist like a bell. Her skin was almost chalk-white, her eyes, nails, and straight, shoulder-length hair jet-black. A surgical mask covered the lower half of her face, and the eyes above them didn't smile as she stepped forward, looming over Kenzie like a rail-thin ghost.

"Mackenzie Chase." The woman's voice, though slightly muffled by the mask, was cultured and breathy. "How nice to see you again. I received your gremlin earlier—it seemed to believe that setting up a meeting today was absolutely essential. But it did not say anything about bringing friends. And so many of them." Her depthless black eyes shifted to the rest of us, becoming slightly pinched. "I don't believe we have met," she said. "I am Madam Dreamer, as I'm sure Mrs. Chase has told you. And whom do I have the pleasure of speaking to?"

"Me," Kenzie said. "You're talking with me, Dreamer. We have some unfinished business to discuss."

Ethan stepped closer to Kenzie, protective and watching the

woman's every move, but Dreamer only sniffed. "I suppose we do," she said. "Though if you and Mr. Chase have broken any of my policies, I am going to be very cross. The rules are there for a reason, you know."

She turned and sashayed back to her desk, the large bustle of the dress bouncing as she walked. Sitting down with a flourish, she laced pencil-thin fingers beneath her chin and raised her eyebrows. "Well, what can Madam Dreamer do for you today, Mrs. Chase?"

Kenzie approached the desk, Ethan beside her and the rest of us close behind. "We're looking for someone," Kenzie explained. "A friend of ours has gone missing. We have reason to believe he is here in the city somewhere. Or at least, very close."

"Looking for someone," Dreamer replied flatly. "And does this someone have a name? Is he half-fey? Is he an exile?"

"He *is* an exile, technically," Kenzie replied. Dreamer gave her a flat, unamused stare, and she sighed. "We're looking for Keirran, King of the Forgotten."

Madam Dreamer's rather large nostrils flared above her face mask. "That is what I was afraid of," she snapped. "I knew that gremlin of yours sounded suspicious." She brought a thin, spidery hand onto the desk surface with a rather weak slap. "You know my policies, Mrs. Chase," she wheezed. "No court fey. No nobles from the Nevernever. I do not deal with the sidhe and their ilk. Certainly not the traitor son of the Iron Queen herself."

My rage flared. I stepped forward, letting ice spread across the floor from my boots, dropping the temperature of the room several degrees. "You'll deal with us," I said quietly, as her head snapped in my direction. "Or you'll suffer the consequences."

"Court fey." Madam Dreamer's voice turned guttural with fear and alarm. She glared at Kenzie, ignoring Ethan, who quickly stepped up beside her. "How could you bring them here?" she said, almost whining. "You know my rules. If you think I will break my policies just because your husband is the Iron Queen's brother—"

"The Iron Queen is here."

Meghan's voice filled the room. Stepping up beside me, she pushed back her hood, revealing her face to the skeletal form of the pale woman. "And as my husband said, you will deal with us, Madam Dreamer," she said calmly. "We wish no harm upon you, but time is of the essence. We are searching for the Forgotten King, and your network of information is said to be vast. We need answers, and we need them now."

"And what makes you think I will bargain with you?" Madam Dreamer brushed past Kenzie, glaring at us with hard black eyes. "Do you think you can come into my lair and bully me into compliance? I am no longer a mere human, thanks to your kind. Would you like to see what the fey have done to me?" She stepped closer, and I gripped the hilt of my sword. "Years ago, I dared win a game against one of your kind, a game where we competed for the affections of the same man. I won, not because I was beautiful and charming, but because I actually cared for him. I grew to love him, completely and selflessly, a sentiment which the fey know nothing about. When he chose me, she laughed and said she hoped I would enjoy my victory…looking like this for the rest of eternity!"

She tore away her mask, revealing a wide, gaping mouth, and the curving black fangs of a spider. The front of her dress parted, as two shiny jointed legs poked out, clicking against the tile. "She cursed me," Madam Dreamer hissed, the curving fangs wiggling as she spoke, "to a life of seclusion and terror. To never knowing human contact again. My love…" She covered her face with claw-tipped hands. "I could not bear for him to see me like this, for *anyone* to see me like this. I would be branded a monster and hunted down. And so I fled human society forever, finding my way into the forgotten corners and hidden crevices of the world, hiding my hideous form from everyone. Eventually, I found those like me, other monsters exiled from their homes. When I realized I was not completely alone, I started building my nest, my web of information, with myself at the center. And slowly, I began attracting others like me, those who have run afoul of the fey, as I had done. Now, my home is a bastion for those like me—poor souls with nowhere else to go, outcasts and exiles and those whom humanity would consider monsters. I take them in, and I give them shelter and safety, and in return, I ask that they do me small favors from time to time. After all…" Those black fangs curved up in a blasphemous parody of a smile. "That is the way of Faery.

"But," the spider-faced woman continued, and stabbed a black nail in our direction. "I have my policies. And the first, the most important, is no deals with court fey. Never again will I have any dealings with those still bound to the Nevernever. Once was enough, and the price was far too high."

"I dunno," Puck mused, crossing his arms. "I will admit, that is one hell of a nasty curse. But a truly creative, evil person could think of ways to make it even worse." An wicked smile crossed his face for just a moment as he shrugged. "Just saying."

"I do not fear you, Robin Goodfellow." Madam Dreamer gave Puck a venomous look. "I do not fear you, or the son of Mab, or even the Iron Queen. Look at me." She raised both arms in weary resignation. "What can you do to me that has not already been done? Slay me here?" She gave a bitter laugh. "I have lived through the worst types of hell, endured constant torment and suffering. I have nothing left to lose but my life, and sometimes I think that would be a blessing."

Anger battled pity, and I gripped the hilt of my blade to keep myself from drawing it. Fey curses were nasty, unpredictable, and usually unfair. Sometimes the punishment was justified, but often, it was the vengeance of a scorned, angry, or just spiteful fey who wanted to make the object of their wrath suffer. Afterward, the faery would forget about the incident and move on; this was impossible for the human who was now the victim of permanent misfortune.

But she was also an obstacle keeping us from finding Keirran.

As if sensing my thoughts, Meghan took a step forward. "Madam Dreamer," she said, and the spider woman eyed her with a mix of defiance and fearful acceptance. "I was human once, just like you," she said. "I know the cruelty of faery. Many years ago, I witnessed someone who was the victim of a faery curse, and I remember the chaos it wreaked on their life. It's not something anyone, human or otherwise, should go through."

"Kind words, Iron Queen," Madam Dreamer said. "But I've learned that kind words are merely a manipulation tactic for the fey." She raised a claw to her skinny chest. "I, too, have perfected the art of manipulation now. I, too, know how to promise one thing while only delivering regret. And I have survived this long by not trusting anything that comes from the mouth of Faery."

"Then let me show you how this is different." Meghan raised an arm, indicating the room and the cursed woman before her. "How long have you been like this, Madam Dreamer?" she asked. "How long ago did the faery curse you? Given the size of your network, it must have been a considerable amount of time."

"Fifty years," the spider woman hissed. "Give or take a few, those years where I lost all sense of time to despair and hopelessness. I have been like this for half a century."

"Fifty years," Meghan repeated. "Did you have family then? Any that could still be alive?"

"I do not know." The cursed woman covered her face with her hands. "I could have found out, but I did not dare. What was the point? It would just be too painful." Her thin shoulders heaved, before she raised her head to glare at Meghan again.

"Why do you ask, Iron Queen?" she spat. "To remind me of my misery? To drive the nail in deeper?"

"No," Meghan replied calmly. "But I am a queen of Faery, Madam Dreamer. I am connected to the Nevernever, as you said. And as a queen of the fey, I have powers that only the rulers of the courts possess. I do not know the name of the faery who cursed you, but there is one thing the rulers of Faery can do. Should you wish it, I can remove your curse. I can't give you back the years you lost, but I can make you human again."

"What?" For the first time, Madam Dreamer seemed stunned. Her dark eyes glazed over, and she staggered back a few steps, spider legs clicking over the floor. "You…can do that?" she whispered. "Return me to my human form?" She trembled, then raised herself up, her voice becoming hard again. "At what cost? What impossible thing would you have me do?"

"Only this." As she spoke, Meghan's character changed. The aura of power around her disappeared, as did the Iron Queen's presence. Meghan was no longer a faery queen, but a normal girl, who held out a beseeching hand to the spider woman. "You said you had family, and that losing them was the most painful thing that had happened to you. I am looking for the King of the Forgotten, not as a faery or a queen, but as a mother who is worried for her son. All I want is information that will help us find him. That is all I am asking. Please, aid us in tracking Keirran down. If you do this, I will lift your curse, and make you human again."

"Human again." Madam Dreamer shook violently, the tips of her pointed legs clicking against the floor. Her hands clutched at her chest. "Walking the streets in the sunlight, not having to hide in the cracks and shadows. My face. I had almost given up hope that I would see it again…" She raised a spindly arm toward the ceiling, claws opening like bird talons, as if trying to snatch the life that had been taken from her.

She yanked back her arm and shook her head. "No," she whispered. "No, I mustn't. Never trust the sidhe. If I accept, how will I know that this bargain will not be worse?"

"Worse than having a spider as a face?" Puck snorted loudly from the corner. "Don't see how that's possible." He sauntered forward, earning an angry look from Madam Dreamer, which he ignored. "But let me, as Robin Goodfellow, alleviate your concerns. If this bargain was any other faery queen—Mab, Leanansidhe, Titania…especially Titania—you would be right to worry. They would try to twist the deal so the outcome would be favorable for them, and screwy for you. But when I say this fey queen isn't like that, I can't tell a lie. There's no hidden meaning here, no funny word play, and this is coming from someone with centuries of funny word play under their belt. If the Iron Queen herself is offering to make you human again, you're not gonna get a better deal, trust me on that."

Madam Dreamer wrung her hands. "My only chance to be human again," she whispered, not talking to any of us. "Dare I take it? What will happen if I do? What will happen if I *don't*?"

"Nothing," I said coldly. "Nothing will change. You'll remain here, in your den of exiles and outcasts, and you will never see the above world again."

"The son of Mab is right." She straightened. "If I don't accept, nothing will change. I will stay like this for the rest of eternity, or however long my miserable life endures. But do I dare return to the above world?" She cast a fearful glance up at the ceiling, as if seeing the city above through the concrete and dirt. "I have been away for so long. Everyone I used to know is dead or has moved on. Here, I am queen. Here, I have an entire kingdom that is mine."

Puck frowned. "Um, I'm confused now. I thought you said you'd give anything to be human again, and now you're backing out?" He gestured to Meghan, who continued to watch the spider woman with a mix of caution and sympathy. "Meghan just offered you a chance to go home. To live a normal life. Trust me when I say that's not gonna come around again."

"Home." Madam Dreamer tore her gaze from the ceiling. "No," she murmured. "Not home. Not anymore. It has been too long. Should I return to the surface, I would have to start over again. I would have nothing." Her thin shoulders trembled. "I am safer in my web. My home. I am safe…here."

Puck glanced at me, the expression on his face saying he thought the spider woman was a fool to turn down the offer.

But Madam Dreamer looked to Meghan, a steely resolve settling over her thin shoulders as she raised a pointed chin. "Iron Queen," she said in a stronger voice. "I will help you. Not because I accept. But because you offered to lift the curse, and though it has been a long time since I have been human, I remember what it is like to lose the one you love."

Meghan drew in a slow breath. "So, you'll help us find Keirran?"

"I will," Madam Dreamer said. "And I do not believe it will be difficult. The arrival of someone like the Forgotten King to the mortal realm does not go unnoticed." She turned and began walking across the room, beckoning us to follow. "I will start collecting information. All news on the street eventually finds its way here. Someone will have seen the King of the Forgotten, and then we will be able to track him down from there."

"I appreciate this, Madam Dreamer," Meghan said as we followed the spider woman across the room. A bloodred door stood against the far wall, black curtains draped to either side, a bright copper Keep Out sign displayed prominently in the middle of the frame. The spider woman waved a rail-thin arm.

"No, Iron Queen. It is I who should be grateful." Madam Dreamer glanced back, touching her collar with a curved black nail. "You have shown me exactly what I have. For so long, I have mourned my human life, the existence I believe was stolen from me. I thought myself a lonely monster, cut off from humanity, doomed to wallow in darkness and isolation. I thought this, because I believed there was no way for me to return to my human life. But, now I see how wrong I have been. Should I return to the mortal world at this time, I would have to start over. My youth is gone—I am not the beautiful young maiden that I was before. And the human world has changed so much since I was a part of it. I would not know what to do should I become human again."

We reached the door, and Madam Dreamer drew a tiny golden key out of the bodice of her dress, then inserted it into the lock below the door handle. "It is better this way," she whispered, back to talking to herself again. "I am…too afraid to return to the human world. This is my world now. My kingdom. I am safe in the center of my web. I am queen."

She pushed open the door, which swung back without so much as a creak. Beyond the frame was a room painted in black and red, though the color was difficult to see through the thick white webbing that covered every inch of the wall. The floor, too, was carpeted in webs, and thin strands, barely visible in the dim light, hung from the ceiling. A black-and-red divan sat in the very center of the room, surrounded by wispy white curtains and glimmering thread.

"Oh, a giant spiderweb, that's just great," Puck remarked, peering through the doorway. "That doesn't make me nervous at all. If she tells us to step into her parlor, I'm outta here."

Madam Dreamer walked daintily to the divan in the center of the web, her pointed spider legs making no sound or vibration on the threads. We followed her, but no matter how lightly we tread, the strands rustled loudly as we passed. I could imagine thousands upon thousands of hidden eyes on me; spiders attracted by the vibrations of the web, only held back by the presence of

Madam Dreamer. I glanced at Puck, who looked a little paler than normal—it appeared he was thinking the same thing.

"Now…" Madam Dreamer perched on the divan, drawing her legs up beside her. She looked more spiderlike than ever, her bottom half huge and bulbous, and Puck gave a shudder as she settled onto the seat. "I can find your son, if he is to be found, but the more information I have, the easier it will be. Is he alone? Is there something or someone hunting him? I often find that, if one is having difficulty finding a certain person, that person could be in hiding because something is after them. If we find the ones hunting the Forgotten King, we will find the Forgotten King."

"He isn't alone," Meghan said. "He was forced to flee with the survivors of his court from their city in the Between. Since Keirran himself is exiled from the Nevernever, they had no choice but to come to the mortal realm."

"And why here?" Madam Dreamer wondered. "Why this city, in particular? There are millions of places on Earth he could have gone to escape pursuit."

"We believe he was trying to contact Ethan and I," Kenzie answered, causing Madam Dreamer's black eyes to glance her way. "We're the only family he has in the mortal world—it would make sense that he would try to find us."

"I see." Madam Dreamer reached up and curled one finger over a single strand. "So, you believe he is close. But what force is chasing him? I find it hard to believe an army could invade a kingdom so easily, especially one in the Between."

I stepped closer to Meghan, and the spider woman eyed me warily. Out of everyone in the room, she trusted me the least, and I was fine with that. "It wasn't an army. It was a single crea-ture, a monster of rage and hate. It had the ability to turn his own Forgotten against him."

The spider woman's gaze flicked to me. "A monster of rage

and hate," she half whispered. "Like the strange shadowy creatures that cling to the humans nowadays? They also appear to foster negative emotion. But you say there is a bigger one?"

"Yes," I replied. "Much bigger than the nightmare piskies we've seen. And not just one, either. We fought and killed another before this. There might be more of them out there."

"This is disturbing news." Madam Dreamer fiddled with the thread under her nails. "I do not know what these new creatures are, but I do know that they either cause humans to become angry and violent, or they are attracted to their negative emotions. Or both. But if there is a larger creature out there..." She shivered. "Perhaps these smaller creatures will turn into a larger version eventually. I am only theorizing, but it does seem like they are related. It is a place to start, at the very least."

She raised her other arm, winding her nails around a second strand, and glanced at all of us. "The lines of information can be subtle," she told us. "Often, they are drowned in the flood of voices and events happening on the surface. Picking out an individual strand and following it to the end is a talent that requires absolute concentration. I ask for complete silence as I attempt to discover what we are looking for. If this is not possible, please wait for me in my office."

All of us looked at Puck, who blinked. "What are you all looking at me for?" he asked, a faint grin creeping across his face. "You won't even know I'm here. I'm as quiet as a mouse when I want to be."

"Yes, if only you wanted to be more often," Grimalkin sniffed.

Madam Dreamer took a deep breath and closed her eyes. Raising her pointed chin, she began mumbling, and a low, droning voice began resonating through the chamber.

"Let the information flow," she whispered, the curved black fangs wiggling as she spoke. "Down the strands, to the center of the web. Let me see the channels, let me hear the voices as they pass over the strands. The city is my web, and all things eventually find their way to the center. Show me what I am looking for."

For several minutes there was silence. Nothing could be heard except the deep breathing of Madam Dreamer, and the occasional rustle of the webs around us.

"The streets are filled with fear," Madam Dreamer whispered suddenly. "Fear, and anger, and uncertainty. Shadows stalk the streets, mortals grow unsatisfied, rage and confusion and violence run rampant through the city. No one is safe."

"This is cheery," Puck mumbled under his breath. Nyx glared at him, narrowing her eyes, and he bit his lip with a shrug.

"There is...a warehouse," Madam Dreamer went on. "On the outskirts of the city. Abandoned by mortals, it was a haven for questionable activities, but now it is swarming with shadow creatures. They are everywhere, climbing the walls and clawing at the windows. They have frightened away all the fey in the area, but they do not leave. Something is within, but no one can get to it. A barrier from inside keeps everything out."

"A barrier?" Meghan repeated.

"Keirran." I felt a cold rage spread through me, and clenched my fingers around my sword hilt. Kierran would only put up a barrier if something was trying to get at him or the ones he was trying to protect. "If he's there, we need to reach him quickly. Where is this warehouse located?"

"The north end of town," Madam Dreamer replied, still with her eyes closed. "On a road called Stonerun. The warehouse stands at the end of a concrete lot, surrounded by chain-link and barbed wire. If you are looking for it, it is rather difficult to miss."

"Let's go." I looked at the others, feeling anger and violence churn the pit of my stomach. My son was in trouble, and if I had to cut my way through an army of enemies to get to him, there would be sea of blood and death before the night was over. I saw concern on Puck's face, as if he could sense my thoughts, and ignored it.

Meghan nodded, but she hesitated at the foot of Dreamer's chair, gazing at the cursed human in sympathy. "Madam Dreamer, your life has been hard, but I hope you can find some measure of peace after this. I know you don't hear these words very often, but thank you."

"You are welcome, Iron Queen." Madam Dreamer opened her eyes, shiny black orbs both grateful and sad as they met the queen's gaze. "Good luck to you and yours. I hope you can find your son."

7

THE SWARM

The warehouse in question was difficult to miss, as Stonerun Road dead-ended at an abandoned industrial park. Since her favor with the goblins had expired, and the warehouse in question was still a few miles away, Kenzie had to call for an Uber. Normally, this would be a problem for regular fey, as sitting in a box of metal and steel was highly unpleasant. But Meghan and I were immune to iron sickness, and Puck and Nyx both had amulets that countered the effects of iron to the fey system. It still wouldn't be pleasant for them, but there wouldn't be any lasting harm. Nyx did keep her hood up the entire time we were in the van, as she silently withdrew into her cloak, but I noticed her fingers interlaced with Puck's, gripping them tightly as the iron sickness pressed down upon her.

The van came to a stop at the end of a gravel road, where skeletal, gutted structures loomed in the distance. As we stepped from the vehicle, I gazed at the scene before us, feeling anger, worry, and impatience gnawing my insides. Crumbling buildings sat beyond a barbed-wire fence, the stench of rust and stagnant water heavy in the air. Somewhere in that maze of iron and cement was Keirran.

"Looks pretty empty," Ethan muttered, as Kenzie finished paying the driver, and the vehicle sped off in a spray of gravel and dirt. I suspected he thought something illegal or dangerous was happening here, and didn't want to be a part of it. "I hope it's as abandoned as it appears."

"If it was," I said darkly, "Keirran wouldn't still be here. He would already have found us."

"Which means we have to be ready for a fight," Meghan added. She glanced at Kenzie, who was walking up to join us with Puck and Nyx close behind. Razor grinned at us from her shoulder, the light from his neon blue teeth dancing over the sides of the truck. "Be on your guard," Meghan continued. "Watch out for each other. We don't know what to expect here."

"It's always so cheerful before a fight," Puck sighed. "Come on, then. Before Nyx or ice-boy gets impatient enough to stab me. Let's go get the princeling."

The barbed-wire fence surrounded the area, and rusty No Trespassing signs were posted every dozen or so feet. Nyx shuddered and held herself away from the barrier of decaying iron, but I drew my sword and slashed through the chains around the gates with one decisive swipe. No more delays. No more waiting around. Keirran was close, and I would stop at nothing until I found him.

Bits of concrete and broken glass crunched under our feet as we made our way through the industrial park, scanning the darkness for movement and glowing eyes. I led the way with Meghan at my side, both of our swords drawn and ready. I could feel the power circling the Iron Queen; the static energy that crackled the air around her. Puck and Nyx trailed at our backs, with Ethan and Kenzie bringing up the rear. Grimalkin was nowhere to be seen, but I wasn't thinking of the cat. I wasn't thinking of what we would find once we reached the warehouse. I wasn't thinking of anything but getting to my son and eliminating the threat that stood between us.

As we turned the corner between two old buildings, the warehouse suddenly came into view at the end of the lot, a crumbling square building of brick and glass, with a steel roof and bars over the many broken windows. It squatted in the weeds and broken cement, its walls covered in what looked like a mass of living shadows. Tiny, twisted things clung to the bricks and swarmed around the base, their eyes white pinpricks in the darkness.

"Oh, wow," Kenzie muttered, staring up at the writhing mass of fey. Piskie creatures zipped through the air, wings buzzing, and I was suddenly reminded of a hornet's nest, of clouds of insects swirling around the hive. "There's...a lot of them."

Whispers hissed in my ear, carried by the wind. They were fragmented, too rapid and disjointed to make out, snatches of words and phrases I couldn't understand. It felt as if I was hearing the entire mass of creatures whispering in my ears all at once, and I felt anger stir in response.

"Ugh, my ears are crawling," Puck muttered at my back. I glanced over my shoulder to see him stick a finger in the side of his head and wiggle it vigorously. "Wish I had some cotton balls to jam into my eardrums, but then you guys would probably get annoyed with me yelling 'what?' all the time."

"Do you think they can be killed?" Nyx wondered. We were now only a few hundred feet from the warehouse, and the mass of crawling, buzzing creatures swarming over it. They didn't seem to notice us, their attention entirely focused on what was inside. "If they're related to the Monster, they could be immune to glamour."

I took a breath and felt the cold, killing rage in me expand. "Kenzie," I said without turning to look at her, "take Razor and get back. There's a lot of small, fast creatures, and we don't know what they're capable of. A dozen enemies we could kill quickly, but there might be thousands of these things, and if they're immune to glamour…"

"Say no more." Kenzie sighed, and I felt her take a step back, surprising me. I had half expected her to protest. "Razor and I will be leaving the battle zone now, don't worry about us. I know when to hold my ground and when to get the hell out of the way so the big powers can handle things. Ethan…" I felt her and Meghan's brother share a look. "Be careful."

"I will," Ethan promised, and Kenzie walked away, her footsteps crunching over gravel, until she and Razor disappeared into the shadows.

As soon as the footsteps had faded, Meghan moved beside me, power and glamour rising around her and making the air crackle. "All right," she murmured, as my own magic swirled up in response. Overhead, the sky darkened, the moon and stars disappearing as black clouds formed, billowing and ominous. "Let's get to Keirran. Ash?"

That's what I had been waiting for. I gave a vicious smile and threw out an arm, sending a wave of winter glamour at my enemies.

A storm of glittering ice daggers streaked through the air, slamming into the hordes clinging to the warehouse walls. Several of them instantly exploded into coils of black smoke that dissolved in the wind, leaving a shrieking echo ringing in my head.

"Oh, well," Puck said, as the entire swarm immediately exploded into motion, wings droning as they rose into the air. I had kicked the hornet's nest, and now they were coming for us. "Here we go. I always forget to bring that can of OFF! for these adventures."

The mass of nightmare piskies descended toward us, thousands of wings a droning hum in my ears. As they drew close, the cloud seemed to shift and change, as hundreds of tiny bodies merged into one huge, looming creature. A giant appeared, glowing eyes peering down on us, as it opened a gaping, shifting mouth and roared.

Lightning streaked from Meghan's hand, slamming into the giant's center, and the creature instantly exploded into thousands of swarming fey. Hissing, they rose up and came at us like wasps, and the air was suddenly filled with tiny black creatures zipping around us.

Whispers surrounded me, buzzing in my ears and making my teeth vibrate. This close, the creatures were a condensed cloud of anger and fury, a mire of frantically swirling emotion. And suddenly, I could feel a different type of glamour in the air around us, one of rage and hate, violence and fear. The ugliest of human emotions, with nothing to filter them. My Unseelie nature stirred, and I was tempted to reach out, to use the fury spinning around us. There was power there; I could feel it, an anger that called to the Unseelie within, urging it to let go, to draw that glamour to me and release it in a violent explosion of ice and death.

The piskies descended on us, blurs of motion and darting wings. I felt several land on me, driving needle teeth into my skin with tiny, red-hot jabs of pain. Vaguely, I was aware of Puck fighting at my side, of Nyx being a whirlwind of deadly grace, darting in and out of the swarm. I could sense Meghan and Ethan behind me, felt the flare of Meghan's power snapping at our enemies, but even they were blips of motion in my consciousness.

I closed my mind to it all, and reached out to the nightmare glamour.

There was a flare of power, along with an immediate spike of rage. I felt my Winter glamour surge up, cold and deadly, bolstered by the infusion of strange magic. There was strength in anger, in fury and hatred, and the Unseelie side reveled in the power coursing through my veins.

I directed that rage at the creatures swirling around us, and released that energy into the cloud.

There was a burst of frigid glamour, and for a moment, everything went completely silent. The sound of their wings stopped, the shrill hisses and shrieking cut out, and everything hung in icy stillness. I looked up to see nearly all of the swarm frozen in midair, wings iced over, tiny bodies rimmed in frost. For a split second, they hung there like crystal ornaments. Then, as one, the entire frozen horde dropped to the ground, shattering like glass against the pavement.

I breathed deep, feeling the rage subside and the ripple of strange glamour fade. The others lowered their arms, watching as the rest of the few remaining piskies scattered, flying over the tops of buildings and out of sight. None of them gave me odd or wary looks, not even Meghan. I had used this particular glamour technique before; it wasn't anything new. But the power I'd felt when tapping in to my anger was instant and overwhelming. For a moment, I'd felt like the Winter prince again.

"Brr," Puck complained, rubbing his arms where a coating of frost had spread over his skin. "Not that I mind when you do the whole instant-blizzard thing, ice-boy, but a little warning would be nice. I hate it when my nose hairs freeze."

Kenzie appeared, walking back across the lot with Razor buzzing irritably on her shoulder. The gremlin kept glancing up, scanning the sky as if he feared piskies would dive-bomb him from above.

"That was fast," Kenzie remarked, observing the carpet of dead, melting piskies fading to nothing on the ground. "So, now that the bugs are gone, we should be able to see what they were so attracted to."

"Hopefully the princeling," Puck said. "And a lot of Forgotten. Unless that's a honey factory in there."

Meghan caught my gaze, a shadow of worry crossing her face. But she turned toward the warehouse, hope and fear mingling with concern as she gazed up at it.

"I can feel a barrier surrounding the building," she murmured. "It's weak, flickering, but composed of all three magics—Summer, Winter, and Iron."

All three glamours. "It's Keirran," I growled, and strode across the lot with the rest of them at my heels.

As I vaulted up the steps to the heavy steel doors, I could suddenly feel what Meghan was talking about. A shield of glamour encased the whole warehouse like a shell, pulsing with energy that made part of me—the winter side—want to recoil and back away.

"Ouch," Puck said, shivering as he took a step back. "That's a pretty impressive barrier. Summer-, Winter-, *and* Iron-repellant, huh? Whoever is on the other side definitely doesn't want anyone coming through."

"Hang on," Ethan said, coming up the steps. "I'm immune. Glamour doesn't affect me, so it shouldn't—ow!"

He'd reached for the door handle, but there was a soundless crackle of energy, and Ethan jerked his hand back with a curse. Puck shook his head.

"You're not immune to iron glamour, kid." Crossing his arms, he regarded the doors appraisingly. "Looks like our princeling wasn't taking any chances."

"How do we break it?" Kenzie wondered, staring up at the warehouse. On her shoulder, the gremlin hissed and muttered incoherently, baring his teeth at the doors. "I was going to send Razor in, but I don't think even he'll be able to get through."

"You do not want to break it." It was Grimalkin's voice, and the feline appeared on a nearby stack of wooden crates. "The barrier is directly tied to whomever is keeping it up. Shattering it by force could damage their psyche and even cause them physical harm."

I glared at the invisible wall before me, stifling the urge to draw my blade and cut through the doors. *Dammit, Keirran*, I thought. If he was trying to protect his people, he would spare himself no discomfort, and he would pour everything he had into keeping up the barrier. *I didn't want to bring this down by force if it would hurt him. How did we let him know it was us?*

The barrier flickered and snapped threateningly, warning me back. Setting my jaw, I raised an arm and pressed my palm to the door.

Instantly, I felt a searing pain through my hand, like I had grasped a live, burning coal. My winter glamour recoiled from the agonizing burn of Summer magic, but I didn't pull back. Closing my eyes, I tried finding the person on the other end, the one we had come all this way to find.

Keirran, I thought, hoping my thoughts would reach him, that he could sense who was pushing against his barrier. *It's us. You're safe now. Let us in.*

For a few moments, nothing happened, except the burning pain in my hand continued to worsen. Then, I felt the faintest glimmer of emotion coming through the barrier wall so fast I might have imagined it. Surprise, and then utter relief.

The barrier flickered once and vanished, taking the searing pain of Summer magic with it. I put my shoulder to the doors and bashed them open, and we all rushed inside.

A sea of glowing yellow eyes instantly turned to face us, surrounding the room. The space beyond the frame was dark, with corroded beams lining decaying concrete walls. Shards of glass littered the floor, and the tang of rust and iron clogged the back of my throat as we stepped farther inside, glass and debris crunching under our feet. The glowing eyes didn't move, and in the pitch-dark, it was impossible to tell what was fey and what was shadow.

In the center of the open space, surrounded by Forgotten, a figure knelt in a shaft of moonlight coming through the broken windows. The light gleamed off his silver hair, though the rest of him was shrouded in black, from his cloak to his gloves. He hunched there with his head bowed, his shoulders heaving with deep, ragged breaths, but he looked up as we entered the room. His face was haggard, his skin pale and wan with exhaustion, but his blue eyes shone with relief as our gazes met through the crowds of Forgotten.

"Keirran!"

Meghan strode forward, through the ranks of fey, who quickly parted for her. Ignoring the Forgotten, she dropped to her knees in front of Keirran and pulled him close. He slumped against her, closing his eyes and letting all his defenses drop, if only for a moment.

The ice in my veins thawed, and I let relief sweep through me as I strode forward, joining my family in the center of the room. Keirran was safe; we had gotten to him in time, and he hadn't turned into that soulless, blank-eyed stranger from my dream. I wouldn't have to fight my son; the relief of that real-ization was nearly as great as the joy of finding him.

Keirran looked up as I stopped above him and Meghan. "How did you find me?" he whispered. His voice was ragged, and dark circles crouched under his eyes. He looked completely spent, and I wondered how long he had been keeping up the magi-cal barrier.

"Long story," I answered, holding out a hand. He grasped it, and I drew him to his feet, gripping his arm to steady him as he swayed. "After we heard what happened in Touchstone, we went to the Between, then Leanansidhe's, then finally to Ethan and Kenzie. They were the ones who led us here."

Keirran looked over my arm at the rest of the group as they approached, a tired smile crossing his face. "Looks like everyone is here," he observed, a little of that wry humor returning to his voice. "I'm touched that I warrant such a rescue." He might've said something more, but Kenzie rushed up to throw her arms around him, making him grunt as she squeezed hard.

"Don't be stupid, Keirran." Kenzie's words were softened by the clearly affectionate look she gave him as she pulled back. "You'd drop everything and go combing every corner of the Nevernever for us if the tables were turned."

Nyx stepped forward, the relief in her golden eyes evident as she bowed her head to her king. "Your Majesty, I am pleased to see you are safe. When we saw what happened to Touchstone, we feared the worst."

"Touchstone." Keirran's face grew serious, a mantle of grief, anger, and regret descending on him. He sighed, and the air around him turned a little colder. "It happened so fast," he muttered. "I would have fought that thing to the death, but when it started corrupting the Forgotten, I knew I had to save as many as I could. I left so many behind…" He closed his eyes, bowing his head. "What kind of king am I, to abandon my city like that?"

I gripped his shoulder. "Touchstone isn't completely destroyed," I told him. "The anchor is damaged, but not gone. It can still be rebuilt."

Keirran nodded, then took a quick breath, shaking off his melancholy. "I tried sending out messages," he went on, glancing up at me. "Before those piskie things trapped us in here, I sent a couple Forgotten to find you. Did any of them make it?"

"One," Meghan said. "At Leanansidhe's. We stopped there when we heard what had happened in Touchstone, and one of your Forgotten did track us down. But something had happened to it. It attacked as soon as it saw us."

Keirran winced, shaking his head. "They must've been corrupted," he said. "I'm sorry—this was before I knew how many of these things were out there. As soon as we got to the mortal realm, those creatures seemed to target us. And with the attack on Touchstone, I don't believe it's a coincidence. Whatever they are, I think they want us—or me—dead." He took another breath, as if gathering his strength, and stabbed his fingers through his hair to push it back. "So," he ventured, "what do we do now?"

Meghan frowned, looking thoughtful for a few moments. "Before we do anything, we need to get you and the rest of the Forgotten to a safe place," she said, gazing around at the still silent Forgotten. "And then, we need to get the other rulers together to warn the Nevernever. These creatures, whatever they are, are clearly a threat. The rest of Faery needs to be aware of them. But first…" She gave Keirran an appraising look, her brow furrowed in thought. "Where can we send you and the Forgotten? For whatever reason, these Monsters seem to be after you, specifically. Is there any spot in the mortal world that is safe?"

Keirran frowned. "I don't know," he sighed. Taking a few steps back, he sank onto a wooden crate, running his hands through his hair. "We haven't been in the mortal realm long, and wherever we turned, it seemed there were more of these things coming after us. But even if there weren't these new Monsters, it isn't safe for us here. The Forgotten aren't suited for long periods in the human world."

"They fade too easily," Nyx stated, and Keirran nodded.

"It's bad enough for exiles," he said. "But the Forgotten have no glamour of their own to sustain them. They either have to steal it from the traditional fey, which is against the law now, or find enough of a natural glamour source to slow the Fade."

"What about the Between?" Kenzie asked. "There have to be other places besides Touchstone. Can you go back there, just for them to be safe?"

The Forgotten around Keirran cringed, and the Forgotten King shook his head. "Not if there's a chance that the bigger Monsters are still wandering the Between," he replied. "As far as I can tell, they haven't been able to cross into the mortal realm. Not like these smaller ones. But I don't want to take my people back through the Veil when they're actively being hunted. You saw what happened to Touchstone. Another attack like that, and the Forgotten could be gone forever."

"Well, we're kinda stuck between a rock and a hard place, then," Puck said. "The Forgotten can't stay in the mortal realm, they can't go back to the Between, and you can't go into Faery." He broke into a toothy grin. "Get it? Stuck *Between*, a rock, and a hard place." When we all just stared at him, he rolled his eyes. "Everyone's a critic."

Keirran sighed. "I don't know what we're going to do," he admitted in a weary voice. "There's no place that is safe anymore. Not without going into the Nevernever. And obviously I can't do that."

"You are wrong, Forgotten King," said a voice, and Grimalkin appeared atop a rusted-out barrel. "There is a way."

We all stared at the cat, who, once all eyes were upon him, made a great show of stretching, turning in a circle, and finally resettling himself atop the barrel. Curling his tail around his feet, he blinked down at us lazily.

"You have been exiled from the Nevernever," the cait sith began as he stared at Keirran, who gave a single grave nod of agreement. "Because of the nature of your exile, all the rulers would have to be present, and in agreement, for the banishment to be overturned. The Iron Queen cannot simply lift it herself.

"However," Grimalkin went on, "your exile is only valid in the places where Faery law holds sway. In this case, where the rulers of Faery are present—in Summer, Winter, Iron, and the wyldwood. Within those boundaries, the rules and decrees must be obeyed. But," he added, raising his head, "there is a place where Faery rule does not extend, where there is no law and no regulations to abide by."

Momentarily puzzled, Keirran furrowed his brow, but Kenzie drew in a quick breath.

"The Deep Wyld," she guessed immediately.

Grimalkin nodded. "As usual, the mortal girl is on top of things," he sighed. "I fear for the rest of the Nevernever. Yes, the Deep Wyld. Faery law does not exist on the far side of the River of Dreams. The Deep Wyld does not recognize any type of authority—it is a truly neutral plane of existence where the only real law is kill or be killed. If the Forgotten King and his people take refuge in the Deep Wyld, technically they are not breaking any law, as the law does not exist there."

"But the Deep Wyld is extremely dangerous," Keirran argued with a worried glance at the Forgotten. "The things that make their home across the River of Dreams are nearly as dangerous as the Monster itself. The Forgotten won't be any safer there then they would in the Between."

"Yes," Grimalkin said, "the things that make their home in the Deep Wyld are very dangerous. Dangerous enough to challenge even the Monsters we have encountered. One creature, in particular, is as much a ruler of his domain as the kings and queens here, though he would never call himself one." The cat's golden eyes shifted to me. "You should know whom I am talking about."

I did know. I think everyone knew, at that point. "The Wolf," I said simply.

Keirran's brows rose. The Wolf, or *The Big Bad Wolf*, as was his official name, was an ancient, primordial creature from the dawn of time. He was, quite simply, a huge black wolf the size of a grizzly bear, but he was also much more than that. The Wolf was the culmination of every story, fable, and cautionary tale about wolves. From Little Red Riding Hood, to the Boy Who Cried Wolf, to the terrible monsters in media and film, the Big Bad Wolf had existed since the beginning of time, and was as old as mankind's fears surrounding him.

He was also immortal, and rumored to be impossible to kill. He had already almost killed me once, when Oberon had sent the great hunter to track me down, thinking Meghan had been kidnapped. But the Wolf had also been vital in the quest of earning my soul, traveling to the End of the World with me and Puck, and helping us on the journey.

I exchanged a look with Meghan, both of us thinking the same thing. The Wolf was strong, extremely dangerous, and normally wanted nothing to do with fey politics. But he was honorable in his own way, and more than a match for any monster in the Nevernever and beyond. If anyone could keep a group of outcast fey safe in the Deep Wyld, it would be the Big Bad Wolf.

The only question was, would he agree to it? No one ordered the Big Bad Wolf to do anything, and if he was bored, or irritated enough, he might bite off the heads of the intruders in his territory as much as help them.

"I think we're going to have to set up a meeting with the Wolf," Meghan said, sounding like she had the same concerns. "Grimalkin, do you think you can do that?"

The cat's whiskers curled back in distaste. "I suppose I must," he sighed. "It should not be too difficult. Though the Deep Wyld is quite large, and the Wolf tends to roam wherever his nose takes him. Dogs." Grimalkin gave a sniff of disgust. "Might I suggest a temporary safe house for the Forgotten until the Wolf can be found?"

"Where?" Keirran wondered. "I can't send them to Leanansidhe's—she's made it very clear that the Forgotten are not welcome there. And neither am I, to be honest."

"They can stay with us," Kenzie said. "Our place should be

safe enough. It might be a little crowded in the basement, but I think everyone will be able to fit. They should be fine."

Ethan nodded with a somewhat resigned sigh. "I'll just have to increase the security measures around the house by a million or so," he muttered.

Keirran bowed his head. "I'm in your debt," he told them. "Thank you both. Hopefully, we won't be there long. Though I'm not entirely sure how I'm going to get into the Deep Wyld."

"Do not concern yourself overmuch, Forgotten King," Grimalkin said. "There are ways to get into the Deep Wyld from the mortal realm, though they are difficult, and sometimes dangerous, to find." He yawned, showing a flash of teeth, and gave us all a lazy stare. "Luckily for you, I happen to know where one of them is located."

8

INTO THE DEEP WYLD

After some initial reluctance on Keirran's part, we left the Forgotten with Ethan and Kenzie, after both assured him numerous times that they would all be fine. The remaining survivors of Touchstone were put into Ethan's faery-proof basement, and though it was a tight fit, the Forgotten were quite adept at squeezing into small spaces and tiny cracks. No fey would be able to get to them without going through the wards, which were strong enough to repel some fairly powerful creatures. Of course, they couldn't stay there long; even with Keirran's intervention, he'd already lost a couple to Fading since they had been forced to flee to the real world. They needed a place in the Nevernever to be safe from the Fade, which was why we were going into the Deep Wyld.

"I'll keep doing research on InSite," Kenzie told us as we prepared to leave. "Once Keirran and the Forgotten are safe, I think we really need to know what's going on there. Why these new creatures seemed to have first sprung up inside that building."

"Agreed," Meghan said. "And we'll need more information if we're going to call on the other courts. You know how fickle they are when it comes to taking action against perceived threats."

"Take this." Kenzie handed Meghan something small and plastic, a key-fob-shaped device that fit in the palm of her hand. "It's something I came up with myself. Since phones don't work in the Nevernever, this will let Razor hone in on your location in Faery. He'll be able to find you if we need to send a message quickly."

Meghan blinked. "That's amazing, Kenzie," she said, slipping the device into her pocket. "We're always looking for new ways to blend magic and tech together, but it's still hard, even with iron glamour. I might have to send our own engineers your way for pointers."

Kenzie shrugged, but she was clearly pleased. "If people need their own gremlin-tracking device, I'll be happy to show you how to make them," she said. "I take no responsibility for a gremlin infestation, though."

It was late morning when we stepped outside, finding Grimalkin waiting for us in the front yard. The forest surrounding the house was silent; nothing moved in the bushes or through the branches of the trees. I saw Keirran turn once, glancing over his shoulder at the fey he was leaving behind, his jaw set in determination. Nyx hovered close to him, but her gaze was on the surrounding forest, watching for enemies. If any nightmare creature came hurtling out of the shadows at him, I suspected the assassin's blades would be the first to cut it down.

"So, where is this trod, Grim?" Meghan wondered as we left the Chase residence, following the cat back through the woods. "I find it hard to believe that there's a trod into the Deep Wyld close to where we need it to be. Especially since Keirran can't go into the Nevernever the normal way."

"It is not close," Grimalkin responded without looking back. "The closest physical trod to the Deep Wyld is hundreds of miles from here."

"What?" Puck exclaimed. "You couldn't have mentioned that earlier, Furball? Seems like an important bit of information to conveniently forget."

"I do not forget, Goodfellow." Grimalkin flattened his ears. "If you recall, at no point did I say that we were going to the Deep Wyld by trod. However, someone owes me a favor, and that favor is going to be called in today."

He stopped in the center of a small clearing, with pine and spruce trees surrounding us, and glanced over his shoulder with a faintly smug look. "We are here. You might want to step back."

We all moved warily to the edges of the clearing. Grimalkin sat down in the center, curled his tail around his feet, and waited.

For several minutes, nothing happened. The wind rustled the leaves and hissed through the pine branches, creating a mournful howling. Grimalkin didn't move, sitting patiently in the center of the grove, eyes closed in the sunlight.

And then, I heard something else. A faint snapping sound, getting louder as it came through the forest. As it got closer, I started to realize that whatever was making the noise was huge: the trees shook and the ground trembled as something crashed through the forest toward us. From the corner of my eye, I saw Puck shift nervously and Nyx call her moonlight blades into her hands as whatever was coming stomped closer. From the commotion it was making, it sounded like it was the size of a house.

The trees across the clearing fell with a crash, and something large and bulky pushed its way into the grove. It was…a house. An ancient-looking cottage with warped wooden sides, peeling shutters, and a thatched roof that left a trail of straw behind it. The whole structure stood on a pair of enormous yellow chicken legs, blunt claws sinking into the dirt. Swaying and bobbing, the house walked across the clearing and stood before Grimalkin, who looked completely undisturbed that one of those giant feet could stomp him like a bug.

I felt my hand stray to my sword hilt. I knew this house. It was, of course, impossible to forget. But the last time Puck and I had seen it, the owner of the house had tried to kill us.

"Oh, great," Puck muttered next to me. Apparently, he remembered as well. "Look who it is, ice-boy. Do you think she still remembers the time we stole her broom?"

"*You* stole her broom."

"Details."

The house stood there for a moment, and then sank into a crouch in front of Grimalkin, like a giant bird settling itself on the ground. After a moment, the single wooden door creaked open, and a hunched figure peered out from atop the steps. She was old and withered, a beady-eyed crone with steel-gray hair and hands like grasping talons. The Bone Witch of the Deep Wyld looked exactly the same as she did years ago, when Puck and I last crossed her path.

Staring down at Grimalkin, her gaze shifted to the rest of us, bloodless lips curling up in a smirk.

"Well." The creaky, rusty voice reached us even on the other side of the clearing. "I figured Grimalkin would call in his favor sooner or later. I did not expect him to use it like this. Good afternoon, Iron Queen. I see you have arrived with your whole entourage. Robin Goodfellow." Her lips curled a bit as she said his name. "Son of Mab." She nodded at me across the grove. "Last I saw of you, Ash who is no longer a prince, you were on your way to earn your soul. I see you managed to do so. My condolences."

Before I could answer, the witch glanced down at Grimalkin again. "All right then, cait sith. You have called me here for a reason, dragged me out of the Deep Wyld, in the middle of the culling season no less. Let us get on with it. The rest of you can stop hovering, you know. I am not going to put you in my cauldron. At least, not today. What do you want of me?"

"We require passage into the Deep Wyld," Grimalkin said calmly, not moving a whisker as one of the chicken talons scratched the ground, leaving deep gouges in the earth. "Without traveling through the territory of any of the courts."

"All of you?" The witch sniffed, looking up at us as we approached the front of the cottage. "Why do you need to…ah, I see the reason." Her beady gaze fixed on Keirran, and she flashed a toothy grin. "Got the little exiled prince with you, eh? Trying to get around the rules? Well, Iron Queen, I'm scandalized." She cackled loudly, and I set my jaw, trying to stifle the instant anger rising within. "But, this entire mess came of you and the former Winter prince breaking the laws, so I suppose it is to be expected. Now you see why there are rules and Faery law. You'll just have to live with the consequences."

"And I would do it again," Meghan stated calmly. "A hundred times over. If I knew exactly what would happen, nothing would change."

Though she wasn't looking at me as she said it, I felt my throat tighten. I'd lived in Faery my whole life; sometimes I'd forget that Meghan had been born a human, and that she'd left her entire world behind to live in the Nevernever. I never doubted she loved me, and she would give up everything she knew to be with me and rule in the Iron Kingdom even now, but it was always nice to hear her confirm it.

"Hmph." The Bone Witch gave a loud sniff. "We'll see if you can still say that in the future, child." With a final chuckle, she stepped back, gesturing to us with a withered claw. "Come inside then, all of you. Try not to touch anything. I do not want to spend the night having to craft a cure frog potion. And, Goodfellow, if I see your fingers drifting anywhere near anything, I'll turn them into slugs."

"Not the worst thing that's happened to me," Puck said, and grinned. But he stuck both hands in his hoodie pocket, and we all followed the witch up the rickety steps into her cottage.

It was surprisingly tidy, all things considered. A large black cauldron bubbled out some kind of greenish mist against the fireplace, but the wooden floor was free of clutter. Shelves ran the length of the wall and were filled with boxes and jars of what you would expect to find in a witch's hut: snake eyes, piskie wings, hen's teeth, and the like. Puck bumped his head on a string of dried crow's feet hanging over the door, and wrinkled his nose when he saw what hit him.

"I'd offer you tea," the witch said, taking a gnarled root from the top shelf and casually tossing it into the cauldron, "but I don't believe you'll be staying very long." She looked at Grimalkin, who had taken a seat atop the only large chair in the room. "What part of the Deep Wyld were you hoping to get to?"

Grimalkin flattened his ears. "*His* territory, unfortunately," he said, as if saying the Wolf's name was somehow distasteful. "Whatever part of the Deep Wyld he is currently roaming in."

"I see. Don't ask for much, do you?" The Bone Witch sniffed and took a kettle off the fire. "One does not simply find the great Hunter in the Deep Wyld," she said, "especially since he could be anywhere." She turned and poured a thin stream of greenish liquid into a cracked teacup on the table, then put the kettle back over the fire. "Fortunately for you, I happen to know where he is. Or, at least his last known location. Let us hope he has not moved on, because it would be difficult to track him down again."

"Excuse me." This from my son, who had been worryingly silent until now. Ever since his banishment from Faery, Keirran had become very withdrawn, speaking only when he had to and hovering at the edges of conversation. It concerned me; before the war with the Forgotten, my son had always been cheerful and outgoing. Now, I saw shadows of my old self in him; quiet, somber, purposefully detached from the world. He carried the guilt of what he'd done on his shoulders, but he was also part Unseelie, and that legacy of darkness clung to him as well. I wished I knew how to help him, but I recognized, better than anyone, that he had to come to terms with his past himself.

"Oh, the Forgotten King speaks." The witch shot Keirran a toothy smile that looked like jagged bits of bone. "And so polite, just like his sire. What can I do for you, Your Highness?"

"How are we getting to the Deep Wyld?" Keirran asked. "According to Grimalkin, the nearest trod is many miles away. Are we going to walk there in this…lovely house?"

The Bone Witch chuckled.

"Of course, we're going to walk there," she said. "But don't worry. As I'm sure you've already surmised, this is not a normal house." She took a sip from her teacup, sighed happily, and sat down on a stool that was made of bones. "I would hold on to something, if I were you."

She snapped her fingers, and the floor beneath us gave a violent lurch, as the house stood up like a giant bird getting to its feet. I braced myself, catching hold of Meghan as the entire hut swayed from side to side. Puck stumbled, falling against a wall and barely managing not to knock over an entire shelf, while Nyx and Keirran shifted their weight to account for the sudden upheaval under their feet. The witch cackled and took another sip of her tea.

"Off we go," she announced, and the house surged forward.

I had been on a ship once, in the middle of a violent storm. I remembered the wild swaying of the deck, pitching from side to side. I recalled the floor roiling and bobbing under my feet, the ship at the mercy of the huge waves crashing against the sides.

This was probably worse.

I put my back to a wall, braced my feet, and locked my arms around Meghan as we waited for the wild ride to be over. She pressed herself back into me, crossing her arms and ignoring the tempting handholds dangling from the ceiling. Walls creaked, furniture rattled, and the items on the ceiling clattered against each other as the shack loped steadily through the forest, smacking aside branches and crushing things underfoot. Keirran and Nyx had claimed another corner, and seemed to be keeping their feet, though Keirran would occasionally put a hand against the wall when the house jerked or turned in an unexpected direction. Nyx, I noticed, barely moved, perfectly balanced through the entire wild ride. After a few times of being jostled against the wall, Puck finally gave up and sat on the floor.

Finally, the house slowed, going from a jarring lope to a less bouncy walk, before finally coming to a halt. I glanced down at Meghan, who looked relieved that it was over. Her body was stiff against mine, though she was trying not to appear tense.

"Are you all right?" I asked softly.

She nodded, uncoiling a bit in my arms. "I think I prefer our spider carriages back home."

With a final, violent heave, the floor dropped several feet as the house sank to the ground, then shuffled a bit as it got comfortable. I then noticed that the sky through the single cottage window was no longer sunny; somehow, and without any of us noticing, it had become pitch-black.

"We are here," announced the witch in a creaky, singsong voice. "You have arrived in the Deep Wyld, without having to go through Summer, Winter, Iron, or the wyldwood. Have a lovely time, and say hello to the big dog if you find him. Now, if you would please leave my cottage as soon as you are able, I must be going. I sense something on the wind, and the rumors circulating through Faery have not been pleasant of late."

We had started to leave the tiny room, but Meghan paused, glancing back at the witch with a frown. "What do you mean?" she asked. "What kinds of rumors?"

"Ominous rumors." The witch shook her head. "Frightening ones. Rumors of End Times, sightings that point to the twilight of all living things. Shadow creatures clawing at the very fabric of Faery, wanting in. The Nevernever is not going to be safe much longer. I am taking my home, and we are fleeing into the Deep Wyld, as far as we can go. Maybe, if we are lucky, we will reach the End of the World, though I fear even that will not be far enough."

I felt a chill crawl up my back. I hadn't ever fought the Bone Witch directly, but I knew what she could do. Legends of her and her unique house still existed in the mortal realm, making the witch extremely powerful in her own right. If even *she* feared what was coming, things were serious indeed.

And by the look on Meghan's face, I knew she was thinking the same.

"So, farewell, all of you," the witch said, gesturing us toward the door again. "The house enjoyed having you here, but it is time for you to go." She looked at Grimalkin, still sitting in her chair, and her nose wrinkled. "Cait sith, we are done. Your favor has been repaid, and our business is now complete. I do not think you will see me again for a very long time. Now get out of my house."

Grimalkin yawned, stretched, and sauntered out the door without speaking. The rest of us followed, ducking crow's feet and dried rat heads as we headed across the floor.

"Son of Mab." The witch's voice stopped me at the doorframe. I turned back to find her watching me, pointed fingers steepled under her chin. "You have changed," she observed. "When last I saw you, you were a pure Unseelie fey, drowning in grief and rage. A Winter prince driven by anger and violence. You are different now."

"I earned my soul," I said simply. "I have a family. They are the most important things in my life now. That Unseelie prince is gone."

"He is still there," the witch countered. "Different, perhaps. Given new purpose. But he will always be a part of you." She raised a withered finger. "I extend this warning, son of Mab. Now that you have much more to lose, be cautious that you are not consumed trying to protect it."

Witches and oracles, I'd found, loved extending cryptic warnings. It was a waste of time to argue, or to try to get more information out of them, so I simply nodded and left the cottage, joining the others outside. Meghan cocked her head at me as I walked down the steps, her gaze curious.

"Everything all right?" she asked. "Did the witch say anything to you?"

"Nothing important," I replied, feeling a glow of possessive determination from within as I met her gaze. Something was out there, coming closer to our world, something even the witch feared, but I would protect my family. For Meghan and Keirran, there was nothing I wouldn't do to keep them safe.

With a deafening creak, the house stood up, shedding dirt and leaves everywhere, and began striding away on long chicken legs. It crashed into the trees, snapping branches and splitting limbs, and stomped back into the deep forest. In moments, it had vanished into the dark.

I gazed around. The Deep Wyld surrounded us, untamed and overgrown. Unlike the endless twilight of the wyldwood, night reigned supreme here. The sun never rose, and the shadows held eternal dominion over everything. The trees surrounding us were ancient, gnarled giants covered in moss and glowing vines, and the ground was covered with a thick, spongy carpet that left luminescent footprints when stepped on. In the forest, branches rustled, creatures chirped or screamed or cried, and I could feel eyes on us from every angle.

The Deep Wyld hadn't changed. It was still ominous, unfriendly, and extremely dangerous. I only hoped that the most dangerous predator of all still roamed somewhere nearby. I did not want to journey across the Deep Wyld a second time.

A faint exhalation of breath drew my attention to Keirran. He stood a few yards away, gazing up at the massive trees with an almost pained look on his face. Tiny lights danced in the air before him, and against the backdrop of the Deep Wyld, he appeared more fey than before—pointed ears, sharp cheekbones, and pale hair a stark contrast in the gloom.

"Keirran."

He sighed and turned toward us, and the longing in his eyes was suddenly plain to see.

"Sorry. I just…" He gestured helplessly to the trees soaring overhead. Cyan lightning bugs drifted around him, turning his hair neon blue. "I never thought I'd be back," he muttered. "In the Nevernever. Not for a long time, anyway." Raising a hand, he watched as a glowing firefly landed on a fingertip, blinking erratically. "I've missed this place," he murmured.

My heart went out to him, even as anger flickered to life within. Keirran had been born in Faery; he was as much an inhabitant to the Nevernever as the fey who called it home. Exiling him had been especially cruel, because even though he was part human and could handle the real world perfectly well, he had grown up surrounded by magic, monsters, faeries, and glamour. Losing all of that, as well as the only home he'd ever known, had to be tough.

"Hey." Surprisingly, Puck strode forward and put a hand on Keirran's shoulder, causing the fireflies swarming around him to zip away. "I wouldn't stress too much about that, kid," he said. "Take it from someone who has been banished…what, three times now? Four? There's always a way around it. Faery doesn't forget, true, but Faery is also fickle as hell. Just wait until the next catastrophe—they'll call you back right quick if they think you're the only one who can save the world."

Keirran gave Puck a faint smile. "I'll try to keep that in mind."

"If you are all ready." Grimalkin walked by, leaving the faintest glowing paw prints in the moss at our feet. "I suggest we move quickly—the dog gets bored quite easily and will wander off if we do not make haste."

"How do we know he hasn't already left?" Puck wondered.

"I don't think that will be a problem," Nyx said. She had paused beneath a dead pine, and was crouched over something in the moss. As we crowded around, we saw what it was.

An enormous paw print, bigger than my hand, glowing faintly in the luminescent moss.

"This is fairly recent," the Forgotten mused, touching a fingertip to the enormous track. "I think whatever made this is close."

"Well, then," Puck said, peering over her shoulder. "I guess there's no choice but to follow the ominous paw prints of doom and see what they lead us to. Hopefully to a giant wolf and not an irritable manticore or chimera." He winced and scratched the side of his head. "Though, if Wolfman is in a bad mood, I think I'd rather meet the manticore."

9

PACKMATES

We headed into the trees, following the luminescent tracks as they set a long, loping trail through the forest. Around us, the Deep Wyld shifted and rustled, never still, always watching. Puck tossed a ball of faery fire into the air to light our way, and the glowing sphere threw strange dancing shadows over the ground and trees as it bobbed in front of us, making the darkness look like grasping claws coming to extinguish the light.

The tracks led us into the most tangled part of the forest, parting trees and undergrowth, until we stumbled upon an ancient stone ruin. In the past, it might have been a grand structure, but all that was left now were broken archways, mossy floors, and vines hanging from every stone. The paw prints ended at the edge of the ruins, and we ventured in cautiously, suddenly feeling the presence of something huge, even though we couldn't see it.

"Okay, I think we're in the right spot," Puck said, his voice barely above a whisper. Even his quietest voice seemed to echo too loudly in the stillness. "This definitely has all those fun 'monster lair' feels. How close do you think Wolfman is right now?"

"Closer than you think," growled the deepest of voices behind us.

We spun. Two yellow-green eyes, glowing and intelligent, watched us from atop a crumbling stone wall. "A good thing I've already eaten today," the voice continued, as the massive form of the Big Bag Wolf dropped into the space with us. He seemed even larger than before, a massive predator of jaws and teeth and bristling menace. Nyx fell back, moonlight blades appearing in her hands, and Keirran tensed as the Wolf stalked forward, fangs bared in a terrible grin. "Robin Goodfellow, the Unseelie prince, the Iron Queen, the exiled king, a Forgotten and the cat, all invading my territory," the Wolf mused. "This would have been a most interesting hunt, indeed." His shaggy head swung around to me. "Hello, prince. I see you've still managed to hang on to that soul, or whatever you got from the Testing Grounds. And that cub of yours hasn't destroyed the Nevernever yet. Though he is very brave, or very foolish, to show his face here."

I stepped forward, feeling the wary looks of Nyx and Keirran at my back as I approached the huge wolf. "True," I said, "but he is mine. And in a way, this is your fault. You should have eaten me when you had the chance."

The Wolf snorted a laugh, and the immediate tension dissipated, if only a little. "That can still be remedied," he growled, though the tone was begrudgingly amused. He sat down, still managing to tower over us as he gazed at me. "It has been a while since our paths have crossed, prince. What do you want this time?"

"Wait," Nyx said, causing us all to glance at her. She stared at the Wolf, recognition dawning in her golden eyes. "I know you," she whispered. "I've seen you before. But, how can that be? I've never been to the Deep Wyld."

"I was alive when the Lady ruled, Forgotten," the Wolf told her. "I remember those days, though it was very long ago. There was no wyldwood and Deep Wyld back then—there was only Faery. The arrival of Summer and Winter and the creation of the courts made it much more civilized, and much more suffocating. Those of us who had no desire to be part of their new laws and regulations left and made our way across the River of Dreams, into dangerous, unclaimed lands where we could be free. That territory, the lands beyond the reach of the courts, became known as the Deep Wyld. There are no laws here, no decrees, no kings or queens that must be obeyed. There are only the Old Ways—eat or be eaten. Kill or be killed. That is the way it has always been, and that is how it will remain, if I have anything to say about it."

"Um, right," said Puck. "Speaking of laws and rulers..."

Meghan stepped up to join me, causing the Wolf to prick his ears at her. "We have a problem, Wolf," she began, wasting no time in coming right to the point. Unlike the rulers of Faery, the Wolf would only grow impatient with empty niceties and superfluous words. I could appreciate that. "Something only you can help us with. I hope you will hear me out."

"Iron Queen." The Wolf peeled his lips back in a grin, tongue lolling out of his jaws. "I remember when you first came to Faery," he said. "I remember a scared, magicless, weak little mortal. But you still decided to take on a legend to save the Winter prince, who was your enemy. Hah." He panted, his grin growing wider. "You had teeth, even if you didn't know how to use them. And now you are a queen, with all the laws, rules, decrees, and regulations that come with becoming the ruler of a court."

His eyes narrowed, the grin fading as his expression turned serious. "Normally, I don't tolerate the rulers of Faery poking their noses into my hunting grounds," he growled. "Not un-less they can offer me an intriguing hunt. However..." The gold-green gaze flickered to me. "You have both proven your strength, and the Deep Wyld respects that. I suppose I can lis-ten. For old time's sake. But make it quick—I have no desire to stand around and listen to pointless blather."

Meghan nodded. "You know of the Forgotten," she went on, and the Wolf snorted.

"Of course I do," he growled. "I fought them in the last war, remember? I entered the Between with your mate to stop this one—" he glared directly at Keirran "—from tearing open the Veil and plunging the Nevernever into chaos."

"Yes," Meghan agreed, sounding perfectly unruffled, though I caught Keirran wincing behind her. "And now, they need your help."

"Do they now?" The Wolf's voice was flat and unimpressed. He lay down, crossing his enormous paws in a vaguely doglike manner. "And I suppose you are going to tell me why?"

"The Between is no longer safe," Meghan went on. "Touch-stone has been destroyed by an unknown monster, one that can twist fey into darker versions of themselves. The Forgotten cannot return home, nor can they stay in the mortal realm. We need a place where they will be safe."

"You chose the wrong territory, then," the Wolf said. "The Deep Wyld has never been safe, for anyone. Bring the Forgot-ten across the River of Dreams, and they will be in just as much danger here as they would in the mortal world."

"Not if *you* are protecting them," I said.

The Wolf curled a lip. "I am not a guard dog," he growled. "I have no interest in helping those too weak to save themselves. If they cannot survive on their own, they are better off extinct. That is the way of the Deep Wyld. That is how it has always been." He yawned with a flash of enormous teeth. "Besides, they are Forgotten. The Forgotten all come from the town where the fey go to die. Their time has passed. They are already not supposed to be here."

I could tell Meghan was about to protest, but Keirran stepped forward at that moment, drawing the Wolf's baleful glare. A low growl rumbled in the air between them, making me tense. It was just a warning; I knew the Wolf wouldn't directly attack Keirran while I was standing right here, but a threat from one of the most dangerous, primordial creatures in the Nevernever was nerve-wracking all the same.

Keirran didn't pause or hesitate, as he joined Meghan in facing down the huge predator. Watching him, I felt a flare of pride. Keirran couldn't have known it, but this was probably the best thing he could do; the Wolf respected strength, and showing no fear in the face of an obvious threat would establish him as a hunter and not prey.

"I know you don't think much of us," Keirran began, which made the Wolf snort. "And I know you probably consider me an enemy, because of what I've done in the past."

"Don't flatter yourself, boy," the Wolf rumbled with a glitter of fangs. "If I considered you an enemy, you would be nothing but a few scraps of bloody bones waiting for the scavengers to claim you. You think that I was concerned by what you did?" He sniffed, tossing his head. "You were like a rabid cub, lashing out at those more powerful. Be thankful that your sire and your dam have my respect. In a pack, those that turn on their fellows are immediately put down."

"I know," Keirran almost whispered. "I know I have a lot to make up for. I know that the rest of Faery will never fully trust me again. But the Forgotten shouldn't have to share my punishment. I..." He hesitated, wincing, then continued in a steady voice. "I knew what I was doing in the war. I was fully aware of my choices. The Forgotten had been manipulated and deceived by the Lady. They were only trying to survive a world where they were destined to Fade away. The Lady promised she could save them, and they followed her because it was the only way they knew to keep existing. I know it's not an excuse, but it was a matter of survival."

"I can understand doing anything to survive," the Wolf said, his tone still flat and unconvinced. "But I am not in the habit of helping those who cannot help themselves. If the Forgotten are destined to Fade and cannot change that fate on their own, then they should accept it. The strong survive, and the weak perish—that is how the world works. I will not protect the weak on sentiment alone."

"Then do it as a favor," I said quietly. "For a fellow pack member."

The Wolf snorted. "I have no pack."

"We traveled together," I continued, holding his gaze. "You, me, and Goodfellow. We journeyed together all the way through the Deep Wyld, past the Briars, and to the End of the World. We have fought together, killed together, faced unspeakable danger together, because it was the only way we would have survived. We are as much a pack as any of your cousins that roam the Nevernever and the wyldwood.

"This is my kin," I went on as the Wolf continued to give me a baleful stare. "He may only be a cub, but he is mine. He is part of our pack, and the pack protects its own. I am asking you, as a friend who accompanied me to the End of the World, will you help us? Will you make the Forgotten your pack, and protect them until they can return to their own territory?"

The Wolf bared his fangs, then let out a long-suffering sigh. "Fine," he growled. "For you and your mate, not him. The Forgotten are welcome here, *temporarily*. I will make sure nothing hunts or troubles them while they are within the Deep Wyld. But you owe me a favor, prince." He curled a lip at me. "We might be pack, but as I said before, I am not a guard dog. I don't make a habit of defending the sheep from the wolves. I am usually the one that must be defended against."

I nodded, and Keirran visibly relaxed. "I'm grateful," he told the Wolf. "You have my thanks, and the gratitude of the Forgotten. Maybe someday we'll be able to return the kindness you've shown us."

"Keep your gratitude, cub." The Wolf shook his head. "It means nothing to me. Actions are what speak loudest in the Deep Wyld, and yours have shown me all I need to know. I don't expect that you or any of your Forgotten will repay me anytime soon."

"He is still young, Wolf," Meghan said quietly. "We have all made mistakes, and Faery is a harsh teacher. How long are we supposed to punish someone for the past, especially if they are trying to change?"

"I do not know," the Wolf replied. "Nor do I care. Regardless…" He narrowed his eyes at Keirran. "I have given my word. Go fetch your Forgotten—I will protect them while they remain in the Deep Wyld. However, if they leave, they are on their own." He sighed and looked around the ruins of the castle, then shook his shaggy head. "I suppose they will have to stay here. Two legs seem to be illogically attached to having a roof over their heads."

"Slight problem," Puck said, and made a walking motion using two fingers. "Our ride in seems to have walked off. How are we going to get back to the real world?"

The Wolf sighed and pointed his muzzle at a path that led out of the ruins. "There is a trod on the other side of the forest," he said. "I never use it, but it goes to a place in the mortal realm." He glanced at Keirran. "If I take you to the human world, you can get to your Forgotten from there, is that right?"

"Yes." Keirran nodded, and turned to Meghan. "But there's

no reason we all have to return to Ethan and Kenzie's," he said. "I can do this myself."

Puck frowned. "Trying to get rid of us, princeling?"

"The Forgotten aren't the only ones in danger," Keirran went on, ignoring Puck. "These creatures, whatever they are, are getting more numerous every day. They're already roaming the Between and the human world. What happens when they make their way into the Nevernever itself? The rulers of Faery need to know about this, before it's too late and the wyldwood is swarming with these things."

"You know these creatures are after you, Keirran," I said. "If they find you again and we're not there to help, you could find yourself in the same predicament you were in earlier."

"I will take care of my people," Keirran said, sounding more like the King of the Forgotten now. "If the Wolf accompanies me, there isn't much that can threaten us. We will get the Forgotten safely to the Deep Wyld, have no fear of that. But we're going to need all of Faery standing together to fight these creatures. We don't even know what they are, or where they're coming from, but we do know they spread rage and hate. What happens when they invade the Nevernever? You saw what one of them did to Touchstone. Imagine if it got into the Summer or Winter Courts. Faery would tear itself apart."

Meghan sighed. "I know," she said. "You're right, I think it's time we warned the other courts. It's not just one monster, anymore. All of Faery will fall to chaos if even a few of those creatures cross into the Nevernever." She glanced at Keirran, a mix of pride and concern crossing her face. "The Forgotten King will go to the mortal realm, gather his people, and bring them here to the Deep Wyld. The rest of us will return to the Nevernever. It's time to call a meeting with the other rulers of Faery."

I set my jaw. I could feel Meghan's worry, knowing she had to send our son back alone when we had come so far to find him. But she was the Iron Queen, and she knew her duty. Our kingdom was in danger, and as much as she wanted to make certain Keirran was safe, she knew she had to put the safety of the Iron Realm and Faery first. Even if it meant letting him walk into danger alone.

Inside, the anger of the Unseelie stirred again. Keirran might be safe for now. But the threat was still out there, looming closer to Faery, my world, and everything I cared for. What would I have to sacrifice this time? What more would I lose before this was over?

That anger flickered quietly to rage. *Nothing*, the Unseelie side whispered. *No more. I will defend them. Whatever it takes.*

"Nyx." Keirran looked at the Forgotten standing quietly beside Puck. "I want you to go with them," he ordered. "Back to the Nevernever. I want you there when the council of Faery rulers is called."

The Forgotten blinked. "My place is here, Your Majesty," she said. "My one obligation is to protect you. I am ashamed that I was not there in Touchstone when it fell—I should have been at your side. I have failed in my duty."

"No." Keirran shook his head. "There was nothing you could have done. And I want you to be present for this meeting. Once the Iron Queen returns to the Nevernever, a Faery council will be called to discuss this new threat. I need you there, to be my voice, and the voice of the Forgotten. They need someone representing them. Otherwise, the rulers of Summer and Winter will not think of them at all."

Nyx set her jaw. I could tell she was reluctant, not wanting to leave her king behind, but she bowed her head all the same. "As you wish, sire. If these are your orders, I will carry them through."

"Don't be too ecstatic or anything," Puck said, masking the flutter of emotion with a smirk. "I know we're not that exciting to hang around, but we try."

Nyx gave him a strange look as the Wolf rose gracefully to his feet, stretched once, and shook himself vigorously. "Come on, then," he growled at Keirran. "The trod is this way. The sooner we fetch your pack, the sooner I can be done with this."

Keirran looked at us all and smiled. "I'll be fine," he said, backing up toward the Wolf. "Don't worry about me, or the Forgotten. We'll be here when you come back."

"Be careful, Keirran," Meghan said.

"Call if you need us," I added.

"I will." Keirran nodded. "Good luck to you both," he said formally, and for a moment, I marveled at how different he looked. Not like Keirran or an exiled prince any longer, but the King of the Forgotten. He had grown up too fast, and that made me both proud and melancholy at the same time. "Until we meet again."

The Wolf padded out of the courtyard, melting into the night with Keirran beside him, and both vanished into the darkness.

Meghan closed her eyes, but only for a moment. When she opened them again, the pure determination of the Iron Queen stared back at us. "All right," she said. "We have work to do. Grim, where's the quickest trod to Arcadia?"

PART
II

10

THE FAERY COUNCIL

I stood on the balcony of our private chambers, gazing out on the city of Mag Tuiredh, the capital of the Iron Realm. Which, I was pleased to discover, had not burned down or erupted into chaos in our absence. After returning to the Nevernever, Meghan and I had gone straight to Arcadia to call a Faery council, which was set to meet in the wyldwood the following night. We quickly returned to Mag Tuiredh, having not been home since Puck and Nyx first arrived with news of the Monster attacking the Between the first time. But there was no time to linger; the council beckoned, and we had only dropped in to check that our realm was still safe before heading out again.

Meghan entered the room, dressed in full Iron Queen regalia; flowing metallic cape that looked like liquid mercury, a silver-and-steel crown on her head. It was designed to impress and intimidate, both imperative if you wanted to be heard in a Faery council. I, too, had dressed for the occasion, my black armor and silver-lined cloak falling around me. I knew Meghan hated dressing up, but she understood fey politics. If it meant protecting her kingdom and family, she would play the part of the Iron Queen without hesitation.

"Glitch has sent for a carriage," she said, stepping onto the balcony as well. "It should be in the courtyard now. We should probably get going."

Her voice was determined, but her eyes were haunted. Flashes of emotion—worry, sadness, determination—pulsed from a glamour aura she wasn't quite able to hide. I reached out and caught her arm, gently drawing her back. "Breathe," I told her softly. "Your emotions are bleeding all over the place right now. The other rulers will be able to sense it."

"I know." Meghan took a deep breath, and the aura of tension and worry surrounding her faded somewhat. Being born into the mortal world, she didn't have the decades of practice in shielding her emotions from other fey, but she had gotten much better in her time as queen. Rarely did she let her glamour aura slip now, and it was usually in moments of high emotion or stress. "I'm sorry," she sighed, "I just… I'm worried for Keirran. I know he's a king and we have to trust him but…" A furrow creased her brow. "Ever since the war with the Lady, I can't stop thinking of what the first oracle told us. About our child, bringing nothing but grief."

My stomach tightened. I remembered that prophecy. Several years ago, before Meghan and I were even married, we had gone to the last oracle for help. She had wanted Meghan's first-born child as payment, and when Meghan refused, she responded with one line. One line that neither of us had thought much of in the moment, but now haunted our thoughts ever since.

You will not give it up, even though it will bring you nothing but grief?

Meghan covered her face with a hand. "What if it's not over?" she whispered. "Maybe the war with the Lady and the Forgotten was only the beginning. What if that monster does get to Keirran, and he turns on us again?"

I took her by the shoulders, gazing into her eyes. "Then we will save him again," I said firmly. "And again, as many times and as often as it takes. If he turns on us, we'll bring him back. If something threatens him, we will eliminate it. No matter what he does, no matter what happens to him, he will always be our son. I will never stop trying to save him." Putting a hand on her cheek, I stroked her skin as her eyes grew misty. "You and Keirran," I said quietly, "are my entire life."

She leaned into me, and I wrapped my arms around her, wishing I could take all her worry, all her grief and despair, onto myself. "I'll protect you both," I said darkly, a promise to myself. "Even if the world stands against you, I will be at your side. No matter what it takes."

No matter what I have to become.

Meghan shivered against me. "I'm worried for you, too, Ash," she whispered. "Ever since Touchstone, you've been acting… different." Her hand slid up my chest, resting over my heart. "I can feel your anger," she went on. "Not often; you've always been able to hide it well, but…it's the same as when you were the Winter prince. It's intense."

"I am angry," I said simply. "The thought of losing you and Keirran…" I shook my head, unable to explain the depth of rage that brought on. "Those creatures," I murmured. "You saw what they did to Puck. To the Forgotten in Touchstone. To the humans walking around the mortal world. My greatest fear is someday looking up…and finding that we're enemies again. Dealing with Puck was hard enough —I thought he'd forgiven me and moved on, but…"

My gut clenched as I remembered the hate in his eyes, the sneering face of Robin Goodfellow when he said we were still enemies. The Monster's influence had brought out the worst in him, but it was still a shock when my best friend informed me, in complete seriousness, that I had better watch my back.

I didn't want to fight Puck again. We'd both had our fill of it, years of anger and hatred and grief. Of trying to hurt each other while wishing we didn't have to go through with it. I was done fighting those I cared about. The nightmare of fighting and having to kill my son still lingered, but it was another nightmare that terrified me. One from long ago, when I was still trying to earn a soul to be in the Iron Realm with Meghan. A nightmare where the enemy facing me across the bloody battlefield was not Keirran or Puck, but the woman in my arms right now.

"If anything like that happened to you," I continued, feeling my voice start to choke up a little, "I…don't know what I would do. Probably let you kill me, because a world where we are enemies is not one I'd want to exist in."

"Ash." Meghan looked up at me, a dozen emotions warring across her face. One hand rose, her palm pressing gently against my cheek. "I have the same fear, sometimes," she confessed. "The war with the Lady showed me how fragile my own perceptions were, how easily someone you thought you knew can turn against you. The prophecy said Keirran could end up betraying everything, but I didn't truly believe it until it happened. If I had to fight both you and Keirran…" Her other hand clenched on my chest. I covered it with my own, feeling her fingers tremble in mine.

"But then, I remind myself what we've been through," she went on. "That we were enemies once, but we overcame it. Both the Summer and Winter Courts, hell, the entire realm of Faery, told us we couldn't be together, that our destiny was to fight each other, because our courts were eternal rivals and Faery law forbade it. Look where we are now."

"And I wouldn't change anything," I added softly. "Well, maybe the part where Keirran nearly destroyed the Nevernever.

But other than that…" My comment brought the tiny smile I was looking for, and I ran my fingers through her hair. "I love you, Meghan," I told her. "I would fight the world for us, and Keirran. I've never had so much to protect, but this is all I've ever wanted."

And if I have to tap into my Unseelie side once more, so be it. I will not let anything take my family away. Even if I have to become a monster myself.

"Still a sweet talker," Meghan whispered, blinking rapidly to clear her eyes. She leaned up and kissed me, making my stomach cartwheel, then gently pulled back. "The carriage will be waiting," she said, and took a breath as if to steel herself. "Ready to go try to change the minds of a bunch of impossible faery rulers?"

"My favorite thing," I sighed, and Meghan slipped her arm through mine. Together, we walked down the halls of the Iron Palace to the carriage that awaited us outside.

The site where the council of Faery agreed to meet was relatively new, having been established once the Iron Court became a real power in the Nevernever. Traditionally, faery councils were held either in Arcadia or Tir Na Nog to prove the goodwill of the ruler hosting, but none of the regular fey could enter the Iron Realm without dying from iron poisoning. Rather than continuously having to travel to Summer or Winter, Meghan and I suggested all meetings between the rulers of the kingdoms take place in the wyldwood, where none of the courts held sway. After some initial resistance—the rulers of Faery did not react well to change—they finally agreed.

"Looks like Oberon is already here," Meghan observed as we stepped out of the carriage. Around us, the trees of the wyldwood soared overhead, ancient and gnarled and as gray as mist, twisted branches blocking out the sun. Twilight reigned eternal in the wyldwood, with everything cloaked in gloom and shadow, except for occasional and startling splashes of color scattered throughout the gray.

Before us, a pair of enormous white trunks rose into the air, twining branches forming an arch overhead. Through the space between, I could just make out a tunnel of trees, pale trunks acting as columns and twisting branches forming a roof above. A pair of Seelie knights guarded the entrance, long-haired sidhe in gold and green armor, leafy capes draping their shoulders and fey swords at their sides.

I stifled a sigh. Even before the council had started, the faery games and power struggles were already in effect. In the long years where I'd attended Elysium and other councils, Oberon and the Summer Court had always been the first to arrive. I suspected it was because the Seelie King wanted his pick of the seats, but also because Titania, when she even bothered to come, wanted to be the first thing everyone saw when they got there. A queen looking down upon her subjects as they entered her presence. Mab, on the other hand, was always fashionably late to every event except the ones she hosted herself, and it would be a loud, extended showing when she did finally arrive. I knew Mab, and I knew she wanted everyone to look at her, while at the same time declaring the queen of Winter would not be told what to do; she would get there on her own time and everyone else could just wait.

Meghan and I were always right on time, as befitting the only court that had working clocks. And because it was just polite.

Meghan glanced at me with a faint grimace. She knew this had to be done, but it was never a pleasant experience dealing with fickle, easily offended faery rulers. "You think Titania will be there today?"

"Let's hope not," I muttered back, and extended an arm to her. "Otherwise, it's going to be a long meeting."

The Seelie knights bowed their heads as we approached, and we followed the tunnel of trees until it opened up into a massive chamber of trunks and intertwining branches. Glowing lanterns hung from the limbs and balls of faery fire floated among the leaves, lighting up the room. They drifted alongside thousands of icicles dangling from the branches, some as long and thick as my arm. The faint breeze ghosting through the chamber set the icicles to tinkling in a cheery but ominous way, as if anything stronger would cause the whole ceiling to plummet. Delicate crystalline snowflakes danced through the room, catching the light like diamonds.

In the center of the chamber, an enormous table rose from the frosty ground, dominating the middle of the room. A perfect circle, the surface was covered in different-sized spinning cogs and gears. Our kobold engineers had spent months on it, blending tech and iron glamour together, and now the table could show the other territories and their borders with a press of a button. Pull a lever, and a miniature Tir Na Nog would appear on the map, looking like the inside of a snow globe. Turn a dial, and Arcadia would bloom across the surface, with all the rivers, trees and flowering meadows that made up the Summer Court.

It was definitely an anomaly within Faery, and only those who wore the special amulets of the Iron Realm could stand that close to the table without fear. This was the ruler's way of trying to incorporate every court into the design for the new Faery Council. Summer, Winter, and Iron all had a presence here, a reminder that while we stood in this room, we were on equal ground. Of course, in trying to make certain no court was overlooked, all they had succeeded in doing was ensuring that no one was comfortable.

Lord Oberon of the Seelie Court already stood at one end of the table as we entered the room. Facing the entrance, I noticed. Which was the reason Meghan and I had made certain the meeting table was round. Had it been rectangular or even square, Oberon would certainly put himself at the head of it every single time. The Summer King was dressed in green and gold, long silver hair falling down his shoulders and his antlered crown rising tall on his head.

Unfortunately, he was not the only one present. Queen Titania stood beside him, her lips already pulled into a nasty smile as she watched us come in. I felt Meghan's inner sigh, and a cold fire flickered to life as the Summer Queen met my gaze, cruelty shining from those crystal-blue eyes. Of everyone in this council, Titania would give us the most trouble, simply because she despised us all and wanted us to suffer. I was not in the mood to play games with fickle faery queens, not when my court and my family were in danger.

Thankfully, Oberon spoke before Titania could make any snide comments. "Iron Queen," the Summer monarch greeted. "I am pleased that you have arrived." *On time*, was the unspoken implication, as we were the only ones to ever do so. "I am unsure as to why you have called this council," Oberon continued. "The courts are at peace, and to my knowledge none of the treaties have been broken. I am curious as to what could be so important that you felt the need to call every ruler of Faery into the same space."

"Not every ruler," Meghan said calmly. "The Forgotten King is not here." A subtle reminder that, while Keirran could not enter the wyldwood, he was still a king of Faery in his own right.

Titania sniffed. "Is he truly a king of Faery if he has been banished from the Nevernever?" she asked, her tone and wide-eyed innocence making it appear that she was truly curious, but we all knew it was just a barb. "Should not a king be able to attend these Faery Councils? How can he represent his court and subjects if he has no voice?"

"I will be his voice," said someone behind us. We turned, and

Nyx melted from the shadows, golden eyes hard as she came into the light. "I was sent as a representative of the Forgotten King," Nyx went on as Titania's narrowed gaze landed on her. "I will speak for him, and the Forgotten of the Between."

"Is that so?" Titania asked. "And what makes you think that you, a lowly assassin, can stand among the kings and queens of Faery?"

"Uh, the same reason a court jester can." It was Puck's voice, as the Summer faery sauntered in behind Nyx. He was smiling, but his eyes were flat and dangerous as he met Titania's glare. "Unless I'm not wanted here, in which case I'll be sad."

Titania's predatory look curled into one of pure contempt. "You are never wanted here, Robin Goodfellow," she spat, but Puck simply grinned. As much as Titania hated Puck, she couldn't make him leave, and they both knew it.

"Nyx is welcome at this council," Meghan said calmly. "The King of the Forgotten sent her, and he is still a ruler of Faery even if he cannot be present. Besides, she knows a great deal about the threat we are facing."

"Threat?" Titania said, her tone mocking. "What threat? Faery has been at peace—the courts have been calm. Unless you cannot control your own subjects and they are rising up against us."

"Nothing like that," Meghan said, still unperturbed. "I will explain everything once Queen Mab arrives."

Queen Mab finally did arrive in a flurry of snow and trumpets, stalking into the chamber like she owned it. The temperature of the room dropped several degrees as the Winter Queen appeared, blue-black hair and fur-lined cape fluttering behind her. She nodded once to me and Meghan before gliding around to the empty side of the table, ice and snow flurries swirling in her wake. Like Titania and Oberon, she hesitated at the edge of the table, fighting her centuries-old fear of iron, before deliberately placing her palms atop the surface, as if to prove she was not afraid.

"Well," she crooned by way of greeting, "we are all here, then. Iron Queen, I assume this is important for you to drag me out of Tir Na Nog at this time of year. What is this great threat that you keep hinting at?"

"Touchstone has been destroyed," Meghan said without preamble. "Though I expect none of you have heard the news, or what happened to the Forgotten."

There were a couple of raised eyebrows from the rulers at the table, except for Titania, who smiled in gleeful delight. Meghan ignored her.

"A creature unlike anything we've seen before entered the Between and tore the Forgotten capital apart," she went on. "The king was forced to gather the survivors and flee to the mortal realm. He is safe, but the creature is still in the Between, so the Forgotten have been unable to return."

"One creature?" Titania's voice was incredulous. "Did so much damage that the King of the Forgotten was forced to retreat before it? Is he that weak, to be unable to protect his own kingdom?"

"Keirran is not weak," I said, trying to keep the icy fury from my voice. "We've fought one of these Monsters before. It took all of us—" I indicated Meghan, Puck, and Nyx "—working together to bring it down. These creatures are immune to nearly all types of damage, including glamour. But that's not the worst of it."

"They emit a type of aura," Nyx explained. "One of rage, hatred, anger, despair. It can transform fey into…darker versions of themselves, is the best way to put it. King Keirran was forced to flee Touchstone because the Forgotten were being twisted and turning on him."

"The Forgotten attacked their own king." This time, it was

Mab who spoke, though she sounded skeptical at the news. "They are proving to be troublesome indeed. Are you saying that we can expect a war with the Forgotten again?"

"No," Meghan said. "I'm saying that we need to prepare for these creatures coming *here*, to the Nevernever."

"One or two monsters is not enough to cause a panic, Iron Queen," Oberon said.

"No?" Puck asked. "How about a few thousand, then?"

"We tracked Keirran to the mortal realm," Meghan continued into the grave silence that followed. "What we found there was hundreds of these creatures, much smaller versions, but they were both attracted to and emitted the same kind of negative glamour of the large monster. These creatures were...almost fey-like, though I've never seen them before."

"Another type of faery?" Oberon wondered. "Have they come from the Deep Wyld, then, like the Forgotten?"

"We don't know what they are," Meghan admitted. "Or where they come from. But the new oracle mentioned something called Evenfall, if that means anything to anyone."

Mab frowned. "Evenfall," she repeated softly. She had a strange look on her face, as if trying to recall a memory that kept just out of reach. "I do not believe I have heard that prophecy before, but it feels important."

"Yes," Oberon agreed, "Evenfall. It is familiar, though I cannot seem to remember why."

I shared a look with Puck. Fey memory was long, able to hold grudges and remember slights for centuries, and the rulers of the courts were not prone to forgetting. If the rulers of Faery could not remember a name, it wasn't a coincidence. Something was blocking that memory.

Which made things even more serious.

"Something is coming," Meghan went on, after a few seconds of obvious frustration from the Faery rulers. They didn't like the notion that something was deliberately blocking their memories, either. Only Titania, who had a pleased smile on her face as she watched Mab, seemed unconcerned. "I think Faery needs to prepare for the worst," Meghan continued. "If these creatures make it through the Between and invade the Nevernever, it will be chaos."

"Are you certain they are that much of a threat, Iron Queen?" Titania asked. "Perhaps they cannot enter the Nevernever at all. If they are content to remain in the Between and the mortal realm, we need not do anything. After all—" her lips curled in a smug smile "—there is little in the Between worth saving."

In that moment, I wondered how hard it would be to kill the Summer Queen.

"We cannot take that chance, Queen Titania," Meghan replied, unaware of my murderous musings. "Faery is surrounded by enemies. Unknown creatures stalk the Between, turning fey into monsters, and only the Veil separates them from the Nevernever. We have delivered our warning; make of it what you will. But the Iron Realm will be prepared should these creatures invade Faery. I suggest the other courts do the same."

"Agreed," Oberon said. "Something larger is happening, and I find the fact that something may be obstructing our memories troublesome." He rose, drawing his robes around himself in a regal manner. "I will return to Arcadia and gather my forces. If it is to be another war, the Summer Court will be ready."

"War is something we know very well," Mab stated. "Whatever the threat, the Winter Court will meet it with ice and death. Should these Monsters invade the Nevernever, they will find Tir Na Nog will be waiting for them."

Meghan nodded, but as the council seemed to draw to a close, there was a sudden, high-pitched beep that caused everyone to jerk up. Frowning, she pulled out the strange device Kenzie had given her, watching as it buzzed and flickered with a neon blue light.

"What is that—?" Titania began, sounding horrified. But before she could finish, there was a flash of blue, and a tiny, bat-eared gremlin winked into existence on Meghan's arm.

All three rulers of the other courts recoiled in some fashion at having an Iron faery suddenly appear in the heart of the Faery council. Titania's reaction was the most extreme; her lip curled and she made an expression like she had swallowed a spider. Mab rolled her eyes and Oberon simply frowned, but though it was clear none of them were happy about the intrusion, no one shouted or ordered the abomination taken away. Strangely enough, a gremlin popping into even the most sacred of areas had become almost commonplace now.

"Razor." Meghan held up her arm as the tiny Iron fey buzzed frantically, bobbing up and down. "What happened? Are Ethan and Kenzie all right?"

"No!" The gremlin shook his head frantically, huge ears flopping from side to side. "Not all right. Pretty girl says come back right away. Monsters! Monsters outside the window!"

11

The Chase residence didn't look any different as we emerged from the woods late that night. The ranch house sat peacefully in the moonlight, intact and undisturbed. No chittering hordes surrounded the walls, no blank-eyed Monsters lurked in the trees beyond the fence line. The air was still, the shadows empty, as if everything was holding its breath.

But the woods *felt* menacing as we slipped through the trunks toward the distant house, and I could feel eyes on me in the branches. There was something here, lurking in the forest, a predator keeping just out of sight. Thankfully, I was certain it was not the Monster. Its presence would be impossible to conceal. Nor did I didn't think it was the small piskie things, either. Whatever prowled the trees with us, it was something new.

"Something is here," Nyx said quietly, confirming my suspicions. "I can feel its glamour. Like the piskie creatures, only stronger."

"We should check on Kenzie and Ethan," Meghan said. Razor

had already fled, zipping back to Mackenzie as soon as we were back in the real world. "We need to make sure they're safe before we go searching for whatever is out here."

We started toward the house, but as one, everyone suddenly paused. There was a ripple in the shadows, an almost silent rustle of air over the leaves, and I knew we weren't alone.

"It's close," I growled.

"No, Winter prince," whispered a voice, the sound slithering out of the trees behind us. "It is here."

We turned, hands on our weapons. A figure stood in the trees a few yards away, watching us. Different than the hordes of monsters we'd seen before, this creature was human-size and had an almost human body, though the differences were disturbing. It was tall and almost emaciated, with thin, withered arms that reached all the way to the ground, and long, long fingers that ended in points. It wore a bleached stag's skull over its face, the empty eye sockets blank and hollow as the mask swiveled on its neck to face us. "Wait," the thing commanded as we tensed, swords and daggers flashing as they were pulled free. Its voice grated in my ears like metal scraping against metal, causing a shiver to crawl up my back. It was a voice that didn't belong, to anything, in either Faery or the human world. Like the Monster and the nightmare piskies, the creature radiated negative glamour: fear, anxiety, and a very subtle disquiet that made my skin crawl. It was akin to being in a pitch-black room, seeing nothing, but knowing something was there with you. "Creatures of the overrealm, stay your blades," it whispered. "I would speak with you."

"What are you?" Meghan demanded.

"The dark mirror of your world," rasped the creature. "The things you fear in the abyss. The shards of emotions you reject. We are...Evenfey."

Evenfey. The anger in me stirred. So, I finally had a name for my enemies. Not that it mattered. I didn't care what they were called; if they were a threat, if they were here to harm my family, I would destroy them. Simple as that.

Nyx drew in a sharp breath. "You are fey, then."

"Fey." The figure made a dismissive gesture with one long, thin arm. "Good neighbors. Demons. Words. Only words. We are what we are. It matters not what they call us."

"Us," I repeated, narrowing my eyes. "Then you are the same as them—the nightmare piskies and the Monsters."

The creature gave a raspy choking sound. A moment later, I realized it was a chuckle. "Your labels," it told me, "are amusing. And closer to the truth than you think. But you cannot know us. You, who stole our names and our world, you will never know us. You have already proven that we cannot exist together. Why should I tell you anything more?"

"What do you want here?" Meghan asked in a steady voice. The Evenfaery, if it really was some type of faery, stared at her a moment, its skull mask giving nothing away. Finally, it rasped:

"Where is he?"

"He?" Puck echoed, sounding nonchalant, though his stance was tense and both daggers were in hand. Nyx hovered beside him, her moonlight blades unsheathed and ready to kill. "There are a lot of *he's* in the world, friend. Count Dracula is a *he*. Godzilla is a *he*. You're gonna have to be a bit more specific if you want a better answer."

"The Soulless King." The creature's empty eye sockets bored into mine. "The ruler of those who once were ours. The traitor of this world. Where?"

Keirran. Cold, murderous rage shot through me, flaring Unseelie magic to life. "You'll never find him," I told the figure, tightening my grip on my sword. "He is in a place you will never touch. But it doesn't matter if you try to seek him out or not, because in another moment you'll be dead."

I lunged, sweeping my blade at the creature's middle. It winked out of sight, vanishing in the blink of an eye, and my sword passed through empty air. With a curse, I spun, searching the trees for the creature, expecting an attack from behind.

"You will not stop us." The voice came from overhead, at the same time I spotted the figure in the branches of a tree. It stood on an impossibly thin branch, barely a twig, as it gazed down at us all. "Our own king awakens. The anger and hatred of this world stirs him from his slumber. Soon, it will be enough to open the way to Evenfall."

A chill coursed through me. At the same time, there was a pulse of Summer glamour, and the tree the Evenfey was standing on came to life. With a grinding creak, clawed branches reached for the spindly figure as Meghan raised her hand, her eyes hard as she clenched her fist. The Evenfey vanished, blinking out of sight just before leafy talons would have crushed the life from it. I scanned the trees around us, searching the branches for long limbs and a stark white mask, but the figure did not reappear.

"Quickly," Meghan said, and began hurrying through the trees, back toward the Chase residence. "We need to check on Ethan and Kenzie. Let's hope they're all right."

"Well, I'm completely creeped out, now," Puck announced, sheathing his daggers as he fell into a jog beside us. "What was that thing? An Evenfey? Has anyone heard of that before? Where the hell is Furball when you need him?"

"I am here," sighed Grimalkin, appearing from behind a tree as we hurried by. "And before anyone asks, no, I do not know what an Evenfey is. Although, it did seem…familiar somehow."

"Yes," Nyx murmured. "It was old, like the Wolf. I feel like I might have met it once, before."

"Given what the creature told us," Grimalkin said as he trotted along, "I would assume Even*fall* is where these Evenfey are coming from. Perhaps a place in the Nevernever that is either sealed away or lost, though that is unlikely. Why would they be infesting the Between and the mortal realm if they come from the Nevernever?"

"Also," Puck added, "did anyone else catch that little tidbit about their king waking up?"

Nyx looked grave. "'The anger and hatred of this world stirs him from his slumber,'" she whispered. "It doesn't sound pleasant. But..." Her smooth brow furrowed. "I don't remember any king before the Lady. There was no mention of another ruler. And yet, the Evenfaery was speaking the truth. Or, it thought it was, anyway."

"Meghan! Ash!"

Ethan's voice echoed through the darkness, and a few moments later he appeared, twin short swords in both hands. Seeing us, he relaxed, though his eyes still scanned the darkness for threats.

"Is it gone?" he asked, glancing at Meghan.

She nodded. "You saw it as well, I assume?"

"Ugly thin thing with a deer skull on its face? Yeah, we did." Ethan turned and gestured back toward the house. "Kenzie is inside. She's fine, but we found something that you guys are going to want to see. Come on."

We followed Ethan into the house, after he deactivated the numerous anti-faery charms he had around the entrance and front yard, and into a small office. Kenzie was seated at a desk, Razor perched on the chair back above her, and she glanced up with a somber look as we came in.

"Oh, you're here. Thank goodness, Razor found you. Did you all see the creepypasta thing lurking outside?"

"We did," I told her. "It's gone now. Though it might return later—we didn't manage to kill it."

"It was looking for Keirran," Meghan added. "It must've thought he was still here." She gave Ethan a grave look. "I know

156

you don't want to hear this, Ethan, but I think you two need to leave and come back with us to Mag Tuiredh. If these creatures are looking for Keirran, they might try to use you to get to him. It's not safe for you and Kenzie to stay here any longer."

"No," Ethan growled. "I'm not going to let the fey chase me out of my own home. The anti-faery measures are working well enough, and I can get even stronger ones if I have to. We can't go running into Faery every time something dangerous comes through. You have to trust us, Meghan," he insisted, looking the Iron Queen in the eye. "We know how to deal with the fey. We can take care of ourselves."

Meghan's lips thinned. I could tell she wanted to argue, but she and her brother had had this argument many times before. Her title and the fact that she ruled and commanded an entire kingdom of Faery didn't mean anything to the younger Chase sibling. Ethan was determined to live his life his own way, and he was just as stubborn as his sister.

"Fine." Meghan finally relented, though she didn't look happy about it. "I certainly can't drag you into the Nevernever if you don't want to go. But promise me that you'll contact us if things get too dangerous. We don't know anything about these creatures, what they are or where they're coming from. We don't have any idea what they're capable of."

"Actually," Kenzie interjected, speaking up from the computer chair, "I think I know where they're coming from."

Everyone turned to her. "I decided to do a bit more research about our friends from InSite," she said, swiveling in the chair to face the laptop again. "And look what just popped up on their feed. Most of what they send out nowadays is trolling or 'news' specifically designed to generate outrage, but this definitely caught my attention."

She leaned back a bit, giving us a better view of the screen.

I gazed down at the text, feeling a quiet dread bloom in my stomach from two short, simple lines.

Evenfall approaches, it read. *Are you prepared?*

Meghan straightened. "Who are these people?" she whispered. "If they know about Evenfall, what are they trying to accomplish?"

"Besides pissing people off in large numbers?" Puck shrugged. "I dunno. Maybe they *want* to bring about the End of the World? I've never understood it, but there are people like that, you know. There's always some cult who somehow thinks blowing up reality is preferable to actually existing in it." He sighed, scratching the back of his head. "I guess we know where we're going next."

Nyx furrowed her brow. "I don't like it," she muttered, crossing her arms. "I don't know anything about technology or whatever you call it, but I do know when something seems too easy. This feels like a trap. Why would they send out that message, if only to draw us to them?"

InSite. I stared at the laptop screen, feeling that cold anger spread through me like frost. Somehow, they knew about Evenfall, what it meant for the rest of the world. "Maybe it is a trap," I said in a voice of icy calm. "But if they're the cause of what's been happening, then we need to pay InSite a visit. I don't think we can afford not to." I looked at Kenzie. "You said you've been there before. Where are they located?"

"Washington, DC," she answered. "Right in the heart of downtown. Weird place for an ancient faery summoning site, or whatever it is, but there you go. I have the address in my email somewhere, just gimme a second." She started to turn back to her computer, but gave me a defiant look over her shoulder. "You *do* know we're coming with you, right?"

Leaning against the doorframe, Ethan abruptly straightened. "Kenzie…" he said, and his voice was a warning.

She gave him an irritated look. "I can't sit here and do nothing, Ethan," she said. "I can't stay behind and do normal things while they go marching off to risk their lives and possibly save Faery again. The only worse thing is if you go with them while I stay behind. I hate feeling useless."

"You've never been useless," Ethan said immediately. "And I'm not leaving you, not with these weird new fey lurking around. But we talked about this, Kenzie. We can't blindly go throwing ourselves into risky situations anymore, especially now. Please." He took a step forward, eyes beseeching. "I don't want anything happening to you."

I straightened, suddenly knowing exactly what was going on. Watching them, Meghan did, too, for she drew in a slow breath and looked at the girl sitting in the computer chair. "Kenzie," Meghan began, her voice hesitant and hopeful at the same time. "Are you...?"

Kenzie let out a long sigh. "Probably," she admitted. "I tested myself a few days ago, and it came up positive. I have a doctor's appointment next week." She glanced at Meghan, unable to keep the faint, wry grin from crossing her face. "We were going to tell you when we knew for certain."

Meghan crossed the room in two strides, bent down and hugged her. "That's amazing, Kenzie," she said, a joyful smile on her face as they drew back. "Congratulations. I'm so happy for you both."

"Aw, Aunt Meghan," Puck added, also grinning broadly. "And Uncle Ice-boy. Doesn't it just warm your heart? Our little family just keeps growing."

"Yes," I added, glancing at Ethan, who looked faintly relieved to have the secret out in the open. I was happy for them, though I doubted Meghan's brother knew the huge changes that awaited him once he was a father. "But now, there is no way we're taking you with us to InSite."

"I'm afraid I have to agree, Kenzie," Meghan said, making Kenzie sigh in resigned acceptance. "I absolutely do not want to put you in harm's way if you could be pregnant." She put a hand on Kenzie's arm. "Besides, you and Ethan are the only ones I can trust in the mortal realm. These Evenfey are after Keirran, and if something happens to us, I need you and Ethan here if he needs help."

Kenzie's shoulders slumped. "Right, I see your point," she agreed reluctantly, and Ethan let out a breath of relief, making her frown at him. "Fine, we'll be here if Keirran needs us. And we'll keep an eye on these new fey that keep popping up."

She grabbed the computer mouse and clicked a few links, then scribbled several lines on a piece of paper. "This is InSite's address," she told Meghan, spinning around to hand her the note. "Call if anything world-ending happens. If the earth is going to crack open and spill an apocalypse's worth of nightmare faeries into the world, I'd kind of like to know about it."

"We're here if you need us," Ethan added. "Be careful in there."

Meghan nodded. "Thank you both," she told Ethan and Kenzie. "You two be careful as well. If you do see Keirran, let him know where we've gone. And congratulations again." She looked at her brother, a genuine smile crossing her face. "I'll expect daily updates once you know for certain. And call me if there's any trouble at all."

"Aw, look at that," Puck said, grinning broadly. "The kid already has their very own faery godmother."

Ethan snorted. "With our life, they'll need one for sure."

Meghan shook her head. "Let's hope not. Grim…?" She looked around for the cait sith. "Are you here?"

The cat appeared on an empty seat in the corner with a loud sigh. "Yes, Iron Queen," he stated in a weary voice, as if he found our celebrations tiring but knew not to comment on them. "And, yes, I know a route that will take us there. But I do want to mention that this gallivanting about will cost you something. I am not a tour guide, after all."

"Oh, I dunno," Puck remarked, grinning. "Grimalkin's Travel Services has a certain ring to it, don't you think?"

The cait sidhe thumped his tail on the seat cushion, and did not deign to answer.

12

INSITE

I had been to the capital city only once, many years ago, and it was a completely different place back then. For one, I didn't remember the enormous cemetery with the thousands of white graves that greeted us when we stepped out of the trod.

"Arlington National Cemetery," Meghan murmured, gazing around. Her voice was hushed, reverent, as she took in the endless rows of headstones, situated in perfectly straight lines to the edge of the field. Directly behind us stood a small marble structure, white pillars forming the archway we had emerged from, and the air between them shimmered as the trod faded from sight. "Well, we are definitely close to DC." She glanced down at the paper Kenzie had given her, then looked at Grimalkin. "I don't suppose you could've gotten us a little closer?"

The feline sniffed. "Grimalkin's Travel Services does not take responsibility for lost or damaged mortals," he said in a voice of complete seriousness. "Please refer to the 'paid services' section if one wishes to purchase extra amenities like transportation and shorter travel time."

"Holy crap, the cat just grew a sense of humor," Puck gasped, one hand flying to his heart. "The world *must* be ending."

Walking around a human city was very different than walking around the wyldwood, or even the fey cities of Mag Tuiredh and Touchstone. In Faery, you didn't have to worry about things like traffic lights, taxis, or bicycles. Or the throngs of mortals passing each other on the street, each lost in their own world. I lost count of the times I had to dodge a human who had their eyes glued to their phone, or was just oblivious to their surroundings. Normally the obtuseness of mortals amused me, but today I found myself sorely tempted to let a collision happen just for the chance to lash out. Having grown up in the Winter Court, I found it difficult to comprehend the complete lack of awareness to one's surroundings. These mortals wouldn't last a single afternoon in the wyldwood.

Following our navigator Grimalkin, who thankfully did not have to worry about things like phones and internet service, we walked down the streets of the nation's capital as evening fell and the streetlamps flickered to life. And, as we left the cemetery and ventured deeper into civilization, I began to realize how serious the threat actually was.

We weren't the only faeries wandering the streets this night. On nearly every corner, I saw flashes of movement, heard the buzz of ragged wings, as the tiny nightmare fey fled our presence. The city seemed to be infested with them; like a plague of locusts or cicadas, they perched on rooftops and in the branches of trees, watching everything with beady, malicious eyes. The throngs of humans never saw the hordes of fey, but several times I would pass a mortal and catch a glimpse of a tiny body clinging to their neck, or a face peeking out of their hair, baring its fangs at me. They seemed especially attracted to anger or fear; a man in a business suit crossed the street, snarling into his phone, unable to see the swarm of nightmare piskies following him like a cloud of gnats. A woman pushed a stroller down the sidewalk, her eyes darting warily about, as if fearing a kidnapper would leap out of a moving vehicle, snatch her child, and take off. A pair of nightmare piskies crouched on the handle of the stroller, their eyes glowing pinpricks in the approaching dusk.

"Okay, this is bad," Puck commented, gazing around at the growing swarms of fey. "Did we stumble onto the set for *The Birds III, the Nightmare Edition*? Why are there so many of the little buggers flying around?"

"This city is angry," Nyx muttered, her gaze never still as they swept our surroundings. I saw flickers of amazement and wonder on her face, a reminder that the Forgotten had never seen things like modern streetlamps or baby strollers. But it was all overshadowed by the present situation. "I can feel the rage building under the surface," Nyx continued. "It feels…"

"Like a boil?" Puck wondered. "Or a volcano getting ready to erupt?" He wrinkled his nose. "Also, by the by, combining those two images? Bad idea."

Someone barreled toward me, another human staring at his phone. On his shoulder, one of the nightmare piskie creatures looked up and opened its jaws in a menacing hiss, baring its mouthful of razor fangs. I could have easily stepped aside, let the mortal pass. Instead, I stayed where I was, barely feeling the impact as the human ran into me square on.

"Hey! What the f—!" The mortal stumbled back and glared at me, indignation shining from his eyes. "You got a problem? Watch where you're going, asshole."

I ignored him, staring at the creature in my hand. As the human had collided with me, I'd managed to snatch the tiny monster off his shoulder before it could react. The nightmare piskie thing hissed and squirmed beneath my fingers, trying to snap at me with oversize teeth. Its ragged wings buzzed frantically against my palm like a trapped hornet. Pulses of rage thrummed from the tiny Evenfey, invisible needles jabbing my skin, unseen and infuriating.

"Hey, you ignoring me?" The human stepped forward, not seeing Meghan and the others, who were still glamoured and invisible. He glared at me as the Evenfey's hissing grew louder, more frantic. "What, you think you're better than me or something? I'm talking to you. Pay attention when I'm talking, you piece of—"

I clenched my fist, crushing the nightmare faery in my grip. It gave a high-pitched shriek before its tiny body dissolved in my fingers. An oily mist rose from where the piskie had been, seeping through my fingers, and writhed on the air like tiny worms before curling away on the wind.

I suddenly felt dirty, like I had picked up something dead and rotting on the pavement. The human in front of me had paused when I'd crushed the Evenfey, the expletive dying on his lips. I raised my head and gave him a cold glare, and the air of indignant bravado around him faded.

"Go home," I said flatly, and the human went, hurrying away down the sidewalk. I shook my hand free of the last of the oily tendrils and tried to ignore the regret that the human hadn't given me an excuse to hurt him.

"Well, that was amusing," Puck remarked. He wore his trademark grin, but his eyes were wary, as if he could feel the anger pulsing through me. "You okay there, ice-boy? It would've been fun to see him take a swing at you, but I'm not sure you wouldn't have stuck an icicle through his middle."

Meghan was also watching me, a concerned look on her face. I gave my hand a final shake and drew my glamour around me again, becoming invisible to mortal eyes. "I'm fine," I said shortly, suddenly impatient to be gone. "Let's keep moving."

Several minutes later, we turned down a nondescript street and came upon an equally nondescript structure. A five-story office building with no signs or defining features stood on the corner; one could easily walk past it without a thought.

If one didn't notice the literal cloud of glamour roiling off it, releasing smoky tendrils that writhed away into nothingness. Nightmare piskies buzzed over the roof and around the building, sounding like giant locusts, and more perched along fences and even atop cars. The very air surrounding the building was drenched in fear, anger, hate.

Puck coughed and made a gagging sound, waving a hand in front of his face as if he smelled something foul. "Oh, man, those are some strong nasty vibes. How can the humans even breathe around this?"

"This is the source of all the anger," Nyx commented, gazing at the building with a grim look on her face. "I've rarely felt hate this strong. But, it feels strange. Almost...manufactured? Is that even possible?"

Puck snorted and rolled his eyes with a smirk. "Welcome to the internet," he muttered. "Manufactured outrage is all the rage these days."

"The question is, why?" Meghan added, frowning as she stared up at InSite. "Why create such hate and division? What are they trying to accomplish?"

"To fill the world with those delightful nightmare piskies?" Puck mused. "Oh, I know! Maybe some entrepreneur invented a new kind of faery repellant, but it needed a really annoying type of faery to really sell the idea and...yeah, you can all stop looking at me like that."

A group of four humans walked past us on the sidewalk, and we all backed up a few paces to let them through. The group started out talking and laughing, but as they got closer, their demeanor changed. One of them said something jokingly to another, who immediately scowled and snapped an angry reply. Another human jumped in to defend him, and in a few seconds, the entire group was arguing with each other as they walked by, their mouths pulled into snarls and ugly sneers. As they passed us, the anger and contempt surrounding them hit me like a fist to the stomach. The humans continued past us, still arguing, and a swarm of nightmare piskies fluttered down and followed them down the street.

I set my jaw, feeling anger and a grim resolve settle over me. Glancing at Meghan, Nyx, and Puck, I saw that they felt the same. Whatever was happening with InSite, it had to end now. There was no way this much rage and hate were good for either world. "We're not going to find any answers standing out here," I said. "We need to get inside."

"Okay, but how are we gonna do that?" Puck wondered. "We can't just walk into a human office building and magically blow it up. One, that would be uncool. And, two, this is the real world. There are probably a bunch of ignorant but innocent corporate drones wandering around after hours."

"How innocent are they, really?" I asked, causing Puck's eyebrows to arch and Meghan to give me a sharp look. I didn't care. I was tired of this, of monsters invading my world, putting my family at risk. Of humans and their volatile emotions, spawning anger and hate over nothing. That darkness in me boiled, tantalizing and powerful. If I walked through those doors and froze every living thing within the walls of InSite, human and faery alike, would the nightmare creatures disappear?

"Ash." Meghan's voice was quiet, not disapproving, but concerned. "We can't harm any humans while we're here," she said. "Even if they have the Sight, or are working with these new type of fey. We can't start killing mortals. Not when there are other ways to deal with them."

I didn't answer. Years ago, before I'd met Meghan, human lives meant very little to me. As the Unseelie prince, I had killed mortals with the same callousness that I'd shown the beasts I hunted. That all changed after I met the half-human daughter of Oberon, fallen in love, and gained a soul, but I still remembered how easy it was to kill a mortal. How I could snuff the life from them with a flick of my hand. In the years of ruling the Iron Realm with Meghan, that ruthlessness had faded, but, I was quickly discovering, it wasn't completely gone.

Puck sighed. "Well, like ice-boy said, we're not gonna learn anything standing out here," he stated. Glancing at InSite's glass doors, he gave an exaggerated shudder and rubbed his hands. "Let's do this thing. The sooner we go in, the sooner we can see how badly we need to panic."

Nothing stopped us as we walked up the front steps of InSite to the glass doors of the building. Nightmare piskies hissed and fled from us, their wings buzzing like giant wasps as they disappeared around the walls and over the roof. I did spot a security camera tucked away in a corner, watching the front entrance, but mortal technology couldn't pick up the fey, even unglamoured; it certainly wouldn't see us now.

The sliding glass doors were locked, as it was fully dark now, though lights still glowed from somewhere inside. The only evidence that this was, indeed, InSite's headquarters were the letters on the doors indicating such.

"Locked, huh?" Puck muttered, observing the glass barrier critically. "Good thing it's glass, then." He glanced at Nyx, standing silently behind him. "Just out of curiosity, were you around before glass was invented? You know how to get through this, right?"

Nyx gave a tiny smile. "I know what glass is, Goodfellow. I am not *that* old. Incidentally, I know what salt is, too. Though it appears that putting a line of salt across the windowsill has fallen out of favor."

"I know, right? Lucky for us." Puck rubbed his hands together, and the air around him shimmered with magic. "Let's see. Been a while since I've done this, but I think the human expression is: like riding a bike? Once you learn how, it never goes away—"

"Stop talking and just go, Puck," I growled at him.

At our feet, Grimalkin sniffed. "I would save your breath, prince," he sighed. "I have been saying the same thing for millennia, and he only seems to get worse."

"Jeez, impatient much, you two?" Puck raised his arm and pressed a palm against the door. Glancing at Nyx, he grinned conspiratorially. "These are also the two that are constantly annoyed when I leap before I look. I don't think they know what they want, really."

"Puck…"

"Keep your frosty hat on, prince. I'm going." He took a step, and for a moment the doors rippled slightly, like heat waves in the sun, as Puck passed through the glass and stepped into the building.

Nyx followed, though I noticed she briefly closed her eyes as she went through, an older technique where the belief was that if they didn't see the barrier, it didn't exist. I pulled my glamour to me and passed through with Meghan, my magic leaving patterns of frost against the glass for a few seconds after we were through. Grimalkin sauntered in behind us like the door wasn't even there.

As soon as we were through the door, the building changed.

I jerked to a halt as we stepped through the glass and saw the rest of the group stop as well, gazing around in wary confusion. At first glance, the inside of the building was just as drab and unremarkable as the outside. The front lobby was brightly lit, and there was a human sitting at a welcome desk, though, of course, he didn't see four faeries and a cat pass right through the front doors. It wasn't the room itself that caused the shiver down my spine, but what lay beyond.

Just past the desk and the walls, the vague outline of stony ruins, covered in trees and vines, entwined throughout the room, like two photographs that had been merged together. They flickered and rippled like mirages, not completely there, shimmering in and out of existence. You couldn't see them clearly; if I stared directly at the desk, all I saw was a human hunched over a computer screen. But from the corner of my eye, I could just make out the existence of another place, like a sunspot that kept moving the more you focused on it.

There were also nightmare piskies everywhere, in both realities, it seemed, perched on fake plants, crawling along branches, and clinging to the ceiling. Several hovered around the single human at the desk, who was currently not paying attention to the door or the bizarre half-real landscape around him. His eyes were glued to the computer screen, his shoulders hunched in concentration, as the sounds of shouting and artificial gunfire echoed over the speakers.

Meghan gazed around in confusion and shock. "What's happened here?" she wondered. "What is this place?"

"No idea, princess," Puck muttered. "I've never seen anything like this, and that's saying something."

I stared at the two realities, as Meghan continued to gaze around the room. "Are we back in Faery?" she asked. "It's like we're in two places at once."

Nyx suddenly drew in a breath. "Two places at once," she whispered. "This...this is the site of an anchor. We must be on the mortal side. The other place—" she gazed around in wonder "—must exist somewhere in the Between."

"Yes," Grimalkin said solemnly. "I believe that is correct. What we are seeing now is the reflection of both worlds, overlapping because the anchor exists in both places at once."

A shout rang out from the human behind the desk. Abruptly, he straightened with an extremely violent expletive, throwing the mouse to the other side of the desk, where it clattered loudly against a pen holder. The piskies surrounding him hissed and chattered in seeming glee, and the rest of the piskies in the room buzzed their wings, giving the disturbing impression that the building was full of wasps.

I felt the anger of the room spike, felt my own violent nature rise up in response. For a moment, the fury was suffocating; my head was suddenly filled with images of stalking up to the human, grabbing his skull, and slamming it into his keyboard. *He works for InSite*, whispered the dark voice within. *He's an enemy, a threat to everything you care about. Destroy him.*

I pushed down the urges. Attacking a hapless human employee, even if he did work for InSite, would get us no closer to our objective. Even if part of me was sorely tempted.

"Well, he seems fun," Puck commented, as the oblivious mortal retrieved his mouse, muttering under his breath the entire time. The piskies in the room, however, stared at us balefully and bared their fangs at his voice. "Playing games on company time, how shameful. Somehow, I don't think he's going to know anything about our Evenfey friends."

"Probably not," Meghan agreed. "So, there are humans working for InSite that don't seem to know about the fey, even though they're sitting in the Between." She observed the human for another moment, then shook her head. "Something is definitely here, though. The glamour aura of this place is scary. And there's something…below us." She paused a moment, as if sensing something we could not, then shivered. "I think we have to go deeper."

"I only see one hallway," Puck pointed out, nodding to the corridor beside the security desk. "Probably going to lead us right into a death trap, so that's something to look forward to." A swarm of nightmare piskies suddenly fluttered from the hallway, buzzing around the room and making him wrinkle his nose. "Oh, this is gonna get so much worse, isn't it?"

Cautiously, we moved down the hall. The dim corridor stretched before us, flanked by wooden doors that probably led to offices or conference rooms. But from the corner of my eye, I saw crumbling walls choked with moss and vines, and stone pillars lying shattered against the walls. The scene flickered in and out, like the horror movies Meghan was still fond of.

Nyx shook her head. "This place," she muttered. "It's strange. It feels ancient, but I can sense the iron poison here as well. How is this possible?"

"I believe it is due to the nature of the Between," Grimalkin replied. "Nothing in the Between is permanent—it is constantly shifting, moving between the Nevernever and the mortal world at random. Phaed is one such place, if you remember. The site that we stand in now might have existed anywhere, at any time, in the mortal realm or Faery. Until someone found an anchor to hold it in place."

"You're making my head hurt, cat," Puck muttered. "Can't you just say 'nothing ever makes sense in Faery' and leave it at that?"

A figure appeared in the spaces between pillars, the bleached white deer skull staring at me from the darkness. I jerked up, whipping my head toward the figure, only to find myself gazing into an office with a bald human sitting at a desk, busily typing away.

"Ash?" Meghan glanced back at me, eyes shadowed with concern. "Did you see something?"

"I...don't know." The human at the desk continued to type,

and the room around him remained empty, but I knew something had been watching us. "For a moment, I thought I saw something," I went on. "But it was in the other place, in the Between."

"I saw it, too," Nyx said softly, her gold eyes narrowed as she scanned the hall and tiny offices on either side. "I think something knows we're here."

"Well, Furball is gone," Puck said, his voice echoing a bit too loudly in the sudden silence. "So, you know what that means."

We came to a single elevator at the end of the hallway. When Meghan hit the button, the doors slid open, revealing the polished metal box through the frame. A trio of nightmare piskies buzzed out, zipping over our heads, and went flying down the corridor. Nyx recoiled, shrinking away from the opening like it was the open mouth of a dragon.

Puck put a hand on her arm. "Yeah, I know," he said. "Trust me, first time I rode one of these things, I felt like I was going to die. You'll be okay, though," he added. Reaching into his shirt, he pulled out an amulet, a stylized raven on a chain. "You have one of these things, remember?"

Nyx took a steadying breath. "So much iron," she said, looking in disdain at the metal box. "How can any fey exist here? Even those piskies, those Evenfey. How can they survive in this place with so much iron and—and…what is that word? Technalobby?"

"Technology," I offered. "And they can survive because the amount of anger in this place overshadows the effects of iron. They're sustaining themselves off all the negative glamour."

Meghan was staring at the inside of the elevator, her eyes dark. If I turned my head slightly, I could see the opening of a ruined stone staircase, plunging down into the black.

"It's down there," Meghan said. "Whatever it is. Something powerful. And angry."

Puck sighed. "Of course, it is," he said, more in resignation than annoyance. "'Cause it's never something cheerful and happy. We never find a giant smiling bunny, do we? It's always something angry and powerful that wants to eat our faces. Fun times. Well, gang...?" He indicated the open doors. "Into the jaws of death we go. Furball, if you're still listening, we'll see you down there."

I stepped through the elevator doors, with Meghan and Puck behind me. Nyx, after one last moment of hesitation, followed as well. The rest of us stood along the mirrored edges, letting the Forgotten stay in the center, as far away from the walls as she could, and Puck wrapped his arms around her waist from behind.

As the doors slid shut, I saw the hallway we had just come down stretching out before us. For a moment, I caught a thin silhouette standing at the very end, the skull mask watching us with empty eye sockets. I blinked, and the thing was closer, long sharp fingers reaching out like spider legs. Then the doors hissed shut, hiding the creature from view, and the elevator began to descend.

13

THE NIGHTMARES BENEATH

We continued to descend far longer than I thought we should; though I hadn't been in many human elevators, it seemed like too much time passed before the box finally came a shuddering halt, letting out a sharp ding that made Nyx jump and unsheathe her light blades.

When the doors started to open, I tensed, half expecting a horde of enemies on the other side, or perhaps to come face-to-face with the eerie figure that had been shadowing us ever since we got here. Instead, a wave of roiling, angry glamour washed into the elevator. Beyond the frame, the hall was cloaked in shadow, with images of ruined stone and moss-eaten pillars overlapping the real world. The buzz of piskie wings echoed through the corridor, and tiny shapes moved in the shadows, both in the real world and within that other place.

"Can you feel it?"

The voice slithered into the hall, making us drop our hands to our weapons, gazing around warily. A face flickered into sight down the corridor, the stark white deer skull, appearing for just a moment before winking out of sight.

Weapons out, we moved cautiously down the hall, but the figure did not appear again, though the whispers continued, swirling around us.

"The anger, the rage. The beautiful hate. It is almost time. It is very nearly enough. Soon, the king will awaken. Soon, the way to Evenfall will appear."

"What is Evenfall?" Meghan demanded.

As I passed a door to what looked like a maintenance room in the real world, from the corner of my eye, I saw the figure in the doorway, the skull face very close to mine. I jerked and whirled around, half drawing my blade, only to find myself staring into a room of brooms and mop buckets.

"Evenfall," the voice whispered, sounding like it was somewhere in that room, hiding behind discarded cleaning implements. *"You wouldn't know it. No one, in this world or the other, remembers. The memory of Evenfall was stripped from every living creature centuries ago. But I remember now. I remember what was hidden away. When the Veil disappeared the night of the sacrifice, when the mortals were able to see us, even if it was for a moment, I remembered the king. And Evenfall."*

"What king?" Nyx asked. "There was no king of Faery. I served the Lady my whole life—there was no king before her."

"Forgotten," the thing whispered. *"Evenfey. You are like me, the memories of yourself stripped away, sealed behind fear and hate of our kind. No matter. Soon, you will remember. The king awakens. Our king awakens. The rage of this world, the violence and anger and uncompromising chaos of it all, stirs him from his unnatural slumber. I built this site, this place of power, to speed the process. Humans helped me, oblivious to what they were creating. They are easy to manipulate, to prod in the right direction. A few whispers, a suggestion or two, and they created this—this site that lives in the ether of their world, ampli-*

fied by their hateful thoughts and accusations." The voice chuckled. *"InSite. Quite the clever play on words, is it not? The mortals think they are so insightful, that they must share their great wisdom and realizations with their poor, ignorant fellows, and yet, all they do is incite one another. And through it all, the beautiful, violent emotions continue to build. Rage, hatred, fear. They seep through the cracks of this world and into the dreams of the sleeping king. His dreams are terrible in their beauty. You have seen them, have you not? The creatures that roam the Between, terrifying all they come across?"*

"Wait, are you talking about the big nasty Monsters we fought?" Puck echoed, sounding both stunned and horrified. "Those huge ugly bastards who stalked us through the Between and nearly destroyed Touchstone, those were just *dreams?"*

"Yes," whispered the voice. *"The dreams of the king. They are but fragments of his consciousness, tiny slivers that worm their way into your world. Are they not beautiful?"*

"Uh, no," Puck said. "I would say no, they're not beautiful. Those are nightmares, my friend. I think you mixed up the meaning of dreams with nightmares."

"What are nightmares, but the dreams of different emotions?" For just a moment, the creature appeared, sitting on a cracked stone block. *"Your kind, the fey of the Nevernever, were born of the dreams of mortals. Even the iron fey, the new abominations that roam the Iron Realm, were born of dreams. Different dreams, aspirations of technology and progress, but dreams nonetheless. Have you never wondered what the fey born of mortal nightmares would look like?"*

I felt a chill in the dim hallway, a finger of dread tracing my spine at the creature's words. We, the fey—the entire Nevernever—were all born of the dreams and fears of mortals. That was what everyone knew, what we always believed. To mortals, the world of Faery was beautiful, surreal, and sometimes terrifying.

But this thing, this creature, implied that there was another type of fey. Born not of dreams, but of nightmares. Born from the darkest side of human emotion. But if that was true, where *were* they all? It didn't seem possible that an entire race of fey could exist in the Nevernever or the moral realm without anyone realizing they were there.

"The dreams of the king," the voice whispered. *"They are not Monsters—they are so much more. His nightmares, the Elder Nightmares, made real. Forgotten…"* The voice went on, and said a word I didn't recognize. A moment later, the word slipped from my mind, and I couldn't remember what had been said, though I realized the thing had been speaking to Nyx. *"You should be with us,"* it continued. *"How can stand with those who sealed us away? Who cut off access to our home? Why do you help them? You are one of us."*

"I don't know you," Nyx said flatly, even as we all glanced at her. "I don't know anything of Evenfall, and your king is not mine. I serve a different king."

"You will remember," the voice whispered ominously. *"Soon. This world's anger is at its peak. The Veil has never been thinner, and Evenfall has never been closer. And when the king awakens, we will take our revenge against those who erased us from the memories of the world."*

"No, you won't," Meghan said, stepping closer. "It doesn't have to be war between us. We don't have to be enemies, but if you threaten the Nevernever, we will have no choice, and Faery *will* rise up to defend itself. Please, reconsider what you want to do. A war with the Nevernever will only bring chaos and death to everyone involved. If we have to stop that here, we will."

"You will not stop us," the voice hissed. *"I will wake the king, and you will all suffer. Do not think that I am unprepared. You will never reach the site of power. We know your fears, your innermost nightmares. Do you think you can stand against us?"* It flickered into view, raising a bone-thin arm. *"Here is but a small taste of what awaits Faery when the king awakens and we all return."*

The voice, and the Evenfey, disappeared, fading into that

other reality and vanishing behind a stone pillar. But a new sound began filtering through the corridor. Dozens of small, shuffling feet, coming down a side passage where the hallway branched off several paces ahead.

"Uh-oh," Puck muttered, and drew both his daggers. "What is that? It sounds like an army of babies coming at us." He gasped in mock alarm. "Oh, no, maybe it's an *infantry.*"

Ignoring the terrible pun, I drew my sword, as the Unseelie within smiled in cold anticipation. An army of enemies meant more things to kill. More creatures to unleash my rage on. It didn't matter if it was a horde of giant insects or nightmare babies, as Puck had suggested. If they attacked us, they would die, and I would feel no regret. Survive, or be slaughtered; that was the way of the Unseelie.

The shuffling noises got louder. And then, spilling around the corner, came dozens of small, pale bodies. They were goblin-size, and had the large, tattered ears of the goblins we knew in the Nevernever, with subtle differences. Their skin was gray instead of green, and their eyes were huge bulbous orbs peering out of their lumpy heads. But their mouths… Their fang-filled yellow grins stretched literally from ear to ear, and when they opened their jaws, a second mouth, as tooth-filled as the first, could be seen inside.

"Oh," Puck remarked, his voice slightly breathy. "Great. Nightmare fuel. I didn't want to sleep for the rest of the month, anyway."

With piercing shrieks, the army of goblin creatures charged. Their jaws gaped open as they ran, giving the impression of an army of mouths coming down the passageway.

I unleashed my winter glamour, sending a blast of frigid air down the corridor. Snarling, the goblins at the head of the charge ran straight into a storm of deadly spikes that pierced through them. They collapsed, and burst into a writhing mass of oily smoke, scattering teeth and fangs over the tile with sharp clicking sounds. The smoke dissolved into nothing, but the teeth remained, glittering dully under the fluorescent lights.

"Ew, ew, ew!" Puck danced back, wrinkling his nose, as a pair of yellow fangs clicked to a stop near his feet. "That's disgusting. Hey, ice-boy, remember when we stumbled onto that tooth-faery lair? With the wind chimes hanging outside, made entirely of molars? They would love this place."

Meghan pulled a face. "Now *I'm* creeped out," she muttered, and sent a strand of lightning flickering down the hall. More goblin things exploded into smoke, scattering teeth over the tile floor. "Keep moving," the Iron Queen commanded. "The sooner we find this center of power, the sooner we can go home and forget this place ever existed."

We pressed forward, into the swarm of tooth goblins. They hissed and chattered at us, gnashing both sets of teeth in their lumpy faces. Fangs clattered to the floor as they died, and I crushed them under my feet, feeling nothing but vicious glee as they fell before us.

Shrieking and gnashing their teeth, the goblins retreated, scurrying around a corner as they fled. We followed, but came to an immediate stop at the edge of the corridor, gazing at the new obstacle before us.

A door, bright red and made of steel, stood at the end of the hall. A creature stood in front of it, its bulky frame filling the entire hallway. It towered over the throng of goblins, a pale, ogre-type thing with stumpy legs and long arms, one claw holding a gnarled, tooth-studded club. But it had no face, just a gaping maw filled with those double sets of jagged teeth, shiny and glistening in the sickly light. Its pale skin was covered in what at first looked like bone shards jutting from its arms, shoulders, and back. A moment later, I realized they, too, were teeth, poking up from its flesh like razor blades.

"Ugh," Puck muttered. "It just keeps getting worse."

The ogre thing took a step forward, and its large belly split open, revealing another tooth-filled mouth below its chest. The belly jaws bared their fangs and roared, and the goblins around it cackled, emboldened by its presence.

Nyx shook her head. "Why is this so familiar?" she almost whispered. "I feel like I've seen this creature before. Or something like it."

I narrowed my eyes. "It's just another monster," I said darkly. Raising my arm, I gathered my glamour into sharp, frozen knives. "It'll die like everything else."

I hurled the ice shards at the ogre, expecting to see it stagger back and fall, peppered with frozen daggers. Instead, the giant mouth on its stomach snatched the ice shards from the air as they came in, crunching through them like it was eating a mouthful of hard candy. I set my jaw against the sound of grinding glass as the ogre munched down the ice, swallowed, and let out a belch that echoed down the hall.

"Terrifying *and* rude," Puck sniffed. "Also, I think I saw a whole chicken drumstick back there. How many times a day do you floss, my friend?"

With a bellow, the ogre tooth thing charged, lumbering down the corridor with the goblins swarming around it. Raising my sword, I watched the giant creature stomp closer, feeling the ground tremble under my boots, and I breathed in the terrible glamour swirling through the hall.

"Here it comes," Puck announced, raising his daggers. "What's the game plan, guys?"

"I'll clear a path," Meghan said, sparks and energy strands snapping around her. Her calm, determined gaze met mine in the flashing lights. "If I take care of the smaller ones, can you three handle the big guy?"

I nodded, and the Iron Queen sent a bolt of electricity down the corridor, making everything flicker like a strobe light. Fangs clattered off the walls and bounced across the floor as the goblins died in large numbers. The tooth ogre flinched, stumbling to a halt for a moment, as the goblins at its feet thrashed and split apart, scattering bone fragments through the corridor.

I charged through the ranks of dying, shrieking goblins, cutting down several as they got in my way. Looming above us, the nightmare ogre saw me coming and roared. Its tooth-studded club smashed down, and the tight, crowded hallway didn't allow much room to dodge. I twisted aside, feeling the ground shake as the weapon crushed a few goblins into oily smoke, sending teeth tumbling down the corridor.

Darting forward, I lashed out at a pale, tree-stumpy leg, slicing my blade deep into the monster's knee. On the other side of the ogre, I saw Puck do the same, diving between the monster's legs and cutting its hamstrings as he rolled to his feet.

The ogre staggered. I jumped back as it fell to its knees, and saw Nyx streak by me as she went in for the kill. But then I saw the remaining goblins falling back, scurrying away from the ogre, and realized the danger too late.

"Nyx!" Puck called, having seen it as well. "Wait! Incoming!"

With a snarl, the ogre hunched its shoulders, and the teeth covering its body suddenly exploded outward like bits of shrapnel, filling the entire corridor. Instinctively, I raised a hand with a burst of winter glamour, throwing an ice shield in front of my face. I felt razor-sharp bits catch my leg, tearing through skin, and something hit my shoulder, sticking in the flesh, but the vital parts of me were behind a frozen shield. The tooth explosion struck the ice barrier, cracking and nearly shattering it, but the shield held. I heard Puck's yelp of alarm as he did a ridiculous flailing dance, arms and legs jerking, but somehow managing to avoid the teeth that flew at him. Nyx dove into a clump of shadows and disappeared a moment before a storm of fangs peppered the wall she had vanished into.

"Meghan." I spun, searching for my wife, hoping she had somehow escaped the explosion. She had been farther down the hallway, away from the worst of the blast, but I could still see the floors and walls of the corridor strewn with holes and places where the teeth had stuck in the plaster. My shoulder throbbed, and I could feel places where the teeth had found their mark, but barely felt the pain.

"Get down, Ash."

Relief swept through me. The Iron Queen stood several paces away, surrounded by teeth and broken bits of wall, a gusting whirlwind surrounding her. It whipped at her hair and clothes, and the teeth trapped within glinted as the Iron Queen raised an arm, blue eyes narrowed and angry, and sent the shrapnel-laced windstorm right back at the ogre.

I pressed back into the wall as the cyclone roared by, pelting the ogre with a storm of its own teeth. The ogre howled, and the maw on its belly gaped wide again, accepting the wind and the bone fragments that flew into it. Several gashes opened on its rubbery skin from the bone bits that got through, but the majority of the shrapnel went into its cavernous jaws, which ground the teeth into smaller chunks before swallowing the whole mouthful.

"Oh, that's disgusting. I think I'm gonna hurl." Puck mock gagged, though his face did look slightly green. Raising its head, the ogre bellowed, and more teeth grew through its skin, rising along its arms, back, and shoulders like bristling tusks. Glancing at me, the Great Prankster offered one of his evil grins. "My, what big teeth it has. Hey, ice-boy, remember that time that rock giant tried swallowing you whole? I think this cookie monster is about to bite off more than it can chew, what do you think?"

I grimaced, knowing what he was suggesting. I hated doing

183

this, but as I had discovered many times when facing powerful, seemingly invulnerable monsters, the inside was much squishier than the outside. "Fine," I growled, as the tooth ogre swallowed the last of the bone shards and grinned down the hall at us. "Just give me an opening."

"Try not to get eaten, ice-boy." And Puck's body burst into a flock of screaming ravens, which circled up and then flew straight as an arrow down the corridor. Right for the monster, which opened its enormous jaws once again. The shrieking ravens flew into the ogre's mouth, tearing themselves apart on its fangs. Feathers flew everywhere, and the jaws opened even wider, snatching the birds from the air.

I charged through the screaming, flapping diversion, braced myself, and leaped into the monster's jaws, ducking my head to avoid the gnashing fangs. The inside of the mouth was fetid and hot, with feathers, bones, and bits of teeth scattered everywhere. Without stopping to think about it too much, I raised my sword and drove it into the monster's upper jaw, sinking the blade as deep as I could.

The monster recoiled. A garbled howl emerged from its throat, blasting me with hot air and swirling feathers. The jaws bucked, a slimy purple tongue rising up to slap me out of its mouth. I pulled my sword free and slashed at the disgusting thing, making it curl away with another howl from the monster.

With a roar, the jaws clamped shut, teeth grinding together, trapping me inside the jaws and plunging me into darkness. I felt the tongue move beneath me and realized the maw was about to swallow me whole. As I slid toward the back of its throat, I raised my sword and plunged it into the bottom jaw with a burst of winter glamour.

This time, the monster screamed. Light returned as the jaws opened with an agonized wail, revealing huge icicles piercing its mouth and throat. The ogre staggered, and I dove out of the jaws as the monster toppled backward, hitting the ground with a crash and the clatter of breaking teeth. Rolling to my feet, I spun, ready to defend myself or attack, but there was no need. The ogre was on its back, twitching in its death throes. Its belly jaws gaped, clenching and unclenching madly, snapping at nothing. Broken ice spears, bloody and glittering, jutted from its mouth, piercing its throat, its cheeks, through the top of its jaw.

Nyx suddenly appeared, dropping onto the ogre's head and driving her moonlight blades through the jaws on its face. The huge creature gave one last twitch, both maws snapping, before it slumped, purple tongue lolling out of the belly jaws, and finally stopped moving.

I breathed out slowly and sheathed my blade, watching as the ogre's body rippled, turned white for a moment, and then dissolved into thousands of teeth, spreading in a pile across the floor. I felt the rage and hungry glamour in the air fade, though it still lingered within, ravenous and angry.

I turned, and was nearly knocked over as Meghan threw herself against me, hugging me hard enough that my ribs twinged. "Dammit, Ash," she breathed. "My heart nearly stopped when I thought that thing had eaten you. Don't do that again."

Despite the darkness still coiling inside, I chuckled. "This from the girl who flung herself at the giant beetle that nearly crushed her," I said. "Or went right for the head of the giant snake. Or stood in the path of the charging Minotaur because she was certain it would stop."

"It did stop, didn't it?" She eyed me in both annoyance and relief, and pulled a feather from my hair. "I'll admit, that was a little disturbing. Let's hope that was the last surprise this place has for us," she murmured.

Nyx and Puck rejoined us, Puck still making a face every time his boot crunched teeth underneath it. "Ugh. Agh. Gross.

Okay, I've heard losing teeth is a fairly common nightmare, but this is ridiculous," he muttered.

"Is everyone all right?" Meghan asked, gazing around. "Grim, are you still here?"

"Of course, Iron Queen," Grimalkin said, glancing up from one of the only clean spots in the hall. "Where else would I be?" He gazed up and down the hallway and curled his whiskers in disgust. "The lot of you certainly made a mess. Let us hope that was the last of them."

"That creature was guarding something," Nyx said. "It was left here to stop us from going any farther. That means that whatever is beyond that door is important."

Meghan nodded. "Then let's see what's behind it," she said.

Carefully, we walked across the tooth-riddled floor to the door at the end of the hall. As we approached, I could feel the anger and hate pulsing behind the barrier, throbbing in my ears. I could see the ruins around us, the moss-covered stones and slithering vines of the other place, flickering in and out of reality. The door to the computer room was locked, but Meghan put her hand against the steel, and glanced at the rest of us. "Ready?" she murmured.

I stifled the rising anger and gripped the hilt of my blade. "Yes."

With a pulse of iron glamour and a faint click from within, the door unlatched, then swung open with a creak.

I tensed, expecting something to come leaping out of the shadows at me, perhaps a creature with three mouths and a face twisted into a grotesque parody of anything sane. But the space beyond the door was eerily silent, though gazing through the frame, a chill skittered up my back.

The narrow hallways and twisted corridors of InSite had disappeared, and the double realities had vanished. Beyond the frame, the ancient, moss-covered stones of the forgotten ruins could be clearly seen. Giant pillars and crumbling walls surrounded the chamber we stepped into, leaving the shadow of the real world behind. The door behind us closed, and though it remained standing upright on the rocks, the hallway and office building disappeared, and the ruins were all that surrounded us.

We eased forward, gazing around in growing horror. Overhead, the roof had mostly fallen in, revealing a strange night sky through the opening. I didn't recognize the stars in this part of the Between; they were almost too bright, pulsing like distant fires that had grown too fast and were about to burn out. Through the ruined ceiling, a bloodred moon, bloated and ominous, hovered low in the sky. It shone a sickly crimson light into the chamber and the eerie scene surrounding us. Enormous trees grew through the stone floor, but they were odd, twisted things. Along the wall, one tree stood frozen and glittering, but the icicles dangling from the branches dripped with red, and the faces of several screaming fey could be seen within the ice. Another tree bloomed with flowers, but if you looked closer, the trunk and most of the branches were the twisted bodies of hundreds of dead animals, all covered in moss and bark. Nightmare piskies perched in the branches of the trees or stared at us from atop broken pillars and shattered stone. Except for the occasional buzz of their wings, everything was unnervingly silent.

I could feel the energy here, the anger and fear and hate, pulsing through every tree, every stone and leaf and scattered pebble. I breathed deep, and felt my Unseelie side rise up in response, more powerful than it had ever been. The corrupted glamour swirled around us, but the core, the center of it all, came from a raised stone dais in the middle of the chamber. The circular platform radiated a faint light, as the edges were surrounded with glowing sigils that flickered red in the eerie luminance of the blood moon.

Cowled, hooded figures stood around the edges of the plat-form with their backs to us, faces hidden from view. They weren't chanting, or whispering, or even moving; they remained motionless around the perimeter of the circle with their heads bowed; if it wasn't for the slightest ripple of their robes and sleeves, they could have been statues.

But I could feel the power coming from the dais, pulsing against an invisible barrier, an angry giant trying to smash free. I could sense that strange glamour, different yet still similar to my Winter magic, throbbing like a wound from the center of the platform. Rage. Fury. Fear. Hate. With every pulse, the runes flared, sending flutters of glamour throughout the cham-ber, waves of negative energy against my skin.

"You are too late."

The robed figure at the top of the steps turned to face us, gazing down at us with empty eyes in its deer skull face. The light from the blood moon cast its long shadow across the floor, antlers reaching for us like grasping claws.

"You will not stop it," the Evenfey whispered. *"The ritual is al-most complete. All the anger, all the fear and despair and hatred of the human world has flowed into this spot, strengthening the sigils, em-powering the spell. It is nearly complete. Can't you feel it?"* It raised thin arms, black as pitch, toward the broken ceiling. *"When the moon reaches its zenith, the king, the bringer of nightmares, will finally be summoned. Can't you feel the anger?"* it breathed, sounding as if it was in ecstasy. *"The hate? It calls to him. Stirs him from his sleep. He is almost here. And when he comes, the entire world will succumb to darkness and terror. Mortals and fey alike will understand true fear, as the Nightmare King will make himself known once again."*

"The Nightmare King," Puck echoed, and glanced at the rest of us. "Well, that doesn't sound like something we want to happen."

"No," Meghan agreed, as power flickered to life around her. "It's not."

I drew my sword, adding an icy blue light to the sullen red glow of the chamber, as the Iron Queen stepped forward, gazing at the creature atop the steps. "You have one chance," she told it, as I clenched my fingers impatiently around my sword hilt. "Stop the ritual now, or we will end it ourselves."

Fury clawed at me, urging me forward, goading me to attack. I didn't want to talk. I wanted to kill. I wanted to lunge up the steps and drive my blade through my enemy, making sure he would never threaten us or our world again. I could feel the power singing through my veins, fed by the dark energies around us. The legacy of the Unseelie Court.

The Evenfey regarded us with empty black eyes. *"You cannot stop it,"* it whispered. *"The Between knows your nightmares, your deepest, most hidden fears. You are all drowning in anger, fear, regret. Don't you see?"*

It raised a hand, and immediately, the crowd of hooded figures surrounding the circle turned, regarding us from the shadows of their hoods. As one, they stepped forward and began walking down the steps toward us. *"I can taste your fear,"* the Evenfey at the top of the steps said, as the hooded figures glided around him and came silently down the stairs. *"I can see the hidden terrors of your mind, the secrets you keep from everyone. They cripple you, but this only makes us stronger."*

"Fear?" Puck scoffed, brandishing both daggers with a defiant smirk. "Do you know how many scary baddies we've seen, antler-head? Granted, your tooth ogre was disgusting, but you're gonna have to do better than that to scare us."

"The Between knows," whispered the Evenfey, as if Puck hadn't spoken. *"You cannot hide your fears from it. It sees all. You cannot escape."*

The cowled figures reached the bottom of the steps and kept

walking forward. I raised my sword as one of them angled toward me, hood still lowered, hiding its face. A thought flashed through my mind of another challenge, many years ago. A narrow hallway with hundreds of mirrors, and watching my own reflection step out of the glass to fight me. Only it wasn't me, but Ash the Winter King. Ash the soulless monster. As the cowled figure came steadily forward, I braced myself to see my own reflection staring back at me. I had slain the evil part of me before; I was fully prepared to face myself again.

The figure raised its head and looked at me straight on.

"Hello, Father," Keirran said quietly. "I knew you would come."

14

PERSONAL NIGHTMARES

"Keirran."

My voice echoed in the sudden, absolute silence. I turned my head and found myself in a vast, frozen wasteland. The ruins had disappeared, and a forest of twisted, frozen trees, bent under the weight of snow and icicles, stretched away into the darkness. The snow coating the ground was spattered red with the blood of countless bodies, lying in twisted piles around me. Most of them were frozen, lips and features blue, though some had been impaled with spears of ice, or cut apart with an icy blade. I spun slowly and saw a figure floating off the ground, a jagged spike thrust through her middle, raising her into the air. Mab hovered there, impaled from behind, limbs dangling stiffly and eyes staring sightlessly at nothing. Snow drifted softly around her, landing on lips and skin before dancing away on the breeze. My stomach lurched, and I took a steadying breath to gather my thoughts. *This is the Between*, I reminded myself. Reality could be manipulated here, my worst fears and darkest secrets manifesting in front of me. No matter what I saw, no matter who appeared from the mist, I had to remember where I was. The fog curled around me, and my mind floundered. Everything felt hazy and surreal; memories were starting to blend together. It was suddenly hard to recall which images were real and which were imagined.

This is not your world. This is not your reality. Remember that. I shook myself, driving back the confusion clawing at me. *Do not forget where you are.*

Steeling myself, I turned back and looked for Keirran. He now stood a few paces away, black cloak fluttering wildly in the wind. His silver hair and unsheathed sword gleamed like metal in the unnatural light. His eyes were a mix of fury, grief, and a terrible resolve, and I suddenly knew his intentions.

Despair flickered, and I pushed it down. "This isn't going to work," I told the figure of my son. "I know you're not the true Keirran. Using my fears against me is pointless if I know this isn't real."

"Is it not?" Keirran asked quietly. "How would you define what is real and what isn't? Look around you." He gestured to the mountains of bodies, all dead by my hand. "This is real, Father," Keirran murmured. "In this world, the Winter King slaughtered everyone we knew. And now, we all have to face the consequences."

Figures melted out of the trees, stepping into the light. Puck and Meghan, their expressions haunted, met my gaze with grim determination, and my heart sank. *No. Not them. I don't want to do this.*

"Ash," Meghan whispered. "I'm so sorry. This is my fault. I should have seen this coming." Her gaze strayed to the body of Mab, hanging limply from the ice spike, and her lips tightened. "But this cannot continue, and you're too far gone. I had to make the call I never thought I would."

This isn't real. I shook my head. "None of you are real," I told them, as the three people I loved most surrounded me, their expressions somber. "I know I'm still in the Between."

"You brought us here, ice-boy," Puck said, his voice uncharacteristically bleak. He took a step forward, green eyes shadowed and haunted. "You know us better than anyone. Your memories, your thoughts, your emotions brought us to this spot. We are as real as you are, and you know I can't tell a lie."

"It's not the same," I insisted, wondering why I was arguing with shadows. They might be flawless copies, but they were not the same as those I had stepped into the Between with. Meghan and Puck were not here. Keirran was safely in the Deep Wyld with the Wolf. I had to believe that, or I would be lost.

Meghan stepped toward me, her expression one of veiled anguish. The pain in her eyes tore at my heart, exactly as if it was the real Meghan. "I can end this quickly," she whispered, not quite able to hide the tremor in her voice. "I would rather end it quickly, for all our sakes. But I know you, Ash. And I know you are not going to yield. Still, I offer you this one chance — drop your sword, close your eyes…and let me do what I must. No more pain, no more blood or killing or death. This will finally be over."

"Meghan." I gazed at her, feeling that same clenching of my heart. *Dammit, everything about her is perfect. I can't tell the difference between them. It's like she's really standing there.* "I don't want to fight you," I said desperately. "I told you before, a world where we're enemies is not one I want to exist in. But," I went on as her eyes grew suspiciously bright, "I can't let you kill me. Not here. My real family is waiting for me, and I won't fail them."

Meghan bowed her head, but I caught the tear crawling down her face before it dropped to the bloody snow. "If that is your decision," she whispered, and her fingers tightened around her blade. "I swear, we'll make it as painless as we can."

And she lunged at me.

I twisted away on instinct, knocking the steel blade aside, my body reacting even though my mind was still reeling with denial and shock. As I leaped back, I saw Keirran dart in and quickly parried the lightning-quick stab at my face. But then Puck joined the fray, and as skilled as I was, my sword couldn't be in three places at once. The edge of Keirran's blade got through, biting into my arm, as the point of Meghan's sword slashed across my chest.

The pain shocked me, proving that, whatever I thought, this aspect of the world was real. Gasping, I staggered away from them, feeling blood stream from my wounds and drip to the ice. They didn't follow; Keirran stood a little behind Meghan and Puck, his face turned away and his jaw clenched, as if he hated this and would rather be anywhere else.

"Ash, please," Meghan said, and though she stood tall, her voice was slightly choked. "We don't want you to suffer. You don't have to fight this. Let us end it quickly."

"No," I rasped, though I knew it was hopeless. I could handle Keirran, and I could hold my own against Puck, but all three at once? Meghan wasn't using her Iron Queen powers, but the second she brought her Iron glamour to bear, I was in trouble.

I stood very little chance of surviving this. And that was assuming I could actually bring myself to kill my son, my best friend, and the woman I loved. They were shadows; logically I *knew* they weren't real. But knowing and making myself destroy the ones I'd sworn to protect was a different story. Everything about this twisted reality felt like my own personal nightmare. Nothing they said was untrue, nothing was out of character. If the day came where Meghan, Puck, and Keirran decided that I needed to die, this was exactly how it would play out.

I felt the ripple of glamour at my feet, and threw myself aside as a cluster of ice spears erupted from the place I'd been standing. Rolling upright, I sent my own storm of ice daggers back at Keirran, but they passed through a wall of Summer glamour and transformed into tulips before they could reach him. Puck leaped at me, daggers flashing, and for a second it was like old times, fighting desperately, trying to kill each other though we wished it could be different.

But this wasn't the same. This wasn't a simple feud with my best friend. Puck pressed in, his strikes coming fast and vicious, giving me no time to recover. I parried, dodged, and struck back where I could, as the Great Prankster continued his relentless assault, grinning as he came forward.

"What's the matter, ice-boy?" Puck said, dodging a stab to his chest and coming right back with a vicious swipe at my face. I knocked it away, but instantly had to duck as he spun with the second dagger, cutting at my throat. It had been years since I'd fought Puck with serious intent; I'd forgotten how lethal he was when he was really trying. "Stop playing around," Puck went on, as we continued to trade blows. "We always knew it would end like this. With one of us actually killing the other."

Anger flared. I could feel the energy pulsing under my feet, the dark glamour of this place calling to my Unseelie side, urging me to reach out for it. I resisted the urge, shoving back the anger. "You're not real," I told the false Puck. "My feud with Robin Goodfellow ended years ago. You're nothing but his shadow."

Puck's grin was vicious. "Then why are you holding back?" he snarled, as something rose from the ground behind me. I whirled, throwing up an ice shield, as the Iron Queen's blade smashed through the barrier and stuck me in the shoulder. I stumbled, and one of Puck's daggers got through, plunging into my ribs, just as Keirran hit me from behind, his blade slicing across my back.

With a shout, I released my glamour in a burst around me, icicles surging out like spears. Meghan and the others jumped back to avoid being impaled, retreating several paces away as the ground around us erupted with ice daggers, becoming a carpet of needles.

I staggered, gasping, then sank to a knee, feeling my wounds throb, seeing my blood dripping slowly to the ice. My vision blurred in and out, my mind spinning from the realization. I was going to be killed by the shades of my family and best friend. They were more than copies, more than shallow images; they had come from my memories, my emotions, the secrets I kept safe about them all. They weren't the real Meghan, Puck, and Keirran, but they *were* real. In another life, if things had been slightly different, this scene might have come to pass. Mercilessly killed by those I loved, because I had become a monster.

Anger flickered, and that power called to me again, dark and seductive. I *could* become a monster. I could become the thing they feared, the ruthless creature who destroyed the Nevernever and slaughtered everything he came across. Ash the Winter King.

I looked up, and found the three of them surrounding me. Their weapons were still drawn, but none of them seemed eager to deal the finishing blow. Puck stepped forward, his face pulled into a grimace of pain. "Stop fighting us, ice-boy," he pleaded. "This is already killing me. Don't draw this out any further than we have to."

"Father, please," Keirran added, and his voice shook as he spoke. "How many more have to die before you are satisfied? How much more blood and chaos can the Nevernever take? Let us end it quickly."

I looked at Meghan. There were tears in her eyes, streaking her face with the spatters of my blood, but she stood firm with her blade at her side. "I'm sorry, Ash," she whispered again. "I love you, I will never stop loving you, but I can't allow this to continue any longer." She raised her other hand, white-hot energy strands flickering at her fingertips. "As queen of the Iron

Realm, I must sentence you to death. Close your eyes," she ordered softly. "This is over."

My arms trembled. I ached, the pain from my wounds like fiery bands across my whole body. The mist coiled around me, and for just a moment, staring into the anguished gaze of my queen, my wife, I almost did what she asked. My body slumped, and my eyes started to close, surrendering to the inevitable.

No, I will not die here. If the shades of Meghan, Keirran and Puck killed me now, what would happen to my real family? What would happen to the Nevernever if the Evenfey summoned the Nightmare King? I remembered the nightmare piskies swarming the warehouse in the real world, trying to get to Keirran. I remembered the tooth goblins and the horror of the ogre creature in the hall. If any of those Monsters got into the Nevernever, there would be chaos and terror and death, which was what the Evenfey wanted.

I clenched my fist against the blood-spattered ice, and opened myself to the rage. Power surged through me, cold and furious, stirring the Unseelie within to life. I drew that anger to me, feeling the power of Winter freeze my wounds, turning the blood in my veins to liquid ice. Strength flowed into me, killing any weakness, doubt, or regret. I was Ash the Winter prince once again, and I would not be defeated.

I felt the shift in the air as the others realized what was happening. Puck gave a curse, pulled his daggers, and lunged at me, intending to take my life then and there. I rose, power and hatred swirling through my veins, and hurled it like a spear at Puck. There was a flash of blue light, and Robin Goodfellow froze instantly, becoming a statue with his weapons still raised to strike. With a cold smile, I clenched a fist, and Puck shattered, bursting apart and raining to the floor with light tinkling sounds. His daggers hit the icy ground and stood there, hilts up, glittering in the eerie light.

Keirran gave a shout of despair and came at me, ignoring the Iron Queen's cry for him to stop. I didn't move, watching as his blade swept down at my head, then calmly raised a hand with a pulse of Winter glamour. Ice formed in the air between us, right before a huge ice spike surged from the ground, punching into Keirran and impaling him through the torso. His mouth gaped, the sword dropping from his fingers, as the spear carried him high into the air. Keirran slumped, his body going limp against the ice, as his blood streamed down the frozen surface and puddled at the base of the spike.

For just a moment, staring at the motionless body of my son, the horror I felt threatened to consume me. But then the frigid emptiness of Winter rose up, stifling the despair, freezing it entirely. *It's not Keirran,* I told myself. *Not the real Keirran. This is a world of nightmares. Do not falter.*

Then, Meghan screamed, and it was the most terrible sound I had ever heard, causing the mist to writhe and the blood in my veins to freeze. I turned to face the enraged form of the Iron Queen, her eyes filled with fury and sorrow, glaring down at me from several feet overhead. Glittering metallic wings spread out from her back, the edges barbed and razor-sharp. Her hair floated about her shoulders, blue eyes glowing with anger, as lightning flickered and snapped around her. She hovered there like an avenging angel, and for just a moment, for the very first time in my life, I was afraid of the Iron Queen.

"Enough, Ash," she ordered, her voice echoing around the chamber. "No more. No more death. No more losing the ones I love. This ends right now."

I threw up a shield, a thick dome of ice, as a storm of lightning slammed down around me, shattering the ground and sending frozen shrapnel spinning through the air. I staggered, the crackle of power in the air the only warning I had before the Iron Queen smashed through the barrier and came at me with her sword raised and a terrifying glow in her eyes. I barely got my sword up in time, backpedaling under the furious assault of the Iron Queen, the clang of our blades ringing through the chamber and making the icicles tremble.

And still, the power beckoned to me, ruthless and enticing. Urging me to let go, to fully give in to the rage and hate. I could be more powerful still, but I was holding back. I was holding back because, no matter how much I told myself that this wasn't real, all my fury and anger could not overcome the love I felt for the woman before me. Had this been the real Meghan, if this had taken place in the real world or the true Nevernever, it would have never gotten this far. If Meghan ever truly wished for me to die, to kneel down and offer my life to her, I would have done it without hesitation.

Something stirred in me, a glimmer of an idea that brought hope but was so appalling I loathed myself the moment I thought of it. The Meghan I was fighting now was a perfect representation of the true Meghan from my memories. That meant she had the same emotions, mannerisms, thoughts, and feelings of her real counterpart. The real Meghan knew me, better than anyone. She knew the lengths I would go to protect her, and in the same way, I knew her weaknesses as well. Her fears and desires and secret thoughts. If I wanted to survive, if I wanted to defeat the Iron Queen, I would have to do something I would never do otherwise. I would have to lie to her.

I trembled. I had to make this convincing, or it wouldn't work. Which meant this was also going to be fairly painful. When the Iron Queen darted back and thrust a hand toward me with a crackle of lightning, I didn't immediately throw up a shield to block, but braced myself instead. The energy strands hit me square in the chest, hurling me back several feet. I struck the icy ground hard and clenched my jaw around a gasp, feeling the world spin around me.

For another tempting moment, I felt the anger rise up, bringing power with it, but I shoved it down. I couldn't win like that. Not with her.

Grimacing, I looked up and saw Meghan hovering overhead. She was terrifying, powerful, completely beautiful, and my heart twisted with both love and despair. I felt my throat close up, and I took a deep breath to open it, hating what came next. This wasn't going to take much acting at all.

"Wait." I held up a hand, my voice coming out hoarse and choked. Meghan hesitated, and I struggled to my knees, breathing hard. Drops of blood trickled from a gash on my cheek and spattered to the ground as I knelt there, panting. "Enough," I rasped. "Enough, Meghan. I yield. I'm done."

My stomach churned. Saying those words felt wrong, like something vital had been torn out of me and thrown to the winds. Meghan's brow creased, her eyes tightening, as if she was both relieved and fearful of what came next.

My arms trembled. Painfully, I straightened, pushing myself to my feet. Meeting the Iron Queen's gaze, I raised my sword, then tossed it aside. It clattered against the ground and slid across the ice, coming to rest at the base of a frozen tree several yards away.

"End it." Despite my resolve, my voice shook, and there was a stinging sensation in the corner of my eyes. Everything about this felt real, and separating what my head knew from the emotions eating me apart from inside was impossible. "Kill me if you must," I rasped. "I told you before—a world where we are enemies is not a world that I want to exist in."

Meghan's face immediately softened, the fury in her eyes replaced with grief and regret. The storm around her ceased, and she floated gently to the ground. The elegant metal wings folded to her back, before they shimmered into a burst of glittering dust and disappeared.

"I'm sorry, Ash," Meghan whispered. She came no closer,

her sword held loosely at her side. "I wish I didn't have to do this. I wish…" Her gaze strayed to the horrible scene behind us, where Keirran's body still lay impaled on the ice. I couldn't bring myself to look at it. "I wish I could send you to the other side and then follow after," Meghan confessed. "I would die as well, so the three of us could be a family again." Her face crumpled with pain, then hardened. "But I can't. I am queen. I have to look after our people. That is how it has always been." She closed her eyes. "That is how it must be."

She stepped forward. Her eyes glimmered as her gaze met mine, and my breath caught. *Not real*, I reminded myself again. *It is Meghan, but this is not your world. Keirran and Puck are still alive, and your real wife is waiting for you on the other side of this nightmare. If you want to see them again, you know what you have to do.*

Meghan raised a hand, her fingers sliding up my neck to my face. I closed my eyes, hating that this felt so familiar, so right. I desperately hoped the Iron Queen would not mistake the pounding of my heart for the guilt and loathing choking me from within.

"Goodbye, Ash," she whispered, and stabbed her blade toward my heart.

I spun, feeling the iron sword slide along my ribs as it barely missed me, the edge slicing a line of fire across my skin. Whirling behind the Iron Queen, I snaked one arm around her shoulders and thrust my other hand into the middle of her back, releasing a surge of Winter glamour. The ice spike exploded from my palm, punching through the Iron Queen's chest in a spray of blood.

Meghan let out a strangled gasp, arching against me. Her mouth opened, but nothing came out but a few choked breaths. The sword fell from her hand, clattering to the ground, as my wife, my partner, and the queen I'd sworn to protect with everything I had shuddered once and slumped lifelessly in my arms.

I let out a breathless sob and held her to me, feeling a part of myself die within. The fact that it wasn't the true Meghan was of little solace. It still felt entirely real. I had just killed my wife, my son, and my best friend, and my soul felt sick at what I had done. What I was capable of doing.

But deep inside, that hidden, Unseelie nature reveled in this discovery. I had killed a queen of Faery. I could destroy my weakness and open myself to unlimited power if I chose. If I embraced the Unseelie side once more, I would be unstoppable.

Meghan's body rippled, then turned to mist in my arms. Dazed, I watched her disappear, writhing to nothing on the wind, and felt a numb relief spread through me. It hadn't been real, after all.

Slowly, I rose to my feet, seeing the world around me was fraying apart as well. The trees, the stones, even the piles of bodies looked like they were giving off steam that coiled away into nothing, and the sky overhead had turned flat and colorless. Straightening, I gazed around the disappearing reality, wondering what would happen when this world faded away. Would I emerge in the ruins with the Evenfey once more? Or would I vanish as well, becoming lost in the Between like so many others before me?

"Ash?"

The world seemed to stop. I turned, and Meghan stepped out of the mist, a bright, vivid silhouette against the colorless backdrop of gray and white.

My heart leaped, everything inside me reacting to her presence. There was a time when I might have been surprised to see her there. I might have questioned, been wary, demanded to know how she found me. Especially now, after I had just ended the life of another Iron Queen, and my hands were still shaking from what I had done.

I had no proof, no evidence, that this Meghan was the one I had pledged my life to. None, except the way my heart and soul reached out to her, and the feeling of utter relief that spread through me like a flood, searing away any doubt.

She raised her hands as she came forward, her gaze beseeching mine. "I'm real," she said softly, carefully, as if afraid I might not believe her. "It's me, Ash. I'm—"

I took two strides forward, reached out, and pulled her close, crushing her against me. She let out a startled breath, then returned the embrace tightly. Her arms squeezed my ribs, and the wounds on my back, arms, and chest throbbed, but I barely felt them. The world could dissolve around me, but if Meghan was here, that was all I cared about.

"Ash." Meghan's voice was soft. Her fingers moved up my chest, resting over my heart, which was still pounding. "You're shaking," she murmured.

"I had to kill you," I replied softly, and it was an effort to keep my voice steady. "That was..."

"I know." She pulled back and gazed up at me, her eyes bright with sympathy and pain. "And I know it killed you to do it. But, I'm glad, Ash. I'm glad I didn't lose you today, especially to myself." Her hand pressed gently against my jaw. "You did what you had to do. We're still together. So, no regrets."

I could only nod. Meghan leaned into me, and I wrapped my arms around her again. The world around us continued to fray apart, strands of mist pulling free to writhe into nothingness. I was glad to see it go, relieved that the bodies scattered through the snow had been the first to disappear. I didn't want to see them, the proof that I had murdered my family. The false Meghan's scream when I killed Keirran still echoed in my mind, sunk into my consciousness like a bright shard of pain that would never come out. The Unseelie side had been set free today, proving that I hadn't gotten rid of it at all. It was still there, waiting for any moment of weakness to rise up again and wreak havoc. I felt tainted, knowing what I had done. What I was still capable of doing.

And while you're standing here feeling sorry for yourself, the Nightmare King is still coming.

I shook myself. This scene would continue to haunt me, and I could look forward to going through it again in future dreams, but the Nightmare King was still being summoned, and we were still trapped in the Between. For now, we had to focus on what we'd come to do.

Taking a deep breath, I gently drew back. "We need to find Puck," I told Meghan. "And Nyx. They're probably dealing with their own nightmares. If we can find them, maybe we can figure out how to get out of here."

"Yes," Meghan agreed. "Though, I'm not really sure how I got here. After I dealt with…my own thing, all I could think about was finding you. When the world began to come apart, I just started walking, and it led me here. I think…" She gazed around, her brow furrowed, before continuing. "I'm not entirely sure this is right, but…if these worlds represent our personal nightmares, then maybe we have to defeat the core, the essence of what we fear, to destroy it. That would make sense… with what I had to do."

I noted her pale face, the almost haunted look in her eyes, and cursed myself for not seeing it sooner. I had been wrestling with my personal nightmares, but Meghan had been through her own as well.

"What happened?" I asked softly.

She shivered, closing her eyes. "The Iron Kingdom was burning," she replied in a shaky voice. "The Nevernever was destroyed, and everyone I knew and loved was dead. You, Puck, Ethan, my family… He killed them all."

My stomach wrenched in horror and sympathy. I knew which

he Meghan was talking about. "Keirran," I murmured, and she nodded. "Did you…?"

She nodded again. "I knew it was a nightmare," she confessed. "I knew that it wasn't real, that it was just my worst fears coming to pass, but still…"

I drew her to me again, holding her as she composed herself. She trembled for a brief moment, allowing herself to feel the grief and horror of what she had to do, then took a deep breath and straightened, the Iron Queen persona falling into place. Later, if we survived this, she would give in to the emotions I knew were tearing her apart inside. But right now, the rest of our party was missing, and I wasn't about to leave anyone behind. We had to find them before they succumbed to their own worst fears.

"We need to find the others," Meghan said, echoing my thoughts. "I was able to leave my nightmare and find you, but only after I had killed…" She paused, a shadow of pain going through her eyes. "He was the heart of it," she mused, as if just coming to the realization. "The anchor of that nightmare world. Maybe if we can defeat the core of what we fear the most, that nightmare will dissolve."

I nodded. "It makes sense." As much sense as anything did in the Between, which was very little. Only in a terrible nightmare world would I find myself having to kill my entire family in self-defense.

I pushed those memories aside to deal with later. "What do you want me to do?" I asked quietly.

Meghan's hand rose to my cheek, her thumb gently tracing the gash left over from my fight with her shade. The rest of my wounds had closed, or at least had gone numb from the angry Winter glamour swirling through me, but I still bore the marks of that terrible battle.

Her eyes tightened. "These are nightmares," she went on, "but the Between makes them real. We could have died fighting them." She paused, a flicker of pain crossing her face, before she set her jaw. "The sooner we find everyone else, the better," she decided. "I'll look for Nyx and Grim, if you go after Puck."

I nodded reluctantly, silencing my immediate protests. I didn't like the thought of splitting up, but it was probably for the best. Time seemed of the essence, and we would cover more ground if we were searching for different people. And as much as I didn't want to leave Meghan alone, I trusted her. Even in a hellish nightmare world, the Iron Queen, I knew, could take care of herself.

"All right," I said. "I'll search for Goodfellow then. Once I find him, we'll come looking for you and Nyx."

"What about Grimalkin?"

I resisted the urge to snort. "Wherever Grimalkin is, he'll be fine. I'm not sure that cat even has nightmares."

"Ash." Meghan caught my hand before I could turn away. "Promise me we'll see each other again," she said, sounding uncharacteristically unsure. It took me by surprise. Meghan, especially in recent years, had shown very little weakness. As the Iron Queen, she had made decisions without hesitation or regret, but now, gazing up at me with haunted eyes, she looked sixteen again. "Swear to me, that no matter what we see or do, even if we get lost in another nightmare, we'll find our way back to each other."

"We will," I promised, and brushed a strand of hair from her face, tucking it behind an ear. "I will always find my way back to you, no matter where we are."

She leaned forward, and I kissed her, feeling her hands slide up my neck into my hair. "Be careful, Ash," she whispered as she pulled back. "Who knows what kind of nightmares are lurking in Puck's mind."

"You, too," I said, and she drew away. Walking to the edge of the forest, she stepped into the fog and disappeared.

I gazed around, and saw that the frozen wood was nearly gone, slowly being swallowed by the mist creeping out of the darkness. Before the landscape could vanish completely, I turned my thoughts inward, bringing the red-haired Great Prankster to the forefront of my memories. Our fights, our arguments, all the adventures we had; some of them were painful, but in the end, everything we'd gone through had only made us stronger.

All right, Puck, I thought, as the bank of fog crept closer, slowly consuming everything it touched. *Wherever you are, hang in there. I'm coming. Let's see if I walk into a nest of fifty-foot spiders.*

The fog rolled over me, chill and damp, muffling all sound. Holding the image of the Great Prankster firmly in my mind, I started walking.

15

PUCK'S NIGHTMARE

For a few moments of walking through roiling mist, I couldn't see anything. The fog surrounded me, completely opaque, blanketing everything in white. I didn't stop, and I didn't change direction, keeping my thoughts trained on finding Puck. After several minutes of walking, the fog started to thin, and suddenly, I walked out of the fog bank into a bright beam of sunshine.

Squinting and shading my eyes, I looked up to find the world had changed once more. The dead, frozen wood was gone, and the forest that had replaced it was almost *too* bright and alive. Enormous trees surrounded me, fully in bloom, leaves and flowers rustling in the sunlight. Birds trilled from the branches, all sounding like they were trying to outsing each other, and insects swooped past my head, the buzz of their wings vibrating in my ears.

Frowning, I lowered my arm, taking in my surroundings. I didn't appear to be alone in this grove. Faeries surrounded me; a trio of piskies zipped by on shimmering dragonfly wings. Near a pond, a female centaur lay in the grass with her hooves folded beneath her. A few feet away, a wrinkled gnome dangled a fishing pole in the water, beady eyes trained on the creatures darting beneath the surface.

Confusion flickered. I was in the Seelie Court, surrounded by Summer fey. Despite knowing I was still in the Between, everything looked normal. Is this really Puck's *nightmare*? I was expecting at least a little chaos. Or a lot of spiders. Curious, I caught the eye of a pair of dryads, lounging easily under a willow tree as they combed each other's long, pale green hair. Normally, the sudden arrival of a Winter faery in the Summer Court would cause a stir, if not an actual uproar. Though if this was Puck's nightmare, anything could be possible. The two dryads noticed me and blinked, startled for a moment, then quickly averted their eyes. So, they did see me, and from their expressions, it appeared they recognized me as well.

I walked toward them, and the pair immediately rose to their feet, bowing their heads as I approached. "Your Highness," one said as I paused in front of them. "What can we do for you this Elysium?"

Elysium. The annual gathering of the courts to discuss politics and new treaties between them. So, that at least explained why my presence wasn't causing a panic. All the rulers of Faery, and their kin, were expected to be present for Elysium. Prince Ash of the Winter Court had been to many, many Elysiums, and nowadays, Meghan and I attended Elysium as a ruling couple every year. And because fey from all three courts were present at the same time, and still did not trust each other at all, things were always fairly tense. Had this been a real Elysium, it would have been the most peaceful one I had ever attended. If this was Puck's nightmare, the utter lack of chaos just didn't seem right for him.

Unless, utter peace and normalcy *was* his greatest fear. Somehow that wouldn't surprise me.

The dryads, I realized, were still waiting for my answer as I was pondering the Great Prankster and past Elysiums. "I'm looking for Puck," I told them. "Have you seen him lately?"

The first dryad furrowed her brow. "Puck?"

"Yes," I confirmed, wondering if Puck had already caused some sort of mischief and was hiding from Oberon's wrath as we spoke. "Robin Goodfellow. Where is he?"

The dryads exchanged a glance. "I am sorry, Your Highness," the first one said. "But I do not know anyone with that name. But, my sister and I are fairly new to the Summer Court. This is only our second Elysium, so we are still learning who all the important fey are."

That didn't make any sense. Everyone in Faery knew who Puck was. Even if they'd never met him, Puck was one of those fey that the entire Nevernever recognized. I was starting to understand what kind of nightmare this was. "You know who I am, correct?" I asked, and their eyes widened.

"Of course, Your Highness!" the other dryad said quickly. "Please forgive us, we meant no offense to you or your family."

"You are Prince Ash," added the first, "son of her highness Queen Mab, the ruler of the Winter Court. Prince Sage and Prince Rowan were your brothers, and—"

"All right, enough." I raised a hand, and they immediately stopped. I didn't need my entire family line repeated back to me. "I'm just looking for a friend," I went on. "If you see a red-haired faery of the Summer Court, let him know that Prince Ash is—"

A frog suddenly fell from the sky, landing in the lap of one of the dryads with a wet plop. A small, bright green amphibian with huge orange eyes, it gave a chirp and hopped to her shoulder, clinging there like a huge insect. The dryad continued to gaze at me, wide-eyed and attentive, not having any reaction to the unexpected visitor from above. She didn't even appear to have seen it.

A second frog dropped out of nowhere, landing on her head, and she didn't flinch. I muffled a sigh as the rain began, hundreds of frogs and toads falling from the sky and plopping to the ground. Not one faery appeared to notice them. They hopped over the grass and crawled along the ground, between the legs of the crowds of fey, sometimes even getting stepped on, and no one saw them at all.

"I'm sorry, Your Highness," the dryad said, as the rain of frogs continued. One landed on her forehead and slid down her face, and she paid it no attention. "Forgive me, but I didn't quite hear that last request. Would you like us to go looking for this Robin Goodfellow?"

I shook my head. If they didn't see the frogs, they wouldn't see the one who caused them. "No, it's fine," I told them, as a fat brown toad peered at me from the top of her head, blinking lazily. "As you were. I'll find him myself."

"Of course, Your Highness."

I turned and walked away, being careful not to step on the numerous, small green bodies scattered everywhere through the court. Summer fey bowed their heads to me or averted their eyes as I passed, not wanting a confrontation with an Unseelie prince. Their reactions were expected, their behavior typical, except for the continued ignorance of the hundreds of chirping, croaking, peeping frogs climbing over everything. A scene that, had this been the real Summer Court, would have caused mass chaos and confusion, but everyone would have instantly known who was behind it.

So, this is your nightmare, is it, Puck? I stepped aside as a toad fell from a tree branch, landing in the grass with a thump. A world where no one remembered the Great Prankster, or had ever heard the name Robin Goodfellow. A world where no one reacted to, or even noticed, the chaos he caused. I could understand that fear. For humans, being forgotten and ignored was unsettling, frightening even. But they weren't in danger of ceasing to exist. For the fey, it was deadly serious.

And for Puck, perhaps the most famous faery in the Nevernever and the human world...well, it was his greatest nightmare.

Where would he be now? I gazed around the Seelie Court again, thinking. The Between had led me here, so Puck had to be around somewhere. The throne room, perhaps? Thinking back to the rain of frogs, I decided against it. Oberon and Titania wouldn't be there during Elysium, and if there was one faery Puck wanted to see react to his pranks, it would be Titania.

The rulers of Faery, Mab included, would be in the courtyard now, sitting at the long marble table that hosted the kings and queens of the Nevernever. All the Gentry would be there, the important nobles of both the Summer and Winter Court. And, depending on where we were in this timeline—if time and past events even mattered—the queen of the Iron fey would be present as well. I both did and did not want to see Meghan in this world. One, it wasn't the real her; it would be this world's version of her. And two, if this was Puck's nightmare, perhaps he had envisioned a Meghan who had loved him and had died. Or had never existed at all.

I didn't know, and I didn't want to find out. But I did have to track down Puck in this nightmare of his own making, and the courtyard was where I would most likely find the Great Prankster, whom no one remembered.

Setting my jaw, I headed into the thick tangle of briars at the edge of the grove. The wall of thorns and twisting branches surrounded the entirety of the Summer Court, a maze that could either hinder or take you anywhere, depending on how well you knew them. I had been to Arcadia so many times, I knew the hidden paths and twisted passages by heart. The brambles peeled back for me, and I started down the tunnel that would take me into the heart of the Summer Court.

I heard the music not long after, haunting harp and string chords drifting through the branches, and stepped out of the tunnels into a courtyard full of fey. Elysium was in full swing, with Summer and Winter Gentry in their finest parading about or mingling among their own.

A long table of white, green, and gold sat at the back of the courtyard. It was covered with all manner of faery food, but only four fey were seated at the table. Oberon, lord of the Summer Court, sat in the very center, his antlered crown casting its pointed shadow over the tablecloth. His wife, Queen Titania, sat beside him, but she seemed wholly uninterested in her husband, sipping from a golden cup and actively ignoring him. Which probably meant they had gotten into another of their numerous arguments. On Oberon's other side, seated a little farther down, sat the imposing form of Mab, queen of the Winter Court. And judging from the miniature blizzard swirling around her and the frost that had spread over the ground and over the tablecloth, she was not in the best of moods.

Opposite Mab, on Queen Titania's side, the final ruler of Faery looked up and met my gaze, and my stomach tightened. This world's Meghan looked just as perfect and flawless as mine had been, down to the earrings I had given her for her birthday. Would she be the same, I wondered, or did Puck have a different vision than what I knew?

I hesitated a moment longer, before curiosity got the better of me. Stepping away from the trees, I headed across the courtyard.

"There you are," Meghan said, smiling as I walked around the table to stand beside her. "I was wondering where you had vanished to. You missed a riveting conversation between Mab and Titania that nearly led to another war. So that was interesting." She rolled her eyes and lowered her voice, turning her head slightly so that only I could hear. "I understand now why Oberon always puts himself between them—it's like trying to separate two siblings who keep playing the 'I'm not touching you' game."

I resisted the temptation to sit, to take my place at her side. This wasn't real, and I could not let myself get comfortable. A tiny, bright yellow frog hopped onto her forearm and sat there a moment, peeping. Meghan didn't seem to notice, and I clenched my fist to keep from plucking the amphibian off her and tossing it to the grass. "I'm looking for Puck," I said, just to confirm what I already knew. "Have you seen him around?"

"Puck?" Meghan furrowed her brow. "I don't recognize that name. Who is this?"

I smiled sadly. "No one you would know," I replied. "Just a friend, from a long time ago."

Meghan blinked and started to respond, but there was a glint of red from the corner of my eye. For just a moment, I saw him in the crowd, green eyes hooded as he watched us. I jerked up, but when I turned around, no one was there. Just the Summer and Winter Gentry sweeping around the courtyard, looking ethereal and otherworldly. The red-haired prankster of the Summer Court had disappeared.

"Ash?" Meghan frowned up at me. "What's wrong?"

"Nothing," I assured her, still scanning the crowds of fey. No Puck, but he *was* out there, I was sure of it. "I'll be right back."

I strode away before she could argue or ask questions, heading into the courtyard and the place where I had seen that fleeting glimpse of Robin Goodfellow. The look on his face, brief as it was, worried me. Completely blank and without emotion. As if he was on the verge of some terrible breaking point.

The crowds of fey parted for me as I walked through their midst, bowing their heads or nodding in deference. I ignored them. The magnificent gowns, the stunning outfits, the ethereal beauty that could make a human forget everything else, meant nothing to me. The faery I searched for wore a ratty green hoodie and an irreverent smirk everywhere he went. He should have stood out like a fox among swans.

Where are you, Puck?

Abruptly, I felt eyes on my back, and turned my head. A figure in a green sweatshirt was walking away through the crowd. His hood was drawn up, his shoulders hunched as he walked away with his hands in his pockets. As soon as I saw him, a Gentry swept in front of my vision and Puck was gone.

"Goodfellow!"

I strode forward, shouldering aside Winter and Summer fey, until I came to the spot the figure had disappeared. Pausing, I gazed around carefully. I'd come to the edge of the courtyard, where several large trees lined the perimeter just before you reached the wall of briars. Overhead, the branches grew close together, blocking out the sun and casting this area of the Summer Court in deep shadow. For a moment, I wondered if Puck had gone through the briars, but there was no tunnel in the wall of thorns that indicated he had left.

Behind me, the music abruptly stopped. Glancing back, a chill crept up my spine. The Summer Court fey were still there, but their faces were blurred, their lines and edges not quite in focus. I could hear voices drifting to me over the breeze, but they seemed muffled and far away, as if they were all speaking underwater.

There was the faintest sniffle at my back, and I turned.

A figure sat against a trunk a few paces away with his head bowed and one knee drawn to his chest. His red hair seemed duller than before, tinged with gray and almost blending into the shadows around him. Watching him, relief battled a strange sense of dread. I didn't remember seeing him when I first looked around this area. In fact, I was certain no one had been there a second ago.

"Puck."

He didn't acknowledge me when I called his name, didn't look up as I stopped beside him. Glancing down, I saw a frog perched on his knee, throat sack inflating and deflating as it sat there placidly.

"Goodfellow," I said, trying again. "Can you hear me?"

His head moved very slightly, as if hearing something in the distance. "Someone is talking again, Mr. Croaky," he muttered. "Sounds like ice-boy. The frosty princeling himself." He sighed, mouth curving in a faint, sad smile. "You know, we used to be good friends. I least, I think we were. Hard to remember, now." He looked down at his hands, frowning. "Maybe it's always been like this, I don't know anymore. Maybe he never saw me at all."

"I see you," I said, but there was no response. He continued to stare at his hands, not seeming to hear me at all now. "Puck," I said firmly. "This is just a nightmare. Look at me."

I went to grab his shoulder…and my fingers passed right through him, making my stomach lurch in horror. Puck frowned slightly, his brow creasing as if in pain. Where my fingers passed, they left a stain of colorless gray that slowly started to creep up his arm, turning him pale and transparent.

The Fade. No, not now. I knelt in front of him, feeling helpless as I watched the most infamous faery in the Nevernever flicker like a dying light bulb. The truth of the situation threatened to crush me. This was a nightmare world, but we were still in the Between. If Puck Faded away here, he would be gone for real.

Puck raised his arm, watching curiously as his fingers started to vanish, starting at the tips. "You know, I thought I'd be more upset," he muttered, as the frog continued to ignore him. "But, maybe it's better this way. I can't hurt anyone, and no one can hurt me. Though I really did think I had a chance with Nyx.

I wonder if she'll miss me when I'm gone. Forgotten by a For-gotten. Heh." He paused a moment, the half-there smile fad-ing away, then snorted. "Who are you kidding, Goodfellow? She won't remember. No one will remember you. Your stories are gone."

The creeping gray reached the top of his head, turning him completely transparent. The frog on his knee abruptly fell through, plopping to the grass with a soft thump, and Puck closed his eyes. "Take care of Meghan, ice-boy," he murmured, dropping his hand to his lap. "I know you don't remember me, and I'm not even sure if we were ever friends, but I'm gonna miss you both."

"No," I husked out. "Puck, look at me, dammit." He didn't open his eyes, but I saw the faint crease of his brow again, and could only hope that, somehow, I was getting through. "I see you," I told him. "We are friends, we were always friends. Even those times when I was trying to kill you, I could never see my-self going through with it. Meghan and Keirran are my life, but you—you're my brother. You're as much family as they are, and we have known each other for so long. Don't do this. I can't... imagine a Nevernever without you in it, Goodfellow. It would be incredibly boring."

He frowned, and his eyes finally opened, blinking in surprise as they settled on me, as if he'd just realized I had been kneeling there not three feet away. He was still transparent, though, flick-ering dangerously close to oblivion, and my determination grew. "Meghan needs you, Puck," I said quietly. "The Nevernever is counting on us. This isn't over, and there's still work to do. You can't Fade now. You would be missed more than you know."

"Ash."

Puck's voice was barely a whisper, but hope flickered. I rose and held out my hand to him, never dropping his gaze. "So, stop feeling sorry for yourself," I ordered, "and let's go save

Faery. Unless you want me to tell Nyx you just gave up without a fight."

Puck blinked. A spark of defiance glimmered to life in his gaze, breaking through the apathy, and the empty gray pupils were swallowed by green. Looking up, his eyes met mine, awareness and recognition dawning in his expression at last. Reaching out, he firmly grasped my palm.

The second he did, color returned to his fingers, spreading swiftly up his arm and to every part of him that had gone transparent. As color washed back into Puck, it vanished from the woods around us, as if Puck himself was leeching it from the forest. The trees started to unravel, branches turning white before coiling away into mist.

Still gripping my hand, Puck shook himself like a dog coming out of a deep sleep and grinned up at me, his expression absurdly gleeful. "Oh, ice-boy," he crooned, sounding like his old, irreverent self again. "You *do* care, after all. I'm so touched. But, um, why is the world melting?"

I sighed and pulled Puck to his feet as around us, the Summer Court continued to fray apart. Trees, stones, even the fey themselves drifted apart like cobwebs, spinning away into the ether. "This nightmare is unraveling," I told him. "Nothing here is real except us. I don't know how these worlds can exist, but we have to get out of here before this one disappears completely."

"Okay, I'm going to pretend I know what the hell you're talking about and just nod," Puck said, bobbing his head vigorously. "But getting out of here sounds like a good plan. Where's everyone else, by the way?"

"Meghan is looking for them," I answered, wondering if she had found Grim and the Forgotten. We still had the Evenfey and the ritual circle to deal with, but I wouldn't even think of that until we were all together again. "We promised we would meet up again when we'd found everyone else."

"Uh, meet up where, ice-boy?"

Ignoring Puck's question, I thought of Meghan, holding the image of her in my mind and pushing everything else aside.

"After I dealt with my own thing, all I could think about was finding you," she had said. "When the world began to come apart, I just started walking, and it led me here."

"Come on," I told Puck without turning around. "We're leaving. If Meghan found the others, they'll be waiting for us on the other side of the mist."

"Right behind you, ice-boy. I still have no idea what you're talking about, but I am more than done with this place. Let's go."

We strode back through the Summer Court, between the crowds of unraveling fey, and stepped into the fog, leaving that world and Robin Goodfellow's nightmare behind.

We emerged from the mist, and stumbled into what looked like another forest, this one much darker and more tangled than the pristine woods of Summer. Huge trees surrounded us, interlocking branches shutting out the sky, and the world was dim and gray save for small, shockingly bright splashes of color interspersed through the wood.

Puck drew in a slow, wary breath. "Okay," he said quietly, gazing around. "This is the wyldwood from the looks of things, which is better than the void or a giant spider's nest. But I don't see...oh."

I followed his gaze. A figure stood in the center of a clearing, pale hair glowing softly in the gloom of the wyldwood. Meghan turned, relief crossing her face as her gaze met mine, and my own relief soared. I crossed the space between us and pulled her close, and she relaxed against me with a sigh.

"Ash." Drawing away, Meghan smiled as Puck joined us, giving her a quick, one-armed hug in greeting. Her expression was worried as she gazed up at him. "Puck. I'm glad you made it. Are you all right?"

He shrugged, a somewhat wry grimace crossing his face. "Never better, princess. I really thought I was going to be dumped into some sort of freaky upside-down spider world, but apparently, spiders are *not* my biggest fear. Who knew?"

Meghan's face was sympathetic. "I won't ask if you won't."

"I can live with that." Puck sighed and glanced around the wyldwood, obviously searching for someone. "So, where are Nyx and Furball?"

Meghan winced. "I haven't been able to find them," she said apologetically. "I'm sorry, Puck. I followed Grimalkin's trail here, but I haven't seen either one of them. Either Grim is somewhere else, or he doesn't want to be found."

"Dammit." Puck scrubbed a hand through his hair. "And if Nyx is still in her own nightmare, it's going to be hard to find her, too. Cats and assassins, ugh." He shook his head. "Well, I guess we'd better start looking under every rock and behind every twig until we find them."

A faint chuckle. "That won't be necessary."

We spun. At the edge of the trees, the mist parted, and Nyx appeared like a phantom, making no noise as she did. "I'm here," she stated quietly. "No need to go looking for me. I thought it would be best if I found you, instead."

Puck immediately left Meghan's side, walked across the clearing, and pulled her into a relieved, very passionate kiss, which she returned. A wry smile crossed her face as they pulled back, her golden eyes both relieved and amused as she gazed up at Puck.

"Nice to see you, too, Goodfellow."

"Are you all right?" Puck asked, serious for once. "Meghan and ice-boy keep talking about nightmare worlds. Were you able to get out of…wherever you were, on your own?"

She nodded, and a haunted look flickered through her eyes, gone in the next blink. "A few near-death moments with my old Order," she muttered. "The Lady sent them after me, and I had to watch myself kill them all. Every single one, brothers and sisters I had known my whole life, dead by my hand."

"Ah, man, that's screwed up." Puck's brow creased in sympathy, and he pressed his forehead to hers. "I'm sorry, Nyx."

The Forgotten shook herself. "It wasn't real," she said in a practical voice. "My Order has been gone for a long time, as has the Lady. I serve a different king, now. Once I remembered that, it wasn't easier, but I could let myself fight without hesitation or regret. After I'd killed them all, the world started to come apart, and I realized I was still in the Between. I followed a tunnel of light, and it led me here."

"We experienced something similar," Meghan said, coming forward. "I don't know what the Evenfey was trying to do— maybe it thought we wouldn't be able to defeat what we fear the most. But we made it. We came out of our nightmares and found each other again."

I suddenly felt eyes on my back and turned, staring into the trees surrounding us. For just a moment, I saw a huge black shadow fade back into the undergrowth and disappear. Shining, green-gold eyes flashed in the darkness for a single heartbeat and were gone.

I frowned. *Was that the Wolf? What would he be doing here?*

Puck sighed, still keeping his arms around the Forgotten, who seemed content to stay there for now. "Yeah, but now we have to find Furball," he complained. "And who knows what horrible things lurk in that cat's mind. On the other hand..." He gave an evil grin. "I can't wait to see what our high and mighty Furball is afraid of. He's never gonna live it down, that's for certain."

Something snapped in the trees, drawing everyone's attention. We waited, hands straying to our weapons, as the branches started to move, rustling and snapping as something large came toward us through the forest. The ruckus grew louder as whatever it was drew closer, crashing through undergrowth and snapping twigs, as if it was just plowing its way through the tangle. The bushes in front of us shook violently...

...and Grimalkin stepped into the open.

Everyone blinked and stared at the cat, who peered disdainfully up at us. "Ah, and here you are," he stated, as if he had been searching for us for hours. "Standing around again, I see. I will never understand. Are you ready to depart, or do you wish to stay and debate the circumstances a bit longer?"

"Wait, what the hell, cat?" Puck scowled at the feline, who regarded him calmly. "We were about to go looking for you. This isn't fair—what happened to your nightmares?"

"Nightmares? Me?" Grimalkin gave a contemptuous sniff and trotted away, tail held up straight behind him. I noticed then that the wyldwood had gone even paler, the edges starting to fray apart and drift into the air. "What are you implying, Goodfellow? Do I look like the type of creature that would have such things? As it is, the nightmares are dissolving, as things do in the Between. I suggest we depart, now, before the Evenfey can complete their ritual. We should appear in the same place we first vanished into the nightmare. If you wish to stop the Nightmare King, I would hurry."

The Nightmare King. I took a breath, and felt the power stir in me again, angry and violent, reminding me of why we were here. The Evenfaery waited for us, and behind him, closer than ever, a huge, threatening shadow was starting to rise. I could not allow it to invade our world; I had never heard of the Nightmare King, but I knew he was something I did not want to meet in the Nevernever or the real world.

Just before we followed the cait sith into the gloom and fog, I glanced behind us, at where Grimalkin had first stepped out of the trees. At the very edge of the forest, where a trail of snapped limbs and branches led away into the wyldwood, an enormous paw print could be seen in the mud. There was only one creature who made a print like that, but he was miles away in the Deep Wyld, protecting a group of Forgotten and an exiled king.

I looked up, searching for Grimalkin, but the cait sith was already gone.

16

SUMMONING NIGHTMARE

"You will not stop us."

The Evenfey still stood atop the dais with its back to us, thin arms spread to either side, as we stepped out of the fog. Slowly, it turned, facing us with the stark white skull of its face. *"And here you are again,"* it rasped. *"I'm surprised you found your way back so quickly, but it doesn't matter. The fear, anger, hate, and despair generated by your nightmares was the final surge of emotion the Nightmare King needed. He is awake now. And he is very eager to meet you all."*

"He will have to be disappointed," Meghan said, and gestured sharply. Glamour sparked around her, and a bolt of lightning descended from the ceiling, striking the very center of the platform. The Iron Queen, apparently, was done being diplomatic.

But the Evenfey hissed a laugh, lowering its arms as the dust and smoke around it cleared. The platform was undamaged; no cracks or holes showed in the surface, and the runes continued to throb with power. *"It is not enough, Iron Queen,"* it said. *"Not even you, with all your power, can stop what has been started."*

Rage flickered, and I drew my sword. "Very well," I said, hating this faery and all he was trying to do. "If we can't destroy the summoning circle, then we'll just have to kill the summoner."

"You can try." The Evenfaery took a step back, curling its long fingers into claws. *"But you will fail. I will defend this ritual, and our king, with my life."* The creature's skull turned, eye sockets looking directly at Nyx. *"Evenfey,"* it whispered, *"you are one of us, blinded and deceived. I give you this last chance to stand on the right side. Join us, help us summon our king, and come home."*

Nyx didn't falter. "I *am* on the right side," she said calmly.

"Wrong choice." The Evenfey crouched down, dropping to all four on the dais. *"Then you can die with the rest of the traitors. Nightmare King,"* it implored, stroking the runes with long pointed fingers, *"give me strength. Lend me your power, and I will destroy those who would stop you."*

The runes and symbols surrounding the platform flared, and the Evenfey threw back its head and howled. Its body swelled, limbs and neck extending as it started to grow. Rising to its feet, it towered over us, a twisted shadow monster with long arms and thin grasping fingers. Its deer skull face, antlers bristling atop its head like thorn branches, opened its jaws and roared, making the ground shake beneath us.

Swinging its head down, the huge Evenfey eyed us with flat, blank eye sockets, and for a moment, I felt a prickle of fear at how much it resembled the nearly invulnerable Monster from earlier. But then, the anger rose up, a storm of violence and rage, and my doubts vanished. This creature, this thing that threatened my world, would die. I would destroy it here and now, I would slaughter every Evenfey that stood against us, and if the Nightmare King himself appeared before me, I would kill him, too.

The creature howled and leaped down the steps at us in a blur of darkness. As it hit the ground, the floor rippled and turned black, as if swallowed by shadow. I could suddenly hear voices, muffled and indistinct, but filled with fury, grief, hate, and despair. A distant, angry mob on the verge of erupting into violence. The emotions clawed at me, raw and visceral, and I could feel my own fury rising in response.

I threw out my arm and sent a storm of ice spears at the monster. They flashed through the air, lethal and glittering, but were swallowed by the void of the creature's body and disappeared, not seeming to harm it. As the ice flurry vanished, a flock of screaming ravens descended on the monster, flapping around its skull-like head. The monster ignored the birds, but with a crackle of energy, lightning erupted around it, strands of blue-white power flickering madly over the floor and ceiling. It recoiled, flinching in the sudden light, and I charged, seeing a flash of bright red as Puck came at it from the other side. The lightning storm flickered out just as we reached the monster, who saw us coming and reared up with a howl.

With a snarl, it lunged, swiping at me with a long black talon. I stood my ground as the claw swept at my head and brought my blade down with a snarl of my own. The sword cut through the slicing fingers, severing all but one, which immediately dissolved into coils of smoke around me. At the same time, I saw Puck dart beneath the creature's leg and slash the back of its knee. It staggered, and Nyx dropped out of the shadows above, the moonlight blades passing through the beast's neck and out the other side. The creature's body rippled into smoke, the bleached deer skull dropping from the shadowy mass to clatter to the floor.

"Whew." Puck lowered his arms, staring at the ghostly tendrils that writhed away on the air. "That was easier than I thought. This one wasn't nearly as scary as the big guy was. Giant deer skull notwithstanding."

He rapped the skull with the back of his knuckles, and the head moved. It rattled, then swiveled around to glare at Puck with empty eye sockets. Puck let out a yelp and leaped backward as the skull's jaws opened with a piercing hiss, then shot straight into the air, flying high overhead.

I felt a surge of rage and hate, as around us, the shadows began rising from the ground and flowing up toward the skull. A long, thin arm rose from the darkness, reaching toward the skull, and the creature's body followed, rising out of the inky floor. Grasping fingers uncurled, taking hold of the skull and placing it back on its disembodied neck. Lowering its arms, the nightmare creature gazed down at us again, crimson fire sparking to life in its eye sockets.

Puck groaned. "Dammit, why are all of these big nightmare beasties suddenly invincible?" he wondered, staring up at the newly arisen monster. "It used to be so easy to slay a dragon— just stab it in the one tiny place that wasn't armored. They'd never come back to life. How do we stop this thing?"

I gazed up at the nightmare beast and narrowed my eyes. The anger in me burned, cold and searing. "We keep killing it," I said, "until it doesn't come back."

A streak of lightning flashed overhead, slamming into and passing through the creature's body and the nightmare beast roared. Crouching down, it sunk its long fingers into the floor, and a ripple of hate-filled glamour passed under my feet.

The floor shivered, and thousands of shadowy hands rose out of the darkness. Icy fingers clutched at me, trying to drag me down, as wails and angry voices babbled in my ear. I slashed at the limbs clinging to me, turning several into smoke, but more appeared almost instantly, rising from the ground to rake at my skin and clothes. I felt myself sinking, the floor rising up past my knees, as the arms continued to pull me down. A few paces away, Puck and Nyx were also struggling with the sea of hands, trying to stop themselves from being dragged into the shadows.

The voices scraped in my ears, angry, accusing, full of hate. Icy fingers dug into my skin, their touch chilling, numbing my limbs and making them heavy. I could feel the darkness surging around me, felt myself sinking ever deeper into the mire. It was up to my neck now, cold and clammy against my jaw, and I could still feel myself sinking. I was drowning, but it was an ocean of power I was resisting, a sea of rage and hate and violence, pressing against my consciousness. It called to me, hissing at me to let go, and my Unseelie nature surged in response. The darkness crawled up my cheeks, flooding my mouth and nose, and I suddenly couldn't breathe.

Just before I went under, I saw Meghan, a cloud of smoke and vanishing limbs surrounding her, being pulled into the shadows. Then the darkness filled my vision, and everything went black.

Enough.

I breathed deep, and felt the hate, fury, and violence rush in, filling me with power. My Unseelie side howled in response, reveling in the sudden surge of dark energy. All this anger; it wasn't there to be fought, it was there to be used. I drew it in, feeling my Winter glamour swell like a tidal wave, and released it in a violent burst of magic around me.

The hands clinging to me and the sea of darkness vanished, blown away in a vicious explosion of ice and wind. I rose, opening my eyes, as rage and icy glamour swirled around me, tossing my hair and yanking at my coat. I took a breath, feeling the power expand and fill my veins, and smiled.

The nightmare creature stood on the other side of the chamber, towering overhead. It roared when it saw me, causing the ocean of hands to flail and writhe. Gazing up at the beast, I drew glamour to me and took a single step, bringing my foot down on the shadowed floor.

With sharp crinkling sounds, ice spread out from my boot and raced through the chamber, freezing the floor, climbing the walls, coating everything in a layer of frozen crystal. The shadow hands clawing at the air stiffened and turned to ice, freezing in place, and icicles grew from the ceiling with sharp crinkling sounds. The only thing unaffected was the nightmare beast, which howled in fury as the world around it froze, and started toward me, jaws gaping and eyes glowing red as it charged.

I raised a hand, and a massive icicle formed in the air above me, the point angled directly at the charging monster. With a flick of my wrist, the spear shot forward, slammed into the creature's chest, and passed right through. Grimly, I conjured another, though it was nearly upon me now, and there would be no time for a third.

"Not the heart, prince," someone called as I drew back my hand to throw it. Grimalkin's voice, ringing out somewhere behind me. "The head! Destroy the skull!"

The nightmare beast screamed and lunged at me, talons raking. I hurled the icicle, aiming for the naked deer skull, and the huge spear of ice struck the creature directly in the forehead. The ice shattered, fracturing into dozens of glittering shards, but the monster staggered with a wail, reeling back and clutching its head.

Around me, the carpet of hands vanished, turning into clouds of smoke. Puck, Nyx, and Meghan appeared, gasping as the sea of limbs dissolved and coiled away on the air. Lowering its arms, the nightmare beast roared again, and I saw a crack had appeared in the bony skull, right in the center of its forehead.

"The skull!" Grimalkin's voice came again, making Puck, Nyx, and Meghan jerk up, though the cat himself was nowhere to be seen in the dissolving smoke. "The head is its weak point. Destroy the skull, quickly, and the monster should disappear."

"You could have told us that yesterday, Furball," Puck called, raising his arms with a shimmer of Summer magic. A flock of ravens appeared around him, and Puck himself disappeared, as the swarm of birds rose up and flew toward the approaching monster. They didn't stop, but one by one slammed into the creature's skull with little explosions of black feathers. As it staggered, a beam of lightning descended from the ceiling, hitting it in the forehead with flash and a peal of thunder. Screaming, the nightmare beast fell to its knees, and Nyx appeared above it, hurling a trio of light crescents that struck its head with audible cracks.

I raised my arm, opening myself up to the dark power, to the anger and rage and hate swirling around me. Winter glamour flared, and a huge frozen stalactite appeared in the air above the creature's skull. It continued to grow, until it was bigger than the monster, a lethal frozen point angled right at its head.

The nightmare beast swung its skull toward me, and its burning crimson eyes met my own. Staring into the gaze of the monster, I felt an ancient presence peering out at me. Not the nightmare creature itself, but something even older. Something huge and primordial, and hungry. I felt the emptiness within: a hunger that could swallow worlds and lay waste to everything. For a moment, I felt crushed beneath the weight of its gaze. But then the icy rage flooded in, blocking my fears, shielding me from the ancient presence. I stared into the eyes of a sleeping king and bared my teeth in defiance.

You will not enter this world. I will put a stop to this, right now.

I clenched a fist, and the still growing icicle plunged down, striking the center of the bleached skull and crushing the monster's head to the floor. It let out one final cry that was cut short as the ice pierced through the skull and shattered it. Amid the cacophonous grinding of ice against stone, I heard the faint clattering of bone chips against the rocky floor.

The creature's shadowy body dissolved into smoke, writhed into the air, and vanished. As the broken chunks of icicle settled against the floor and stopped moving, an eerie silence descended on the chamber, broken only by the faint crinkling of ice as it continued to expand over the walls and ceiling.

I breathed deep, feeling a euphoric rush of power course through my veins. I remembered this, having the power of Winter at my fingertips, tapping into the darkness of my Unseelie side. I'd given it up to have a soul, but I'd forgotten what it was like; the raw, vicious power of Unseelie rage. Gazing at the remains of the giant deer skull, now shattered and lying in pieces over the floor, I smiled coldly in satisfaction.

Your avatar has fallen, Nightmare King, I thought, wondering if, on some level, he would hear me. *Stay in your dreams, and leave the Nevernever in peace. Or the same will happen to you.*

Puck landed next to me with a swirl of black feathers, shaking them out of his hair as he rose. "Okay, I officially do not like this Nightmare King," he stated, as Meghan and Nyx joined us as well. "If he's going to be spawning creepies like that, he can stay out of the Nevernever and keep his dreams to himself. Faery is crazy enough without all these nightmares."

A faint chuckle reached me in the silence. Frowning, I gazed toward the broken skull to see the body of the Evenfey, surrounded by bone bits and pieces of ice, lying where the monster had fallen. Its empty eye sockets turned toward us as we approached, and another chuckle escaped the much smaller deer skull.

"*Too late,*" it whispered. "*You are still too late. The ritual is complete. The king rises again, and will enshroud this world in a million fears and terrors when he comes. There is no one with the power to break the summoning circle when he is so close. Evenfey,*" it whispered, turning its skull slightly to look at Nyx, "*when the king arrives, tell him I was proud to serve.*"

Its body flattened, becoming as a literal shadow, before melting into the floor and vanishing. The naked deer skull clattered as it hit the rocks and lay there, lifeless and staring.

Behind us on the dais, the circle of runes flared.

The Nightmare King was coming.

17

THE CIRCLE BREAKS

I sprinted up the steps to the platform, hearing the others close behind. The entire dais was glowing now, runes and symbols almost too bright to look at. They snapped and flared as we stepped onto the dais, filling the air with an ominous humming sound.

I could feel the glamour coming off the platform, swirling in the air around us. The maelstrom of rage, hate, and fear that suffused every inch of this place. I could feel it clawing at me, phantom talons digging into my mind, urging me to use it, to pull all that anger from the air and bend it to my will.

"Okay, so how do we turn this off?" Puck wondered, looking frantically around the circle. "Where's the switch to shut this ride down?"

I shook myself free of the choking fury, clearing my mind. "There is no switch," I said. "We have to break it. The entire platform. Shatter the dais and disrupt the runes. That should end it."

"You sure, ice-boy?"

Impatience flared. "We don't have time to wonder about this," I said. "The Nightmare King is almost here. Break the circle and interrupt the summoning, and we finish this now."

Puck shrugged, then drew his daggers, Summer glamour sparking around him. "If you say so. Though, from what that Evenfey told Meghan earlier, this might be harder than we think. We might have to bring out the big guns."

"Wait."

We paused, turning to Nyx, who stood at the edge of the dais, a conflicted look on her face. "Something is wrong," she confessed, staring at the glowing ring around us. "I don't like this."

Meghan frowned. "What do you mean?"

"I…don't know." Nyx shook her head in frustration. "But this whole place…it feels familiar. I don't think we're supposed to be here." She hesitated, then added, "I don't think we should tamper with the seal."

I narrowed my eyes. "That Evenfey said you were one of them," I said in a lethally quiet voice. "Maybe it feels familiar because you subconsciously want the Nightmare King to return." Nyx stared at me, her expression blank, and my anger flickered to life. "Or maybe it's not subconscious at all."

"Hey, ice-boy." Puck stepped forward, his own eyes narrowed in warning. "What are you trying to say? Whatever it is, I don't think I like it."

I ignored him, staring at the Forgotten instead. It would have been easier for her, I realized, to infiltrate our plans from the beginning. We knew nothing about the Lady's assassin, only that she had allegedly pledged herself to Keirran. She could have been with the Evenfey from the start, and we wouldn't have known until it was too late.

Nyx met my gaze calmly, her expression giving nothing away. "I have been with you from the beginning," she stated in a cool, practical voice. "Before we knew about the Evenfey, or InSite, or this place of power. I don't know why this feels familiar, or why the Evenfey says that I am like him. All I know is that I have sworn myself to the King of the Forgotten, and he has ordered me to aid you however I can."

"She's not a spy, ice-boy," Puck added, glaring at me. "All she suggested was that maybe we don't smash sites of power willy-nilly, which frankly sounds like pretty sound advice to me."

"Please stop, all of you." Meghan's voice, though calm, was steely, as the Iron Queen coming to the forefront again. "There's no time—we need to make a decision now. Ash…" Her blue eyes met mine and softened. "I know you're angry, but Nyx has a point. There is a lot of power coming from this thing, and…" She hesitated, brow furrowing. "I have a weird feeling about this, too. I can't explain it, but this whole place feels forbidden. There's this nagging sensation, like we're not supposed to be here. Maybe we shouldn't tamper with what we don't understand. We don't really know what will happen if we destroy the circle."

I took a breath to stifle the anger and impatience that immediately rose up within. I didn't want to argue with Meghan, but I was tired. I was tired of saving my world from things that wanted to destroy it. I was tired of terrible forces always threatening my family. "We can't take that chance," I said coldly. "The Nightmare King is coming, and this circle is summoning him. We destroy it now, we put a stop to this whole thing."

"Do not be hasty, prince." Grimalkin leaped onto the circle with us. The fur of his tail stood on end, and his golden eyes were a little wild. "There is powerful magic here, as the queen said. I do not believe destroying the seal is a sound plan."

The rage inside was reaching a breaking point. "Do you know what this is, Grimalkin?" I demanded, and the cait sith narrowed his eyes at me.

"No." His tail lashed, annoyed with the admission. "But it feels familiar. As if I have been here before. Which only means that the memory of it has been deliberately blocked or sealed. And if it has been blocked, then it was for a reason. I do not believe we should meddle with the circle until we know exactly what we are dealing with."

"Enough!" The runes surrounding the dais flared red, casting everything in crimson light, and my waning temper finally snapped. "I will not stand here and argue when the Nightmare King is waking up in front of us," I told all four of them. "If you will not destroy the seal, then I will do it myself."

I opened myself to the maelstrom of glamour, and power rushed into me. The anger and fear of the mortal world, all drawn into this spot. My Unseelie nature howled in response, stronger than ever. I stretched a hand over the dais, and saw blue-black veins crawling up my arms, pulsing beneath my skin. Power roared in my ears, filling my senses. I shaped that anger into what I wanted and yanked it into the open.

A rumble went through the chamber, and the ground trembled. Meghan and Puck took a step back, eyes widening, as a huge ice spike surged up through the ground. The stone dais split with a deafening crack as the enormous shard pushed its way into the air, parting rock and earth as it rose toward the ceiling. We all leaped back as the two halves of the dais tumbled away, then ground to a halt on the stones. The runes flared once more then winked out, plunging us into darkness.

For a single heartbeat, there was absolute silence.

Then a torrent of noise erupted from beneath the broken dais, a wail like a thousand voices screaming at once. Light and ghostly faces poured from the hole, howling like bean sidhes, and swirled frantically around the room. Images flashed into my head, memories that weren't mine, people, places, and events that I didn't recognize. The memories continued to pour in, too fast to understand, fragments from a thousand strangers all invading my head at once. The Nevernever. A terrible war. Fear, blood, and death. A group of fey standing in a circle in a place that looked much like this one, arms raised and chanting in one unified voice. A great black wolf was part of that circle, a shaggy gray cat standing opposite him.

And I remembered.

Everything.

PART
III

EVENFALL

There was...another Nevernever, once.

It wasn't called the Nevernever. But it was another realm of Faery, one that existed alongside the mortal world. As the fey of the Nevernever were born from mankind's dreams and fears, the faeries of this world came from their nightmares and most primal emotions. Rage, terror, hate, despair; these were the emotions that created this world and the fey within, and this was the glamour that sustained them. A mirror realm to the Nevernever, it was a world of terror and darkness, ruled by a creature few had ever seen, and the ones that did often went insane. Some called him an Elder god, some called him the personification of fear and rage. To the fey of the mirror world, he was the Nightmare King, and he ruled the realm without opposition.

The realm known as Evenfall.

"Evenfall grows too powerful."

I stood at the edge of an enormous table grown entirely from roots and branches, flowering vines weaving together to form the surface. Around the table, a circle of unfamiliar sidhe looked on with grim expressions. In the deep forest around them, even more powerful creatures looked on. An ancient treant crouched several feet from the clearing, blending perfectly into the surrounding woods, his mossy beard nearly reaching to the grassy floor. A massive creature that looked like a pile of boulders come to life looked on silently, the glow of its eyes the only indication that it was a living creature at all.

And something else watched from the forest. Something old and formidable, lurking in the shadows just out of sight. I couldn't see it, but I could feel its eyes on me. Right now, it wasn't a threat; we weren't in any danger, but just knowing it was out there caused the hairs on the back of my neck to stand up. Even more so than the enormous, bulbous form of the Spider Queen, crouched in the center of her cocoon in the branches overhead.

I gazed around at the circle of fey, knowing them and yet not recognizing them. My consciousness was split; part of me realized I was experiencing someone else's memories, but everything was hazy and dreamlike. Of the sidhe lords and ladies, I knew they all were very powerful, the strongest of their kind. But they were not the kings and queens of the Nevernever. There was no Oberon or Titania, no Queen Mab. I didn't know these faeries' names. In fact, I had never seen them before, never even heard of them. They were all strangers to me.

Except for one.

On the other side of the table, watching everything with a calm, appraising gaze, was the Lady. Looking younger and far less bitter than I remembered, though I had only glimpsed her once. Seeing her now, I felt a rush of both anger and regret. Anger at what she had done—or would do—to Faery, to the Forgotten, but most of all, to Keirran. He had followed her blindly, believed her promises, committed terrible acts for her, and had suffered greatly for it. Gazing at the younger, more innocent version of the First Queen of Faery, I found myself hating her, wishing I could leap across the table and drive my sword into her throat. Maybe if I could watch her die here, before she could put Faery in danger and drive my family apart, maybe then it would erase the flood of remorse I felt for waking her up again. Because, despite my son's reckless decisions, despite never regretting my choice to earn a soul to be with Meghan, the one responsible for freeing the First Queen and turning her loose on the Nevernever again wasn't Keirran.

It was me.

I had been in Phaed that day with Puck, Ariella, Grimalkin, and the Wolf. Where, unbeknownst to us all, the Lady had been sleeping, forgotten, for the past few centuries. Maybe it wasn't just me; maybe our combined glamour had been enough to rouse the Lady from her slumber. But it had been my quest, my determination to be with Meghan, that had put us in Phaed in the first place.

I did not regret what I had done. Everything I had gone through, my entire quest to earn a soul, if I had to do it all again, there would be no hesitation. However, if I could change one thing about the journey to gain a soul, I'd wish that we had never stumbled into that silent, eerie town in the fog. If there had been no war with the Forgotten, if the Lady still slept beneath the Town that Wasn't There, maybe Keirran would still be home.

The fey that had spoken, a tall sidhe noble with silver hair, raised his chin and gazed at the assembled crowd as if he expected opposition. "Evenfall must be dealt with," he insisted, though no one was disagreeing yet. "The mortal realm grows violent. The humans are becoming ever more bloodthirsty, and the Nightmare King grows fat on the hate and fear."

"You say that as if we have no knowledge of what is happening, short-lived one," the ancient treant rumbled. Shiny, beetle-black eyes gleamed in the darkness as it peered down upon us all. "The darkness in the human world can be felt even through the roots of the Mother Tree. The fey of Evenfall spread anger and fear, and the mortals respond as mortals do."

"They are going to destroy themselves." This from the other female sidhe, her cold eyes and blue-black hair reminding me vaguely of Mab. Though there were also white feathers woven throughout the strands, and her cloak was split like a pair of giant bird wings. "If the Nightmare King continues to spread his influence, the mortals will turn on each other and destroy themselves. And then there will be no glamour. If the humans die, the Nevernever will vanish, too."

"But if we slay the Nightmare King," said yet a third sidhe noble, a golden-haired youth with a cape of roses and a swarm of bees around him, "we risk war with Evenfall. The fey of the mirror realm will not take kindly to their king being slain. Are we willing to go to war with the whole of Evenfall should we kill the Nightmare King?"

"You are all being foolish."

The deep, guttural voice came from the trees, from the dense shadows beneath the tangled limbs. A pair of gold-green eyes appeared in the darkness, glaring out at the assembled fey.

"The Nightmare King is not a creature that can be destroyed," the presence growled. "He is the embodiment of fear itself. To the Evenfey, he is nearly a god. None of you are strong enough to challenge him."

For the first time, the Lady spoke. "Then, if we cannot slay him," she began, "we can remove the power that sustains him and all the Evenfey. Without human glamour, his influence cannot continue to grow."

The other nobles immediately made noises of contempt. "Impossible," a female sidhe scoffed. "Evenfall runs alongside the human world just like the Nevernever. To do what you are suggesting, we would have to cut off access to the mortal realm entirely."

"Yes," the Lady agreed. "We would."

Silence fell around the table. The Lady's smile as she gazed around the clearing was triumphant and cold. "We seal away Evenfall," she said again. "To the mortal realm and the Nevernever. The Nightmare King will be trapped, and without glamour, he will eventually Fade away and die."

"Sealing off an entire world." One of the sidhe shook his head. "Is such a thing even possible?"

"Even if it were," the treant said, raising one gnarled, mossy arm, "it is not an option. Not only would we trap the Nightmare King, we would doom all the Evenfey as well. They are different than us, yes. But they are still fey."

"We have no choice," the Lady insisted. "Under the Nightmare King's influence, the mortal world grows ever darker with hate and fear. Already, the humans fight each other. Already, wars have begun, and blood is being spilled every day. The very ground screams with violence, fear, anger, and bloodlust. If this continues, the mortal world will tear itself apart."

"So you say," growled the voice in the trees. "But you don't know that for certain." It snorted. "You two-legs are so impatient. It is your own hubris that convinces you that things must be fixed, and you end up making things worse. You interfere with matters you don't understand, when if you just gave it time, the problem would correct itself. Even the Nightmare King's influence must eventually find balance if he and the Evenfey are to survive. They need the mortals just as much as we do."

"And what would you have us do until then?" the Lady asked coldly. "Shall we delay taking action until it is too late? Until the day we wake to find the Nevernever in eternal darkness because Evenfall has swallowed us whole?"

"It will not work," the treant insisted. "Even if you could accomplish such a thing, the Evenfey themselves will not let it stand. We cannot be certain that every single Evenfey will become trapped on the other side. If even one remains in the Nevernever or the mortal realm, they will not rest until they can break the seal to their realm and release the Nightmare King."

"Unless," the Lady said, "they do not remember. Unless their memories of Evenfall are gone completely."

"A dangerous proposition," said a new voice overhead.

All the nobles turned their gazes upward, to the gnarled branches of a tree where a pair of glowing eyes peered down on them all. The speaker was hidden in leaves and shadows; only the golden orbs of its eyes could be clearly seen, hovering in the gloom. But, the creature attached to the eyes looked bigger than I remembered; much shaggier and wild. A gray paw emerged from the darkness, enormous talons curling around the branch with audible cracking sounds.

"You are talking about erasing the Evenfey from existence," the voice said. "Sealing Evenfall and cutting off their access to the human realm and the Nevernever is essentially making the Evenfey extinct, at least in this world. But sealing their memories will not work. The Evenfey would not remember the Nightmare King, but the rest of Faery would. It would be only a matter of time before they release the seal, and then the Nightmare King will return to take his vengeance upon all of Faery."

"Yes," the Lady agreed, smiling. "If even one remembers the Nightmare King and Evenfall, the seal would eventually be broken. Therefore…"

I felt a chill go through the clearing, as everyone realized what was being presented. "Therefore," murmured a noble, her voice slow and thoughtful, "we must seal away not only Evenfall and the Nightmare King, but *all* of our memories of them as well. Everyone's memories."

"The entire Nevernever," said another.

A growl came from the darkness between the trees, along with a flash of very large teeth. "Foolish," said the guttural voice of the creature within. "Madness. Sealing away Evenfall is bad enough. Erasing their memory from the entire Nevernever will only come back to haunt us."

"I agree," said the voice overhead. "I would advise against this course of action, though I can tell those words will not be heeded." It gave a familiar-sounding sniff of contempt. "Do what you wish, but be aware that this will have dire consequences later on."

"We have little choice," the Lady insisted again. "If we must cut Evenfall away from the rest of the world, we must ensure that it can never be reopened. If no one remembers the Nightmare King, no one will go looking for him. He will fade into obscurity, forgotten, and will no longer be a threat to us or the mortal world."

I felt myself nodding, as the noble whose memories I was experiencing seemed to agree with the Lady. At the same time, it was strangely and bleakly ironic, hearing the Lady speak of Fading away and being forgotten. When, centuries from now, she would wake up, become the Forgotten queen, and start a war with the Nevernever to reclaim what she felt she had lost.

"I do not like this plan," the noble said. "But I fear we must carry it out. Break Evenfall's connection to the mortal realm, and seal away the Nightmare King. But this is a monumental task that will require tremendous amounts of our own glamour to accomplish, and even then, it will be dangerous. This entire circle must agree to work together if we are to have a chance of success. Do we dare risk our very existence to end the threat Evenfall represents?"

"Yes," said the Lady immediately. "I will."

There was a pause, and then the silver-haired noble raised his head. "I will as well."

"I, too, will lend my power," said a third, as around the table, all the nobles were nodding in agreement. "I do not relish losing my memories, but it is for the best. The Nightmare King will not be a threat to the Nevernever much longer."

"Hush," growled the voice in the trees, and enormous fangs gleamed in the darkness as he bared them in a snarl. "Something spies upon us."

The faeries at the table jerked up, looking around. At that moment, I saw a blur of movement overhead, almost too quick to see, as something sprang through the branches of the trees.

My stomach clenched. I recognized the faery, with her black leather armor, silver hair, and twilight skin. I gave a start, but the sidhe around the table reacted quickly. Glamour and magic flared, and the trees surrounding us came to life. Branches reached out, coiling and writhing, and the shadow disappeared into a tangle of wood and leaves. The Lady raised her hand, and a branch lowered with a creak, gnarled branches forming a spiky cage around the hunched form of the Evenfey.

A murmur of anger and alarm went around the table. "An Evenfey spy," one of the nobles hissed. "How dare you come into this sacred place, creature of shadow? Do you know whom you spy upon? We are the high lords and ladies of Faery. You overstep your bounds."

A deep growl came from the trees, where the monstrous shaggy creature peered out with glowing green eyes. "You should kill it now," it said. "If it lives, the Nightmare King will know what you are planning. If you don't wish a war with Evenfall, it needs to die here and now."

The captured faery stared out of the web of branches at us, her golden eyes narrowed and hard. "Treachery," she stated in a cold voice, glaring at us all. "It appears the Order was right.

The fey of the Nevernever cannot be trusted. You would kill us all, erase us from existence, for your own comfort and peace of mind."

"We have no choice, Evenfey," the Lady said, her voice surprisingly gentle. "Don't you see how the mortal world is being affected? The Nightmare King's influence is too strong. The humans will destroy each other if we cannot stop him."

The Evenfaery shook her head. "The Nightmare King draws his power from the human realm, not the other way around," she replied. "If humans are growing angrier and more violent, it is of their own volition, not ours."

"Do not twist words, shadow creature." A tall sidhe noble stepped forward, pointing with a long, thin finger. "Your presence, the very existence of all Evenfey, causes terror and fury. Your king is by far the strongest influence the mortal world has seen."

"You cannot seal us away." The trapped faery's voice held the faintest hint of desperation, though she hid it well. "The faeries of the Nevernever and Evenfall are the same, just different reflections of each other. We are born from mankind's darkest fears and nightmares, in the same way you are born from their dreams and imagination. The Evenfey cannot help their nature, but we still deserve to live."

"We are not suggesting otherwise," the Lady soothed. "But we *will* seal away the Nightmare King, and all of Evenfall, from the mortal realm and the Nevernever. It is not a matter of choice. It is a matter of survival. And sadly, so you cannot return home to warn the Nightmare King, I fear you are going to have to die as well."

She gestured, and the tangle of roots, vines, and thorns contracted like a fist closing, crushing the Evenfey within. I winced, but instead of being torn apart, the faery's body shattered into fragments of light, like the reflection of the moon in a pool of water, and disappeared.

"No." The tall sidhe stepped forward, examining the knot of vegetation. "A trick," he exclaimed, shaking his head. "Curse the Evenfaery—we were talking to a shadow. The spy is gone."

"Then there is no time to waste." The Lady turned to the circle, her voice and expression grim. "If she informs the Nightmare King of our plans, the Nevernever will suffer his wrath. We must seal off Evenfey, and the Nightmare King, now. There is a site in the Between," she went on. "A place of power, where the Veil is thin, and the emotions of mankind flow freely, strengthening it with glamour. I will meet you there, and we will do what must be done. Hopefully before the Nightmare King realizes what is happening."

I blinked, and when I opened my eyes, the scene had changed, as had my memories.

The Nightmare King knew.

The Evenfaery had delivered her message, and unsurprisingly, the fey of the Evenfall had responded in kind. With violence, terror, and fury, trying desperately to stop the ritual from happening. The Nightmare King himself was on his way to the Nevernever, and his terrifying presence could be felt for miles, looming ever closer.

Wind whipped at my hair and cloak, as below me, my stag mount bounded madly through the forest. I was someone else now. The faery whose memories I had been inhabiting before was dead, killed before he could ever reach the ritual site. In fact, all the fey who had been at the meeting that night were being targeted. The faery whose head I was in didn't know how they were being killed; the fey nobles were all very powerful, and the peasant fey of the Nevernever feared them, but somehow, impossibly, the Evenfey had managed to kill one of their numbers.

This notion filled the faery's heart with terror. She had never known the fear of death before. The decision to seal away the Nightmare King was a mistake; they never should have agreed to such a thing. It was that one faery's fault, the youngest member of their circle. She was far too ambitious for her own good. But tonight, it would be over. If she could reach the meeting site, the Nightmare King and the Evenfey would be gone, and no one in Faery would even remember what had happened.

Something bright suddenly streaked out of the trees, and her mount gave a squeal as it toppled forward. She was thrown from the saddle and hit the ground hard, rolling to an undignified stop at the base of a tree. Grimacing, she pushed herself upright, seeing the stag lying a few paces away on the path. A thin shaft of moonlight pierced its throat, and as the beast gave a final shudder and was still, she could suddenly feel eyes on her from the shadows between the trees.

Terrified, she turned in a circle, gathering her power as she scanned the trunks, searching for enemies. Eyes appeared in the shadows, golden eyes the color of the moon, razor-thin blades of moonlight shimmering to life around her.

She screamed.

And I was in someone else's memories.

There weren't many of us left.

Of the circle of fey who had attended the meeting that fateful night, only three had survived, including the faery whose memories I was seeing. The rest were gone, mysteriously slain by the vengeful faeries of Evenfall. Two sidhe stood opposite him, the tall noble with silver hair, and the Lady. Around us, I recognized the dim, eerie light of the Between, all sounds and colors swallowed by the endless wall and curtains of mist. I stood on a large, circular stone dais, surrounded by huge columns and ancient pillars. Mist curled around the pillars and crept over the dais like ghostly fingers, seeking to hide the hundreds of runes and symbols carved into the surface of the rock. Gazing down at them through the faery's eyes, I felt her shiver, as dread curled through her stomach. Something about the circle seemed ominous. She tore her gaze away so she didn't have to look at them.

"Are we ready?" The Lady stepped forward, and her voice was calm, almost triumphant. A stark contrast to the cloud of fear and uncertainty swirling through the air around us. The Lady wore a silver white gown that glowed in the fog, and her pale wings cast a faint nimbus of light around her.

"Why here?" the faery whose memories I was seeing asked. "The Between is not a place I would normally set foot in. Why have you called us to this spot?"

"The ritual must be held in the Between," the Lady replied. "Holding it in the Between is the only way to affect both the mortal world and the faery worlds at the same time. Not only that, it will be difficult for something to stumble across the ritual site so deep in the Between. As long as the seal remains, the spell will be permanent, so it must never be tampered with."

"And if the seal is broken?"

"If it is broken, not only will the way to Evenfall be opened once more, but it will also release all the memories of the Nightmare King and the Evenfey," the Lady replied. "Obviously, we cannot allow that to happen. So we will hide it, and hope that it is never discovered."

The silver-haired noble gazed down at the dais, frowning at the complex sigils and runes carved into the stone. "These are dangerous, complicated signs," he said in a grim voice. "The glamour they require will be immense, and there are but three of us left. Will that be sufficient power for what we plan to do here?"

"It must be," the Lady said. "Evenfall is here. The Nightmare

King himself is at the threshold of the Nevernever. All of Faery is counting on us. We cannot afford to fail."

"No, you cannot," said a slow, familiar voice, coming from overhead. We glanced up, and two glowing golden eyes appeared in the tangle of branches above, peering down at us haughtily.

It took a step forward, and a large gray creature dropped out of the branches to crouch atop a broken pillar. A cat, but many times larger than a simple feline, with extremely shaggy fur and long tufted ears. Its legs and tail were banded with black stripes, giving it a wild look, and huge claws curled from its pads as it settled atop the column, watching us with primeval glowing eyes.

"Foolish two-legs," the enormous cait sith said, as the shock of seeing a much older, wilder Grimalkin rippled through me. "We warned you about the danger of meddling with Faery. You have started something that cannot be undone. And now we must all face the consequences."

"I should have killed the lot of you," growled a deep voice, as a massive shadow prowled toward us through the shadows, stopping at the edge of the light. Even in the darkness, however, the terrifying head and muzzle of an enormous black wolf glared at us across the stones. Its fur was spiky, its fangs almost too big for its jaws. And the feral light shining from its green eyes could make even the oldest fey cold with terror. "You should have left well enough alone," the Wolf told us. "Evenfall would have been content and peaceful had you not decided to antagonize them. But now the Nightmare King is aware, and on his way to destroy the Nevernever. The way to Evenfall must be closed. So be it." The Wolf bared his fangs, sharp teeth gleaming in the darkness. "We will seal away the Nightmare King and doom the Evenfey to oblivion. You will get your wish, but you will need our strength to make it happen."

"Yes," agreed the cait sith, leaping up to perch on the rock.

"A terrible decision, but one you have brought on yourselves. Evenfall must be closed, and the memories of the Evenfey and the Nightmare King stripped from the minds of every living creature. Such a task will not be easy—I have my doubts that you will be able to accomplish it." He gave a sniff, sounding dubious. "I do not even think you have realized the true extent of your decision."

"It will work," the Lady insisted. "With your aid, the three of us together will be enough to complete the ritual. We will be able to save the Nevernever."

"At what cost, though?" Grimalkin glanced down at the circle of runes and symbols, and the fur on his tail bristled. "Be aware—a spell of this power is dangerous, and the Nevernever itself might react poorly. It is possible that some of you may forfeit your very existence, but it cannot be helped now. You wished for this to come to pass, and now we must follow this road to the end. So..." Those eyes narrowed, glaring down at us all. "Shall we begin?"

And so, we did.

Beyond this point, the memories grew hazy, fragmented bits of color and emotion pulsing through my head. How long we stood there, chanting words I couldn't quite understand, pouring glamour and magic into the circle at our feet, I didn't know. It might have been hours, or days. I could feel my magic being drained, sucked away by the circle of glowing runes, as the symbols in the rock changed from white to blue to bloodred. I could feel my body fading, growing exhausted, and still, the circle demanded more. More magic, more glamour and energy, a seemingly endless amount.

I blinked, and suddenly, I couldn't remember where I was anymore, or what I was doing. There were two figures standing to either side of me, chanting over a glowing circle of power, but I didn't know them. With a start, I realized I didn't know my own name. But, though I was aware of all of this, I knew that what I was doing was vitally important. I was compelled to finish, no matter the cost.

A deep snarl came from somewhere behind me, raising the hairs on the back of my neck, though I couldn't turn to see what made it.

Too much, I thought, even as the chanting reached a crescendo, my voice rising along with the others. *It's too much. I can't stop. What's happening to me? Why am I here? Who—who am...I?*

The light flared, and for a few seconds, everything went white.

And then, there was nothing.

The Lady opened her eyes.

She blinked, gazing around in confusion. A misty grove surrounded her, fog drifting over the grass to coil away in the breeze, eerily beautiful under the light of the full moon. She recognized this meadow, one of her favorites in the wyldwood, but she couldn't remember how she had come here. The last thing she remembered was traveling rather urgently through the wyldwood, on her way to...

She couldn't remember that, either. Strange.

Rising to her feet, she frowned, trying to recall the events that brought her here. Something had happened, she thought. Something big. The world felt...unstable. The Nevernever itself was in turmoil, though she didn't know the reason. She could feel the anger and confusion in the air, flashes of panic and desperation, as if all of Faery was reacting to some unknown catastrophe. Subconsciously, she turned her thoughts to the land, to the Nevernever itself, trying to understand.

So much chaos. What has happened? What can I do?

She wasn't expecting an answer, but for just a moment, it was as if she could hear everyone's voices, feel all of Faery's terror and confusion. She gasped, one hand going to her face, as the voices screamed in her head, a torrent of noise and emotion. Just as quickly, the maelstrom faded, leaving her breathless and gasping in the center of the grove. She knew, suddenly, what Faery wanted.

Her shoulders felt heavy with the weight of power they bore, the responsibility dropped at her feet. Whatever had happened, it had caused the structure of the Nevernever to be uprooted, and everything was drowning in uncertainty. If Faery was to survive, it needed someone to step forward, to unite everyone under a single banner. The lesser fey needed someone to follow, or they would succumb to their fear and tear each other apart. She would be that for them. The beacon of hope that held Faery together. The symbol of authority that they would come to love…or fear.

She would be content with either.

There was a ripple of movement behind her, and the Lady turned. For a moment, nothing was there. The trunks and branches of the trees, outlined in black and silver moonlight, were empty. But she was certain she had seen something, and could feel eyes on her from the shadows. They didn't feel dangerous or hostile, just confused like everything else.

"I know you are there," she murmured at last. "Please come out. I am not your enemy, or at least, I am not an enemy you want. Show yourself."

A shaft of moonlight rippled through the leaves, seeming to disentangle itself from the shadows, and a figure stepped into view. A slight faery in black leather armor, silver hair the same color as the moonlight. The Lady had not seen this type of fey before, though she had the strangest feeling that she should know her from…somewhere. The other faery did not attack or make any threatening moves, but the Lady felt uneasy knowing, somehow, that she was quite dangerous. Luminous golden eyes regarded her in wary bewilderment.

"Who are you?" asked the Lady.

For several moments, the strange faery hesitated, as if trying to decide whether or not to answer. Finally, her shoulders slumped and she gave a weary sigh.

"My name is Nyx," the faery said. "And...that is all I know."

The Lady frowned. "What do you mean?" she asked. "Where do you come from?"

"I..." Nyx's brow furrowed, those golden eyes filling with anguish for the barest of moments. "I don't know. But something is very wrong, I can feel it. I know I've lost something, but I can't remember what it is. And you..." Those golden eyes shifted to the Lady, narrowing ominously. Her arms moved, and two blades of light appeared in her hands. "I feel I should know you...and that you've done something unspeakable. Who are you?"

The Lady smiled.

Raising her arms, she reached out and felt the magic of the Nevernever flooding into her, a deluge of glamour and power. The ground at her feet rippled, then sprouted with flowers and vegetation, coiling around trees and rising into the air. Overhead, the sky darkened, clouds swirling together, and lightning flickered between them, turning the world white for a moment.

"The Nevernever has spoken," the Lady said. Her voice echoed in the lightning-charged air and rippled through the earth, making the trees shake and the ground tremble. Nyx staggered away, eyes wide, as the Lady stood before her, bathed in the power of Faery. "A new era has begun. Bow before your queen."

19

EVENFALL ARRIVES

"Ash. Ash, get up."

I jerked awake with a start, my hand instantly going for my sword before I recognized the face in front of mine. Meghan raised her hands in a soothing gesture, her eyes bright with worry and relief as they met mine.

"It's me," she whispered, and I relaxed, though something terrible hovered at the edge of my memory, waiting to break free. I was lying on my back, the ground beneath me hard and cold, and there was a sharp object jutting into my ribs. Overhead, lights flickered through the room, and the rumble of stone echoed in my ears.

"Did you see?" Meghan whispered, and with those words, everything came flooding back. Gritting my teeth, I struggled upright, feeling my head throb with pain. My skull felt like it wanted to burst, spilling memories, emotions, and the terrible knowledge of the past all over the floor of the chamber. I remembered now. I knew what happened, to the Nevernever, to the Nightmare King, and all the faeries of Evenfall. The memories that had been sealed away by the Lady and the other fey swirled around my head, screaming in pain and betrayal.

I felt sick with the realization. Evenfall wasn't an event. Evenfall was the other side of Faery, the mirror realm of the Nevernever. An entire world of faeries and creatures just like us. And the fey that had come before had committed an atrocity, sealing away the Nightmare King and cutting Evenfall off from everything. And to make things worse, they sealed the memory of what they had done from the entire world, dooming the Evenfey to obscurity and being forgotten.

The Forgotten. My stomach clenched. How many of the Forgotten were actually Evenfey, hanging on to existence by a thread, longing for a home they couldn't even remember? Rage filled me, echoes of the Lady's betrayal ringing in my head. The Nightmare King might have been a true threat, but to seal off an entire world...

"You saw, didn't you?" Meghan's voice came again, and I nodded. "That they sealed off Evenfall and made everyone forget. Even Grimalkin was in on it, and the Wolf. Was the Nightmare King that big a threat?"

"I don't know," I murmured in reply. "Maybe we should ask him."

"Screw Furball," said another voice behind us, and Puck staggered into view. Blood trickled down one side of his face, and his green eyes were hard as he gazed at something over our shoulders. "I think we have bigger problems to worry about."

I turned, and my heart froze in my chest.

The dais had been shattered, huge ice spikes still jutting into the air through the stone. Broken chunks of rune inscribed rock lay everywhere, the glow completely faded and dead. But where the seal used to be, an enormous tear of darkness had opened, a pit opening into the void, and it was slowly spreading over the ground like a stain of ink.

"Evenfall," Meghan whispered, as the horror of what I had done finally hit me. The circle, the one I had destroyed, hadn't been to summon the Nightmare King. It had been the seal to Evenfall, and all the memories the Lady had erased from the Nevernever. By destroying it, not only had I released those memories, I had also torn open the way to the mirror realm.

The path to the Nightmare King was open. Evenfall had come.

And I was the one who ushered it in.

"At last," whispered a voice.

There was ripple of movement, and a bleached deer skull slid across the floor like the head of a huge serpent, trailing shadows behind it. It slithered up a broken column and rose into the air, and the gloom around it materialized into the Evenfey I thought we had killed. Swinging its naked skull toward the gash of darkness, it raised both arms as if welcoming something home.

"It is open," the Evenfey breathed. *"Evenfall has come. At last, after so many centuries, we can return home."* Its hollow eyes turned to me. *"Unseelie prince,"* it whispered, *"you have my eternal gratitude. For destroying what the Lady accomplished so long ago. My apologies for the deception, but you played your part better than I could have imagined."*

Rage flooded me, and the power of the Unseelie flared to full strength. The Evenfey let out a chuckle that sounded like bone chips rattling against each other. *"It's addicting, isn't it, Unseelie?"* the faery whispered. *"The rage, and the power that comes with it. Only the rulers of Faery, or a fey with equivalent magic, could have any hopes of breaking the seal. You are not a king, but your anger was inspiring. And now, the way to Evenfall is open at last, all thanks to you."*

Abruptly, the top of the pillar where the Evenfey stood exploded with long spikes, frozen spears surging into the air. The faery's shadowy body frayed apart, but the skull flew away un-harmed. Drifting down, it hovered before the ever-widening gash to Evenfall, before a shadow rose from the floor and at-tached itself to the deer skull again.

"*So impressive.*" The skull tilted to the side, regarding me. "*You are very much like us, Winter prince. A pity the Nightmare King is going to destroy this world. Your anger is nothing compared to the fury of a god who has been sealed away for an eternity. Even slumber-ing, one of his nightmares was nearly enough to kill you all. When we fully wake him, the Nevernever will be no more, and the Evenfey will be all that remains.*"

Meghan stepped forward, her own power flaring to life around her, but at that moment, a dreadful howl echoed through the chamber, coming from the pit torn in reality. It swept over us, and the sheer rage and hatred coming through the portal hit me like the force of a typhoon. I staggered back, buffeted by the power and fury of it all, and the Evenfey cackled.

"*It stirs,*" the Evenfaery hissed, sounding ecstatic and trium-phant. "*It remembers. Everyone remembers. All of Faery, all of Even-fall. Sister…*" it called, turning its head to the side. "*Now you know. You understand, do you not? How you were betrayed? Why the fey of the Nevernever are your enemies? Do you remember now?*"

"I remember," said a soft voice in the shadows. "Everything."

Nyx melted from the darkness, coming to stand between us and the pit to Evenfall. I stiffened, as the assassin's cold eyes swept over us. Her blades were out, in both hands, and the look on her face caused my Unseelie nature to stir in warning. I knew that expression. I'd seen it before, on my own face, and knew the assassin was very dangerous right now.

"Nyx," Puck breathed, but for perhaps the first time I'd known him, did not say anything more. But what could he say? We all knew the truth of what had happened. The meeting in the grove with the council of sidhe, and what happened between the Lady and the assassin afterward told us everything.

"I was Evenfey," Nyx stated in a voice of deadly calm. "Evenfall was my realm. Before any of you existed, I served the Nightmare King. Our home was stolen by the faeries of the Nevernever, our king banished and sealed away, and the rest of us doomed to Fade into nothing. To become Forgotten, because we didn't fit into your perfect world."

"Nyx." Meghan stepped forward, making me tense. The assassin's eyes were still hard as they shifted to Meghan, her expression unyielding. "I know this is a shock. I understand you're confused right now, but—"

"No, Iron Queen." Nyx shook her head. "I'm afraid it is you who does not understand. I am not confused. For the first time in centuries, everything is perfectly clear. I know who I am, and where I came from."

"Yes," hissed the Evenfey above her. "The Lady and all her kind betrayed you. You served her for years, when she was the one who took our home and sentenced us all to death. And now, these fey would do the same."

Nyx didn't move. The Evenfey floated down until it was standing behind her, that bleached deer skull inches from her ear. "Now, kill them, sister," it whispered. "They are no better than the ones who betrayed us. They strive to close the way to Evenfall, and keep our king in eternal slumber. The fey of the Nevernever are treacherous, the same as the Lady and her ilk. We cannot exist together in harmony, not now, when you know the truth."

It pointed at us with a long black finger. "Kill them," it urged. "You are one of us. You have always been one of us. Our king wakens, and will destroy this world when he comes, but these fey do not deserve to see his glory. We cannot exist together, and you are a beautiful agent of death. It is the only answer."

"I agree," Nyx said softly.

She spun, her blade coming up in a vicious arc, a flash of light that appeared for a blink before it was gone. The Evenfaery jerked, stood motionless for a second, and then the bleached deer skull toppled from his shoulders, hitting the ground with a crack, before shattering on the stones. The shadowy body frayed apart, becoming tendrils of black fog that writhed away into nothing.

I stiffened, as Puck drew in a slow breath. That was not what we had been expecting.

"I am Evenfey." Nyx lowered her arm as the dark mist curled around her and disappeared. "The Lady betrayed us, but she is gone now. What was done to us, our king, and our realm was unforgivable, but…" She paused, closing her eyes, as if coming to an impossible decision. "If the Nightmare King wakes, he will destroy this world," she whispered. "And I have learned too much, and have seen too much, to let that happen. I swore myself to Keirran, and he has already defeated the Lady. I am Evenfey, but I don't want this world to die."

I felt Puck's relief, though it faded as the assassin opened her eyes, rage and hatred shining from hard yellow eyes. "Mark my words, though," she warned, "I will never forgive what was done to us. I am going back to Evenfall it has been too long since I have seen my homeland, and perhaps I can stop the Nightmare King before he awakens completely. So, this is where we part ways. I'm grateful that I met you, but it is time I go home."

"Nyx, wait." Puck stepped forward, and surprisingly, the assassin paused, glancing back over her shoulder. "Don't go," he pleaded. "Don't run out on us now. Whatever you're planning to do, let us help. We can still stop this together."

"Puck." Her eyes softened for the briefest of moments. "I wish I could have seen the Nevernever with you," she murmured. "I almost wish I didn't know the truth right now. But that doesn't change what has happened. You're part of the Summer Court, and I don't belong there. Maybe someday we'll meet again, but don't try to find me. If I see you in Evenfall, I might have to kill you."

Another howl came through the open portal, like a hundred voices screaming in fear and rage. There was a sound like the flutter of a million dragonfly wings, and a huge swarm of nightmare piskies burst through the opening, shrill voices hissing in my ears. They swirled through the air in a dark cloud, frantic blips of terror and fury, before scattering in every direction and vanishing into the ruins.

When I looked back at the portal, Nyx was gone.

"Dammit." Puck slammed his fist into a pillar, causing it to tremble. "Dammit," he breathed again, bowing his head. "I really liked that one. Did I catch your curse or something, ice-boy?" he asked, glancing at me with a bleak look. "Maybe I should just become a hermit in the woods who only talks to squirrels."

Meghan stepped beside him, putting a hand on his shoulder. "We'll find her," she promised. "Now that Evenfall is open, I'm afraid we're going to have to deal with the Nightmare King. Whether that means reasoning with him, or preventing him from waking up again, I'm not certain. But I bet that's where Nyx is going. Back to her king."

Puck took a quick breath. "Yeah," he said, giving Meghan a weak smile. "Yeah, she's not getting rid of us that easily. If she thinks we're not going to follow her to Evenfall, then she doesn't know me well at all." His smile turned into a somewhat evil smirk. "Besides, we have an appointment with royalty. I'm sure the Nightmare King will go back to his nappy time if we just reason with him."

"You cannot reason with him," said a new voice, as Grimalkin appeared, perched on a stone column several yards away. Anger stirred as the cat peered down at us. He had been there. He had been part of the ritual to close Evenfall. Maybe he hadn't said the actual words, but he knew what was going on. Of course, by that time, the Nightmare King might have been on his way to destroy the Nevernever, so they hadn't had much of a choice. But with all his knowledge, I was almost certain he could have come up with something, some other way, to appease the Nightmare King and save Evenfall.

Grimalkin met my stare with flat gold eyes and pinned his ears, as if he knew what I was thinking. "The Nightmare King cannot be reasoned with," he said again. "He is not fey. Perhaps he was at one point, long ago, or perhaps he was some sort of ancient god. But now, he is a force of hunger, rage, and emotion. He is the darkness of the world given form, the shadow self of mankind and faery alike, and now that he has been sealed away for so long, he will know only two things—hunger and fury. You cannot reason with him. He will not hear you. If he is freed, if the Nightmare King wakes once more, not only will he destroy the Nevernever, he could very well move on to the rest of the world."

Silence fell for a moment after that statement, the gravity of the situation weighing heavily on us all. We had been here before, facing down cataclysmic prophecies, fighting to save the Nevernever from certain doom, but this one…felt different. This one, as Meghan had stated once before, felt like the big one. The prophecy to end them all. Like we really were standing at the brink of The End, and if we didn't succeed this time, that was it for everyone.

"So," Meghan said quietly, "another End of the World situation, huh?"

Puck snorted. "Must be a Tuesday."

A ripple of glamour hissed through the opening, furious and hungry, raising the hairs on the back of my neck. I could sense a tide rising from the pit, swelling and growing ever larger as it came toward us, a tsunami ready to break over us all.

"Heads up," I warned, and raised my sword, feeling the violence and power of Winter course through me. "Something is coming."

Puck and Meghan fell silent, listening, and for a moment, the stillness throbbed against my skin. Then, a new sound began emerging from the portal, a faint clicking, rustling sound. Like hundreds of feet or hands, moving toward us over the stones.

Meghan rose and came to stand beside me, sword at the ready. "Whatever comes out of there," the Iron Queen said, "we can't let them through. If they get past us into the Nevernever, it will be chaos. It's up to us to hold them here."

"Yeah, but for how long, princess?" Puck asked, and raised an arm, gesturing to the hole in reality. "That isn't the entrance to a movie theater, you know. There's a whole freaking world on the other side. How long do you expect us to hold the line?"

"Until they stop coming. Or until something arrives to close it."

The clicking noise got louder. And then several large, bloated creatures crawled out of the opening, wincing as they came into the light. At first they looked like a huge half-spider creatures, with elven heads and torsos welded to an arachnid's body. But then I saw that the spider's "legs" weren't legs at all, but long fleshy fingers, with jagged fingernails scraping against the stone as they crawled forward. A dozen hairless, eyeless heads turned toward us, circular mouths opening to bare dozens of hooked white teeth. They screeched and scuttled toward us over the floor, and Puck leaped to his feet with a curse.

"Oh, what the hell! Just when I thought spiders couldn't get any worse!"

The spider creatures leaped at us, terrible mouths gaping to nearly cover their entire faces. I lashed out as one came at me and sliced its fleshy, shrieking head from its body. The creature collapsed to the stones, burst apart, and turned into swarms of real spiders that scrambled away in all directions.

Puck let out a vehement curse.

"Okay, I am officially done! No. No, no, no." He leaped back, dancing around a trio of spider things that scurried toward him, hissing. "Nope, nuh-uh, no. Do not like. I hate this place. I hate this place, let's kill everything and burn it to the ground so we don't ever have to do this again."

I sneered, slicing multiple legs from a creature's twisted body. It collapsed to the ground, scrabbling with its remaining four, and I plunged my sword through its bloated thorax. "Scared, Goodfellow?"

"Of nightmare spider things with fingers for legs and giant lampreys for a face? Whatever gave you that idea, ice-boy?" A spider creature reared up, revealing a huge mouth on its stomach with a pair of curved black fangs waving in the light, and Puck gave a yelp that was higher-pitched than anything I'd ever heard from him.

Meghan's sword came slashing down, cutting into the spider creature threatening Puck, splitting it in two. Raising her arm, she blasted another pair with lightning, and they reeled back, shrieking, before exploding into tiny spiders. "Get it together, Puck," she ordered, raising her weapon as the rest swarmed in. "If you're going to shriek at every nasty that jumps out and says 'boo,' you'll be exhausted before the second wave ever gets here."

"Ohohoho, touché, princess." Puck grinned, a spark of defiance flickering to life in his eyes. And for a moment, despite the bleakness of the situation, it was like old times again: me, Meghan, and Puck facing unspeakable odds together. "You've been waiting years to say that, haven't you?"

The spider creatures pressed forward, a hissing, scuttling swarm. Despite their horrific appearance, they died easily on my sword as I cut them from the air. Briefly, I wondered why so many had an almost crippling fear of spiders, to the point where giant spiders and spiderlike monsters showed up in almost every culture and stories across time. I supposed some fears were universal. Still, they died quickly, no match for the three of us. Even Puck got his act together, though he still complained every time a nightmare creature erupted into a spider swarm and skittered to all corners of the ruins.

But that was only the beginning. Just the first wave, as Meghan had said.

20

ENDLESS

I lost track of how long we stood against Evenfall. More creatures poured through the opening, monstrous and terrifying. Vipers with human hands that crawled toward us on pale fingers. Silent gray men with glowing white eyes, their feet never touching the ground as they floated forward. Huge crows with skulls for heads that reeked of death and carrion as they swooped through the opening. And the pit to Evenfall continued to widen.

The power of Winter rose ever higher, fed by fury and the nightmare glamour swirling throughout the ruins. The very ground was steeped in it—anger, fear, hate, rage, an intoxicating mix of volatile energy that the Unseelie nature reveled in.

I cut down a nightmare leaping toward me, hating them all, feeling my rage soar with every swing of my blade. Monsters and abominations. If I had to destroy every one of them to protect my family and my world, I would. If I had to become the very evil I was facing to save everyone, so be it. Let the nightmares come. In the end, they would be the ones who would know true fear.

And still, I could feel myself holding back. Not giving in completely. Perhaps it was subconscious. Perhaps it was my very soul that kept me from becoming a true Winter fey again. Though the power beckoned and my Unseelie nature goaded me on, urging me to take that final step and embrace the darkness, I still hesitated.

Puck dropped beside me, breathing hard. "This is never-ending," he muttered, ducking as a winged nightmare swooped over his head, and a few strands of bright red hair went spiraling to the floor. He raised an arm as it swooped back, and a branch from a nearby tree hissed down and smacked the creature from the air. "Ugh, they just keep coming. Not that I don't love a good fight against overwhelming odds, but even we can't keep this up forever."

With a guttural snarl, a massive, wolflike thing clawed its way up from the hole, panting and slavering as it heaved itself into the open. It was even larger than our Wolf, its shaggy head brushing the tops of a few trees as it swung around. It raised its head and howled, and its jaws split its entire chest, baring a maw of fangs to the light. Lowering its head, it bunched its muscles and charged, huge unnatural jaws gaping to swallow us all.

There was a ripple of iron glamour behind me, and several roots broke through the surface, stabbing into the air. The branches glittered with steel thorns as they shot forward, twining around the nightmare wolf, which gave a very human scream of pain as the roots contracted, pinning it in place. I leaped forward and brought my blade down on its neck, and the shaggy head tumbled free, thumping against the stones.

The wolf's body shuddered, slumping against the branches. Panting, I glanced back at Meghan and Puck, who met my gaze wearily. Meghan, especially, looked exhausted, but before I could say anything, the head of the nightmare wolf, lying in the dirt, twitched. Faster than I thought possible, it flipped upright, jaws gaping, and lunged at Meghan. As the slavering maw snapped shut, completely hiding her from view, there was a crackle of energy, and lightning strands erupted from between its teeth. The wolf's disembodied head jerked, twitching and convulsing, until it finally slumped to the ground. Its jaws opened, tongue lolling between its fangs, and it finally seemed to die.

"Meghan!"

I reached the wolf's muzzle, pried it apart, and dragged a grimacing Iron Queen into the open. She was breathing hard, and blood welled from one shoulder where a wolf fang had caught, but she was alive.

"I'm all right," she gasped as I pulled her close. "I'm okay, Ash. I just need...a second to catch my breath." Eerie wails echoed up from the pit, causing Meghan to glance over with a grimace. "Of course, they're not going to give us that, are they?"

Rage battled relief and a growing desperation. This wasn't working. We couldn't keep this up, not with the amount of creatures coming through the gate. Meghan was hurt, Nyx was gone, and we were all reaching the limits of what we could do.

With piercing cries, a flood of creatures spiraled up from the pit, descending on us in a glittering swarm. Their faces were elven and beautiful, but their bodies were wasplike, with serrated limbs like a praying mantis. They surrounded us, slashing with their arms, their movements frantic and quick. Still kneeling, I cut several down, protecting Meghan as best I could. But a curved blade scored my back, tearing a line of fire across my skin, and my rage soared.

Enough. Die, insects!

I reached out, drawing on the glamour surrounding us, and released it in an icy burst. Ice instantly spread over everything, pointed spears glittering off trees and stones, and the swooping creatures went crashing to the ground and careening into rocks as their wings froze, some impaling themselves on the spikes. I breathed in the fury-drenched air, feeling the power surge through me, and slashed a final Evenfey in half as it fell from the ceiling.

Meghan shuddered against me. "Ash, you're freezing," she whispered. "What...?"

She stiffened, and the hand gripping my own turned my palm over, revealing my wrist and forearm. Blue-black veins stood out against my skin, crawling up my arms like inky tendrils. Staring into my face, her eyes widened. I saw my own reflection in her gaze, my eyes glowing icy blue, my pupils shrunk down to pinpricks. More tendrils of darkness crawled up from neck, spreading over my jaw. Meghan touched my cheek, and her fingers were like burning coals against my skin.

"What's happening to you?"

Her voice was suddenly terrified. Blood streamed down her arm, her face was pale, and her muscles shook with exhaustion, but she had not wavered or shown any signs of fear until now. "Ash..."

"I'm fine," I told her. More than fine. I felt powerful again, the strength of my Winter glamour fully restored. The anger and hate swirling through the ruins fed my Unseelie nature and made it stronger than ever. My blood had chilled, all pain, doubt and weakness of the flesh frozen to nothing. My back had been slashed open by the claws of the praying-mantis fey, and I couldn't even feel it.

A stale wind howled through the opening before Meghan could answer, and the rush of glamour accompanying it made my senses prickle. Fear, mixed with pure, undiluted rage. Something was coming, looming ever closer on the other side of the gash. Something...enormous.

A massive claw, nearly as big as I was, suddenly gripped the edge of the portal. Another appeared on the other side, as something huge and terrible began rising up from the depths. A head emerged, chilling and familiar, a massive creature with blazing white eyes and antlered horns crowing its shaggy head. Black tendrils crept out from the portal and spread across the floor, as the Monster, the thing that had destroyed Touchstone, hunted us through the Briars, and nearly ended our lives before, came through the opening, lifted its head, and let out a roar that shook the pillars.

The dreams of the king. His Elder Nightmares brought to life.

"Crap," Puck whispered. He staggered back a pace, grimacing, as the nightmare creature took one thunderous step forward. "Not this thing again. I barely remember how we beat it last time, and I'm not feeling nearly so cheerful now."

Meghan took a deep, shuddering breath. "We've killed it before," she said quietly, though I still held her hand, and felt it tremble under my fingers. Despite her words, she was nearly spent. Even the Iron Queen's power had limits, and her reserves of glamour was almost gone. "We can beat it," Meghan insisted. "We just have to work together."

I glanced at Puck, as doubts prickled. The last time, it had been the Great Prankster who had figured out the Elder Nightmare's weakness. In his ridiculous Goodfellow way, he'd made the rest of us forget our fear by playing a battle tune on his panpipes and dancing around the Nightmare as it tried to stomp on him. Absurd as it was, it had been enough to turn the tables and bring the creature down.

That wouldn't be an option here. Puck did not look up to playing a tune or singing a song now. The anger, despair, and grimness of this place saturated everything, killing any thoughts of hope or happiness. Even if Puck did manage to bounce back to his normal irreverence, I couldn't see it having any effect on the Nightmare in front of us.

And then, another head appeared, twisted and crowned with antlers, as a second monster pushed its way through the gash. A third followed, snarling as it came into the light.

And a fourth.

"Oh, come on," Puck groaned, and Meghan's grip on my hand tightened. Four Nightmares. If even one of them got past us into the Nevernever, they would corrupt it and all the faeries they came across, just like the Monster did in Touchstone. Somehow, we would have to kill all four here, before they could invade the Nevernever.

I knew, with cold certainty, that we wouldn't be strong enough. Not as we were.

The Unseelie within raged at me, furious and defiant. *You can be strong enough*, it snarled. *You know the way. Give up your weakness. Embrace the darkness and become as you were.*

As I was before. My hands trembled. I understood now, what was holding me back. If I wanted to use the power around me to its fullest, I would have to become pure Unseelie again. A full fey, with no human weakness or conscience to hold him back. It meant I could completely lose myself to the rage and violence around me, and that power would be mine.

It meant I would have to give up my soul.

Part of me recoiled in horror. I had gone to the End of the World, faced trials and monsters, endured tests that should have killed me, to become the first faery that was ever granted a soul. I'd done it so I could be with the woman I loved in the Iron Realm, for to gain a soul was to become human. But it also meant I wasn't fully fey. I was something between, neither faery nor mortal, and I had given up a portion of my Winter glamour in exchange. Without a soul, I could become that Unseelie prince again, one that was even more powerful, who used anger and hate to their full effect. Who might even rival Mab and the rulers of the Faery courts.

But at what cost? If I gave up my soul, what would I become? Could I even return to the Iron Realm? If I lost Meghan, would my life be worth anything at all?

Across the ruins, the four Nightmares roared and bared their fangs as inky tendrils crept across the ground and began choking the life from the trees. At the edge of the pit, more things began crawling out, a whole new wave of enemies that filled me with hate and despair. This would never end. The nightmarish glamour in the ruins grew suffocating, drenched in rage, hate, and fear. *And if you die here*, the Unseelie side of me whispered, *what would it matter? If the Nevernever falls, if these Nightmares kill you all right now, you've already lost everything. Being able to return to the Iron Realm will matter for nothing if there is no queen there to rule it.*

Gazing across the ruins at the wave of creatures and the looming Nightmares, the dreams of a sleeping god, I set my jaw. What would I sacrifice for the ones I loved? I had risked my very existence to gain a soul so I could be with Meghan in the Iron Realm.

I would sacrifice it, and my humanity, to save her.

So be it. Ice flooded my heart, as I made my decision. Gently, I lowered Meghan back against a smooth rock, being careful not to jostle her wounds. "Wait here," I told her. "I'll take care of this."

Her blue eyes met mine, anguished and desperate. "Ash, what...?"

I brushed her cheek. "Trust me."

Knowing she would. She had always trusted me, even when I didn't deserve it. I certainly didn't deserve it, now. Glancing at Puck, who was watching us with a wary frown, I felt a brief stab of regret. I was going to betray him, too, in the end. "Stay with her, Goodfellow," I told him. "I won't need your help. Not this time."

His green eyes narrowed. "What are you doing, Ash?"

"Ending this," I said, and whirled, striding toward the Nightmares that waited at the edge of the portal.

21

STOPPING EVENFALL

*T*his is what you always were.

I tried clearing my thoughts as I walked steadily across the chamber, preparing myself for battle as I had a thousand times before. But my thoughts were consumed with anger, and the only thing I could feel was hatred for the creatures before me. The desire to cut them into pieces and watch them writhe away into nothing. The horde of smaller enemies shrieked and bounded toward me, and my bloodlust soared, welcoming the inevitable slaughter.

You were always Unseelie. You were always meant to be cold and violent and ruthless. Hate is your legacy, and the power of Winter has always been fueled by anger. Become the Winter prince again and destroy all your enemies. Destroy everything that stands against you.

I reached out and the power was there, an endless well of fury and rage. It flowed into me, vicious and violent, a maelstrom that coated the pillars and the ground at my feet with ice. Casually, I raised a hand, and the first wave of enemies coming at me froze, turning to ice midlunge before shattering into fragments.

I felt a flat, chilling smile cross my face as the darkness within surged higher. Power and nightmare glamour swirled around me, whipping at my coat and freezing me from within. I could feel myself getting colder, like ice was spreading through my veins, freezing out all emotion or weakness. My skin had gone numb, all the warmth disappearing, and bits of ice began spreading across my cheeks and arms. It wasn't painful at all, and the Unseelie within laughed in glee.

The Nightmares howled and stalked forward. Raising both arms away from my sides, I gathered more anger to me and sent a wave of Winter glamour out before me. Winds whipped into a fury, howling through the air as they became a shrieking blizzard, pelting the approaching mob with ice and snow.

Colder, the Unseelie hissed, as fury and bloodlust surged. The horde of nightmare beasts slowed as they crossed the ruins, fighting wind and driving bits of ice. Drawing my sword, I raised an arm and froze another wave, shattering them into tiny fragments, as the Unseelie goaded me on. *Freeze your weakness. Destroy them all. Claim your destiny, and become the Winter King.*

Deep inside, I could sense a tiny light flickering against the flood of power and darkness, growing dimmer as the rage and fury swirled around it. For just a moment, I faltered, uncertainty overshadowing my thoughts. Once done, there'd be no going back. If I took this final step, I could never return to what I was.

No. I would not waver. I would not back down. If I had to give up my soul to save the Nevernever, I would. If I had to become the Winter King to keep my family and my world safe, so be it. Let the rage and cold consume me; I was Unseelie. I was born in darkness, and my legacy was death. This was what I had always been.

The light inside sputtered, flickering even more weakly

against the cold. The darkness pressed down, suffocating it, and the storm of power and rage tore at it viciously. It pulsed one final time, a last attempt to exist, before snuffing out completely.

"Ash, stop!"

Something grabbed my arm from behind. I spun, power and ice flaring around me, and met Meghan's eyes.

Her expression was anguished as she gazed up at me, and the terror on her face made me pause, the maelstrom inside sputtering for just a moment. The Unseelie snarled at her, urging me to strike her down, the once-human queen who dared challenge me.

"Stop," Meghan whispered again, her fingers shaking as they clutched my arm. "Ash, please don't do this."

"Get back." My voice dropped the temperature of the air between us, and Meghan shivered. Wind tore at her, snow and ice chips pelting her skin, but she didn't flinch or step away. "This must be done." I raised an arm toward the pit, toward the Monsters and the wave of enemies fighting their way through the blizzard. The horde of smaller enemies slowed down the Nightmares, but their combined auras sent pulses of hate and dark glamour rippling through the air, spreading inky tendrils over everything. "We're not going to stop them otherwise. This is the only way."

"At what cost?" Meghan asked. Her grip on my hand tightened, searing hot against my skin as she shook her head. "Ash, look at me. Can't you see what you're becoming?"

I looked into her eyes. A pale, white-haired creature met my gaze, icy veins completely covering his neck and spread across his cheeks. His eyes, empty and completely blue, hovered on the edge of madness as he stared at me.

Shock and unease rippled down my spine. I'd seen that look before, in the eyes of Queen Mab, just before her wrath froze a room, or encased a creature in ice to endure a living death for eternity. I'd felt the fear when she turned that gaze on me, knowing that when that madness took her, no one was safe. Mab ruled through violence and terror, as was the legacy of the Unseelie Court. That heritage, that inheritance of anger and ruthlessness and bloodlust, was mine as well.

Though I had chosen to give it up. To forge a new legacy.

"I feel it, too," Meghan whispered. Her hands shook, and she closed her eyes, her brow creasing as if in pain. "I can feel the power of this place, the anger and the hate, urging me to use it. To give in and let the rage consume me. It's overwhelming." Her eyes opened, defiance and determination shining through the tears. "But if we listen, we're only going to become what we're fighting against. I refuse to rule the Iron Realm through fear and violence. And I refuse to let these creatures turn me into one of them."

She stepped closer, ignoring the ice spreading over her cheeks and forehead, the frozen crystals forming on her lashes as she gazed up at me. "I know what you're doing," she whispered in a shaky voice. "I know you're scared. But we've gone through so much together, Ash. I can't let you do this. You have been my husband, my knight, my partner in everything. I will not watch you turn into the Winter King."

"We could lose everything, Meghan." Unexpectedly, I felt my voice start to choke up, and struggled to hang on to the anger and fury, trying to shield myself from everything else. "Are you…are you all right with sacrificing Keirran, the Iron Realm, the entire Nevernever?"

"No," Meghan replied softly. "Of course not. I will fight with everything I have, and I will continue to fight as long as I have the breath to keep going." Her hands rose, framing my face, her palms searing spots of warmth against my cheeks. "But if I lose *you*, Ash, if you become one of them, even if we win, it wouldn't be worth it. You've fought so hard for your soul—some things are not worth sacrificing."

"Listen to her, Ash." Puck appeared behind her, green eyes solemn as he stared at me. "I've seen the Unseelie side. I know what you can become. Remember Ariella's vision?" He crossed his arms. "I don't want to meet the Winter King, no matter what the circumstances are."

"Would you rather die, then, Goodfellow?"

His eyes narrowed. "I'd rather die fighting beside my friend, than have to face him as an enemy one more time," he snapped, and the emotion in his voice startled me silent. Puck sighed, raking a hand through his hair, and shook his head. "All stories come to a close eventually, ice-boy," he said. "I was planning to live forever, but you know what? This is a good end. So, come on." A wry smile tugged one corner of his mouth. "You, me, and Meghan. Let's make this epilogue unforgettable."

I glanced down at Meghan. She smiled, and her hand rose to my face once more, pressing against my cheek. "I love you, Ashallyn'darkmyr Tallyn," she whispered. "I will be proud to stand with you to the end. If we die fighting, I will die as myself. And trust that Keirran and the ones who come after will be able to stop them."

I closed my eyes, feeling something hot slide down my cheek. The fury and hatred roared, telling me to give in, that we were going to die if I didn't use the power of my rage. Darkness churned through me, anger and hatred feeding the bloodlust, urging me to destroy.

No. I opened my eyes, meeting the gaze of the woman I loved. The reason I went to the End of the World to earn a soul. *I will not become what I'm fighting against. What will it matter if we win, if I become the enemy? The cycle would never end. I would lose everything regardless.*

Meghan was still watching me, her own gaze teary. Bowing

281

my head, I took a deep breath, and released the fury and hatred that had been with me for so long. It wasn't as hard to relinquish as I'd thought. I just had to make the choice, not to hate, not to let fear and rage fuel my every decision. To let it go and forge a new path. The dark vortex swirling around me weakened, dissipating into the air and finally fading into nothing.

As the howling blizzard sputtered and died, a field of half-frozen creatures looked up, blinking away snow and ice. Behind them, four huge silhouettes still loomed, casting their shadows and black tendrils over everything. With renewed snarls and howls, the horde of creatures charged us, bounding over the snowy ruins. The four Nightmares let out challenging roars that shook the pillars and stalked forward, their movements slow but inevitable. They knew they would get to us eventually, and there was no escape.

Watching them approach, I felt resolve spread through me, replacing the churning rage. I would still protect my family. I would still fight with everything I had to keep them safe. But I would not let hate and violence consume me. I was not pure Unseelie, the legacy of death and darkness tainting everything I touched. I was something more. And now, as the fury cleared and released the bloodlust clinging to my mind, I felt as if I had surfaced from the depths of the abyss. I wasn't as strong, but I was free.

I felt a touch on my shoulder, and looked back into Puck's green eyes. "Glad to have you back, ice-boy," he said seriously. I gripped his hand, and the smile he gave us both was a little sad as he gazed across the ruins. "Though I think it's going to be a pretty short reunion. Kinda sad if you think about it; who's going to pester Titania when I'm gone?"

The first wave was almost upon us. Reaching down, I took Meghan's hand, feeling her fingers curl tightly with mine. "All right," I said quietly, "if this is our final stand, I love you both. It has been an honor, and I wouldn't change a thing."

Meghan squeezed my hand, and Puck gave a loud sniff. "Don't turn mushy on me now, prince," he said, though his voice came out rather thick. "It's hard to stab things when I can't see what I'm stabbing." He gazed calmly at the wave of creatures coming for us, and the giant Monsters looming over them all, and smirked. "Didn't really think this was how it would end, but, hey... I can't complain. Standing with the pair of you, trying to save the world. There are worse ways to kick the bucket."

Meghan took a deep breath, still holding on to me tightly, and raised her sword. "We're not done, yet," she said, and took a fearless step forward. "Let's give them one hell of a fight."

The creatures of Evenfall were just a few lunges away now, a screaming, hissing swarm. I braced myself, readying my weapon, but suddenly there was a roar, a blast of wind from overhead, and a column of fire slammed into the ground between us and the horde. The line of fire strafed the ground, setting parts of the ruins ablaze, as something large and scaly wheeled away on enormous wings and soared over the trees.

"What?" Puck gaped, as the nightmare creatures howled and cringed away from the inferno. "Not that I'm complaining, but who ordered the dragon?"

An answering howl, wild and suddenly familiar, rang out behind us.

My stomach clenched. I turned, as a huge black creature hurled itself over a shattered wall and skidded to our side, panting. The Big Bad Wolf stared down at us, tongue lolling between shining fangs, green eyes blazing in the night. A face peered over his shoulder, silver hair standing out against the pitch-black of the Wolf's fur.

"Keirran." Meghan gasped, as the King of the Forgotten gazed down at us. "What are you doing here?"

The Big Bad Wolf snorted and shook his head. "What do you think?" he growled. "When the seal was broken, the memories of Faery were released. I remembered what happened the night the circle closed the other realm. I remembered what that stripling Lady set into motion. And I knew the Nightmare King would never let it stand. So, there's only one logical reason we could be here."

My son gave us both a somber smile. "We've come to help you stop Evenfall."

"We?" Puck shook his head with a smile that was part grimace. "Not to insult our good Wolfman, but I hope you brought an army, princeling."

"Actually, I did."

Another column of fire suddenly slammed into the ground between us and the horde, turning into a curtain as it traveled across the stones. I looked up to see the massive body of a red dragon pass by on leathery wings, tossing leaves and branches in its wake. The quartet of Elder Nightmares roared a challenge, but the dragon continued on, soaring over the trees, and vanished from immediate sight.

Behind us, a bugle sounded, and a ripple of glamour went through the air. As I turned out of the fog, an army of Summer, Winter and Iron fey broke through the trees at the edge of the ruins. I saw Mab, Oberon and, shockingly, even Titania out front on ethereal faery steeds, power glowing around them and throwing back the shadows. I saw Summer knights in silvery armor, Winter knights with weapons and armor made of ice, and the fey of both courts slinking through the shadows. Dryads, redcaps, goblins, ogres, centaurs, and more, all staring at the hordes of Evenfey with fear and hate in their eyes.

With a shimmer of steel and the clanking of boots, the Iron knights appeared, Glitch at the head. The lightning in his hair flickered, casting sporadic purple light through the trees. Beside them, an enormous Iron horse stepped out of the trees, his eyes glowing red against the darkness. Spikerail, leader of the Iron herd, tossed his head with a blast of flame, and more Iron horses appeared behind him, snorting and filling the air with smoke. Coaleater met my gaze across the ruins, crimson eyes hard with determination.

"Protect the queen!" called Glitch, and drew his sword, the lightning in his hair snapping wildly. As one, the Iron knights and the Iron fey around them sprang forward, racing into the ruins. With a roar and a blast of flame, the huge forms of Spikerail and Coaleater reared up, pawing the air with their hooves, and charged, the rest of the Iron herd behind them.

Oberon raised a fist, and the squadron of Summer knights charged, silver lances angled toward the mass of nightmare creatures swarming from the pit. With shrieks and howls, the army of Unseelie also bounded forward, brandishing weapons, claws, and fangs. They thundered past us, making the ground tremble, and the cacophony that arose when the Nevernever and Evenfall clashed shook the ruins.

The rest of us fell back, joining the other rulers of Faery, as the sounds of battle echoed into the night. "Iron Queen," Oberon called from atop his warhorse. The Seelie King swung a terrible gaze at the ruins and the forces tearing each other apart in the center, and his green eyes narrowed. "How long has the rift to Evenfall been open?" he demanded. "Is the Nightmare King coming?"

"No," Meghan replied. "At least, not yet. We think he's still asleep, though with the seal broken he probably won't be for much longer."

"How did you know to come here?" I asked, looking at Mab. "And to bring the armies? None of you were there when the Lady decided to close off Evenfall."

The Winter monarch pursed her lips in distaste. "No, but

those memories were the memories of Faery, not just the Lady and her misinformed circle," Mab replied. Her eyes glittered dangerously, hinting at what she might do had those fey still been alive. "We are connected to the Nevernever," she went on, "so when the seal was broken, we remembered what happened as if we were there ourselves. We remember Evenfall, and the Nightmare King. And we know that if the Nightmare King wakes, he will consume Faery with his vengeance."

"So we have come," Oberon added, "to stop Evenfall. To drive it back so it does not spill into the Nevernever. And to face the Nightmare King when he finally arrives."

A terrible roar shook the surrounding pillars and caused us all to look back. The four Elder Nightmares had reached the armies of Faery, and were scything through them with claws and fangs, tossing them aside like rags. The fey of Summer, Winter, and Iron responded bravely, but with the amount of fear, rage, and violence choking the air, the Nightmares shrugged off blows that would have crippled normal creatures and lashed out in return. The writhing tendrils that proceeded the Nightmares snaked forward, growing out of stones and the ground itself, wrapping around fey and dragging them under. When they emerged, they were changed to creatures of insatiable rage and fear, who either fled or attacked everything around them. I clenched a fist, watching as a Winter knight disappeared into a knot of tentacles, emerging as a creature with pure white skin and icicles growing from his back and forearms. His blue eyes were empty of reason as he shrieked and flung himself at his brothers, then immediately died on their swords.

Puck let out a curse. "Dammit, those big uglies are really getting on my nerves. How are we going to kill these bastards before they turn everyone here into madmen? I don't fancy having to fight all the armies of Faery."

"Oberon." Meghan spun toward the Summer King, who

turned an electric green gaze on her, eyes blazing. "Don't engage the largest creatures," she told the Seelie monarch. "There's too much fear and anger in the area to have any effect on them, and negative glamour only makes them stronger. Have your forces fall back before they turn them all against us!"

"Retreat?" Mab curled a lip, steam and mist writhing off her huge black warhorse, its glacial blue eyes wide with fear and alarm. She yanked the reins savagely to keep it under control. "They cannot stop the entire army," she said. "Eventually, they will be brought down. We cannot let these creatures get past us into the Nevernever. I will see my entire force dead before I allow these Monsters to rampage through Winter."

"That is not acceptable, Queen Mab," Meghan told the Winter monarch, who glared down at her. "We will lose too many people. I will not throw my subjects at the Nightmares only to die."

"Then what do you suggest, Iron Queen?" This from Titania, joining the Winter monarch in glaring down at us. "Or do you simply expect us to watch these abominations stroll into the Nevernever without a fight?"

"No." Atop the Wolf, Keirran suddenly raised his head. "Drive them back," he stated. "Don't focus on killing them, focus on pushing them away." He pointed back into the ruins, at the gaping hole to Evenfall. "Drive the Monsters into the pit and seal it. It will be a temporary solution, but it will buy us time to decide what to do."

The rulers of Faery gazed at each other as, around us, the battle between Evenfall and the fey of the Nevernever shook the ruins. Finally, Oberon nodded.

"Acceptable," he announced, dismounting from his steed in a flurry of green and silver. "We will drive the creatures back and return them to the pit they crawled out of. Knights!" he called, his voice booming over the battlefield. "Fall back! Summer forces, return to me!"

Queen Mab's voice echoed Oberon's, calling her own forces to retreat, as Meghan did the same. Slowly, the armies of the Nevernever began falling back, still battling nightmare creatures as they retreated. In the center of the chaos, the Elder Nightmares howled as they continued to lay waste, inky tendrils thrashing as they lashed out at fey and nightmare alike.

Titania stepped up beside Oberon, watching the battle and the raging Nightmares with a look of distaste. "And where are we supposed to send these abominations back to?" she wondered.

"Back to Evenfall," Meghan told her. "The broken seal is where they're coming from. We need to push them back, and somehow close it before they claw their way out. It's not going to be easy, though."

The Summer Queen sniffed. "Speak for yourself, child," she said, as power began flickering around both her and Oberon, rippling their capes and causing their hair to float around them. "You have only been in the Nevernever a few short years. We *are* the Summer Court."

The Elder Nightmares were nearly upon us, and the armies of the Nevernever had been pushed back until only a hundred or so paces separated them from the gathered rulers. The swarms of Evenfey continued to hound them, but the real threat was the four great beasts and the carpet of swarming tentacles that thrashed and flailed in every direction. The screams of our own people rang through the ruins, as scores of Winter, Summer, and Iron fey succumbed to anger and fear, becoming twisted versions of themselves and turning on their former allies.

Deep below, there was a pulse, and dozens of massive roots broke through the stones, rising into the air with muffled roars. They whipped about like dragon heads, striking at nightmare fey and flinging them in all directions. I saw Titania raise her hand,

and glamour-fueled wind gusted furiously through the ruins, swirling into howling tornados. Faeries and Evenfey were swept off their feet, hurled like rag dolls into trees and broken walls, as the intense storms cut a swath of destruction through the ruins.

The Elder Nightmares roared, their unnatural voices rising even over the howling winds. Roots and vines slashed at them, and furious gusts tore at their flesh and manes of tentacles, but they didn't fall back. Lowering their antlered heads, they prowled toward us, coming a bit faster now, and the scent of fear rose up from the forces out front.

Beneath us, the ground turned to shadows, and inky tendrils began rising from the stones, writhing madly as they reached for us. The Wolf snarled and, with Keirran still on his back, sprang atop a pillar, away from the flood of darkness, as Mab's horse squealed in terror and reared, and the tornado sputtered and died as the Summer rulers turned to the more immediate threat. With a pulse of Winter, Summer, and Iron glamour, the tentacles surrounding us vanished, but more crept forward, a never-ending carpet, and the Nightmares drew closer as well.

As one Elder Nightmare snarled and lurched forward, a trio of spinning crescents flashed through the air, striking it in the face, and it recoiled with a bellow. Startled, I glanced up, as a familiar silver-haired figure melted out of the shadows over-head, peering at us from a stone column.

Puck drew in a sharp breath. "Nyx?" he gasped. "I thought you left."

"I did." The Evenfaery dropped silently to the ground beside Puck, her gaze solemn as she rose. "But then I saw what was on the other side. No matter what I believe now… I don't want you to die, Puck." She glanced at the red-haired fey beside her, and a faint grimace crossed her face. "It appears I've broken the first rule of my Order and have grown rather attached to someone. I hope you're happy, Goodfellow. I don't know whether to kill you now or not."

"Welcome to the club," Puck grinned. "Remind me to get you the VIP pass. That stands for 'Very Interesting to Puck,' if you're wondering."

Nyx shook her head, grabbed the front of his shirt, and pulled him into a kiss. "You are very bad for my good sense, Goodfellow," she said as they parted. "But I'm glad I came back." She turned her head, observing the approaching Monsters with grim determination. "Think we can keep these Nightmares distracted until the rulers can do their work?"

Puck drew his daggers with another wicked grin. "Just try to keep up."

They sprang forward, into the hordes of fey, and a moment later a flock of ravens swooped through the ruins with screaming cries, circling the heads of the closest Monsters, and flashes of silver light caused them to recoil with snarls of rage and confusion.

With a snort the Wolf dropped from the pillar and cast an irritated glance back at Keirran. "Get off, cub," he growled, and the Forgotten King complied. "These creatures don't frighten me," the Wolf stated, narrowing his gold-green eyes at the raging Nightmares. "Let's see how strong they really are."

With a howl, the great Wolf bounded forward, leaped over the heads of the armies, and charged one looming monster. I watched as his huge shaggy form galloped toward his enemy, launched himself off a crumbled wall, and slammed into the Nightmare's chest, knocking it back. The monster roared as it stumbled, regaining its balance, but the Wolf darted in, clamped his jaws around one foreleg, and dragged it off its feet.

"They're distracted," Meghan said quietly, and glanced at me. "But they won't be for long. If everyone can push them back, I think I can close the pit. I just need a little time."

"You'll have it." I took a breath, feeling pure, untainted

Winter glamour rise up within. "Keirran," I said, and my son immediately came to stand beside me. I felt the intense glamour of the Forgotten king—Summer, Winter, and Iron—in the air around him, and called my own magic to the surface. "Ready?" I asked, and felt Keirran's Winter glamour grow even more powerful, overshadowing the other two. He nodded.

Turning back, we each held out an arm, and sent a screaming blizzard into the faces of the Nightmares. Ice formed on the stones, growing inches thick in seconds, shards of frozen daggers pelted the Monsters' hides, and pointed spears rose from the ground, sinking into legs and stomachs as they pressed forward. An icy wind joined the howling tornadoes of Summer, flinging rocks and frozen darts everywhere, and the Nightmares finally flinched back.

I felt a cool hand on my shoulder, and glanced over to see Mab standing behind us, a faint smile on her lips as she watched the chaos in the center of the ruins. "Let me show you how it's done, my boys," she murmured, and a massive flood of power washed through me, adding its strength to ours. The blizzard intensified, screaming winds turning razor-sharp, as the Summer tornado flung debris everywhere and flailing roots lashed out at the Nightmares. Ice coated the ruins, hanging in enormous spikes from pillars and branches, and coating the ground. One of the creatures slipped, digging its claws into the ice to keep from sliding. I saw a flash of red as Puck darted in behind it, slicing its ankle. The Nightmare lost its grip, crashing to the ice, and as its head struck the ground, the Wolf lunged out of the trees and sank his jaws into the side of the shaggy neck.

There was a crinkling sound above me, as Mab raised an arm, and an enormous frozen boulder appeared in the air over her head. With a flick of her wrist, she sent it hurtling into the ruins, and the ice chunk slammed into a Nightmare as it was lurching to its feet, knocking it backward with a snarl.

Slowly, fighting all the way, the Nightmares began falling back, driven by vicious winds, ice, lightning, flailing roots, and the continuous darting blows from Nyx, Puck, and the Wolf. They slid over the ice, claws raking gouges in the frozen surface, giving ground before the fury of Summer, Winter, and Iron.

I glanced to where Meghan knelt, head bowed, hands resting lightly on her sword hilt. I could feel her centering herself, gathering the strength and magic for what needed to be done. Silently, I sent a portion of my magic to her, adding my strength to hers. She breathed deep, and her eyes opened, hard and determined, as she glared at the Nightmares slowly being driven back. Back toward the pit, and Evenfall. Back to where they came from.

The first of the Nightmares reached the edge of the crumbling hole, snarling and digging talons into the stones to keep from moving any farther. But its claws could not find any purchase against the ice, and it tumbled into the darkness with a final howl. A second followed, raking the ground as it slid toward the endless abyss, snarling its rage and hate. Lashing out wildly, it latched on to the leg of a third Nightmare, and both went sliding into the black.

The last Elder Nightmare hunched its shoulders and dug its claws into a stone pillar, bracing itself against the wind and swirling debris. For a moment, it stood there, motionless, as ice and lightning pelted its hide, crawling over its skin and leaving gashes that leaked dark fluid onto the rock.

Then, its twisted, antlered head lifted, blank white eyes fixed on us all, and a chill crawled up my spine. Its jaws opened, and a terrible, droning voice echoed through my thoughts.

"What strange dreams are these?"

I shuddered. It wasn't the monster speaking. It was *him*, the Nightmare King, gazing at us through the eyes of his subjects. Not awake yet, but not entirely asleep, either.

Its gaze shifted fully to me, and staring into the eyes of a sleeping god, I suddenly couldn't catch my breath. The weight of its stare crushed me; beyond anger, beyond rage and loathing and mindless terror. It was pure, unfiltered chaos. I could feel the madness of the Nightmare King clawing at me, chilling my insides to the core. After so long asleep, being sealed away from the world, the Nightmare King had gone mad with his own dreams. Now, all he knew was fury, hate, and destruction.

"I will destroy all." Even asleep, the Nightmare King's words made the ground tremble. *"All dreams will die. This nightmare I find myself trapped in will finally end. I hear the ripples of the world above. I hear the voices calling. The screams, the anger, they pull me from this dream. Soon, I will be among them. Soon, all will know my rage. All will be darkness, and the ones who betrayed us will know nothing but terror. Wait for me, dreams. I will be there, soon."*

Then Meghan rose, the power of the Iron Queen snapping around her, and raised a hand.

The edge of the pit crumbled, as more roots broke through the stones, coiling into the air. Only these glinted in the shadows and flashes of lightning swirling in the winds; infused with the glamour of Iron, they wrapped around the monster's limbs, dragging it down. It howled, bracing itself against the pull, fighting the inevitable. The roots strained, on the verge of snapping, the Nightmare's empty gaze watching us with unfiltered hate.

With shrieking caws, a cloud of ravens descended on the creature, clawing its face and pecking at its eyes, and a flurry of light crescents sliced into its hide. As it flinched, the Wolf thundered forward, lowered his shaggy head, and plowed full-speed into the thick muscled leg.

The Nightmare lost its grip at last, and with a final roar, was dragged into the pit. It clawed futilely at the ground, raking deep gashes in the ice, before its twisted skull vanished over the edge and fell into the blackness.

Meghan raised her other arm, and the Iron roots thrashing at the edge of the pit wove together, forming a knot, a tangle of Iron cables over the mouth of the hole. I felt Oberon and Mab adding their own power to the mix, as tree roots intersected with Meghan's Iron cables, and a sheet of ice spread over the entire thing.

The winds died down, the icy blizzard ceased, and the tornados spun themselves into nothing, taking the lightning with them. A ragged cheer echoed through the ranks of faeries, from Summer, Winter, and Iron, standing side by side. A few nightmare creatures still prowled the edges of the ruins, but the battle with the Nightmare King's strongest minions was over. Evenfall was sealed, and the Nevernever was safe.

At least for now.

EPILOGUE

INTO EVENFALL

I strode over to Meghan, who was kneeling on the rough stones of the ruins, and gathered her in my arms as she collapsed against me, her breaths coming in short gasps.

"That's not the end of it," she panted. "The Nightmare King...he's still coming. Once he wakes up, he'll destroy the Nevernever, and possibly the mortal world as well."

"Breathe," I told her softly, as the rest of the rulers gathered around, all looking grave. They had seen the power of the Nightmare King; even the fragments of his nightmares were enough to have them worried. A triumphant-looking Wolf padded out of the shadows to join us, and a raven swooped in, changing to Puck in a cloud of black feathers. "We're safe for now," I said to Meghan. "You've sealed the way to Evenfall— nothing is coming through, for a little while at least."

"That is not a seal," said a scornful voice, and Grimalkin materialized a few paces away, gazing down at us from a broken pillar. We hadn't seen the cat since the original seal was broken, and I was relieved that he was all right. Though he remained as disdainful as ever as he curled his whiskers at the pit. "That is a plug. And it will not hold for long. Evenfall will keep coming, as will the Nightmare King, when he regains consciousness."

"So, what are we supposed to do?" Puck wanted to know. "We can't sit here and keep replugging the hole forever."

Nyx shimmered into view, crouched on a broken pillar much like Grimalkin. Her golden eyes were hard as she gazed down at us. "The Nightmare King is tied to Evenfall, much as the rulers of the courts are tied to their realms," she began. "His emotions and state of mind affect all those who live in Evenfall. And right now, he is angry, enraged, and full of hate. Even half-asleep, he affects his world, and the fey who live there. I could feel his rage when I crossed over—it frightened even me. If you ever want peace with Evenfall, if there is any hope for reconciliation..."

"We're going to have to take care of the Nightmare King," Keirran said, finishing for her. "Either put him back to sleep, or..."

Everyone fell silent as we realized what had to be done. If it could even be accomplished. Keirran stood quietly a moment, his brow furrowed in thought, then raised his head to the Even-faery perched above us.

"Nyx." The Forgotten King's voice was hesitant, and the cold gaze of the assassin turned on him. "I know how you must feel," he began. "I know you're angry, and you have every right to be. What was done to you and all the fey of Evenfall..." He shook his head. "It's unforgivable. I have no right to command, and I'm in no position to request anything of you, but...if the Nightmare King wakes up, it could be the end, for all of us. I'm asking not as a king, but as a friend; would you take us to him? Would you lead us through Evenfall to find the Night-mare King?"

The Evenfall assassin didn't move for a few heartbeats. Nothing more was said; even Titania was silent as the Evenfaery considered. Finally, she rose and with a ripple of her cloak, dropped gracefully from the pillar to stand before Keirran.

"King Keirran." Her voice was stiff, quietly formal. "I am angry," the assassin went on. "I can only imagine what I've lost—my home, my purpose, myself. My kin." An anguished look passed over her face, but vanished in the next heartbeat. "Everyone I knew is gone. I am the only one of my Order left. We all perished serving the Lady, the very one who sealed our world and sentenced us to die. I will not forgive that. I will never forget again.

"But the Lady is gone now." Nyx raised her head, her voice flat and pragmatic once more. "She tried to take over the Nevernever, and you defeated her. There is no one left to take vengeance on. And the Nightmare King—" her jaw tightened "—is not the king I remember.

"I cannot forgive what happened," Nyx went on. "I cannot forget that my world was taken from me. But the Nightmare King intends to destroy the worlds that are left…and I can't allow that. I've lived here too long." For just a moment, her gaze flickered to Puck, and the shadow of emotion passed between them both. "I see the ones who call this realm their home."

Nyx paused, then gracefully sank to one knee before Keirran. "I swore an oath," she stated calmly. "My allegiance is still yours, Forgotten King. It might make me a traitor to my own kind, but if the Evenfey are lost to rage and madness, then I will not regret what I must do. I will guide you through Evenfall to find the Nightmare King, or the place where he currently sleeps. I cannot promise anything more than that."

Keirran visibly relaxed. "I'm grateful, Nyx," he whispered, which was the closest anyone came to saying "thank you," in Faery. "I know this must be hard."

"We do what we must," the Evenfaery replied. "Though I

doubt any of you will be able to kill the Nightmare King, even if we do find him." She rose, giving the rest of us a solemn glance. "So, now the question becomes, who is going into Evenfall with me?"

"I am," Meghan said, as I knew she would. "Ash and Puck as well," she continued as we both nodded. "I won't ask anyone else."

"I'm coming, too," Keirran announced, making me frown. "The Forgotten could be Evenfey," he went on, glancing at me, as if he could sense my thoughts. "At the very least, they have been hurt so badly by the Lady and her kin. I owe it to them, to try to end this. As King of the Forgotten, I need to make things right."

I set my jaw. I didn't like that Keirran was coming along. But he wasn't just my son; he was the King of the Forgotten, and I couldn't tell another ruler what to do. I would just have to protect him, and Meghan, as best I could. Without giving in to the darkness.

I felt Meghan's sigh, and knew she, too, wanted to say something, to prevent Keirran from coming with us into Evenfall. But Keirran had grown up, and had his own people and kingdom to worry about. The Iron Queen understood that. "Then let's not waste any time," she said quietly. "Grimalkin? Are you with us as well?"

"I am, Iron Queen." The cat gave a solemn bob of his head. "I have not yet been to Evenfall, but it does not matter. Someone must come along to point out the obvious."

The Iron Queen turned to the other rulers. "After we go in, will you seal the way behind us?" she asked.

"Yes," Oberon said gravely. "And we will remain here, to guard the way and prevent anything from coming out." Titania thinned her lips but didn't argue, and Mab gave a grim nod. "And if you fail," the Summer King continued, "if the Nightmare King does awaken and makes his way into the Nevernever, we will be here to welcome him."

We stood a hundred or so paces away from the pit, observing the tangle of cables, vines, ice, and stone that blocked the way to Evenfall.

"Well, this is going to be fun," Puck mused. "I bet all the beasties on the other side didn't just give up and go home. It's going to be like shaking a hornet's nest."

I stood close to Meghan and glanced at my son, waiting quietly beside me. My family and my closest friends were all I needed in the world. I would not fear the Nightmares, the creatures in the darkness, even my own Unseelie nature, if they were at my side.

"Is everyone ready?" Meghan asked. I nodded, and she raised a hand, calling her glamour to life.

With the groan of metal and trees and the shattering of ice, the knot plugging the hole to Evenfall peeled back. Instantly, smaller nightmares began crawling out, hissing and shrieking as they emerged into the light. They swarmed toward us, and we cut them down as we ran, not slowing as we approached the looming pit to Evenfall.

Just as we reached the edge, an enormous, familiar arm rose from the depths, sinking terrible claws into the stones, and the antlered head of an Elder Nightmare began rising from the black.

"Don't stop!" Meghan ordered. "Keep going!"

The Nightmare roared as it spotted us, dark tendrils rising from the ground as it clawed its way from the hole. I felt the glamour surge in the air as all of us—me, Meghan, Keirran, Puck, and Nyx—sent a barrage of magic scything toward the creature. Lightning, ice, and moonlight daggers slammed into it, causing it to scream and reel back, as it lost its grip on the edge of the hole.

With a howl, it plummeted into the darkness, and we were right behind it. I grabbed Meghan's hand as we reached the edge, feeling darkness, anger, hate, and fear swirling up from the abyss. She squeezed my fingers tightly, and we jumped, leaving the Nevernever behind, and plunging into the unknown of Evenfall.

★ ★ ★ ★ ★